W. Y. (William Young) Sellar

The Roman Poets of the Republic

W. Y. (William Young) Sellar

The Roman Poets of the Republic

ISBN/EAN: 9783741126796

Manufactured in Europe, USA, Canada, Australia, Japa

Cover: Foto ©Andreas Hilbeck / pixelio.de

Manufactured and distributed by brebook publishing software
(www.brebook.com)

W. Y. (William Young) Sellar

The Roman Poets of the Republic

THE

ROMAN POETS

OF

THE REPUBLIC.

BY

W. Y. SELLAR, M.A.

PROFESSOR OF GREEK IN THE UNIVERSITY OF ST. ANDREWS, AND FORMERLY
FELLOW OF ORIEL COLLEGE, OXFORD.

EDINBURGH:

EDMONSTON AND DOUGLAS.

1863.

EDINBURGH: PRINTED BY THOMAS CONSTABLE,

FOR

EDMONSTON AND DOUGLAS.

LONDON . .	HAMILTON, ADAMS, AND CO.
CAMBRIDGE	MACMILLAN AND CO.
DUBLIN	. M'GLASHAN AND GILL.
GLASGOW .	JAMES MACLEHOSE.

PREFACE

I HAVE endeavoured, in this volume, to trace the development of Roman Poetry from the origin of Latin literature to the fall of the Roman Republic. I hope to be able, at some future time, to carry on the subject at least to the end of the Augustan age. As my main object has been to show the native spirit by which the imaginative literature of Rome is animated, I have not thought it necessary to include the writers of Roman Comedy under this inquiry.

In examining the first period of Roman Poetry I have made constant use of the editions of the Fragments of the early writers by Klussman, Vahlen, Ribbeck, and Gerlach. I have availed myself also of the German histories of Roman literature, by Bernhardy, Bahr, and Munk, and of the chapters on the early Literature in Mommsen's Roman History. To the first of these writers I am especially indebted for many references to passages in later Latin literature, in which the works of the early writers are quoted or commented on. In writing the second chapter, I derived much of my information from a small treatise on the origin of Roman Poetry, by Corssen, and from the chapter in Sir G. C. Lewis's work on *The Credibility of Early Roman*

History, in which Niebuhr's hypothesis of a ballad poetry is discussed.

During my whole study of the subject I have made constant use of Smith's *Dictionary of Greek and Roman Biography and Mythology.* I have especially to acknowledge my debt to the articles, in that work, written by Professor Ramsay, which, besides nearly exhausting the ascertained information about the lives of the Roman Poets, contain the most clear and judicial summing up of all legitimate inferences on the subject with which I am acquainted.

In quoting from Lucretius I have used the text of Mr. Munro's edition. I have to acknowledge also the help which I have got in understanding some of the difficulties in the philosophical argument of Lucretius from reading Mr. Munro's articles in the *Journal of Classical and Sacred Philology.* In quoting from Catullus I have generally adhered to the text of Rossbach.

I have, in conclusion, to return my warm thanks to my friend, Mr. Theodore Martin, for his kind permission to make free use of his spirited and accomplished translations from Catullus.

W. Y. S.

St. Andrews, May 1863.

CONTENTS.

CHAPTER I.

GENERAL CHARACTER OF ROMAN POETRY.

CHAPTER II.

VESTIGES OF EARLY INDIGENOUS POETRY IN ROME AND ANCIENT ITALY.

CONTENTS.

FIRST PERIOD.

CHAPTER III.

THE BEGINNING OF ROMAN LITERATURE—LIVIUS ANDRONICUS—CN. NAEVIUS, B.C. 240-202.

CHAPTER IV.

Q. ENNIUS, B.C. 239-170—HIS LIFE, TIMES, AND PERSONAL TRAITS—HIS VARIOUS WORKS—NATURE OF HIS GENIUS AND INTELLECT.

CHAPTER V.

EARLY ROMAN TRAGEDY—M. PACUVIUS, B.C. 219-129—L. ATTIUS, B.C. 170-ABOUT B.C. 90.

CHAPTER VI.

THE ORIGIN AND NATURE OF EARLY ROMAN SATIRE—C. LUCILIUS.
B.C. 148-B.C. 103.

CHAPTER VII.

REVIEW OF THE FIRST PERIOD.

SECOND PERIOD.

LUCRETIUS AND CATULLUS.

CHAPTER VIII.

LUCRETIUS—PERSONAL CHARACTERISTICS.

CHAPTER IX.

THE PHILOSOPHY OF LUCRETIUS.

CONTENTS.

CHAPTER XII.

CATULLUS.

THE ROMAN POETS OF THE REPUBLIC.

THE

ROMAN POETS OF THE REPUBLIC.

CHAPTER I.

GENERAL CHARACTER OF ROMAN POETRY.

A GREAT fluctuation of opinion has taken place, among modern scholars and critics, in regard to the worth of Roman poetry. From the revival of learning till comparatively a recent period, the poets of ancient Rome, and especially those of the Augustan age, were generally esteemed the purest models of literary art, and the best exponents of the life and sentiment of antiquity. Their works were used as the chief instruments in education. They were studied, imitated, and translated by some of the greatest poets of modern Europe ; and they supplied their favourite texts and illustrations to moralists and humorists, from Montaigne to the famous English essayists who flourished during the last century. Up to a still later period, their words were habitually used by statesmen to add weight to their arguments or point to their invectives. Perhaps no other writers have produced so powerful an effect, not only on the style, but on the character and understanding, of the most refined and influential men in the leading nations of the modern world.

It was natural that this excessive deference to their au-

A

thority should be impaired both by the ampler recognition
of the claims of modern poetry, and by a more intimate
familiarity with Greek literature. Since, in the present
day, the study of the ancient languages is directed more to
the discipline of the understanding than to the refinement
of taste, and general cultivation has become more enlarged, the Roman poets have no longer been able to maintain the foremost place either in the education of youth,
or among the intellectual resources of riper age. They
have suffered, in the estimation of literary critics, from
the change in poetical taste which commenced about the
beginning of the present century, and, in that of scholars,
from the fresher and superior attractions of the great
epic, dramatic, and lyrical poets of Greece. ˙ They have
thus, for some time, been exposed to undue disparagement rather than to undue admiration.   The perception of the great debt which they owed to their Greek
masters, has led to some forgetfulness of their original
merits.   Their genuine Roman character and fresh Italian feeling have been partially hidden under the foreign
forms and metres which they adopted.   It is said, with
some plausible admixture of truth, that Roman poetry is
not only much inferior in interest to the poetry of Greece,
but that it was the work merely of cultivated imitators,
not of creative artists ; that other forms of literature
were more adapted to the genius of the Roman people
than any form of imaginative composition ; that their
poets have brought nothing new into the world ; that
they have enriched the life of after times with no
fresh vein of native feeling, or any impressive record of
national experience.

   It is indeed neither possible nor desirable to read
Roman literature with the deference which it received
from men of letters in the last century. But that
literature may still be studied with as much sympathy and appreciation as in former days. It is one

of the best results of modern studies, that if, in some
departments of knowledge, there is less learning, there
is in general a truer discernment of the spirit of the
past, and of the points of resemblance and difference
between ancient and modern civilisation.   In many
provinces of inquiry it may be seen that criticism is
striving, with a genuine sympathy, to penetrate to the
heart of earlier times, and to separate the treasures
of lasting worth from the materials of trivial value,
which have been borne down casually among the accumulated spoils of time.   It is an important question
to determine in which of these classes the works of
the Roman poets of the Republic and the Empire are
to be ranked.   In poetry, more than in any other
field of literature, only works of high and original excellence deserve the permanent attention of the world.
If the famous works of Roman poetry shall long continue
to be prized among the masterpieces of literature, this
result must depend on the conviction that they are not
only finished compositions, but that they are inspired by
original impulses and ideas, and that they stand in a
true relation to the heart and mind of the Romans in
the time of their vigorous growth or established greatness.

It is impossible to claim for Roman poetry the unborrowed glory or the ever-fresh and manifold inspiration of
the earlier art of Greece.   To the genius of Greece only
can the words of the bard in the Odyssey be applied,

αὐτοδίδακτος δ' εἰμί, θεὸς δέ μοι ἐν φρεσὶν οἴμας
παντοίας ἐνέφυσεν.[1]

Besides possessing the charm of poetical feeling and
harmony in unequalled measure, Greek poetry is to
modern readers the immediate revelation of a new
world of thought and action, in all its lights and shadows and ever-moving life.   Like their politics, the

[1] Self-taught am I; God implanted in my heart strains of every kind.
Hom. Od. xxii. 318.

poetry also of the Greeks sprang from many independent centres, and renewed itself in each of the great
epochs of national civilisation. Roman poetry, on the
other hand, has not the same freshness or variety of
matter ; nor did it assume new shapes under the influence of a many-sided creative energy, like that which
gave birth in succession to the epic, lyrical, dramatic,
and idyllic poetry of the Greeks. But the poets of
Rome still possess a real independent value. There is
a charm in their language and sentiment which belongs
to no other literature in the world. They express certain modes of feeling and thought, which are nowhere
else so happily exhibited. Certain deep and abiding impressions are stamped upon their words, which have
penetrated deeply into the cultivated life of modern
times. If the imagination is not stimulated, as by a
new, rich, and very varied prospect, yet, in the elevated
tones of Roman poetry, there is felt to be a permanent
affinity with the strength and dignity of man's moral
nature ; and, in the finer and softer tones, a power to
move the heart to sympathy with the beauty, the enjoyment, and the natural sorrows of a bygone life.
The sense of the eager hopes and buoyant fancies of the
dawn of song has passed away, but there is still a peculiar brightness and glory around the latest phase in
which the genius of antiquity was revealed.

While the literature and civilisation of Greece were
still unknown to them, the Romans had produced certain rude kinds of metrical composition : they preserved some knowledge of events in various kinds of
chronicles or annals : they must have been trained to
a primitive oratory by the contests of public life, and
by the practice of delivering commemorative speeches
at the funerals of famous men. But they cannot be
said to have produced spontaneously any works of
literary art. Their oratory, history, poetry, and philo-

sophy owed their first impulse to their intellectual contact with Greece. But while the form and expression of all Roman literature were moulded by the teaching of Greek masters and the study of Greek writings, it may be urged, with some show of truth, that the debt incurred by the poetry and philosophy of Rome was much greater than that incurred by her oratory and history. The two latter appear to have assumed a more distinct type, and to have adapted themselves more naturally to the genius of the people and the circumstances of the State. They were the accomplishments of men who took an active and prominent part in public affairs ; and they bore directly on the practical wants of the times in which they were cultivated. Even the structure of the Latin language testifies to the oratorical force and ardour by which it was moulded into symmetry ; as the language of Greece betrays the plastic, harmonious power of her early poetry. There is no great improbability in supposing that, if Greek literature had never existed, or had remained unknown to the Romans, the political passions and necessities of the Republic would have called forth a series of powerful orators ; and that the national instinct, which clung with unusual tenacity to the past, would, with the advance of power and civilisation, have produced a type of history, capable of giving adequate expression to the traditions and continuous annals of the commonwealth.

But their poetry, on the other hand, came to the Romans after their habits were fully formed, as an ornamental addition to their power,—ϵηπίον καὶ ἐγκαλλώπισμα πλούτου. Unlike the poetry of Greece, it was not addressed to the popular ear, nor was it an immediate emanation from the popular heart. The poets who commemorated the greatness of Rome, or who sang of the passions and pursuits of private life, in the ages immediately before and after the establish-

ment of the Empire, were men born in the distant provinces of Italy, neither trained in the formal discipline
of Rome, nor taking any active part in practical affairs.
Their tastes and feelings are, in some respects, rather
Italian than purely Roman; their thoughts and convictions are rather of a cosmopolitan type than moulded
on the national traditions. They drew the materials of
their art as much from the accumulated treasures of
Greek poetry, as from the life and action of their own
times. Their art is thus a composite structure, in which
old forms are combined with altered conditions; in which
the creations of earlier genius reappear clothed in a
new language, and the spirit of Greece interpenetrates
the grave temperament of Rome, and the genial nature
of Italy.

But, although oratory and history may have been
more essential to the national life of the Romans, and
more adapted to their genius, their poetry still remains
as their most complete literary monument. Of the many
famous orators of the Republic only one has left his
speeches to modern times. The works of the two greatest
Roman historians have come down to us in a mutilated
shape; and the most important epochs in the later history
of the Republic are not represented in what remains of the
works of either writer. Tacitus records only the sombre
and monotonous annals of the Empire; and the extant
books of Livy contain the account of times and events
from which he himself was separated by many generations. Roman poetry, on the other hand, is the contemporary witness of several marked eras in the history of the
Republic and the Empire. It includes many authentic
and characteristic fragments from the great times of the
Scipios,—the works of the two poets of finest genius, who
flourished in the last days of the Republic,—the masterpieces of the brilliant Augustan era;—and, of the works
of the Empire, more than are needed to exemplify the

decay of natural feeling and of poetical inspiration under the long-continued pressure of Imperialism. And, besides illustrating different eras, the Roman poets throw light on the most various aspects of Roman life and character. They are the most authentic witnesses both of the national sentiment and ideas, and of the feelings and interests of private life. They stamp on the imagination the ideal of Roman majesty; and they bring home to modern sympathies the charm and the pathos of human life, under conditions widely different from our own.

Roman poetry was the living heir, not the lifeless copy, of the genius of Greece. It was, indeed, rather a highly-trained accomplishment than the spontaneous outpouring of a natural faculty; but it was an accomplishment, based upon original gifts of feeling and character, and marked by its own peculiar features. The creative energy of the Greeks died out with Theocritus; but their learning and taste, surviving the decay of their political existence, passed into the education of a fresh and vigorous race, endowed, above all other races of antiquity, with the capacity of receiving and assimilating alien influences, and of producing, alike in action and in literature, their greatest results through persistent and concentrated purpose. It was owing to their persevering industry, and to their fine powers of appreciation, that the Roman poets, in the era of the transition from the freedom and vigour of the Republic to the pomp and order of the Empire, succeeded in producing works which, in point of execution, may be compared with the masterpieces of Greece. It was due to the spirit of a new race,—speaking another language, living among different scenes, acting their own part in the history of the world,—that the ancient inspiration survived the extinction of Greek liberty, and reappeared, under those altered conditions, in a fresh succession of powerful works, which owe their long existence as much

to the genuine feeling as to the artistic perfection by
which they are characterised.

From one point of view, therefore, Roman poetry may
be regarded as an imitative, from another, as an original
art. For the form, and for some part of the substance,
of their works, the Roman poets were indebted to
Greece : the inner spirit and feeling, and much also of
the substance of their poetry, are native in their origin.
They betray their want of inventiveness chiefly in the
forms of composition and the metres which they employed ; occasionally also in the cast of their poetic
diction, and in their treatment of ancient materials. But,
in even the least original aspects of their art, they still
bear the national stamp. Although, with the exception
of Satire, they struck out no new forms of poetic composition, yet those adopted by them assumed something of a new type, owing to the weight of their
materials, the massive structure of the Roman language,
the gravity and fervour of the Roman temperament, and
the practical bent and logical mould of the Roman
understanding.

They were not equally successful in all the forms
which they attempted to reproduce. The original limitations of their genius,—perhaps, among other causes,
their marked inferiority to the Greeks in social vivacity,
—prevented their attaining success in dramatic poetry.
They betray the want of dramatic genius in other fields
of literature, especially in epic and idyllic poetry, and
in philosophical dialogues. Their poets give utterance to
vehemence of passion, or heroism of sentiment, either
directly from their own hearts and convictions, or in
great rhetorical passages, attributed to the imaginary personages of their story—to Ariadne or Dido, to Turnus or
Mezentius. But this utterance of passion and sentiment
is not often united in them with a vivid delineation of
the complex characters of men. There is thus, as com-

pared with Homer and Theocritus, a deficiency of human
interest in the epic, descriptive, and idyllic poetry of
Virgil. The natural play of characters, acting and react-
ing upon one another, scarcely, if at all, enlivens the
divinely-appointed action of the Æneid ; nor adds the
charm of personal associations to the poet's deep and
quiet pictures of rural beauty, and to his graceful expression of pensive and tender feeling.

The Romans, as a race, were wanting also in speculative capacity; and thus their poetry does not rise,
or rises only in Lucretius, to those imaginative heights
from which the great lyrical and dramatic poets of Greece
contemplated the wonder and mysterious solemnity of
life. Yet both the epic and the lyrical poetry of Rome
have a character and perfection of their own. The Æneid,
with many resemblances in points of detail to the poems
of Homer, is yet, both in design and execution, a true
national monument. The lyrical poetry of Rome, if
inferior to the choral poetry of Greece in thought, in
idealism, and in ethereal grace of expression, and
scarcely equalling the few fragments of the early Æolic
poetry in the force of passion, is yet an instrument of
varied power, capable of investing the lightest moods or
most transient joys of life with an unfading charm, and
rising into fuller and more commanding tones to express
the national sentiment and moral dignity of Rome. The
didactic poetry of Lucretius and Virgil was constructed
after the models of Empedocles and of Hesiod ; but it is
to the Roman, not to the Greek poets, that this form of
composition owes its substantial value. It was by their
skill that poetic art was made to embrace within its province the treatment of a great philosophical argument,
and of a great practical pursuit. The elegiac poets of
the Augustan age, while borrowing the outward form
of their compositions from the early poets of Ionia and
the later writers at the court of Alexandria, have taken

the substance of their poetry to a great extent from their own lives and interests ; and have treated their materials with a fluent brilliancy of style, and often with a graceful tenderness of feeling, unborrowed from any foreign source. It may thus be generally affirmed that the Roman poets, although adding little to the great discoveries or inventions in literature, and although not successful in all their adaptations of the inventions of their predecessors, have yet left the stamp of their own genius and character on some of the greatest forms which poetry has hitherto assumed.

The metres of Roman poetry are also seen to be adaptations to the Latin language of the metres previously employed in the epic, lyrical, and dramatic poetry of Greece. The Italian race had, in earlier times, struck out a native measure, called the Saturnian,—apparently of a rapid irregular flow,—in which their religious emotions, their festive raillery, and, perhaps, some of their patriotic memories were rudely expressed. But after this measure had been rejected by Ennius, as unsuited to the gravity of his greatest work, the Roman poets, from their deficiency in inventive faculty, continued to imitate the metres of their Greek predecessors. But, in their hands, they became characterised by a slow, stately, and regular movement, not only differing widely from the ring of the native Saturnian rhythm, but also, with every improvement in poetic accomplishment, receding further and further from the freedom and variety of the Greek measures. The comic and tragic measures, in which alone the Roman writers observed a less strict rule than their models, never attained among them to any high metrical excellence. The rhythm of the Greek poets, owing in a great measure to the frequency of vowel sounds in their language, is more flowing, varied and richly musical than that of Roman poetry. Thus, although their verse is constructed on the same metrical

laws, there is the most marked contrast between the
rapidity and buoyancy of the Iliad or the Odyssey, and
the slow and weighty movement of the Æneid. Notwithstanding their outward conformity to the canons of
a foreign language, the most powerful and characteristic
measures of Roman poetry,—the Lucretian and Virgilian
hexameter, and the Horatian alcaic,—are distinguished
by a grave, orderly, and commanding tone, symbolical
of the genius and the majesty of Rome. In such cases,
as the Horatian sapphic and the Ovidian elegiac, where
the structure of the verse is too slight to produce this
impressive effect, there is still a remarkable divergence
from the freedom and manifold harmony of the early
Greek poets to a uniform and monotonous cadence.

The language, also, of Roman poetry betrays many
traces of imitation. Some of the early Latin tragedies
were literal translations from the works of the Athenian
dramatists; and fragments of the rude Roman copy
may still, in a few cases, be compared with the polished
expression of the original. Some familiar passages of
the Iliad may be traced among the rough-hewn fragments of the Annals of Ennius. Even Lucretius, whose
diction, more than that of most poets, produces the
impression of wonderful freshness and originality, has
described outward objects, and clothed his thoughts, in
language borrowed from Homer and Empedocles. The
short volume of Catullus contains translations from Sappho and Callimachus: and, from the extant fragments
of Alcæus, Anacreon, and others of the Greek lyric poets,
it may be seen how frequently Horace availed himself
of some turn of their expression to invest his own experience with old poetic associations. Virgil, whose
great success is, in no slight measure, due to the skill
and taste with which he used the materials of earlier
Greek and native writers, has reproduced the heroic
tones of Homer in his epic, and the mellow cadences of

Theocritus in his pastoral poems; and has blended something of the antique quaintness and oracular sanctity of Hesiod with the golden perfection of his Georgics.

But besides the direct debt which each Roman poet owed to the Greek author or authors whom he imitated, it is difficult to estimate the extent to which the taste of the later Romans was formed by the familiar study of a foreign language so much superior to the rude speech spoken by their fathers. The habitual study of any foreign language has an influence not on style only, but even on the structure of thought and the development of emotion. The Roman poets first learned, from the study of Greek poetry, to feel the graceful combinations and the musical power of expression, and were thus stimulated and trained to elicit the same effects from their native language. It is for this gift, or power over language, that Lucretius prays in his invocation to the creative power of nature,—

> Quo magis æternum da dictis, diva, leporem ;

and it is this which Catullus claims as the characteristic excellence of his own poems.

The Augustan poets attained a still greater success in the variations of words and rhythm; but they scarcely show the same freshness and intensity as their immediate predecessors show in availing themselves of the newly discovered resources of their native tongue.

Yet the Latin language appears, in its adaptation to poetry, to have lost some of its power as an immediate vehicle of thought. In Virgil and in Horace, words are combined in a less natural order than in Homer and the Attic dramatists. Their language does not strike the mind with the spontaneous force of Greek poetry, nor does it seem equally suited to impress or move a popular audience. The power of direct, natural speech, stamped upon the rude fragments of the early epic and tragic poetry of Rome, passed away before the elaborate art of the Augustan poets. Catullus is perhaps the only great Roman poet who can express himself at once with perfect grace and with the happiest simplicity. Yet the studied and compact diction of Latin poetry, if wanting in fluency, ease, and directness, lays a strong hold upon the mind, by its power of presenting objects and ideas in their logical connexion and interdependence. The thought and sentiment of Rome have been engraved on her poetical literature, in deep and enduring characters. And, notwithstanding all manifest traces of imitation, the diction of the greatest Roman poets attests the presence of genuine creative power. A strong vital force is immediately perceptible in the fresh and vigorous diction of Ennius and Lucretius; and, though more latent, is not less really present under the stateliness and splendour of Virgil, and the subtle moderation of Horace.

Roman poetry owes also a considerable part of its substance to Greek thought, art, and traditions. This reproduction of old materials is, indeed, the chief source of that conventional element which detracts from the originality of some of the masterpieces of Roman genius. The old religious belief of Rome and Italy was thus merged in the poetical restoration of the Olympian Gods; the story of the origin of Rome became inseparably connected with the personages of Greek poetry; the familiar manners of a late civilisation appear in unnatural association with the idealised features of the heroic age. Even the expression of personal feeling, experience, and convictions is often coloured by light reflected from earlier representations. Hence a great deal of what is most beautiful in Latin poetry appears to come less directly from nature, and to fit less closely to the facts of human life, than the best poetry both of Greece and of modern nations. This imitative and composite workmanship is more apparent in the

later than in the earlier poets. The substance and
thought of Ennius, Lucretius, and Catullus, even when
they are reproductions of Greek materials, appear to be
fresher and more vivified by their own feeling than
the substance and thought of the Augustan poets. The
beautiful and stately forms of Greek legend, which lived
a second life in the young imagination of Catullus, were
becoming trite and conventional to Virgil :—

Cetera, quæ vacuas tenuissent carmina mentes,
Omnia jam vulgata.

The ideal aspect of the golden morning of the world has
been seized with a truer feeling in the Epithalamium of
Peleus and Thetis than in the episode of the 'Pastor Aris-
tæus' in the Georgics. Not only are the main features in
the story of the Æneid of foreign origin, but the treatment
of the story betrays the want of any sincere conviction
of its reality, or any vital sympathy with the elements
out of which it is composed. The poem is a religious
as well as a great national work ; but the religious creed
which is expressed in it is a composite result of Greek
mythology, of Roman sentiment, and of ideas derived
from an eclectic philosophy. The manners represented
in the poem are a medley of the Augustan and of the
Homeric age, as seen in vague proportions, through the
mists of antiquarian learning. It must, indeed, be remembered that Greek traditions had penetrated into the
life of the whole civilised world, and that the belief in
the connexion of Rome with Troy had rooted itself in
the Roman mind for two centuries before the time of
Virgil. Still, the tale of the settlement of Æneas in
Latium, as told in the great Roman epic, bears the
mark of the artificial construction of a late prosaic era,
not of the spontaneous growth of imaginative legend,
in a lively, creative age. So, also, in another sphere
of poetry, while there are genuine touches of nature in
all the odes of Horace, yet the mythological accessories

of some of those which celebrate the praises of a god, or the charms of a mistress, must have been more in contrast than in harmony with his genuine convictions.

Roman poetry, from this point of view, appears to be the old Greek art reappearing under new conditions : or rather the new art of the civilised world, after it had been thoroughly leavened by Greek thought, taste, and education. The poetry of Rome was, however, a living power, after the creative energy of Greece had disappeared, so that, were it nothing more, that literature would still be valuable as the fruit of the later summer of antiquity. As in Homer, the earliest poet of the ancient world, there is a kind of promise of the great life that was to be ; so, in the Augustan poets, there is a retrospective contemplation of the life, the religion, and the art of the past, —a gathering up of 'the long results of time.' But the Roman poets had also a strong vein of original character and feeling, and many phases of national and personal experience to reveal. They had to give a permanent expression to the greatness of Rome, and to perpetuate the charm of the old Italian life. In their highest tones, they embody the patriotic spirit, the dignified and commanding attributes, and the moral strength of the Imperial Republic. There is, however, another side to their art, in which they manifest the receptive and pleasure-loving temper, and that open susceptibility to the influences of nature, which, in ancient as in modern times, have characterised the Southern nations. Like the patrician and plebeian orders in the old commonwealth, these diverse elements, naturally antagonistic, combined at last to produce the majesty and the beauty of Roman poetry. Either of these elements would by itself have been unproductive and incomplete. The pure Roman temperament, on the one hand, was too austere, too unsympathetic, too restrained and formal, to create and foster a luxuriant growth of poetry : while the

genial nature of the south, on the other hand, when dis-
sociated from the control of manlier instincts and the
elevation of higher ideas, rapidly degenerated into licentious and voluptuous effeminacy, both in life and literature. The fragments of the earlier poets indicate
the predominance of the gravity and the masculine
strength inherent in the Roman temper, almost to
the exclusion of the other element. In Lucretius,
Virgil, and Horace, moral energy is most happily combined with susceptibility to the charm and the power of
nature. Catullus and the elegiac poets of the Augustan
age, — although the first at least was endowed with
fine gifts of heart as well as of genius, — abandoned
themselves to the passionate enjoyment of their lives,
under little restraint either from the pride or the
virtue of their forefathers. Their vices, and still more
their weaknesses, are of a type most opposite to the
tendencies of the purely Roman character. Yet even
their faults may be looked upon as a kind of indirect
testimony to the ancient vigour of the race. Catullus,
in his very coarseness, betrays the grain of that strong
nature, out of which, in a better time, the freedom and
energy of the Republic had been developed. Ovid, even
in his libertinism, displays his vigorous and ardent vitality.
The effeminacy of Tibullus looks like the reaction of a
nature, enervated by the circumstances of his age, from
the high standard of manliness, which a sterner and
better time had maintained.

Among the most original characteristics of Roman
poetry, the national and patriotic sentiment of those poets
especially who lived in the early Republican era and in
the Augustan age is prominently conspicuous. Among
the poets of the Republic, Nævius and Lucilius were
animated by strong political as well as national feeling.
The chief work of Ennius was devoted to the commemoration of the ancient traditions, the august institutions,

the growing power, and the great character of the Roman State. In the works of the Augustan age, the fine episodes of the Georgics, the whole plan and many of the details of the Æneid, show the spell exercised over the mind of Virgil by the ancient memories and the great destiny of his country, and bear witness to his deep love of Italy, and his pride in her natural beauty and her strong breed of men. Horace rises above his irony and epicureanism, to celebrate the imperial greatness of Rome, and to bear witness to the purity of the Sabine households, and to the virtues exhibited in the best types of Roman character. The Fasti of Ovid, also, is a national poem, owing its existence to the strong interest which was felt by the Romans in their mythical and early story, so long as any living memory of their political life remained.

The poets of the latest age of the Republic, on the other hand, express little sympathy with national interests or with any great public cause. The time in which they flourished was not favourable to the pride of patriotism or to political enthusiasm. The contemplative genius of Lucretius inclined him to keep apart from active life ; and his philosophy taught the lesson that to acquiesce in any government was better than to engage in the strife of personal ambition which he saw raging around him ;—

> Ut satius multo jam sit parere quietum
> Quam regere imperio res velle et regna tenere.

Catullus, while eagerly enjoying his life, seems, in regard to all the grave public questions of his time, to 'daff the world aside, and bid it pass :' yet there is often, as has been well said,[1] a rough republican flavour in his careless satire ; and he retained to the last, and boldly asserted, what was the earliest, as well as the latest, instinct of ancient liberty—the spirit of resistance to the arbitrary rule of any single man.

[1] Smith's *Dict. of Greek and Roman Biography*, Art. Catullus.

B

Roman poetry is pervaded also by a peculiar vein
of imaginative emotion. There is no feeling so characteristic of the works of Roman genius as the sense of
majesty. This feeling is called forth by the idea or
appearance of strength, stability, order, or immensity;
and by whatever impresses the imagination as the symbol of power and authority, whether in the aspect of
nature, or the works, actions, and institutions of man.
It is in their most serious and elevated writings, and
chiefly in their epic and didactic poetry, that the Romans
have given expression to this grave and dignified emotion. Even the plain, rude diction of Ennius rises into
a kind of rugged sublimity when he is moved by the
vastness or massive strength of outward things, or by
the pomp and circumstance of war, or by the august
forms and symbols of government. The majestic tones
of Lucretius seem to give a voice to the deep feeling of
the order and immensity of the universe, which possessed
him. The sustained dignity of the Æneid, and the
splendour of some of the finest passages in that poem—
such for instance as that which brings before us the
solemn and magnificent spectacle of the fall of Troy—
attest how the imgination of Virgil was moved to
sympathy with the attributes of ancient and powerful
sovereignty.[1]

Further, in the fervour and elevation of their moral
feeling, the Roman poets are true exponents of the
genius of Rome. Their moral purpose is more direct,
their lessons more imperative, than the speculative and
ethical spirit in Greek poetry. They speak rather from
the will or conscience than from the wisdom that has

---

[1] The following lines, for instance, may be quoted as a specimen of the
majesty of the Æneid :—

Hæc finis Priami fatorum ; hic exitas illum
Sorte tulit, Troiam incensam et prolapsa videntem
Pergama, tot quondam populis terrisque superbum
Regnatorem Asiæ.—Æn. ii. 554-7.

searched and understood the ways of life. The tendency of the Greek poets is to sound the depths of every ethical question ; that of the Roman poets is to proclaim the plain course of duty or expediency. The former strengthen the will or purify the heart indirectly, by their truthful representation of the tragic situations in human life ; the latter appeal directly to the manlier instincts and magnanimous impulses of our nature. This glow of moral emotion pervades not the poetry only, but the oratory, history, and philosophy of Rome. It has cast a kind of religious solemnity around the fragments of the early epic, tragic, and satiric poetry : it has given an intenser fervour to the stern consistency and desperate fortitude of Lucretius : it has added the element of strength to the pathos and fine humanity in the Æneid. It is by his moral, as well as his national enthusiasm, that Horace reveals the Roman earnestness that tempered his genial nature. The language of Lucan and Juvenal still breathed the same spirit in the deadening atmosphere of the Empire. Of all the great poets of Rome, Catullus alone seems not to have come under the influence of this grave ardour of feeling, which is the more usual accompaniment of the firm temper of manhood than of the prodigal genius of youth.

There are, however, as was said above, other feelings expressed in Roman poetry, which are, perhaps, more akin to modern sympathies. In no other branch of ancient literature is so much prominence given to the enjoyment of nature, the passion of love, and the record of personal character and experience. The gravity and austerity of the old Roman life, and the predominance of public over private interests in the best days of the Republic, tended to repress, rather than to foster, the birth of these new modes of emotion. They are like the flower of that more luxuriant but less stately Italian life which spread itself abroad under the shadow of Roman institutions, and

came to a rapid maturity after her conquests had given
to Rome the accumulated treasures of the world, and left
to her more fortunate sons ample leisure to enjoy them.

The love of natural scenery and of country life is
certainly more prominently expressed in Roman than in
Greek poetry. Homer, indeed, among all the poets of
antiquity, presents by far the most vivid and true description of the outward world ; and the imagination
of others among the great Greek poets, especially of
Pindar, Æschylus, and Sophocles, appears to have been
strongly, though indirectly, affected both by the immediate aspect and by the invisible power of nature. Thucydides and Aristophanes testify to the enjoyment which
the Athenians found in the ease and abundance of their
country life, and to the affection with which they clung
to the old religious customs and associations connected
with it. But the great poets of Greece were too deeply
penetrated by the thought of the mystery and the grandeur in human life, to yield their hearts absolutely to the
charm of nature. Though their delicate sense of beauty
was unconsciously cherished and refined by the air which
they breathed, and the scenes by which they were surrounded, yet they do not, like the Roman poets, care to
dwell on the passive pleasure derived from contemplating the scenes of the natural world ; nor do they express
the happiness of passing out of the tumult of the city
into the peaceful security of the country. The difference
between the two nations in social temper and customs is
connected with this difference in their feeling towards
nature. The spirit in which a Greek enjoyed his leisure,
was one phase of his sociability, his communicativeness,
his constant passion for hearing and telling something
new,—a disposition which made the 'Λέσχη' a favourite
resort so early as the time of Homer, and which is
seen still characterising the most typical representatives
of the race in the days of St. Paul. The Roman states-

man, on the other hand, prized his *otium* as the healthy
repose after strenuous exertion. The chief relaxation
to his proud, self-dependent temper consisted in being
alone, or at ease with his household and his intimate
friends. This desire for rest and retirement was one
great element in the Roman taste for country life ;—a
taste which was manifested among the foremost public
men, such as the Scipios and Laelius, long before any
trace of it is betrayed in Roman poetry. But, as the
practice of spending the unhealthy months of autumn
away from Rome became general among the wealthier
classes, and as new modes of sentiment were fostered by
greater leisure and finer cultivation, a genuine love of
nature,—taking the form either of attachment to particular places, or of enjoyment in the life and beautiful
forms of the outward world,—was gradually awakened
in the minds which were by nature most open to such
influences.

The poetry of the Augustan age and of that immediately preceding it is deeply pervaded by this love of
nature. Each of the great poets manifests the feeling
in his own way. Lucretius, while contemplating the
majesty of nature's laws, and the immensity of her
range, is, at the same time, powerfully moved to sympathy with her ever-varying life. He feels the charm
of simply living in fine weather, and looking on the
common aspects of the world,—such as the sea-shore,
rich pastures and full-flowing rivers, or the new loveliness of the early morning. He represents, under the
symbol of the punishment of the Danaides, the incapacity
to enjoy the natural charm of the recurring seasons of
the year, among the miseries which the restless spirit
of man entails upon him. Catullus, too, has many fine
images from nature in his poems. He delights in comparing the grace and the passion of youth with the
bloom of flowers and the stateliness of trees ; he asso-

ciates the beauty of Sirmio with his bright picture of
the happiness of home ; he feels the return of the genial
breezes of spring as enhancing his delight in leaving the
plains of Phrygia, and in hastening to visit the famous
cities of Asia. Virgil's early art was characterised by
his friend and brother poet in the lines,—

> Molle atque facetum
> Virgilio annueruut gaudentes rure camenæ.[1]

The love of natural, and especially of Italian, beauty
blends with all his patriotic memories, and with the
charm which he has cast around the common operations
of rustic industry. The freedom and peace of his country life, among the Sabine hills, kept the heart of Horace
fresh and simple, in spite of all the pleasures and flat-
teries to which he was exposed ; and enabled him, till
the end, to mingle a clear fountain of native poetry with
the stiller current of his meditative wisdom.

The passion of love was a favourite theme both of the
early lyrical poets of Greece, and of the courtly writers
of Alexandria, but their works have reached us only
in inconsiderable fragments ; and it is thus in Roman
literature that the power of that passion over the men of
antiquity is most distinctly declared. Few among the
poets who have recorded their own experience of love, in
any age, have expressed a feeling so true or so intense
as Catullus. He has all the ardent, unselfish devotion, if
he has not the romance and purity, of modern sentiment.
He has painted the love of others also, with graceful
fidelity. He has shown the finest sense in discerning,
and the finest power in delineating the charm of youthful passion, when first awakening into life, or first unfolding into a true and deep affection. Virgil has imparted
the chief personal interest to the story of the Æneid
by his delineation of the agony of Dido. If he has failed

---

[1] 'The muses, who delight in the country, have granted tenderness and
grace to Virgil.'—HORACE, Sat. 1. 10, 45.

to embody any complex type of character, he has described the tumult and pathos of this particular passion at least with a powerful hand. Horace is the poet of love, in its lighter, gayer moods. Without ever losing self-command, he experienced enough of its pains and pleasures, to enable him to paint the fascination or the waywardness of a mistress with the equable feeling of an epicurean, but, at the same time, with the refined observation of a poet. The elegiac poets of the Augustan age, as pleasure was the chief pursuit of their lives, allowed the weaker and the baser moods of the passion of love to enter too largely into their poetry. Yet the effeminacy of Tibullus is redeemed by real tenderness of heart; and the profligacy of Ovid is, if not redeemed, at least relieved, by his buoyant wit and his brilliant fancy.

Roman poetry is also interesting as the record of personal experience and character. The biographies of ancient authors are altogether untrustworthy; and thus it is chiefly through the conscious or unconscious self-portraiture in their writings that the actual men of antiquity are brought into close contact with the modern world. Few men of any age or country are so well known to us as Horace; and it is from his own writings, exclusively, that this intimate knowledge has been obtained. The lines in which he describes Lucilius are more applicable to himself than to any extant writer of Greece or Rome,—

> Ille velut fidis arcana sodalibus olim
> Credebat libris: neque si male cesserat, usquam
> Decurrens alio, neque si bene: quo fit, ut omnis
> Votiva pateat veluti descripta tabella
> Vita senis.[1]

He has described himself, his tastes and pursuits, his

---

[1] 'He, in old days, used to intrust all his secret thoughts to his books, as to friends on whom he could rely, turning nowhere else, either in evil fortune or in good; and thus it is, that the whole life of the old poet lies before our eyes, as if it were portrayed on a votive picture.'—Sat. II. i. 30.

thoughts and convictions, with perfect frankness and
candour, and without any of the triviality or affectation of literary egotism. Catullus, although sometimes
wanting in proper reticence, and altogether devoid of
that meditative art with which Horace transmutes his
own experience into the common experience of human
nature, is known also as a familiar friend, from the
force of feeling with which he realised, and the transparent sincerity with which he recorded, all the pain
and the pleasure of his life. The elegiac poets of the
Augustan age have written, neither from so strong a
heart as that of Catullus, nor with the good taste and
self-respect of Horace ; but yet one of the chief sources
of interest in their poetry arises from their unreserved
communicativeness, and from the light they thus throw
on one phase of the life and character of antiquity.
This record of their own lives is especially to be prized
from the rarity with which personal experience is ob-
truded in the best ancient literature.

Nor are these indications of individual character confined to the poets who profess to communicate their
own feelings, and to record their own fortunes. All the
works of Roman poetry bear emphatically the impress
of their authors. While the finest Greek poetry is a
pure, almost impersonal emanation of genius, Roman
poetry is, to a much greater extent, the expression of
character. The great Roman writers manifest that kind
of self-consciousness which accompanies resolute, successful effort ; while the Greeks enjoy that happy self-forgetfulness which attends the unimpeded exercise of a
natural gift. The epitaphs composed for themselves
by Nævius, Ennius, and Pacuvius, and the assertion
of their own originality and of their hopes of fame,
which occurs in the poetry of Lucretius, Virgil, and
Horace, were dictated by a strong sense of their own
personality, and of the importance of the task on

which they were engaged. Catullus, although he is
most frank in communicating his feelings and pursuits,
has much less of the consciousness of genius, is much
more humble in his aspirations, and more modest in
his estimate of himself. In this, as in other respects,
he approaches nearer to the type of Greek art than any
of his brother-poets of Rome.

It is a common remark that the very greatest poets
are those about whose personal characteristics least is
known. It is impossible in their case to determine
where they have expressed the real sympathies of their
heart, and the real convictions of their conscience.
They rise above the prejudices of their country and the
accidents of their time, and can see the good and evil
inseparably mixed in all human action. No criticism
can throw any trustworthy light on the personal position, the pursuits and aims, the outward and inward
experience of Homer. It cannot even be determined
with certainty how much of the poetry which bears his
name is the creation of his own inexhaustible genius;
and how much is the 'divine voice' of earlier singers
still 'floating around him.' Such inquiries are ever
attracting and ever baffling a high curiosity. They leave
the mind perplexed with the doubt whether it is discerning, in the far distance, the outline of solid moun-
tain-land, or only the transient shapes of the clouds.
Hesiod, on the other hand, a poet of equal or nearly
equal antiquity, but of an infinitely lower order of genius,
has left his own likeness graphically delineated on his
remains. There is much to interest a reader in the old
didactic poem, 'The Works and Days,' but it is not the
interest of studying a work of art or of creative genius.
The charm of the book consists partly in its power of
calling up the ideas of a remote antiquity and of human
life in its most elemental conditions; partly in the distinct impression which it bears of a character of an an-

tique and primitive and yet not unfamiliar type;—a character of deep natural piety and righteousness, but with a
quaint intermixture of other qualities,—homespun sagacity and worldly wisdom;—genuine thrift, and horror
of idleness, of war, of seafaring enterprise;—sardonic
dislike of the airs and vices of women, and a grim discontent with his own condition, and with the poor soil
which it was his lot to till.[1] It is through his want
of those gifts of genius which have made Homer immortal as a poet, and a mere name as a man, that Hesiod
has left so distinct a picture of himself to the latest
times. In like manner Roman poetry, while it never
rises to the height of creative, impersonal genius, from
this very defect, is a true revelation of the poets themselves. The Æneid supplies ample materials for understanding the temper, affections, and convictions of Virgil. Lucretius makes his personal presence felt through
the whole march of his argument, and supports every
position of his system not with his logic only, but with
the intensity of his being. The fragments of Ennius
afford the most authentic evidence from which it may
be judged what manner of man he was.

It thus appears that, over and above their higher and
finer excellencies, the Roman poets have this additional
source of interest, that, more than any other authors in
the vigorous times of antiquity, they satisfy the modern
curiosity in regard to personal character and experience.
These poets have themselves left the most trustworthy
record of their happiest hours and most real interests; of
their standard of conduct, their personal worth and their
strength of affection; of the studies and the occupations

---

[1] The strange parallel which Mr. Ruskin draws (*Modern Painters*, vol. iii.
p. 194), between an ancient Greek and 'a good, conscientious, but illiterate
Scotch Presbyterian Border farmer of a century or two back,' becomes
almost intelligible, if we regard Hesiod as a normal type of the Greek
mind.

in which they passed their lives, and of the spirit in which they awaited the certainty of their end.

It remains to say a few words in regard to the historical progress of this branch of literature. The history of Roman poetry may be divided into four periods :—

I. The age of Nævius, Ennius, Lucilius, etc., extending from about B.C. 240 till about B.C. 100 :

II. The age of Lucretius and Catullus, immediately before the fall of the Republic ; from about B.C. 60 to about B.C. 46 :

III. The Augustan age :

IV. The whole period of the Empire after the time of Augustus.

The poetry of each of these periods is distinctly marked in form, style, and character. There is evidently a great progress, in artistic accomplishment and in poetical feeling, from the rude cyclopean remains of the annals of Ennius to the stately proportions and elaborate workmanship of the Æneid. Yet this advance was attended with some loss as well as gain. With infinitely less accomplishment and less variety, the older writers show signs of a robuster life and a more vigorous understanding than some at least of those who adorn the Augustan era. They attempted to work after the model of the great masters, who had made the most heroic passions and most serious interests of men the subject of their art. They were men also of the same fibre as the chief actors on the stage of public affairs, living with them in familiar friendship, while at the same time they maintained a close sympathy with popular feeling and the national life. Their fragments are thus, apart from their intrinsic merits, especially valuable as the contemporary language of that great time, and as giving some expression to the strength, the dignity, and the freedom which were stamped upon the old Republic.

For more than a generation after the death of Attius and Lucilius, no new poet of any eminence appeared at Rome. The vivid enjoyment of life, and the sense of security which usually accompany and foster the successful cultivation of art, had been rudely interrupted by the convulsions of the State. A new birth of Roman poetry took place during the brief lull between the storms of the first and second civil wars. The new poets arose independently of the old literature. They appealed not to popular favour, but to the tastes of the few and the educated; they gave expression not to any public or national sentiment, but to their individual thought and feeling. Their works reflect the restless agitation of a time of revolution; but they show also all the vigour and sincerity of republican freedom. While greatly superior to the fragments of the older poetry in refinement of style, and in depth and variety of poetical feeling, they want the simple strength of moral conviction, and the interest in great practical affairs, which characterised their predecessors. They are inferior to the poets of the Augustan age in artistic skill; but they show greater power of thought, greater intensity of passion, a stronger and livelier inspiration, a bolder, more independent character.

Between the date of the latest poems of Catullus and of the Bucolics of Virgil only five or six years intervened. This short interval marks the beginning of a new era in literature and in history:

Magnus ab integro saeclorum nascitur ordo.

Catullus, dying almost contemporaneously with the extinction of popular freedom, is, in every nerve and fibre, the poet of a republic. Virgil, even before the final success of Augustus, proclaimed the advent of the new Empire; and he became the sincere admirer and interpreter of its order and magnificence. Most of the other poets of that age, though born before the final extinction of ancient liberty, show the influence of their time, not only by sympathy with or acquiescence in the new order of things, but by a perceptible lowering in the higher energies of life. Still, the poetry of the Augustan age, if inferior in natural force to that of the Republic, is the culmination of all the previous efforts of Roman art; and is, at the same time, the most complete and elaborate representation of Roman and Italian life.

The chief interest of Roman poetry, considered as the work of men of natural genius and cultivated taste, and as the expression of great national ideas or of individual thought and impulse, ceases with the end of the Augustan age. Under the continued pressure of the Empire, true poetical inspiration and pure feeling for art were lost. One certain test of this decay is the absence of musical power and sweetness from the verse of the later poets. Yet some of the poets of the Empire have their own peculiar greatness. Lucan and Juvenal express the masculine tone and fervid feeling of the old Roman character, liberalised, but not enervated, by the progress of thought and education. In the Satires of Persius, there is an atmosphere of purer morality than in any earlier Roman writer, with the exception of Cicero. There is much vigour, sense, and wit, intermingled with the coarseness of Martial. Yet it is owing rather to their rhetorical or their intellectual ability than to their genius or taste that these writers are still read and admired. The artificial epics of Silius Italicus and Valerius Flaccus may be occasionally read in the interests of learning; but it is hardly probable that they will, or desirable that they should, ever be permanently restored from the neglect and oblivion into which they are gradually subsiding.

This review of Roman poetry will bring before us the origin and progressive growth of a branch of literature, moulded, indeed, on the forms of earlier art, but executed

with native energy, and expressive of native character.
In this poetry not the genius only, but the inner nature
and sympathies of some of the most interesting men of
antiquity are displayed. It throws light on the influences which determined the action of different epochs
in Roman history. The great qualities of Rome—her
strength, dignity, sagacity, and virtue—mould and ani-
mate her poetry. These qualities are found in harmonious union with the spirit of enjoyment and the sense
of exuberant life, flowing from the genial air of Italy ;
and with a refinement of taste drawn from the purest
source of human culture which the world even now possesses. After all deductions have been made for their
want of inventiveness, it still remains true, that the
Roman poets of the Republic and of the Augustan age
have added to the masterpieces of literature some great
works of true native feeling as well as of elegant and
elaborate execution.

CHAPTER II.

THE Romans themselves traced the origin of their
poetry, and of all their literature, to their contact with
the mind of Greece.   As it is expressed in the familiar
lines of Horace,—

> Græcia capta ferum victorem cepit, et artes
> Intulit agresti Latio.[1]

The first productive literary impulse was communicated to the Roman mind by the Greek slave, Livius
Andronicus, who, in the year B.C. 240—one year after
the end of the First Punic War—brought out, before a
Roman audience, a drama translated or imitated from
the Greek.   From this time Roman poetry advanced
along the various literary channels which the creative
energy of Greek genius had formed.

But it has been maintained, in recent times, that this
was but the second birth of Roman poetry, and that a
golden age of native minstrelsy had preceded this historical development of literature.   The most distinguished
supporters of this theory are Niebuhr and Macaulay.   In
the preface to his *Lays of Rome*, Macaulay says that ' this
early literature abounded with metrical romances, such as
are found in every country where there is much curiosity
and intelligence, but little reading and writing.'   Niebuhr
goes so far as to assert that the Romans in early times

[1] ' Vanquished Greece vanquished her fierce conqueror, and brought art
into rude Latium.'

possessed epic poems, 'which in power and brilliance of imagination leave everything produced by the Romans in later times far behind them.' He considers the flourishing period of this native poetry to have been the fifth century after the foundation of the city. He holds that the early lays were of plebeian origin, strongly animated by plebeian sentiment, and familiarly known among the mass of the people ; that they disappeared after the ascendency of the new literature, chiefly through the influence of Ennius ; whose immediate predecessor, Nævius, was the last of the genuine native minstrels. He professes also to find clear traces of these ballads and epic poems in the fine legends of early Roman history. The theory is supported by arguments founded on the testimony of ancient writers ; on indications of the early recognition of poetry by the Roman State (as, for instance, the worship of the Camenæ) ; on the poetical character of early Roman story ; and on the analogy of other nations.

Although there may be no more ground for believing in a golden age of early Roman poetry than in a golden age of innocence and happiness, yet the question raised by Niebuhr deserves to be examined, not only from a regard to his authority, but also as opening up an inquiry into the probable nature and value of the rude germs of literature which the Latin soil produced. There may be no substantial evidence of the existence among the Romans of anything corresponding to the modern ballad or the early epic of Greece ; yet certain kinds of metrical composition did spring up and flourish among the Italians, previously to and independently of their Greek culture. The controversy that has arisen out of Niebuhr's theory must, like the Ossianic controversy in modern times, be regarded as one, not so much concerning the existence of some kind of indigenous poetry or verse, as about its nature and importance.

It has been observed in the former chapter that the
metres of all the great Roman poets were founded on the
earlier metres of Greece. But there was a native Italian
metre, called the Saturnian, which was employed apparently in various kinds of composition, and was quite
different in character from the heroic and lyric measures
adopted by the cultivated poets of a later age. This metre
was used not only in the rude extemporaneous effusions
of nameless bards, but also in the long poem of Nœvius,
on the First Punic War. Horace indicates his sense of
the roughness and barbarism of the metre, in the lines,

Sic horridus ille
Defluxit numerus Saturnius, et grave virus
Munditiæ pepulere.[1]

Ennius speaks contemptuously of the verse of Nœvius,
as that employed by the old prophetic bards, before any
of the gifts of poetry had been received or cultivated—

Quum neque musarum scopulos quisquam superarat
Nec dicti studiosus erat.[2]

The irregularity of the metre may be inferred from a
saying of an ancient grammarian, that, in the long epic
of Nævius he could find no single line to serve as a
normal specimen of its structure. From the few Saturnian lines remaining, it may be inferred that the verse
was of a rapid as well as an irregular movement; and
it seems first to have come into use as an accompaniment to the beating of the foot in a primitive rustic dance.
The name, connected with Saturnus, the old Land-
God of Italy, points to the rustic origin of the metre.
It seems first to have been employed in ritual prayers
and thanksgiving for the fruits of the earth, and in the
grotesque raillery accompanying the merriment and
license of the harvest-home. Virgil is speaking evi-

[1] 'So that rough Saturnian measure passed away, and that rank humour
yielded to a finer culture.'—*Epist.* II. i. 157.
[2] 'When no one had climbed the cliffs of the muses, or gave any care to
style.'

dently of the Saturnian verse in the lines of the second
Georgic,--

> Nec non Ausonii, Troja gens missa, coloni
> Versibus incomptis ludunt risuque soluto.[1]

As the long roll of the hexameter and the stately march
of the alcaic were expressive of the gravity and majesty
of the Roman State, so the ring and flow of the Saturnian verse may be supposed to have been derived from
the primitive freedom and geniality characterising the
Italian peasantry.

The kind of metrical or rhythmical compositions
which were produced in early times, under purely native
influences, may be classed as,

1. Religious, i.e., ritual and prophetic verses.
2. Festive and satiric strains.
3. Commemorative odes sung or recited at banquets
and funerals.

1. The earliest extant specimen of the Latin language
is a fragment of the hymn of the Fratres Arvales, a
priestly brotherhood, who offered, on every 15th of May,
public sacrifices for the fertility of the fields. This fragment is variously written and interpreted, but there can
be no doubt that it is the expression of a prayer, for
protection against either blight or pestilence, addressed
to the Lares and the god Mars, and that it was uttered
with the accompaniment of dancing. The following is
the reading of the fragment, as given by Mommsen :---

> Enos, Lases, juvate.
> Ne veluerve, Marmar, sins incurrere in pleores.
> Satur fu, fere Mars.
> Limen sali.
> Sta berber.
> Semunis alternis advocapit conctos.
> Enos, Marmar, juvato.
> Triumpe, triumpe, triumpe, triumpe, triumpe.[2]

[1] 'And so the Italian peasants, a race sprung from Troy, disport themselves
in rude strains with wild bursts of laughter.'—Georg. ii. 385.

[2] It is thus interpreted by the same author:—Nos, lares, juvate. No
malam luem, Mamers, sinas incurrere in plures. Satur esto, fere Mars. In

The word *pleores* is by some interpreted as equivalent to *plures*, by others as equivalent to *flores*. According to the first interpretation, the prayer is directed to avert pestilence from the people ; according to the second, to avert a blight from the crops. The latter rendering appears more appropriate to the functions of the brotherhood. The address to Mars ' Satur fu,' or, according to another reading, ' Satur furere,' ' be satisfied or done with raging,' might refer to the severity of the winter and early spring.[1] This meaning of the words points to the earlier form of the Italian and Greek religion, under which the various powers of nature were deified and worshipped. The other expressions in the prayer appear to be, either directions given to the dancers, or the sounds uttered as the dance proceeded.

Another short fragment has been preserved from the hymn of the Salii, also an ancient priesthood, supposed to date from the times of the early kings. The hymn is characterised by Horace, among other specimens of ancient literature, as equally unintelligible to himself and to its affected admirers.[2]

From the extreme antiquity of these ceremonial chants it may be inferred that metrical expression among the Romans, as among the Greeks and other ancient nations, owed its origin to a primitive religious worship. But while the early Greek hymns or chants in honour of the gods soon assumed the forms of pleasant tales of human adventure, or tragic tales of human suffering, the Roman hymns retained their formal and ritual character unchanged among all the changes of

limen insili. Desiste verberare (limen) ! Semones alterni advocate cunctos. Nos, Mamers, Juvato. Tripudia.
  ' Help us, Lares. Suffer not, Mamers, pestilence to fall on the people. Be satisfied, fierce Mars. Leap on the threshold. Cease beating it. Call, in turn, on all the demigods. Help us, Mamers.'—MOMMSEN, *Rom. Geschichte*, vol. i. ch. xv.
  [1] Such is the interpretation of Cormen, *Origines Poësis Romanæ*.
  [2] *Epist*. II. i. 80.

creed and language. In the lines just quoted there is
no trace of creative fancy, nor any germ of deep devo-
tional feeling, such as might have been matured into
lyrical or contemplative poetry. They sound much like
the words of a rude incantation. They are the obscure
memorial of a primitive, agricultural people, living in a
blind sense of dependence on their gods, and restrained
by a superstitious formalism from all activity of thought
or fancy. Such compositions cannot be attributed to
the inspiration or skill of any early poet, but seem to
have been copied from the uncouth and spontaneous
shouts of a simple, unsophisticated priesthood, engaged in
a rude ceremonial dance. While the religious sentiment
of the Greeks kindled their imaginative sympathy with
nature and with human life, and thereby gave birth to
poetry and art, the ritualism of Roman superstition re-
pressed all novelty of thought, feeling, and imagination,
and was more calculated to check than to promote any
literary impulse.

The verses of the Fauns and Vates spoken of by Ennius, with allusion to the poem of Nævius, in the lines,

Scripsere alii rem,
Versibu' quos olim Fauni vatesque canebant,

were probably as far removed from poetry as the ritual
chants of the Salii and the Fratres Arvales. The Fauni
were the woodland gods of Italy, and were supposed to
be endowed with prophetic power. The word *Vates*
originally means not a poet, but a soothsayer. The
Camenæ or Casmenæ (another form of which word is
Carmenta, the prophetic mother of Evander), were worshipped, not as the inspirers of poetry, but as the fore-
tellers of future events.[1]   Both the Greeks and the
Romans sought to obtain a knowledge of the future,
either through the interpretation of omens, or through
the voice of persons supposed to be divinely endowed

[1] Cf. Schwegler, *Röm. Gesch.* i. 24, note 1.

with foresight. But the Greeks, even in the regard which they paid to auguries and oracles, were influenced, for the most part, by their lively, susceptible imagination; while the Romans, from the earliest to the latest eras of their history, lived under the bondage of a scrupulous and unreasoning ceremonialism. The notices in Latin literature of the functions of these early Vates — as, for instance, the counsel of the Etrurian seer to drain the Alban Lake during the war with Veii, and the prophecy of Marcius uttered during the Second Punic War,

Amnem Trojugena Cannam Romane fuge, etc.,[1]

suggest no more idea of poetical inspiration than the occasional notices, in Latin authors, of the oracles of the Sibylline books. The language of prophecy naturally assumes a metrical or rhythmical form, partly as an aid to the memory, partly as a means of giving to the words uttered the effect of a more solemn intonation. In Greece, the oracles of the Delphian priestess, and the predictions of soothsayers, collected in books or circulating orally among the people, were expressed in hexameter verse and in the traditional language of epic poetry; but they were never ranked under any form of poetic art. The verses of the Vates, so far as any inference can be formed as to their nature, appear to have been products and proofs of the unimaginative superstition, rather than of any imaginative inspiration among the early inhabitants of Latium.

2. Another class of metrical compositions, of native origin, but of a totally opposite character, was known by the name of the 'Fescennine verses.' These arose out of a very different class of feelings and circumstances. Horace attributes their origin to the festive meetings and exuberant mirth of the harvest-home among a primitive, strong, and cheerful race of husbandmen. He

[1] Livy xxv. 12.

points out how this rustic raillery gradually assumed
the character of fierce lampoons, and had to be restrained
by law :—

> Fescennina per hunc inventa licentia morem
> Versibus alternis opprobria rustica fudit ;
> Libertasque recurrentes accepta per annos
> Lusit amabiliter, donec jam sævus apertam
> In rabiem cœpit verti jocus et per honestas
> Ire domos impune minax. Doluere cruento
> Dente lacessiti ; fuit intactis quoque cura
> Conditione super communi ; quin etiam lex
> Pœnaque lata, malo quæ nollet carmine quemquam
> Describi : vertere modum, formidine fustis
> Ad bene dicendum delectandumque redacti.[1]

The change in character, here described, from coarse
and good-humoured bantering to libellous scurrility, may
be conjectured to have taken place when the Fescennine
freedom passed from villages and country districts to
the active social and political life within the city. That
this change had taken place in Rome at an early period,
is proved by the fact that libellous verses were for-
bidden by the laws of the Twelve Tables.[2] The original
Fescennine verse appears, from the testimony of Horace,
to have been in metrical dialogue. This rude amusement,
in which a coarse kind of banter was interchanged during
their festive gatherings, was in early times characteristic
of the rural populations of Greece and Sicily, as well as
Italy, and was one of the original elements out of which
Greek comedy was developed. The more probable ety-

[1] ' The Fescennine raillery in this way, arose and poured forth its rustic
banter in responsive strains ; its free spirit, made welcome, as the season
came round, played a genial part ; until the jests first grew savage, then
passed into utter madness, and began, with impunity, to threaten and
assail honourable households. Men smarted under the sharp edge of its
cruel tooth : even those who were unassailed felt concern for the common
weal. A law was passed, and a penalty enforced, forbidding any one to be
branded in libellous verse. Thus they changed their style, and were
brought back to a kindly and pleasant tone, under fear of a beating.'—Epist.
II. i. 144-55.

[2] Sei quis occentasit, carmenue condisit, quod infamiam faxit flacitiomque
alterei, fuste feritor.

mology of the word *Fescennine* [1] indicates also an
affinity between these verses and the phallic odes of
the Greeks. They both appear to have sprung out of
the rudest rites and the grossest symbolism of rustic
paganism. The Fescennine raillery long retained traces
of this original character. Catullus mentions the 'pro-
cax Fescennina locutio' among the accompaniments of
marriage festivals; and the songs of the soldiers, in the
extravagant license of the triumphal procession, betrayed
unmistakably this primitive coarseness.

The original characteristics of the Fescennine verses
appear thus to have been a gross symbolism, arising out
of an unconscious sympathy with the productive power
of nature, on the one hand, and a bold and censorious
freedom of speech on the other. To the first the origin
of ancient pastoral poetry, to the second the origin of
Roman satire, may be traced.

Sicily was the birthplace of pastoral poetry, and
the rude germs of that form of composition appear to
have first existed among the native Sicilian people—
a people of the same origin as the Italians—before they
assumed a cultivated form under the plastic influence of
Greek genius. [2] The purely pastoral idylls of Theocritus,
—such as the first in which the lament of the shepherds
for Daphnis occurs, are supposed to have been founded
on some older native poems or traditions. The idylls
which describe the passions or the humours of the city—
as, for instance, the second and the fifteenth—look as if

[1] According to Corssen, from *fascinum*, used by Horace (*Epod.* viii. 18)
and others, as equivalent to *phallus*.

[2] 'The first bucolic poem is said to have been sung by Diomus, a cowherd
in Sicily, a country abounding in cattle. The hero of this pastoral poetry
was the shepherd Daphnis (celebrated in Theocritus), who had been beloved
by a nymph, and deprived by her, out of jealousy, of his sight, and with
whose laments all nature sympathised.'—K. O. MÜLLER, *Literature of Ancient
Greece.*

According to Müller, this rude strain of merely local interest was first
raised to a classical branch of Greek poetry by Stesichorus.

they were drawn directly from the contemporary life of
Alexandria or Syracuse. But many of the others stand
in no immediate relation to the tastes and manners familiar to Greek civilisation; and yet, from their fresh, uncon-
ventional character, they cannot be supposed to be without a root in nature and human experience. The most
probable account of their origin appears to be that they
are artistic reproductions of some features of rustic life
in Sicily, which either actually existed in the time of
Theocritus, or had been handed down from an earlier
time in some kind of native poetry. The raillery of his
herdsmen and reapers recalls Horace's description of the
Fescennine poetry :—

> Versibus alternis opprobria rustica fudit ;

and, not unfrequently, the coarser characteristics suggested by the name. It might, perhaps, be conjectured
that the genial enjoyment of nature, in Theocritus,
which is more like the spirit of Roman than of Greek
poetry, was instilled into him by contact with that
Sicilian life, which he has represented with the ideal
colouring of Greek art and feeling, and with his own pictorial power and musical sweetness.

It is seldom that the pastoral poetry, either of ancient
or modern times, has reproduced the real life of peasants
and herdsmen. Even the idylls of Theocritus present
this life only in 'the second intention.' If they are
fresher than the bucolics of Virgil, they are yet far
from being a true, or at least a complete picture of
the manners of such shepherds and shepherdesses as
have ever lived in the world. The Fescennine verses
must have been a more real and natural expression of
the rude country life of antiquity. The pastoral poetry
of Scotland is, perhaps, more directly drawn from real
experience than any other similar poetry in modern
times. Many of the older Scotch songs and ballads
exhibit a vein of coarse sentiment and humour, not un-

like to that which revealed itself in the Fescennine verses of Italy and Sicily.

While it seems probable that native Sicilian verses, analogous to the Fescennine verses of Italy, contained the germ which ultimately unfolded into the rich flower of Greek idyllic poetry, the indigenous verses of Italy bore a very different fruit. In Rome this vein of raillery, allying itself with the freedom and boldness of the plebs, assumed the form of personal lampoons. These rude and inartistic verses were the first expression of that aggressive, censorious spirit which afterwards animated Roman satire. But the original satura, which also was familiar to the Romans before they became acquainted with Greek literature, was somewhat different both from the Fescennine verses, and from the lampoons which arose out of them. The word *satura* is said to be derived from the *satura lanx*,— a plate filled with various kinds of fruit offered to the gods,—and properly means a medley. It was originally a kind of dramatic entertainment, accompanied with music and dancing, differing from the Fescennine verses in being regularly composed and not extemporaneous, and from the drama, in being without a connected plot. The origin of this composition is traced by Livy[1] to the representation of Etrurian dancers, who were brought to Rome during a pestilence. The Roman youth, according to his account, being moved to imitation of these representations, in which there was neither acting nor speaking, added to them the accompaniment of verses of a humorous character; and continued to represent these jocular medleys, combined with music (*saturas impletas modis*), even after the introduction of the regular drama.

These scenic saturae, which, from Livy's notice, appear to have been accompanied with good-humoured

[1] vii. 2.

hilarity rather than with scurrilous raillery, prepared
the way for the reception of the regular drama among
the Romans, and will, to some extent, account for its
early popularity among them. The later Roman satire
long retained traces of a connexion with this primitive
and indigenous saturn, evinced both by the miscellaneous character of its topics, and by its frequent
employment of dramatic dialogue.

3. But it is not from any of these sources that Niebuhr
supposed the poetical character of early Roman history
to be derived. Nor is there any analogy between the
religious hymns, or the Fescennine verses of Italy, and
the modern ballad. But there is evidence of the existence, at one time, of other metrical compositions of
which scarcely anything is definitely ascertained, except
that they were sung at banquets, to the accompaniment
of the flute, in celebration of the praises of great men.
These are supposed by the supporters of Niebuhr's
hypothesis to have been heroic lays, and, in some cases,
regular epic poems. There is no direct evidence of the
time when they existed, or when they fell into disuse.
Cato, as quoted by Cicero in the Tusculan Disputations,
and in the Brutus,[1] is our earliest authority on the subject. His testimony is to the effect that many generations before his time, the guests at banquets were in
the habit of singing, in succession, the praises of great
men, to the music of the flute. Cicero in the Brutus
expresses a wish that these songs still existed in his
own day; 'utinam exstarent illa carmina, quæ multis
sæculis ante suam ætatem in epulis esse cantitata a
singulis convivis de clarorum virorum laudibus in Ori-
ginibus scriptum reliquit Cato.' Varro again is quoted,
to the effect, that boys used to be present at banquets,
for the purpose of singing 'ancient poems,' celebrating
the praises of their ancestors. Valerius Maximus men-

[1] *Tusc. Disp.* iv. 2; *Brutus*, 19.

tions 'that the older men used at banquets to celebrate in song the illustrious deeds of their ancestors, in order to stimulate the youth to imitate them.' Passages are quoted from Horace and from Dionysius, supposed to imply a belief in the ancient existence of these songs.[1]

Besides the odes sung or recited at banquets, there were certain funeral poems, called *Næniæ*, originally chanted by the female relatives of the deceased, but afterwards by hired women. As the practice of public speaking advanced, these gradually passed into a mere form, and were superseded by funeral orations.

The facts ascertained about these commemorative poems amount to no more than this,—that they were sung at banquets and the funerals of great men,—that they were of such length as to admit of several being sung in succession,—and that they fell into disuse some generations before the age of Cato. The inferences that may fairly be drawn from these statements are opposed to some of the conclusions of Niebuhr. The evidence is all in favour of their having been short lyrical pieces, and not long narrative poems. As they were sung at great banquets and funerals, it seems probable that, like the custom of exhibiting the ancestral images on the same occasions, they owed their origin to the patrician pride of family, and thus could not have been animated by strong plebeian sentiment. If they had been preserved at all, they were thus more likely to have been preserved by members of the great houses living within the city walls, than by the peasantry living among the outlying hills and country districts. If ever there were any golden age of early Roman poetry, it had passed away long before the time of Ennius and Cato.

---

[1] All the passages here referred to are quoted in Macaulay's preface to *The Lays of Rome*, which contains the clearest and most interesting exposition of the hypothesis.

The fact, however, remains, that the Romans did possess, in early times, some kind of native minstrelsy, in which they honoured the memory and the exploits of their great men. But is there any reason to suppose that these compositions were of the nature and importance assigned to them by Niebuhr, and had any great value in respect of invention, sentiment, and execution? The theory which attributes the impressive character of early Roman legend to a strong spring of native genius, pouring itself out in numerous ballads and epic poetry, really proves too much. If all their early legends were the creations of poets, the Romans, before the time of Nævius and Ennius, must have been among the most poetically gifted races that ever existed. It is difficult to believe that such a native force of feeling and imagination could have been frozen so near its source ; or that a rich, popular poetry, not scattered through thinly-peopled districts, but the possession of a great commonwealth—one most tenacious of every national memorial —could have entirely disappeared, under any foreign influence, in the course of one or two generations. But even on the supposition that a great national poetry might have passed from the memory of men—as, possibly, the poems existing before the time of Homer may soon have been lost or merged in the greater glories of the Iliad and the Odyssey—this early poetry could not have perished without leaving permanent influence on the Roman language. The growth of poetical language necessarily accompanies the growth of poetical feeling and inspiration. The sensuous, passionate, and musical force by which a language is first moulded into poetry is transmitted from one generation of poets to another. The language of Homer, by its natural and musical flow, by its accumulated wealth of meaning, by the use of traditional epithets and modes of expression, that penetrate far back into the belief, the feelings, and the life of an earlier time, implies the existence of a long line of poets who preceded him. On the other hand, the diction of the fragments of Ennius, in its strength and in its rudeness, is evidently the creation of his own time and his own mind. He has no true discernment of the characteristic difference between the language of prose and of poetry. The materials of his art had not been smoothed and polished by any long, continuous stream of national melody, but were rough-hewn and adapted by his own energy to the rugged structure of his poem.

While, therefore, it appears that the actual notices of the early commemorative poems do not imply that they were the products of imagination or poetical feeling, or that they excited much popular enthusiasm, and were an important element in the early State, their entire disappearance among a people so tenacious of all their gains, and, still more, the unformed and prosaic condition of the language and rhythm used by Nævius, Ennius, and the other early poets, lead to the presumption, that they were not much valued by the Romans at any time, and that they were not the creations of poetic genius and art. This presumption is further strengthened by such indications as there are of the recognition, or rather the non-recognition, of poets or of the poetic character at Rome in early times.

The worship of the Camenæ was indeed an old and genuine part of the Roman or Italian religion ; but, as was said before, their original function was to predict future events, and to communicate the knowledge of divination ; not like that of the Greek Muses, to imagine bright stories of divine and human adventure, —

λησμοσύνη τε κακῶν ἄμπαυμά τε μερμηράων.[1]

Even the names by which two of the Camenæ were known —Postvorta and Antevorta—suggest the prosaic

[1] 'To give forgetfulness of sorrow, and a rest from cares.'—HESIOD, *Theog.* 55.

and practical functions which they were supposed to fulfil.
The Romans had no native word equivalent to the Greek
word ἀοιδός, denoting the primary and most essential of
all poetical gifts, the power to awaken the music of language. The word *vates*, as was seen, denoted a prophet.
The title of *scriba* was applied to Livius Andronicus ;
and Nævius, who has by some been regarded as the last
of the old race of Roman bards, applies to himself the
Greek name of *poeta*,—

Florent divæ Camenæ Nævium poetam.

The commemorative odes appear to have been recited
or sung at banquets, not by poets or rhapsodists, but
by boys or guests. There is one notice, indeed, of a
class of men who practised the profession of minstrelsy.
This passage, which is quoted by Aulus Gellius from the
writings of Cato, implies the very lowest estimation of
the position and character of the poet, and points more
naturally to the composers of the libellous verses for-
bidden by the laws of the Twelve Tables, than to the
authors of heroic and national lays :—' Poeticæ artis
honos non erat : si qui in ea re studebat, aut sese ad
convivia adplicabat, grassator vocabatur.'[1]

It appears that, on this ground also, there is no reason
for believing in the existence of any golden age of
Roman poetry before the time of Ennius, or in the
theory that the legendary tales of Roman history were
created and shaped by native minstrels. To what
cause, then, can we attribute their origin ? These tales
have a strong human interest, and represent marked
and original types of antique heroism. They have the
elements of true tragic pathos and moral grandeur.
They could neither have arisen nor been preserved
except among a people endowed with strong capaci-

[1] ' Poetry was not held in honour : if any one devoted himself to it, or went
about to banquets, he was called a vagabond.'—*Noct. Att.* xi. 2.
A similar character at one time attached to minstrels in Scotland.

ties of feeling and action. But the strength of the
Roman mind consisted more in retentive capacity than
in creative energy. Their art and their religion, their
family and national customs, aimed at preserving the
actual memory of men and of their actions : not like the
arts, ceremonies, and customs of the Greeks, which aimed
at lifting the mind out of reality into an ideal world.
As one of the chief difficulties of the Homeric controversy arises from our ignorance of the power of the
memory during an age when poetry and song were in
the fullest life, but the use of letters was still unknown ;
so there is a parallel difficulty in all attempts to explain
the origin of early Roman history, from our ignorance of
the power of oral tradition in a time of orderly civilisation, but yet unacquainted with any of the forms of
literature. The ignorance and indifference of barbarous
tribes in regard to their past history can prove little or
nothing as to the tenacity of the national memory among
a civilized people like the Romans. Nor can the analogy of early Greek traditions be fairly applied to those
of Rome, owing to the great difference in the circumstances and the genius of the two nations. Many real
impressions of the past might fix themselves indelibly in
the grave and solid temperament of the Romans, which
would have been lost amid the inexhaustible wealth of
fancy that had been lavished upon the Greeks. The
strict family life and discipline of the Romans, the unity
of a single state as the common centre of all their interests, the slow and steady growth of their institutions,
were all conditions more favourable to the preservation of tradition than the lively social life, the numerous
centres of political organization, and the rapid growth
and vicissitudes of the Greek Republics.

It cannot, indeed, be disputed that although the legendary tales of Roman history may have been founded more
on memory than on imagination, yet there is no criterion
by which the amount of fact contained in these traditions

can be separated from the other elements of which they
were composed. Oral tradition among the Romans, as
among other nations, was founded on impressions originally received without any careful sifting of evidence ;
and these first impressions must gradually have been
modified in accordance with the feelings and opinions of
each generation, through which they were transmitted.
Deliberate falsification, and the systematic reconstruc-
tion of forgotten events, have also entered into the composition of Roman history. But these admissions do
not lead to the conclusion that the art or fancy of any
class of early poets was added to the unconscious opera-
tion of popular feeling in moulding the impressive tales
of early heroism, partly out of real events, partly out of
the ideal of character, latent in the national mind. It has
been remarked by Sir. G. C. Lewis that many even of the
Greek myths, abounding 'in striking, pathetic, and interesting events,' existed as prose legends, and were handed
down in the common speech of the people. In like
manner, such tales as those of Lucretia and Virginia, of
Horatius and the Fabii, of Camillus and Coriolanus,
which stand out in marked outline through the twilight
of Roman history, may have been preserved in the *fama
vulgaris*, or common speech of the people, till they were
gathered into the poem of Ennius and the prose narra-
tives of the early annalists. In so far as they are shaped
or coloured by imagination, they do not bear traces of
the conscious art of a poet, but rather of an unconscious
conformity to the national ideal of character. The most
impressive of these legendary stories illustrate the primitive virtues of the Roman character, such as chastity,
frugality, fortitude, and self-devotion ; or the national
characteristics of patrician pride and a stern exercise of
parental authority. There is certainly no internal evidence that any of them originated in a pure poetic
impulse, or gave birth to any work of poetic art deserving a permanent existence in literature.

The analogy of other nations might suggest the inference that a race which in its maturity produced a genuine poetic literature must, in the early stages of its history, have given some proof of poetic inspiration. It is natural to associate the idea of poetry with youth both in nations and individuals. Yet the evidence of their language, of their religion, and of their customs, leads to the conclusion that the Romans, while prematurely great in action and government, were, in the earlier stages of their national life, little moved by the active power of imagination. The state of religious feeling or belief which gives birth to or co-exists with primitive poetry has left no trace of itself upon the early Roman annals. It is generally found that a fanciful mythology, of a bright, gloomy, or grotesque character, in accordance with the outward circumstances and latent spirit or humour of the particular race among whom it originates, precedes and for a time accompanies the poetry of romantic action. The creative faculty produces strange forms and conditions of supernatural life out of its own mysterious sympathy with nature, before it learns to invent tales of heroic action and of tragic calamity out of its sympathy with human energy and passion, and its marvellous discernment of the course of destiny, and the vicissitudes of life. The development of the Roman religion betrays the absence, or at least the weaker influence of that imaginative power which shaped the great mythologies of different races out of the primeval worship of nature. The later element introduced into Roman religion was due not to imagination but to reflection. The worship of Fides, Concordia, Pudicitia, and the like, marks a great progress from the early adoration of the sun, the earth, the vault of heaven, and the productive power of nature ; but it is a progress in the understanding and the moral consciousness, not in poetical feeling nor imaginative power. It shows

D

that Roman civilisation advanced without this vivifying
influence ; that the mind of the race early reached the
maturity of manhood without passing through the dreams
of childhood and the buoyant fancies of youth.

The circumstances of the Romans, in early times,
were also different from those by which the growth of a
romantic poetry has usually been accompanied. Their
orderly organisation,—the early establishment of their
civic forms,—the strict discipline of family life among
them,—the formal and ceremonial character of their
national religion,—and their strong interest in practical
affairs,—were not calculated either to kindle the glow
of individual genius, or to dispose the mass of the
people to welcome the charm of musical verse. The
wars of the young Republic, carried on by a well-
trained militia, for the acquisition of new territory,
formed the character to solid strength and persistent
energy, but could not act upon the fancy in the same
way as the distant enterprise, the long struggles for
national independence, or the daring forays, which have
thrown the light of romance around the warlike youth
of other races. The tillage of the soil, in which the
brief intervals between their wars were passed, was a
tame and monotonous pursuit compared with the mari-
time adventure which awoke the energies of Greece, or
with the wild and lonely, half-pastoral, half-marauding
life, out of which a true ballad poetry arose in modern
times. Some traces of a wilder life, or some faint
memories of their Sabine forefathers, may be dimly discerned in the earliest traditions of the Roman people ;
but their youth was essentially practical,—great and
strong in the virtues of temperance, gravity, fortitude,
reverence for law, combined with sturdy resistance to
wrong. These qualities are the foundations of a powerful
and orderly State, not the root nor the sap by which a
great national poetry is nourished.[1]

[1] Cf. Schwegler, Röm. Gesch. i. i. 24.

If the pure Roman intellect and discipline had spontaneously produced any kind of literature, it would have been more likely to have taken the form of history or oratory than of national song or ballad. It was from men of the Italian provinces, and not from her own sons, that Rome received her poetry. The men of the most genuinely Roman type and character long resisted all literary progress. The patrons and friends of the early poets were the more liberal members of the aristocracy, in whom the austerity of the national character and narrowness of the national mind had yielded to new ideas and a wider experience. The art of Greece was communicated to 'rude Latium,' through the medium of those kindred races who had come into earlier contact with the Greek language and civilisation. With less native strength, but with greater flexibility, these races were more readily moulded by foreign influences ; and, leading a life of greater ease and freedom, they were more susceptible to all the impulses of nature. While they were thus more readily prepared to catch the spirit of Greek culture, they had learned, through long years of war and subsequent dependence, to understand and respect the majesty of the State in which their own nationality had been merged. It is important to remember that the time in which Roman literature arose was not only that of the first active intercourse between Greeks and Romans, but also that in which a great war, against the most powerful State outside of Italy, had awakened the sense of an Italian nationality, of which Rome was the centre. The Imperial Republic derived her education and literature from the accumulated stores of Greek thought and feeling ; but these were made available to her through the willing service of poets who, though born in alien provinces, looked to Rome as the head and representative of their common country.

CHAPTER III.

THE historical event which first brought the Romans
into familiar contact with the Greeks, was the war with
Pyrrhus and with Tarentum, the most powerful and
flourishing among the famous Greek colonies in lower
Italy. In earlier times, indeed, through their occasional
communication with the Greeks of Cumæ, and the other
colonies in Italy, they had obtained a vague knowledge
of some of the legends of Greek poetry. The worship
of Æsculapius was introduced at Rome from Epidaurus
in B.C. 293, and the oracle of Delphi had been consulted
by the Romans in still earlier times. As the Sibylline
verses appear to have been composed in Greek, their
interpreters must have been either Greeks or men acquainted with that language.[1] The identification of the
Greek with the Roman mythology had probably commenced before Greek literature was known to the
Romans, although the works of Nævius and Ennius
must have had an influence in completing this process.
Greek civilisation had come, however, at an earlier
period into close relation with the south of Italy; and
the natives of that district, such as Ennius and Pacuvius, who first settled at Rome, were spoken of by the
Romans as 'Semi Græci.' But, until after the fall of
Tarentum, there appears to have been no familiar intercourse between the two great representatives of ancient
civilisation. Before that time there is no trace of free

[1] Cf. Lewis, *Credibility of Early Roman History*, vol. I. chap. ii. 14.

Greeks residing at Rome, nor of Romans being settled
in any of the famous colonies planted by Greece on the
Italian shores. Till the war with Pyrrhus, the knowledge
that the two nations had of one another was slight and
vague. But, immediately after that time, the affairs of
Rome began to attract the attention of Greek historians,[1]
and the Romans, though very slowly, began to obtain
some acquaintance with the language and literature of
Greece.

Tarentum was taken in B.C. 272, but more than
thirty years elapsed before Livius Andronicus represented
his first drama before a Roman audience. Twenty years
of this intervening period, from B.C. 261 to B.C. 241,
were occupied with the First Punic War ; and it was
not till the successful close of that war, and the com-
mencement of the following years of peace, that this
new kind of recreation and instruction was made familiar to the Romans.

> Serus enim Græcis admovit acumina chartis ;
> Et post Punica bella quietus, quærere cœpit
> Quid Sophocles et Thespis et Æschylus utile ferrent.[2]

Two circumstances, however, must in the meantime
have prepared the minds of the Romans for the reception of the new literature. Sicily had been the chief
battle-field of the contending powers. In their intercourse with the Sicilian Greeks, the Romans had great
facilities for becoming acquainted with the Greek language, and frequent opportunities of being present at
dramatic representations. Many Greeks also had been
brought to Rome as slaves after the capture of Tarentum,
and were employed in educating the young among the
higher classes. Thus many Roman citizens were pre-

[1] Cf. Lewin, *Credibility of Early Roman History*, vol. i. chap. ii. 14, 15.
[2] 'For it was late before the Roman applied the sharpness of his wit to
the writings of the Greeks ; and, reposing after the Punic wars, began to
ask what worth there was in Sophocles, Thespis, and Æschylus.'— *Epist.* ii.
i. 161.

pared, by their circumstances and education, to take
interest in the legends and in the dramatic form of
literature introduced from Greece; while the previous
existence of the satura, and other scenic exhibitions
at Rome, must have made the new drama acceptable to
the great mass of the population.

The earliest period of Roman poetry extends from the
close of the First Punic War till the beginning of the
first century B.C.   During this period of about a century
and a half, in which Roman oratory, history, and comedy,
were also actively cultivated, we hear only of five or six
names as eminent in different kinds of serious poetry.
The whole labour of introducing and of keeping alive,
among an unlettered people, some taste for the highest
literature thus devolved upon a few men of ardent
temperament, vigorous understanding, and great productive energy; but with little sense of art, and endowed
with faculties seemingly more adapted to the practical
business of life than to the idealising efforts of genius.
They had to struggle against the difficulties incidental
to the first beginnings of art and to the rudeness of the
Latin language.   They were exposed, also, to other dis-
advantages, arising from the natural indifference of the
mass of the people to all works of imagination, and from
the preference of the educated class for the more finished
works already existing in Greek literature.

Yet this long period, in which poetry, with so much
difficulty and such scanty resources, struggled into existence at Rome, is connected with the age of Cicero
by an unbroken line of literary continuity.   Nævius, the
younger contemporary of Livius, and the first native poet,
was actively engaged in the composition of his poems till
the time of his death; about which period his greater successor first appeared at Rome.   For about thirty years,
Ennius shone alone in epic and tragic poetry.   The poetic
successor of Ennius was his nephew, Pacuvius. He, in

the later years of his life, lived in friendly intercourse with his younger rival Attius, who, again, in his old age, had frequently conversed with Cicero. The torch, which was first lighted by Livius Andronicus from the decaying fires of Greece, was thus handed down by these few men, through this long period, until it was extinguished during the stormy times which fell in the youth of the great orator and prose writer of the Republic.

The forms of serious poetry, prevailing during this period, were the tragic drama, the annalistic epic, and satire. Tragedy was earliest introduced, was received with most favour, and was cultivated by all the poets of the period, with the exception of Lucilius. The epic poetry of the age was the work of Nævius and Ennius. It has greater claims to originality and national spirit, both in form and substance, and it exercised a more powerful influence on the later poetry of Rome, than either the tragedy or comedy of the time. The invention of satire, the most purely original of the three, is generally attributed to Lucilius; but the satiric spirit was shown earlier in some of the dramas of Nævius; and the first modification of the primitive satura to a literary shape was the work of Ennius, who was followed in the same style by his nephew Pacuvius.

No complete work of any of these poets has been preserved to modern times. Our knowledge of the poetry of this long period is derived partly from ancient testimony, but chiefly from the examination of numerous fragments. Most of these have been preserved, not by critics on account of their beauty and worth, but by grammarians on account of the obsolete words and forms of speech contained in them,—a fact, which probably leads us to attribute to the earlier literature a more abnormal and ruder style than that which really belonged to it. A few of the longest and most interesting fragments have come down in the works of

the admirers of those ancient poets, especially of Cicero
and Aulus Gellius. The notion that can be formed of
the early Roman literature must thus, of necessity,
be incomplete. Yet these fragments are sufficient to
produce a consistent impression of certain prevailing
characteristics of thought and sentiment. They are
stamped with a genuine Roman strength, and with the
freedom and boldness of the time in which they were
written. They are almost the sole contemporary expression of the grave and authoritative bearing, the plain
sincerity of speech, the manly interest in practical affairs,
which were marked features in the men of the old
Republic. Many of the fragments are valuable from
their own intrinsic worth and greatness; others again
from the grave associations connected with their antiquity, and from the authentic evidence they afford
of the moral and intellectual power, the prevailing
passions and occupations of the strongest race of the
ancient world, in one of the most interesting epochs in
their history.

The two earliest authors who fill a period of forty
years in the literary history of Rome, extending from
the end of the First to the end of the Second Punic War,
are Livius Andronicus and Cn. Nævius. Of the first
very little is known. The fragments of his works are
scanty and unimportant, and have been preserved by
grammarians merely as illustrative of old forms of the
language. The admirers of Nævius and Ennius, in
ancient times, awarded only scanty honours to the older
dramatist. Cicero, for instance, says of his plays 'that
they are not worth reading a second time.'[1] There is no
ground for believing that Livius was a man of original
genius. The importance which attaches to him consists
in his being the accidental medium through which literary
art was first introduced to the Romans. He was a Greek,

_____
[1] *Brutus,* 18.

and, as is generally supposed, a native of Tarentum. If he was among the captives taken after the fall of that city, he must have resided thirty years at Rome before he ventured to reproduce a Greek drama in the Latin language. He educated the sons of his master, M. Livius Salinator, from whom he afterwards received his freedom. The last thirty years of his life were devoted to literature, and chiefly to the reproduction of the Greek drama in a Latin dress. His tragedies appear all to have been founded on Greek subjects ; most of them, probably, were translations. Among the titles, we hear of the *Ægisthus*, *Ajax*, *Equus Trojanus*, *Tereus*, *Hermione*, etc.—all of them subjects which continued to be popular with the later tragedians of Rome. No fragment is preserved sufficient to give any idea of his treatment of the subjects, or of his mode of thought or feeling. Little can be gathered from the scanty remains of his works, except some idea of the harshness and inelegance of his diction.

In addition to his dramas, he translated the Odyssey into Saturnian verse. This work long retained its place as a school-book, and is spoken of by Horace as forming part of his own early lessons under the rod of Orbilius.[1] One or two lines of the translation still remain, and exemplify its bald and prosaic diction, and the extreme irregularity of the Saturnian metre. The lines of the Odyssey,[2]

οὐ γὰρ ἔγωγέ τί φημι κακώτερον ἄλλο θαλάσσης
ἄνδρα γε συγχεῦαι, εἰ καὶ μάλα καρτερὸς εἴη ;

are thus rendered :—

Namque nilum pejus
Macerat hemonem, quamde mare saevom, viris quoi
Sunt magnae, topper confringent importunae undae.

He was appointed also, on one occasion, near the end of the Second Punic War, to compose a hymn to be sung by ‘ virgines ter novenæ,’ which is described by Livy, the historian, as rugged and unpolished.[3]

[1] *Epist.* II. L 71.   [2] VIII. 138.   [3] XXVII. 17.

Livius was the schoolmaster of the Roman people rather than the father of their literature. To accomplish what he did required no original genius, but only the industry, learning, and tastes of an educated man. If his long residence among his grave and stern masters, and the hardships and constraint of slavery, had subdued in him the levity and gaiety of a Tarentine Greek, they did not extinguish his love of his native literature and the intellectual cultivation peculiar to his race. It was creditable to his taste that he strove to introduce to the Romans the works of the old masters of Greek poetry, in preference to the Alexandrian literature. In spite of the disadvantage of writing in a foreign language, and of addressing an unlettered people, he was able to give the direction which Roman poetry long followed, and to awaken a new interest in the legends and heroes of his race. It was necessary that the Romans should be educated before they could either produce or appreciate an original poet. Livius performed a useful, if not a brilliant service, by directing those who followed him to the study and imitation of poets who combined, with an unattainable grace and art, a masculine strength and heroism of sentiment congenial to the better side of Roman character.

Cn. Nævius is really the first in the line of Roman poets, and the first writer in the Latin language whose fragments give indication of original power. He is believed to have been a Campanian by birth, on the authority of Aulus Gellius, who characterised his famous epitaph as 'plenum superbiæ Campanæ.' Though the arrogance of Campania may have been proverbial, yet the expression could scarcely with propriety have been applied, except to a native of that district. If not a Roman by birth, he became, like his successor, Ennius, a genuine Roman in character and sympathies. He served as a soldier in the First Punic War, and recorded

his services in his epic poem on that subject. The earliest
drama of Nævius was brought out in B.C. 235, five years
after the first representation of Livius Andronicus. The
number of dramas which he is known to have composed
affords proof of great industry and activity, from that
time till the time of his banishment from Rome. He was
more successful in comedy than in tragedy, and he used
the stage, as it had been used by the writers of the old
Attic comedy, as an arena of popular invective and
political warfare. A keen partisan of the commonalty,
he attacked with vehemence some of the chiefs of the
great Senatorian party. A line, which had passed into a
proverb in the time of Cicero, is attributed to him,—

Fato Metelli Romæ fiunt consules ;[1]

to which the Metelli are said to have replied in the pithy
Saturnian,

Dabunt malum Metelli Nævio poetæ.[2]

It is, however, doubted whether the first of these lines
was really written by Nævius, as the Metelli did not enjoy
their rapid succession of consulships till nearly a century
after his death ; but even at the time of the Second
Punic War they were powerful enough to procure the
imprisonment of the poet, in consequence of some
offence which he had given them. Plautus[3] alludes to
this event, in one of the few passages in which Latin
comedy deviates from the conventional life of Athenian
manners to notice the actual circumstances of the time.
While in prison, he composed two plays (the *Hariolus*
and *Leon*), which contained some retractation of his former attacks, and he was liberated through the interference of the Tribunes of the Commons. Being afterwards banished, he took up his residence at Utica, where
he is said by Cicero, on the authority of ancient records,

1 'It is fate, which makes the Metelli consuls at Rome.'
2 'The Metelli will make Nævius the poet pay for this.'
3 *Miles Gloriosus*, II. ii. 27.

to have died, in B.C. 204,[1] though the same author adds that
Varro, 'diligentissimus investigator antiquitatis,' believed
that he was still alive for some time after that date.[2]　It is
inferred, from a passage in Cicero,[3] that his poem on the
First Punic War was composed in his old age.　Probably
it was written in his exile, when removed from the sphere
of his active literary efforts.　As he served in that war,
some time between B.C. 461 and B.C. 441, he must have
been well advanced in years at the time of his death.

The best known of all the fragments of Nævius, and the
most favourable specimen of his style, is his epitaph :—

> Mortales immortales flere si foret fas,
> Flerent divæ Camenæ Nævium poetam,
> Itaque postquam est Orcino traditus thesauro,
> Obliti sunt Romæ loquier Latina lingua.[4]

It has been supposed that this epitaph was written as a
dying protest against the Hellenising influence of Ennius ; but as Ennius came to Rome for the first time
about B.C. 204, it is not likely, even if the life of Nævius
was prolonged somewhat beyond that date, that the
fame and influence of his younger rival could have
spread so rapidly as to disturb the peace of the old
poet in his exile.　It might as fairly be regarded as
proceeding from a jealousy of the merits of Plautus, as
from hostility to the innovating tendency of Ennius.
The words of the epitaph are simply expressive of the
strong self-consciousness and independence which Nævius maintained till the end of his active and somewhat
turbulent career.

He wrote a few tragedies, of which scarcely anything

---

[1] *Brutus*, 15.
[2] Mommsen remarks that he could not have retired to Utica till after it
fell into the possession of the Romans.
[3] *De Senectute*, 14.
[4] 'If immortals might weep for mortals, the holy Camenæ would weep for
Nævius the poet : for since he passed to the chambers of Orcus, men have
forgot, in Rome, how to speak in the Latin tongue.'

is known except the titles,—such as the *Andromache*, *Equus Trojanus, Hector Proficiscens, Lycurgus*,—the last founded on the same subject as the Bacchæ of Euripides. The titles of nearly all these plays, as well as of the plays of Livius, imply the prevailing interest taken in the Homeric poems, and in all the events connected with the Trojan War. The following passage from the Lycurgus has some value as containing the rude germs of poetical diction :—

> Vos, qui regalis corporis custodias
> Agitatis, ite actutum in frundiferos locos,
> Ingenio arbusta ubi nata sunt, non obsita.[1]

He composed a number of comedies, and also some original plays, founded on events in Roman history, —one of them called *Romulus*, or *Alimonia Romuli et Remi*. The longest of the fragments attributed to him is a passage from a comedy, which has been, with less probability, attributed to Ennius. It is a description of a coquette, and shows considerable power of close satiric observation :—

> Quasi pila
> In choro ludens dadatim dat se, et communem facit :
> Alii adnutat, alii adnictat, alium amat, alium tenet ;
> Alibi manus est occupata, alii percellit pedem ;
> Alii spectandum dat annulum ; a labris alium invocat ;
> Cum alio cantat, attamen dat alii digito literas.[2]

The chief characteristic illustrated by the scanty fragments of his dramas is the political spirit with which they were animated. Thus Cicero[3] refers to a passage in one of his plays (*ut est in Nævii ludo*) where,

[1] 'Ye who keep watch over the person of the king, hasten straightway to the leafy places, where the copsewood is of nature's growth, not planted by man.'

[2] 'Like one playing at ball in a ring, she tosses about from one to another, and is at home with all. To one she nods, to another winks ; she makes love to one, clings to another. Her hand is busy here, her foot there. To one she gives a ring to look at, to another blows a kiss ; with one she sings, with another corresponds by signs.'
The reading of the passage here adopted is that given by Munk.

[3] *De Senectute*, 6.

to the question, 'Who had, within so short a time, destroyed your great commonwealth?' the pregnant answer is given, applicable to other times in modern as well as ancient history,

> Proveniebant oratores novi, stulti adolescentuli.[1]

The nobles, whose enmity he provoked, were probably attacked by him in his comedies. One passage is quoted by Aulus Gellius, in which a failing of the great Scipio is exposed.[2] Other fragments are found indicative of his freedom of speech and bold independence of character :—

> Quae ego in theatro hic meis probavi plausibus,
> Ea nunc audere quemquam regem rumpere ?
> Quanto libertatem hanc hic superat servitus ![3]

and this also :[4]—

> semper pluris feci potioremque ego
> Libertatem habui multo quam pecuniam.[4]

He is characterised by an old author, who places him immediately after Plautus in the rank of comic poets, as ' Naevius qui fervet.' He has more of the stamp of Lucilius than of his immediate successor Ennius. By his censorious and aggressive vehemence, by boldness and freedom of speech, and by his strong political feeling, Naevius in his dramas represents the spirit of Roman satire rather than of Roman tragedy. He holds the same place in Roman literature as the Tribune of the

---

[1] 'A set of new orators came forward, some foolish striplings.'

[2] Etiam qui res magnas manu saepe gessit gloriose,
Cujus facta viva nunc vigent, qui apud gentes solus praestat,
Eum suus pater cum pallio ab amica abduxit uno.

[3] 'What I in the theatre here have made good by the applause given to me, think you that any of these great people will now dare to interfere with? How much better thing is the slavery here' (i.e., represented in this play) 'than the liberty we actually enjoy ?'

[4] 'I have always held liberty to be of more value and a better thing than money.' The reading is that given by Munk.

Commons in Roman politics. He expressed the vigorous independence of spirit that supported the Plebs in their long struggle with the Patricians, while Ennius may be regarded as expressing the majesty and authority with which the Roman Senate ruled the world.

But the work on which his fame as a national and original poet chiefly rested was his epic or historical poem on the First Punic War. The poem was originally one continuous work, written in the Saturnian metre; though, at a later time, it was divided into seven books. The earlier part of the work related to the mythical origin of Rome and of Carthage, the flight of Æneas from Troy, his sojourn at the court of Dido, and his settlement in Latium. The mythical background of the poem afforded scope for poetical treatment and invention. Its main substance, however, appears to have been composed in the spirit and tone of a contemporary chronicle. The few fragments that remain from the longer and later portion of the work, evidently express a bare and literal adherence to fact, without any poetical colouring or romantic representation.

Ennius and Virgil are both known to have borrowed much from this poem of Nævius. There are many passages in the Æneid in which Virgil followed the track of the older poet with slight deviations. Nævius (as quoted by Servius) introduced the wives of Æneas and of Anchises, leaving Troy in the night-time,—

> Amborum
> Uxores noctu Troiade exibant capitibus
> Opertis, flentes abeuntes lacrimis cum multis.[1]

He represented Æneas as having only one ship, built by Mercury,—a limitation which did not suit Virgil's account of the scale on which the war was carried on,

---

[1] 'The wives of both were going forth at night from the Trojan land, with their heads veiled, weeping, departing with many tears.'

after the landing in Italy. The account of the storm in the first Æneid, of Æneas consoling his followers, of Venus complaining to Jupiter, and of his comforting her with the promise of the future greatness of Rome (one of the cardinal passages in Virgil's epic), were all taken from the old Saturnian poem of Nævius. He speaks also of Anna and Dido, as daughters of Agenor, though there is no direct evidence that he anticipated Virgil in telling the tale of Dido's unhappy love. He mentioned also the Italian Sibyl and the worship of the Penates—materials which Virgil fused into his great national and religious poem. Ennius followed Nævius in representing Romulus as the grandson of Æneas. The exigencies of his chronology compelled Virgil to fill a blank space of three hundred years, with the shadowy forms of a line of Alban kings.

Whatever may have been the origin of the belief in the connexion of Rome with Troy, it certainly prevailed before the poem of Nævius was composed, as at the beginning of the First Punic War the inhabitants of Egesta opened their gates to Rome, in acknowledgment of their common descent from Troy.[1] But the story of the old connexion of Æneas and Dido, symbolising the former league and the later enmity between Romans and Carthaginians, most probably first assumed shape in the time of the Punic Wars. The belief, as shadowed forth in Nævius, that the triumph of Rome had been decreed from of old by Jupiter, and promised to the mythical ancestress of Æneas, proves that the Romans were possessed already with the idea of their national destiny. How much of the tale of Æneas and Dido is due to the imagination of Nævius it is impossible to say; but his treatment of the mythical part of his story,—his introduction of the storm, the complaint of Venus, etc.,—merits the praise of happy and suggestive invention, and of a

[1] Cf. Lewis, Credibility of Early Roman History, vol. i. chap. ix. 6.

real adaptation to his main subject. There was more meaning in the mythical foreshadowing of the deadly strife between Romans and Carthaginians, at a time when the two nations were fighting for their very existence, and for the ultimate prize of the empire of the world, than in the age of Virgil, when the power of Carthage was only a memory of the past, and the immediate danger from which Rome had escaped had arisen from no foreign enemy, but from the fierce passions of her own sons.

The mythical part of the poem was a prelude to the main subject, the events of the First Punic War. Nævius and Ennius, like others among the Roman poets of a later date, allowed the provinces of poetry and of history to run into one another. They composed poetical chronicles without any attempt to adhere to the principles and practice of the Greek epic. The work of Nævius differed from that of Ennius in this respect, that it treated of one particular portion of Roman history, and did not profess to unfold the whole annals of the State. The slight and scanty fragments that remain from the latter part of the poem, are expressed with all the bareness, and, apparently, with the fidelity of a chronicle. They have the merit of being direct and vigorous, but are entirely without poetic grace and ornament. Rapid and graphic condensation is their chief merit. There is a dash of impetuosity in some of them, suggestive of the bold, impatient, and disorderly temperament of the poet; as for instance in the lines

Transit Melitam Romanus exercitus, insulam integram
Urit, populator, vastat, rem hostium concinnat.[1]

But the fragments of the poem are really too unimpor-

[1] 'The Roman army crosses to Melita, burns, ravages, wastes the whole island, makes a clean sweep of all the enemy's property.' Mommsen remarks that, in the fragments of this poem, the action is generally represented in the present tense.

tant to afford ground for a true estimate of its general
merit. They supply some evidence in regard to the irregularity of the metre in which it was written. The uncertainty which prevails as to its structure may be inferred
from the fact that different conjectural readings of every
fragment are proposed by different commentators. A
saying of an old grammarian, Atilius Fortunatianus,
is quoted to the effect that he could not adduce from
the whole poem of Nævius any single line, as a normal
specimen of the pure Saturnian verse. Cicero bears
strong testimony to the merits of the poem in point of
style. He says in one place, 'the Punic War delights us
like a work of Myron.'[1]   In the dialogue 'De Oratore,'
he represents Crassus as comparing the idiomatic purity
which distinguished the conversation of his mother-in-
law, Lælia, and other ladies of rank, with the style
of Plautus and Nævius.   'Equidem quum audio soc-
rum meam Læliam (facilius enim mulieres incorrup-
tam antiquitatem conservant, quod, multorum sermonis
expertes, ea tenent semper, quae prima didicerunt) ; sed
eam sic audio, ut Plautum mihi aut Nævium videar
audire.   Sono ipso vocis ita recto et simplici est, ut nihil
ostentationis aut imitationis afferre videatur ; ex quo
sic locutum ejus patrem judico, sic majores.'[2]   Expressions from his plays were, from their weight and
compact brevity, quoted familiarly in the days of Cicero ;
and one of them 'laudari a laudato viro,' like so many
other pithy Latin sayings, is still in use to express a
distinction that could not be characterised in happier

[1] Brutus 10.

[2] 'I, for my part, as I listen to my mother-in-law, Lælia (for women more
easily preserve the pure idiom of antiquity, because, from their limited
intercourse with the world, they retain always their earlier impressions), in
listening, I say to her, I fancy that I am listening to Plautus or Nævius.
The very tones of her voice are so natural and simple, that she seems absolutely free from affectation or imitation ; from this I gather that her
father spoke, and her ancestors all spoke, in the very same way.'—Cicero,
De Oratore iii. 12.

or shorter terms. It is to be remarked also that the
merit, which he assumes to himself in his epitaph, is the
purity with which he wrote the Latin language.

Our knowledge of Nævius is thus, of necessity, very
limited and fragmentary. From the testimony of later
authors it may, however, be gathered that he was a
remarkable and original man. He represented the
boldness, freedom, and energy, which formed one side
of the Roman character. Like some of our own early
dramatists, he had served as a soldier before becoming
an author. He was ardent in his national feeling ; and,
both in his life and in his writings, he manifested a
strong spirit of political partisanship. As an author, he
showed great productive energy, which continued unabated through a long and vigorous lifetime. His high
self-confident spirit and impetuous temper have left
their impress on the few fragments of his dramas and
of his epic poem. Probably his most important service
to Roman literature consisted in the vigour and purity
with which he used the Latin language.. But the conception of his epic poem seems to imply some share of
the higher gift of poetical invention. He stands at the
head of the line of Roman poets, distinguished by that
force of speech and character, which appeared again, at
long intervals, in Lucilius and in Juvenal ; distinguished
also as having suggested to Ennius first, and after him
to Virgil, the idea of using their poetical faculty to raise
a monument in commemoration of the power and the
glory of Rome.

CHAPTER IV.

Q. ENNIUS, B.C. 239 170—HIS LIFE, TIMES, AND PERSONAL
TRAITS—HIS VARIOUS WORKS—NATURE OF HIS GENIUS
AND INTELLECT.

Q. ENNIUS occupies by far the most prominent position
among the early Roman poets. His remains will repay a
more minute examination than those of any other author
of this era, both from their intrinsic worth and from
their representative character. The Romans themselves
esteemed him as the father of their literature,—the
Homer of Italy. While owing his fame chiefly to his
success in epic and tragic poetry, he displayed an extensive learning and very varied activity in other branches
of literature. He did more than any other man to fix the
permanent character of Roman poetry, by his bold application of Greek metres and forms of art to the Roman
language and to subjects of Roman interest ; and by the
moulding influence which his genius exercised over the
sentiment and the style of two of the greatest among his
successors in poetry. It has happened also that the
fragments of Ennius are more numerous and important,
and more expressive and characteristic, than those of any
other poet of this epoch. In him the serious moral spirit
and intellectual vigour of the early Republican literature
are found most clearly expressed ; and he alone possessed original creative power, and that vein of imaginative sentiment by which the noblest type of Roman
poetry is pervaded. His personal nature, sympathies
and convictions, are strongly stamped on many of his

remains. Something too is known, from other sources, of his circumstances and manner of life, of his relation to the time in which he lived, and to the greatest among his contemporaries.

1. LIFE, TIMES, AND PERSONAL TRAITS.

I. He was born at Rudiæ, a village in Calabria, in B.C. 239, the year after the first representation of a drama on the Roman stage. He first entered Rome about B.C. 204, in the train of Cato, who, when acting as quæstor in Sardinia, found the poet in that island, serving, it is said, in the Roman armies. It is recorded that he rose to the rank of centurion, and he is fancifully represented, in the poem of Silius Italicus, as distinguishing himself in personal combat like one of the heroes of the Iliad. After this time, according to the Eusebian Chronicle, he resided at Rome, 'living very plainly, on the Aventine' (the Plebeian quarter of the city), 'attended only by a single maid-servant'[1] and supporting himself by teaching Greek and by his writings. He accompanied M. Fulvius Nobilior in his Ætolian campaign. Through the influence of his son, he afterwards obtained the honour of Roman citizenship, —a distinction he has himself recorded in a line of the Annals :—

> Nos sumu' Romani, qui fuvimus ante Rudini.

He lived on terms of intimacy with influential members of the noblest families in Rome, and became the familiar friend of the great Scipio. When he died at the age of seventy, his bust was placed in the tomb of the Scipios, beside that of his illustrious friend. The most famous of his works were his Tragedies and the Annals, a long historical poem written in eighteen books. But, in addition to these, he composed several miscellaneous works,

[1] Panco admodum sumptu contentus et unius ancillæ ministerio.

under the name of Saturn, of which only very scanty
fragments have been preserved.

Among the circumstances which gave an impulse to
his career, and prepared him to be a great national poet,
and the founder of a new literature, his origin and birthplace, and the time of his appearance at Rome, are first
to be taken into account. He was born among the hills
of Calabria, overlooking the Grecian seas, and the coasts
planted with the famous colonies of lower Italy. In a
line of the Annals he spoke of his birthplace among
these mountains,

In patrius montes et ad incunabula nostra :

and Horace speaks of his poetry under the name of
the 'Calabrian Muses.' This district came earlier than
other parts of Italy under the influence of Greek civilisation; but it must have preserved something of its old
Italian character and of its own ancient memories. Ennius spoke the Oscan as well as the Greek and Latin
languages,[1] and claimed descent from the old kings of
Messapia,[2]—a circumstance probably not unconnected
with his high and independent bearing, and with the
patrician sympathies manifested both in his life and
writings. His knowledge of the Greek, Oscan, and
Roman languages, may be regarded as a type and sign
of the threefold gifts, accomplishments, and sympathies
which fitted him for his task,—the old wisdom and
culture of Greece, the fresh inspiration of Italy, the
patriotic and earnest sentiment of Rome. In him, more
than in any of the early poets, were thus united the
various conditions out of which a new national literature was destined to arise.

The momentous events of the time, in which his youth

<hr/>

[1] Compare the remarkable saying attributed to Ennius by Aulus Gellius,—
'Quintus Ennius tria corda habere sese dicebat, quod loqui Græce, et Osce,
et Latine sciret.'—GELL. xvii. 17.

[2] Virgil is said by Servius to allude to this at Æn. vii. 691.

was cast, were of a nature to call forth, in the strongest degree, his ardent and steadfast Roman sympathies. Through all the years in which the impressions of life are most vivid, he was a witness of that long protracted and long doubtful conflict between the two greatest powers in the world, which decided the fate of future civilisation. The critical importance of that time was described more than a century and a half afterwards, in these weighty and powerful lines of Lucretius :—

> Ad confligendum venientibus undique Pœnis,
> Omnia cum belli trepido concussa tumultu
> Horrida contremuere sub altis ætheris oris :
> In dubioque fuere utrorum ad regna cadendum
> Omnibus humanis esset terraque marique.[1]

In that war the virtue of Rome had culminated. It proved the vigour and tenacity of her life, the strength of her institutions, the great qualities of her citizens. It called forth many men of the old Roman stamp of character, and one at least of still more commanding genius,—men ' great in council and great in war,'—the soldiers and statesmen, the orators and administrators of the old Republic. The age was one not so much of romantic incident as of sagacious and deliberate action ; full of grave and stirring interests, but more calculated to nerve all the moral energies than to stimulate the imagination to creative activity. The genius of Ennius was in thorough harmony with the national cause, with the strong characters among whom his lot was cast, and with the momentous issues in which all were concerned. Although not bred under the discipline of Roman institutions he had imbibed what was grandest in their spirit ; while his richer culture and more genial nature seem to have kept him clear of all sympathy

[1] ' When the Carthaginians were coming from all sides to the conflict, and all things, beneath high heaven, confounded by the hurry and tumult of war, shook with alarm : and men were in doubt to which of the two the empire of the whole world, by land and sea, should fall.'—III. 833-7.

with the narrow austerity of the Roman character and
the ruthless policy by which the Roman arms were tar-
nished.

He entered on his work in the security that had been
gained for Rome and Italy by the the battle of Zama;
and, for more than thirty years afterwards, he witnessed
the spread of the Roman conquests in all directions;—
over the old monarchies of the East, rich in the accumulated wealth of centuries, and over the hardy barbarians
of the North and West. He died one year before the
crowning victory of Pydna. During all his career, his
sanguine spirit and patriotic sympathies were buoyed
up by the success of his country abroad; while in his
time the worst results of conquest, moral corruption
and political disorganization, though not altogether in-
operative, were as yet unapparent.

The intellectual conditions of the age in which Ennius
first appeared at Rome are also to be taken into account,
as affecting the nature of the work which he performed.
For a generation previous to his time, the Romans had
been familiar with the forms of dramatic poetry, and
with the outline of many of the legends of Greek poetry
and mythology. The Odyssey had been translated into
the native Italian verse; and a long narrative poem,
representing a part of the national history, had been
written, and may have been recited to listening crowds.
A popular literature had not yet been established, or,
if at all, only in the adaptations of Greek comedy;
but the minds of men were prepared to receive such
a literature. The forms which it was to assume had
been, to a great extent, determined by the influence
of Livius and Nœvius; but the spirit by which it was
animated, and the style in which it was executed, were
due partly to the original genius of Ennius, partly to the
intellectual conditions of his age. Prose literature, in
the forms of oratory and history, were springing up

simultaneously with poetry. . The simplicity of religious belief had been broken by the identification of the gods of Olympus with the native deities of Italy. The state of opinion was undergoing a remarkable change. Common sense and the experience of life were contending with the faith and the superstition of ages. The confidence which the Romans were beginning to feel in their own power to govern the world, loosened their sense of dependence on the formal ritualism which outwardly remained unchanged. It is true that, in a people so tenacious of all impressions and convictions, it required centuries of unbelief to obliterate the stamp of this ancient creed, even from the more advanced and cultivated minds ; but it was natural that the provincial origin and the Greek education of the early poets should incline their minds to the sceptical and cosmopolitan, rather than to the traditional modes of thought on religious subjects. The definite tenets of Stoicism and Epicureanism were not generally adopted at Rome till after the death of Ennius ; yet the results of Greek speculation, diffused in various channels through the world, contributed to, if they did not originate, the gradual change in men's deepest convictions. All these tendencies of the time acted on Ennius, so as to stimulate his mental activity in various directions ; blending, however, at the same time, a strongly prosaic and sceptical element with his fervent, sometimes even mystical, enthusiasm. In point of accomplishment, he lived too late for that spontaneous flow of poetry which springs out of the heart of a lively, impressible people ; too soon for the delicacy of taste and refinement of thought with which the masterpieces of a more advanced age are produced.

Of his early life scarcely anything is known. There is no reason to believe that he had obtained any eminence in literature before he settled in middle age at Rome.

His genius was of that robust order which grows richer and livelier with advancing years. The Annals was the work of his old age,—the ripe fruit of a strong, sagacious, and energetic manhood, prolonged to the last in vigorous and cheerful activity. The fragments of the work, even at this day, testify to his freshness of feeling, his real experience of life, and his vital interest in the affairs of his time. Cicero speaks of ' the cheerfulness with which he bore the two evils of old age and poverty.'[1] Wherever the poet speaks of himself, his words reveal a sanguine and contented spirit; as, for instance, in that fine simile, where he compares himself, at the close of his active and successful career, to a brave horse which has often won the prize at the Olympian games, and in old age obtains his well-deserved repose :—

> Sicut fortis equus, spatio qui saepe supremo
> Vicit Olimpia, nunc senio confecta' quiescit.

In none of his fragments is there any trace of that melancholy, the usual accompaniment of meditative genius, which pervades the poetry of his greatest successors, Lucretius and Virgil. From the humorous exaggeration of Horace,

> Ennius ipse pater nunquam, nisi potus, ad arma
> Prosiluit dicenda ;[2]

and from the poet's own confession,

> Nunquam poetor, nisi si podager,[3]

it may be inferred that, like other famous poets, of a lusty and social nature, no less than those of an Epicurean or Anacreontic temperament, he enjoyed the pleasures of wine ; and the fact that he translated the *Hedyphagetica* into Latin may be regarded as a sign that he was

---

[1] *De Senectute*, 5.

[2] ' Father Ennius himself never girt himself up to sing of battles, till after he had well drunk.'

[3] ' I never write poetry, except when I have got the gout.'

not indifferent to other forms of good cheer. The well-known anecdote, told by Cicero, of the interchange of visits between Scipio Nasica and Ennius,[1] though not perhaps a favourable specimen of Roman humour, is interesting from the light which it throws on the easy terms of intimacy in which the poet lived with the members of the most eminent Roman family. Such testimonies and traits of personal character make us think of Ennius as a man of genial and social temper, as well as of ' an intense and glowing mind.'

The outline thus suggested may be filled up from a remarkable passage, quoted by Aulus Gellius, from the seventh book of the Annals. In this passage the poet is stated, on the authority of L. Ælius Stilo[2] (an early grammarian, a friend of Lucilius, and one of Cicero's teachers), to have drawn his own portrait, under an imaginary description of a confidential friend of the Roman general, Geminus Servilius. The portrait has the air of being drawn from the life, with a rapid and forcible hand, and with a minuteness of detail significant of close personal observation :—

Hæce locutu' vocat quocum bene sæpe libenter
Mensam sermonesque suos rerumque suarum
Congeriem partit, magnam cum lassu' diei
Partem fuisset de summis rebu' regendis
Consilio, indu foro lato sanctoque senatu :
Cui res audacter magnas parvasque jocumque
Eloqueretur, cuncta simul malaque et bona dictu
Evomeret, si qui vellet, tutoque locaret.
Quorum multa volup ac gaudia clamque palamque :
Ingenium cui nulla malum sententia suadet
Ut faceret facinus levis aut mali', doctu', fidelis,
Suavis homo, facundu', suo contentu', beatus,
Scitu', secunda loquens in tempore, commodu', verbum
Paucum, multa tenens antiqua sepulta, vetustas
Quem facit mores veteresque novosque tenentem,
Multorum veterum leges divumque hominumque ;

[1] De Oratore, II. 68.
[2] 'L. Ælium Stilonem dicere solitum ferunt Q. Ennium de semet ipso hæc scripsisse, picturamque istam morum et ingenii ipsius Q. Ennii factam esse.'—Gell. XII. 4.

Prudenter qui dicta loquive tacerere posuit.
Hunc inter pugnas Servilius sic compellat.[1]

There are many touches in this picture, which recall
the intimacy between Ennius himself and his exalted
friends. So he may have borne himself when accompanying Fulvius Nobilior in his Ætolian campaign, or
when taking part in the grave councils and the light
or serious talk of the Scipios. The learning and copious
readiness of speech, the vast knowledge of antiquity
and of the manners of the day, attributed to this
friend of Servilius, were gifts very rare among the
Romans of that time, but possessed in remarkable measure by Ennius himself. The good sense, tact, and reticence, the cheerfulness in life and conversation, the
high honour and the integrity of character represented
in the same passage, and obviously drawn from the life,
are among the personal qualities which, in all ages,
attach men eminent in great practical affairs to men
eminent in literature. Such were the qualities that,
according to his own account, recommended Horace to
the intimate friendship of Mæcenas. Many expressive
fragments from the lost poetry of Ennius give assurance
that he also was a man in whom the ardent temperament
of genius was happily united with the real worth and
good sense described in this nameless portrait.

[1] ' He finished : and summons to him one with whom he often, and right
gladly too, shared his table, his talk, and the whole weight of his business,
when weary with debate, throughout the day, on high affairs of state,
within the wide Forum and the august Senate,—one to whom he could frankly
speak out serious matters, trifles, and jest ; to whom he could pour forth and
safely confide, if he wanted to confide in any one, all that he cared to utter,
of good or bad import ; with whom, in private and in public, he had much
entertainment and enjoyment,—a man of that nature which no thought ever
prompts to evil act through levity or malice : a learned, honest, pleasant
man, of fluent speech, contented and cheerful, of much tact, speaking well
in season ; courteous and of few words ; with much old buried lore ; whom
length of years had made versed in old and recent ways ; in the laws of
many ancients, divine and human ; one who knew when to speak and when
to be silent. Him, during the battle, Servilius thus addresses.'

His intimacy and friendship with many of the foremost men of his time, may be attributed to the worth and manliness of his character even more than to the force of his genius. By his personal merit he broke through the strongest barriers ever raised by national and family pride, and made the name of poet, instead of a reproach, a name of honour with the ruling class at Rome. The favourable impression which he produced on the old Roman sagacity and 'primitive virtue' of Cato, by whom he was first brought to Rome, was more probably due to his force of character than to his genius and literary accomplishment, — qualities seemingly little valued by his earliest patron, who, in one of his speeches, reproached Fulvius Nobilior with allowing himself to be accompanied by a poet in his campaign. But the strongest proof of the worth and the wisdom of Ennius is his intimate friendship with the greatest Roman of the age, and the conqueror of the greatest soldier of antiquity. It is honourable to the friendship of generous natures, that the poet neither sought nor gained wealth or rank from this intimacy, but continued to live plainly and contentedly on the Aventine. Yet after death the two friends were not divided ; and the bust of the provincial poet found a place among the remains of that time-honoured family, the record of whose grandeur has been preserved, even to the present day, in the grave and august simplicity of their monumental inscriptions.

The feeling which Ennius expresses towards Scipio is one of enthusiastic admiration for personal greatness. While he pays due honour to the merits and services of other famous men of the time, of Scipio he said that Homer alone could worthily have uttered his praises.[1]

[1] Ἐννίοιο γὰρ ἔθος καὶ ἐπὶ μέγα τὸν ἄνδρα ἐξαίρει βουλόμενος φησὶ μόνον ἂν Ὅμηρον ἐπαξίως ἐπαινέσαι τίνσ δὲ Σκιπίωνα.—ÆLIAN, as quoted by SCIPAN, vol. i. p. 1258. Ed. Clainford. (T. VAHLEN.)

Besides devoting a separate poem to commemorate his achievements, he has left also two short pieces, written apparently as epitaphs over his illustrious friend :—

Hic est ille situs cui nemo civi' neque hostis
Quivit pro factis reddere opis pretium ; [1]

and this also,

A sole exoriente supra Maeoti' paludes
Nemo est qui factis me aequiperare queat.
Si fas endo plagas caelestium ascendere cuiquam est,
Mi soli caeli maxima porta patet. [1]

That this admiration was no emotion of blind or transient enthusiasm, but the sincere tribute of genius to personal greatness, may be gathered from the calm verdict of history on the high qualities and momentous services of the conqueror of Hannibal.

With many marked differences, which distinguish a man of active, social, and national sympathies from the eager student of nature and the passionate thinker on human life, there is much affinity of character and genius between Ennius and Lucretius. Their enthusiastic admiration of personal greatness is one prominent feature in which they resemble one another. But while Lucretius is the ardent admirer of contemplative and imaginative greatness, it is greatness in action and character which moves the admiration of Ennius. There is a marked resemblance between them in another personal characteristic. They both were men of that type of genius which is most conscious of itself, and has the highest estimate of its function and position. Cicero mentions that Ennius applied the epithet *sanctus* to poets. Lucretius uses the same epithet in those lines of strong affection and reverence, which he applies to Empedocles—

---

[1] 'Here is he laid, to whom no one, neither countryman nor enemy, has been able to pay a due meed for his services.'

[1] 'From the utmost east, beyond the Maeotian marsh, there is no one who in actions can vie with me. If it is lawful for any one to ascend to the realms of the gods, to me alone the vast gate of heaven is opened !'

Nil tamen hoc habuisse viro praeclarius in se,
Nec sanctum magis, et mirum carumque videtur.[1]

The well-known inscription which Ennius composed for
his own bust directly expresses his sense of the greatness
of his work, and his confident assurance of fame, and of
the lasting sympathy of his countrymen—

Aspicite, O cives, senis Enni imagini' formam.
Hic vestrum panxit maxima facta patrum.
Nemo me lacrimis decoret nec funera fleta
Faxit. Cur? Volito vivo' per ora virum.[2]

Two lines from one of his satires—

Enni poeta salve qui mortalibus
Versus propinas flammeos medullitus,[3]

indicate in still stronger terms his burning consciousness
of power.

Some of the greatest of modern poets have also manifested a proud self-confidence, like that expressed by
Ennius and Lucretius. It is when genius is allied with
an intense nature, and is exercised with serious purpose,
rather than when combined with subtle discernment and
wide sympathy, that it is most self-assured and most
intolerant of opposition. Although appearing in strange
contrast with the wonderful modesty or self-forgetfulness
of the highest creative art (as seen in Homer, in Sophocles, and in Shakspeare), this strong self-confidence is yet
widely removed from the turbulent or petulant self-
assertion of lower and coarser natures. But the least
pleasing side of the feeling, even in men of high and
generous nature, is the scorn,—arising not from a narrow

[1] 'Yet nothing more glorious than this man doth it (the island of Sicily)
seem to have contained, nor aught more holy, nor more wonderful and
beloved.'

[2] 'Behold, my countrymen, the bust of the old man, Ennius. He built
up the record of your fathers' mighty deeds. Let no one pay to me the
meed of tears, nor weep at my funeral. And why? because I am borne,
still living, through the mouths of men.'

[3] 'Hail, poet Ennius, who pledgest to mortals thy fiery verse from thy
inmost marrow.'

envy, but from imperfect sympathy, - which they are
apt to entertain towards rival genius or antagonistic
convictions. Something of this spirit appears in the disparaging allusion of Ennius to his predecessor Naevius :—

> Scripsere alii rem
> Versibu', quos olim Fauni vatesque canebant,
> Quum neque Musarum scopulos quisquam superarat
> Nec dicti studiosus erat.[1]

The contempt here expressed is, indeed, only for the metre
employed by the older poet, and seems to be the counter-
part of his own exultation in being the first to introduce
what he called ' the long verses' into Latin literature.

Another point in which there is an affinity between
Ennius and Lucretius is their religious temper and convictions. There is no ground for attributing to Ennius
the rigid intellectual consistency of Lucretius, nor to
Lucretius any gleam of that imaginative mysticism which
Ennius inherited from the speculations of Pythagoras.
But in both a deep and reverential sense of the power
and mystery encompassing the world was combined with
an impatient disbelief of the superstition of their time.
They both apply the principles of a prosaic rationalism to
resolve the fair creations of the old mythology into their
original elements. Ennius, like Lucretius, seems to have
denied the providence of the gods ; at least he puts
the following sentiment into the mouth of one of his
characters—

> Ego deum genus esse semper dixi et dicam caelitum,
> Sed eos non curare opinor, quid agat humanum genus ;
> Nam si curent, bene bonis sit, male malis, quod nunc abest :[2]

and he exposed, with shrewd caustic sense, the false pre-

---

[1] ' Others have treated the subject in the verses, which in days of old the
Fauns and bards used to sing, before any one had climbed the cliffs of the
Muses, or gave any care to style.'

[2] ' I have always said and will say that the gods of heaven exist, but I
think that they heed not the conduct of mankind ; for, if they did, it would
be well with the good and ill with the bad ; and it is not so now.'

tences of augurs, prophets, and astrologers. He translated the Sacred Chronicle of Euhemerus,—a work
conceived in that spirit of vulgar rationalism which is
reprobated by Plato in the Phædrus,—and in this
way contributed to shake the faith of his countrymen
in their religious traditions. But while led to these
conclusions by the spirit of his age, and by the study
of the later speculations of Greece, he was at the same
time a believer in the Pythagorean doctrine of the transmigration of souls. He fancied that the soul of Homer,
after many changes,—at one time having animated a
peacock,[1] again, having been incarnate in the sage of
Crotona,—had finally passed into his own body : and he
told how the shade of ·his great prototype had appeared
to him from the invisible world,—

> Quo neque permaneant animæ neque corpora nostra
> Sed quædam simulacra modis pallentia miris,[2]

and explained to him the whole plan of nature. These
were vague dreams of the imagination ; but they may
have had some effect in enabling Ennius to rise clear
above all the gloom which ' eclipsed the brightness of
the world' to Lucretius. The light in which the world
appeared to the older poet was strangely coloured by
the blended rays of common sense and of imaginative
mysticism. He thus seems to stand midway between
the spiritual dreams and aspirations of Empedocles and
the more positive spirit of Lucretius. While living in
the vigorous prime of Italian civilisation he had inherited
both the bold fancies of the earlier Greeks and the dull
rationalism of their later speculation. His religious ideas,
as the result of his natural understanding, of his circumstances, and his varied reading, appear thus to have been

[1] Cor jubet hoc Enni, postquam destruit eas
Mæonides, Quintus pavone ex Pythagoreo.
                                    Persius, vi. 10 (Ed. Jahn).
[2] ' Where neither our souls nor bodies abide, but only certain phantoms
wondrous pale.'—Lucret. i. 121.

without the unity arising from a simple unreflective
faith, or from the basis of philosophical consistency.

II. HIS WORKS.—(1.) MISCELLANEOUS WORKS.

11. (1.) In laying the foundations of Roman literature, Ennius displayed not only fervent sympathies and
original genius, but also great energy and industry, and,
for his age, vast and varied, though probably not very
exact, learning. The composition of his tragedies and of
the Annals, while making most demand on his original
power, implied also a diligent study of Homer and the
Greek tragedians, and a large acquaintance with the traditions and antiquities of Rome. ·But besides the works
on which his highest poetical faculty was employed,
other writings, of a philosophical, didactic, and miscellaneous character, gave evidence of the variety of subjects
in which he was interested, and of the extent of his
reading and his industry. It does not appear that he
was the author of any prose writing. His version of the
Sacred Chronicle of Euhemerus was more probably a
poetical adaptation than a literal prose translation of
that work. The object of Euhemerus was to explain
away the fables of mythology, by representing them as
being merely a supernatural account of historical events.
Several extracts of the work quoted by Lactantius, as
from the translation of Ennius, look as if they had been
reduced from a form originally metrical into the prose
of a later era.[1] There is thus no evidence, direct or
indirect, to prove that Ennius had any share in forming
the style of Latin prose. But if verse was the sole
instrument which he used, this was certainly not due
to the poetical character of all the topics which he
treated, but, more likely, to the fact that his acquired
aptitude, and the state of the Latin language in his time,

[1] Vahlen.

made metrical writing more natural and easy than prose composition.

One of his works in verse was a treatise on good living, called Hedyphagetica, founded on the gastronomic researches of Archestratus of Gela,—a sage who is said to have devoted his life to the study of everything that contributed to the pleasures of the table, and to have recorded his varied experience and research with the grave dignity of epic verse. A few lines from this translation or adaptation of Ennius, giving an account of the coasts on which the best fish are to be found, have been preserved by Appuleius. The information contained in the passage has probably lost any value that it may have originally possessed; but the lines are curious from their being written in that tone of half-serious enthusiasm, which all who treat, either in prose or verse, of the pleasures of eating seem naturally to adopt. The language in which he speaks of the *scarus* implies a very real appreciation of that lordly fish :[1]

> Quid tantum, merulam, melanuram umbramque marinam
> Praeterii, atque scarum, cerebrum Jovi' paene supremi ?
> Nestoris ad patriam hic capitur magnusque bonusque.[2]

He wrote also a philosophical poem in trochaic tetrameters, called Epicharmus, either translated from, or founded on some work of the old Sicilian poet of that name, who besides being one of the earliest writers of comedy, was a disciple of Pythagoras, and one of the physical philosophers and poets of the same class as Empedocles and Parmenides. A few slight fragments have been preserved from this poem. They speak of the four elements or principles of the universe as ' water, earth,

---

[1] Cf. Pliny, *Hist. Nat.* ix. 29. 'Nunc scaro datur principatus, qui solus piscium dicitur ruminare, herbisque vesci, non aliis piscibus, mari Carpathio maxime frequens.'

[2] 'Why have I omitted' (so and so, names of certain fish which cannot be identified) 'and the *scarus*, the brain almost of almighty Jove ? By the native shores of Nestor that fish is caught, both large and good.'

air, the sun ;' of ' the blending of heat with cold, dryness
with moisture ;' ' of the earth bearing and supporting all
nations and receiving them again back into herself.' The
following is the longest fragment from the poem :—

> Istic est is Jupiter quem dico, quem Graeci vocant
> Aërem : qui ventus est et nubes ; imber postea
> Atque ex imbre frigus : ventus post fit, aër deuuo,
> Haece propter Jupiter sunt ista quae dico tibi,
> Quoniam mortalis atque urbes beluasque omnis juvat.[1]

   These fragments and a passage from the opening lines
of the Annals, where the shade of Homer was introduced
as discoursing to Ennius (like the shade of Anchises to
Æneas), on ' the nature of things,' are specimens of that
vague curiosity about the facts and laws of nature, which,
in ancient times, supplied the absence of scientific knowledge.   Physical speculation continued to attract many
among the later Roman poets.   The fragments of Pacuvius indicate that his thoughts were turned to the same
subject.   The ardour with which Lucretius devoted himself to explore the laws and observe the processes of
nature is visible in every page of his poem.   Virgil
represents the knowledge of the secrets of nature as the
great gift of the Muses, and as the first lesson imparted
by the spirits of the dead to the living : and in the latter
years of his life, he regarded the prosecution of his philosophical studies as more important than the composition
of the Æneid.   Physical speculations are introduced also
into the Metamorphoses of Ovid ; and Propertius professes
to look forward to the study of nature as the calm solace
of his age, after spending his youth in the strenuous
gratification of his passions.
   Another of these miscellaneous works was known by

[1] 'This is that Jupiter which I speak of, which the Greeks call the air ;
it is first wind and clouds ; afterwards rain, and after rain, cold ; next it
becomes wind, then air again.   All those things which I mention to you are
Jupiter, because it is he who supports mortals and cities and all animals.'

the name of Protreptica, and was evidently a work of a moral or didactic character. It is probable that all of these works,[1] as well as the Scipio, were included in the Saturæ, or Miscellanies, under which title Ennius composed four, or, according to another authority, six books. The Romans looked upon Lucilius as the inventor of satire in the later sense of that word;—he having been the first to impress upon the satura the character it has borne since his time. Satire was used first by Lucilius, as an instrument of censorious criticism on morals, politics, and literature; of contemptuous and ludicrous representation of individuals and classes of men; and of moral teaching, enforced by wit and humour. But there was another kind of satura, of which Ennius and Pacuvius in early times, and Varro at a somewhat later time, were regarded as the principal authors. This was really a miscellany treating of various subjects, in various metres, and, as employed by Varro, was written partly in prose, partly in verse. This kind of composition, as well as the Lucilian satire, arose out of the old indigenous satura or dramatic medley, familiar to the Romans before the introduction of Greek literature. When the scenic element in the original satura was merged in the new comedy introduced from Greece, the old name was first applied to a miscellaneous kind of composition, in which ordinary topics were treated in a serious but apparently prosaic way; and even as employed by Lucilius and Horace the satura retained something of this character. The satires of Ennius were written in various metres, iambic, trochaic, and hexameter, and treated of various topics of personal and public interest. The few fragments that remain from them are not of much value in themselves, but when taken in connexion with the ancient testimonies as to their character, they are of some interest as showing that this kind of composition was a

[1] Mommsen.

form intermediate between the old dramatic satura and
the satire of Lucilius and Horace. It is recorded that
in one of his satires, Ennius introduced a dialogue between Life and Death ;—thus transmitting in the use
of dialogue (which appears very frequently in Horace
and Persius) some vestige of the original scenic medley.
Ennius also appears, like Lucilius and Horace, to have
communicated in his satires his own personal feelings
and experience, as in the fragment already quoted :—

Nunquam poetor, nisi si podager.

Again, it has often been remarked that all poetry among
the Romans had a tendency to become didactic. Satire,
in the hands of its chief masters, aimed at practical
moral teaching, not only by precept, ridicule, and invective, and by portraiture of individuals and classes, but
also by the use of anecdotes and fables. This last mode
of combining amusement with good advice is common in
Horace. It appears, however, to have been first used by
Ennius. Aulus Gellius mentions that Æsop's fable of
the field-lark and the husbandman ' is very skilfully and
gracefully told by Ennius in his Satires ;' and he quotes
the shrewd practical advice, appended to the fable,
' Never to expect your friends to do for you what you
can do for yourself :'

Hoc erit tibi argumentum semper in promptu situm :
Nequid expectes amicos, quod tute agere possies.

These miscellaneous works of Ennius were the fruits
of his extensive learning, and of his great literary industry, rather than of his imagination. Such works
might have been written in prose, if the art of prose
composition had been as familiar as that of verse. It
is in the fragments of his dramas, and still more of the
Annals, that his whole power is most apparent, and that
the influence which he exercised over the Roman mind
and literature is best discerned.

(2.) DRAMAS.

(2.) Before the time of Ennius, the Roman drama, both tragic and comic, had established itself at Rome, in close imitation of the tragedy and the new comedy of Athens. The latter had been most successfully cultivated by Nævius and his younger contemporary, Plautus. The advancement of tragedy to an equal share of popular favour was due to the severer genius of Ennius. He appears however to have tried, though without much success, to adapt himself to the popular taste in favour of comedy. The names of three of his comedies, viz., the *Ambracia*, *Cupuncula*, and *Pancratiastæ*, have come down to us; but their fragments are too insignificant to justify the formation of any opinion on their merits. His warmest admirers in ancient times nowhere advance in his favour any claim to comic genius. Volcatius Sedigitus, an early critic, who wrote a work *De Poetis*, and who has already been referred to as assigning the third rank in the list of comic poets to Nævius, mentions Ennius as tenth and last, solely 'antiquitatis causa.' Any inference that might be drawn from the character exhibited in the other fragments of Ennius, would accord both with the negative and positive evidence of antiquity, as to his deficiency in comic power. He has nothing in common with that versatile and dramatic genius, in which occasionally the highest imagination has been united with the most abundant humour. The real bent of his mind, as revealed in his higher poetry, is grave and intense, like that of Lucretius or Milton. Many of the conceits, strained effects, and plays on words, found in his fragments, imply want of humour as well as an imperfect poetic taste. Thus, in the following fragment from one of his satires, the meaning of the passage is rather obscured than pointed by the forced iteration and play upon the word *frustra* :—

Nam qui lepide postulat alterum frustrari,
Quom frustrast, frustra illum dicit frustra esse.
Nam qui se frustrari quem frustras sentit,
Qui frustratur frustrast, si ille non est frustra.[1]

The jingle of sounds in the following line of the Annals
is an instance of a straining after verbal effect, incompatible not only with a cultivated taste, but with any
sense of the ludicrous :—

O Tite tute Tati tibi tanta tiranne tulisti.

Many of his fragments show indeed that he possessed
the caustic spirit of a satirist ; but it was through the
light of common sense, not of humour, that he viewed
the follies of his time.   This striving after a spurious
kind of ornament, of which his fragments afford frequent
instances, though a natural accompaniment of the rude
efforts of the earliest art, and of the new formative energy
applied by Ennius to the Latin tongue, is in marked
contrast with the good taste and case characteristic of
the style of Roman Comedy.

The general character of Roman Tragedy, so far as it
can be ascertained from ancient testimony, and the extant
fragments of the early tragedians, will be examined in
the following chapter.   It is not possible to determine
what dramatic power Ennius may have displayed in the
evolution of his plots or the delineation of his characters.
His peculiar genius is more distinctly stamped on his
epic than on his dramatic fragments. Still many of the
latter, in their boldness of conception and expression,
and in their strong and fervid morality, are expressive of
the original force of the poet, and of the Roman temper
of his mind.   Some of them will be brought forward
in the sequel, along with passages from the Annals, as
important contributions to our estimate of the poet's
genius and intellect.

[1] The meaning of the passage amounts to no more than this, that the man
who tries to 'sell' another, and fails, is himself 'sold.'

It was certainly due to Ennius that Roman tragedy was first raised to that pitch of popular favour which it enjoyed till the age of Cicero. While actively employed in many other fields of literature, he carried on the composition of his tragedies till the latest period of his life. Cicero records, that the *Thyestes* was represented at the celebration of the Ludi Apollinares, shortly before the poet's death.[1] The titles of about twenty-five of his tragedies are known, and a few fragments remain from all of them. About one-half of these bear the titles of the heroes and heroines connected with the Trojan cycle of events, such as the *Achilles, Achilles Aristarchi, Ajax, Alexander, Andromache Æchmalotis, Hectoris Lustra, Hecuba, Iphigenia, Phœnix, Telamo, Thyestes.* One at least of his tragedies, the *Medea*, was literally translated from the Greek of Euripides, whom he seems to have made his model, in preference to the elder Attic dramatists. Cicero[2] speaks of it, along with the Antiope of Pacuvius, as being translated word for word from the Greek; and a comparison of the fragments of the Latin with the passages in the Medea of Euripides shows how closely Ennius followed his original. In one place he has mistranslated his author,—the passage (Eur. *Med.* 215),

οἶδα γὰρ πολλοὺς βροτῶν
σεμνοὺς γεγῶτας, τοὺς μὲν ὀμμάτων ἄπο
τοὺς δ᾽ ἐν θυραίοις,

being thus rendered in Latin,—

Multi suam rem bene gessere et publicam patria procul.

The opening lines of the Medea of Ennius may be quoted as probably a fair specimen of the degree of faithfulness with which the early Roman tragedians translated from their originals. There is some nervous force, but little either of poetical grace or musical flow in the language :—

[1] *Brutus,* 20.   [2] *De Fin.* i. 2.

> Utinam ne in nemore Pelio securibus
> Caesa accidisset abiegna ad terram trabes,
> Neve inde navis inchoandae exordium
> Cepisset, quae nunc nominatur nomine
> Argo, quia Argivi in ea dilecti viri
> Vecti petebant pellem inauratam arietis
> Colchis, imperio regis Peliae, per dolum;
> Nam nunquam era errans mea domo ecferret pedem
> Medea, animo aegra, amore saevo saucia.[1]

In his Hecuba, also, and · probably in his Iphigenia,
Ennius made free use of the dramas founded on the
same subjects by Euripides. But in many of· his dramatic fragments the sentiment expressed is clearly
that of a Roman, not of a Greek mind.[2]   It was
by Ennius that Roman tragedy was impressed with
that grave moral and didactic character which it bore ·
through all this early period.   Although it is impossible to judge how far his conceptions of character
may have been original or consistently worked out,
yet a few short scenes preserved in his remains give
indication of power and imagination in delineating passionate emotion.   One of his most striking dramatic
passages is a short dialogue between Hecuba and Cassandra, quoted from the Alexander, with great admiration, by Cicero.   Cassandra (at the end of the scene),
under the influence of Apollo, reluctant and *ashamed*
(perhaps in this feeling the hand of a Roman rather than
of a Greek poet may be recognised), yet mastered by prophetic fury, bursts forth in wild, agitated tones, casting
a stormy light around the fatal crime of Paris :—

[1] Cf. Eur. *Med.* 1-8 :—

> Εἴθ' ὤφελ' Ἀργοῦς μὴ διαπτάσθαι σκάφος
> Κόλχων ἐς αἶαν κυανέας Συμπληγάδας,
> μηδ' ἐν νάπαισι Πηλίου πεσεῖν ποτε
> τμηθεῖσα πεύκη, μηδ' ἐρετμῶσαι χέρας
> ἀνδρῶν ἀριστέων, οἳ τὸ πάγχρυσον δέρος
> Πελίᾳ μετῆλθον· οὐ γὰρ ἂν δέσποιν' ἐμὴ
> Μήδεια πύργους γῆς ἔπλευσ' Ἰωλκίας
> ἔρωτι θυμὸν ἐκπλαγεῖσ' Ἰάσονος.

[2] Several of these fragments will be examined later.

Adest, adest fax obvoluta sanguine atque incendio :
Multos annos latuit : cives ferte opem et restinguite.
Iamque mari magno classis cita
Texitur : exitium examen rapit.
Advenit, et fera velivolantibus
Navibus complevit magna litora.[1]

(3.) THE ANNALS.

(3.) But the poem which really represented this epoch
was the Annals of Ennius. This was the master-work of
his genius,—a truly national poem, inspired by Roman
feeling, and built up with Roman energy and solidity.
On the composition of this work he rested his hopes of
popular and permanent fame—

Hic vestrum panxit maxima facta patrum :[2]

and again, apparently at the opening of the Annals, he
thus writes—

Latos per populos terrasque poemata nostra
Clara cluebunt.[3]

On the execution of this work he had concentrated his
highest faculties : he had gathered up in it the manifold
results of his learning and his life, and the whole weight
of his moral and national sympathies. At the conclusion of the poem, he claims for his old age the repose
due to a brave and triumphant career. He composed the
eighteenth book, the last, in his sixty-seventh year, three
years before his death. The great length to which the
poem extended, and the vast amount of materials which
it embraced, imply a long and steady devotion to this
task. It was a task requiring learning, as well as original
powers. The fragments of the poem afford proofs of a

[1] 'Here it is ; here, the torch, wrapped in fire and blood. Many years
it hath lain hid ; help, citizens, and extinguish it. For now, on the great
sea, a swift fleet is gathering : a mighty swarm of men " is crying havoc."
They come : a fierce host lines the shores with sail-winged ships.'

[2] 'He hath built up the record of the great deeds of your fathers.'

[3] 'Far and wide through lands and nations the fame of my poems shall
sound.'

familiarity with Homer, and of acquaintance with the
Cyclic poets.[1] It is impossible to say how much of the
early Roman history, as it has come down to modern
times, is due to the diligence of Ennius in collecting, and
to his genius in giving life to the traditions and ancient
records of Rome. He was certainly the earliest writer
who gathered them up, and united them in a continuous
form. And his work required not only the antiquarian
lore of a man

'Multa tenens, antiqua, sepulta,'

and a power of imagination to give a new and permanent
interest to the past, but also a true and sympathetic discernment of the spirit of his age, and an intimate personal
familiarity with the great affairs of the time, and with
the character of his great contemporaries.

The poem was written in eighteen books. Of these
books about six hundred lines have been preserved in
fragments, varying from about twenty lines to half a line
in length. From the minuteness with which comparatively unimportant matters are described, it is inferred
that the separate books extended to a much greater length
than those either of the Iliad or of the Æneid. Of
the first book there remain about 120 lines, including
the dream of Ilia in seventeen lines, and the auspices
of Romulus in twenty lines. In it were narrated the
mythical events from the time

Quum veter occubuit Priamus sub marte Pelasgo,

to the death and deification of Romulus ;

Romulus in caelo cum dis genitalibus aevum
Degit.

There is no allusion in these fragments to the Carthaginian adventures of Æneas, which Nævius had introduced into his poem on the First Punic War. Æneas
appears at once to be brought to Hesperia, a land,

---

[1] He speaks of Eurydice as the wife of Æneas. This statement he is
supposed to have derived from the Cypria.

Quam prisci casci populi tenoere Latini.

Ilia is represented as the daughter of Æneas, and the
birth and infancy of Romulus and Remus appear to
have been described at great length. In commenting
on Virgil's fine lines at Æneid VIII. 630—

> Fecerat et viridi fetam Mavortis in antro
> Procubuisse lupam : geminos huic ubera circum
> Ludere pendentes pueros, et lambere matrem
> Impavidos ; illam terreti cervice reflexam
> Mulcere alternos, et corpora fingere linguâ.—[1]

Servius says 'Sane totus hic locus Ennianus est.' The
second and third books contained the history of the
remaining Roman kings. Virgil imitated the description
given in these books of the destruction of Alba (the
story of which is told by Livy also with much poetic
power), in his account of the capture of Troy, at
Æneid ii. 486—

> At domus interior gemitu miseroque tumultu, etc.

One short fragment of the third book contains a picturesque notice of the founding of Ostia—

> Ostia munita est ; idem loca navibu' pulchris
> Munda facit ; nautisque mari quaerentibu' vitam.[2]

This line also

> Postquam lumina sis oculis bonus Ancu' reliquit

is familiar from its reappearance in one of the most
solemn passages of Lucretius.

The fourth and fifth books contained the history of
the State from the establishment of the Republic till just
before the beginning of the war with Pyrrhus. One

---

[1] 'The cave of Mars was dressed with mossy grecas ;
There, by the wolf, were laid the martial twins.
Intrepid on her swelling dugs they hung.
The foster-dam lolled out her fawning tongue—
They suck'd secure ; while, bending back her head,
She lick'd their tender limbs, and formed them as they fed.'
DRYDEN.

[2] 'Ostia was built ; he too made her shores gay with fair ships, her
mariners seeking their living on the deep.'

short fragment is taken from the night attack of the
Gauls upon the Capitol. The sixth book was devoted
to the war with Pyrrhus ; the seventh, eighth, and
ninth, to the First and Second Punic Wars. In the
fragments of the sixth are found a few lines of the
speeches of Pyrrhus, and of Appius Claudius Crocus.[1] In
the account of the First Punic War, the disparaging
allusion to Nævius occurs—

Scripsêre alii rem, etc.

It is mentioned by Cicero that Ennius borrowed much
from the work of Nævius ; and also that he passed
over (reliquisse) the First Punic War, as it had been
treated by his predecessor. Several fragments however
must certainly refer to this war ; but it is probable that
that part of the subject was treated more cursorily than
either the war with Pyrrhus, or the later wars. The
passage in which the poet is supposed to have painted
his own character under the form of a friend of Servilius
Geminus,[2] occurred in the seventh book. Two well
known passages have been preserved from the ninth
book — viz., that characterising the ' sweet-speaking '
orator, M. Cornelius Cethegus --

Fos delibatos populi suadæque medulla.

and the lines in honour of Q. Fabius Maximus,

Unus homo nobis cunctando restituit rem, etc.

The tenth and eleventh books, beginning with a new
invocation to the muse—

Insece Musa manu Romanorum induperator
Quod quisque in bello gessit cum rege Philippo,

treated of the Macedonian war, and of the deeds of T.
Quinctius Flaminius. In the later books, Ennius told
the history of the war with Antiochus, of the Ætolian
War carried on by his friend, M. Fulvius Nobilior, of the
exploits of L. Cæcilius Denter and his brother (of whom

scarcely anything is known except that the sixteenth
book of the Annals was written in consequence of the
poet's especial admiration for them), and lastly, the
Istrian War, which took place within a few years of the
author's death.

Neither in general design nor in detail could the
Annals be regarded as a pure epic poem. Like the
Æneid, which connects the mythical story of Æneas
with the glories of the Julian line and the great destiny
of Rome, the poem of Ennius treated of fabulous tradition, of historical fact, and of great contemporary events;
but it did not, like the Æneid, unite these varied materials
in the representation of the fortunes of one individual
hero. The action of the poem, instead of being limited
to a few days or months, extended over many generations. Nor could the poem terminate with any critical
catastrophe, as its object was to unfold the continuous,
still advancing progress of the State. From the name
it might be inferred that the Annals must have been
more like a metrical chronicle than like an epic poem ;
yet, as being inspired and pervaded by a true and grand
idea, the work was elevated above the level of matter
of fact into the region of poetry. The idea of a high
destiny, unfolding itself through the old kingly dynasty,
and the long line of consuls—through the successive
wars with the Italian races, with Pyrrhus and the Carthaginians—rapidly advancing, though not fully accomplished in the age when the poem was written—gave
unity of plan and consistency of form to its rude and
colossal structure. The word Annales, as applied to
Roman story, suggests something more than the mere
record of events in regular annual sequence. It in-
volves also the idea of unbroken continuity. In the
Roman Republic, the unity and vital action of the State
were maintained and manifested by the delegation of
the functions of government on magistrates appointed

from year to year, as the life of a monarchical state is
maintained and manifested in its line of kings. In
the spirit animating the work, and in the conception
of a past history, stretching back in unbroken grandeur until it is lost in fable, but yet vitally linked to
the interests of the present time, the Annals of Ennius
may be compared with the dramas in which Shakspeare
has represented the national life of England—in all its
greatness and vicissitudes—with the glory and splendour, as well as the dark and tragic colours with which
that story is inwoven.

. The poem, although laying no claim to the perfection
of epic form, had thus something of the genuine epic
inspiration. While treating both of a mythical past
and of real historical events, it was pervaded by a living
and popular idea,—faith in the destiny of Rome. It was
through the power and presence of that same idea in his
own age, that Virgil was able to impart a vital and
enduring meaning to a fabulous tradition, and to create,
out of the imaginary fortunes of a Trojan hero, a poem
most truly representative of Roman feeling. It is the
absence of any such living idea which renders the artificial epics of refined and civilised eras,—such poems,
for instance, as the *Thebais* of Statius, or the *Argo-
nautics* of Valerius Flaccus,—in general so flat and
unprofitable. If, on the other hand, we look upon it
as a historical poem, the Annals appears to have been
written under more favourable conditions than the
Pharsalia of Lucan, or the *Punic Wars* of Silius Italicus
—in being the work of an age to which the past had
come down as popular tradition, not as critical history.
The imagination of the poet may employ itself more
happily and legitimately in filling up or modifying a
story that has been shaped by the fancies and feelings of
successive generations, than in venturing to recast the
facts that stand out prominently in the actual march of

human affairs. By treating of contemporary events, the poem must have receded still further from the pure type of epic poetry; yet the later fragments of the work, while written with something of the minute fidelity of a chronicle, bear many traces of imaginative fire. They reveal to us the insight and power of a poet able to embody the living spirit of his age.

There must have been many drawbacks to the popularity of the poem in a more critical time, when strong enthusiasm and forcible conception are little regarded, unless they are combined with harmonious execution. Even from the extant fragments, the rude proportions and the unwieldy mass of the original work may be inferred. It is still possible to note the bald, annalistic style of many passages which sink below the level of dignified prose, the barbarisms of taste shown by a fondness for alliterative lines and plays upon words, the more common faults of careless haste and redundance of expression, and of a rugged and irregular cadence. There must have been some peculiar excellencies or adaptation to the Roman taste, through which, in spite of these defects, the popularity of the poem was sustained far into the times of the Empire. This late popularity may have been due in part to antiquarian zeal or affectation, but some degree of it, as well as the favour of his own age, must have been founded on more substantial grounds. Apart from other literary interest, this poem first drew forth and established, for the contemplation of after times, the ideal latent in the national mind. The patriotic tones of Virgil appear to be an amplification of such lines as these :—

> Audire est operæ pretium procedere recte
> Qui rem Romanam Latiumque augescere vultis ;[1]

[1] 'It is worth your while to listen, ye who wish that the Roman State should hold its onward course, and that Latium should wax in power.'

G

and of that other line which Cicero compared to the
utterance of an oracle—

Moribus antiquis stat res Romana virisque.[1]

While in his other works Ennius was a teacher of his
countrymen, in his Annals he represented them. He set
before them the best image of themselves ;—an image
combining the strength and commanding features of his
own time, with the proud memories and traditional traits
of the past. As it is by sympathy with what is most
intense and of deepest meaning in actual experience that
a great poet can form his ideal of what transcends experience, so it is by a very vivid apprehension of the present, that he is able to re-animate the past. Dante and
Milton gained their vision of other worlds through their
intense feeling of the spiritual meaning of this life ; and,
in another sphere of art, Scott was enabled to immor-
talise the romance and humour of past ages, partly
through the chivalrous and adventurous spirit which
he inherited from them, partly also through the strong
interest and enjoyment with which he entered into the
actual life and pursuits of his contemporaries. It is in
ages of transition, such as were the ages of Sophocles, of
Shakspeare, and of Scott, in which the traditions of the
past blend with and colour the active pursuits and enjoyments of the present, that great representative works
are produced. Living in such an era, and deeply moved
by all the memories, the hopes, and the impulses which
acted upon his contemporaries, Ennius was able to create
a national literature, and to gather the life of centuries into
one representation. He was enabled to tell the story of
Rome, if without the accomplished art, yet with something
of the native force and genius of early Greece ; he could fix
in language the patriotic feelings and associations which
had hitherto been kept alive by the statues, monuments,

[1] 'By the manners of the olden time and by her men the Roman State
stands firm.'

and commemorative ceremonies of earlier times ; he
could uphold the standard of national character with a
fervent enthusiasm ; and could address the understanding of his contemporaries with a practical wisdom like
their own, and a large knowledge both of ' books and
men :'—

Multa tenens antiqua sepulta, vetustas
Quem fecit mores veteresque novosque tenentem.

The manifest defects, as well as the peculiar power of
the poem, show that it was no mere imitation of the
Greek epic. In spirit and design, as well as proportions
and execution, it was a truly Roman work,—of the era
in which the language of Rome was first moulded into a
literary form, and the people first became conscious of
their aims and saw their destiny before them. The vast
dimensions and solid structure of the poem are proofs of
that power of long labour and concentrated interest on
one great object, which was the source of Roman success
in other spheres of action. So vast a mass of materials held
in union only by a pervading national enthusiasm would
have been utterly repugnant to Greek taste, intolerant
above all things of monotony, and most exacting in its
demands of artistic unity and completeness. The fragments of the poem give no idea of careful finish ; they
produce the impression of massiveness and energy,
strength and uniformity of structure, unaccompanied by
beauty, grace, or symmetry. The creation of an untutored age may be recognised in the rudeness of design,
—of a Roman mind in the national spirit, the colossal
proportions, and the strong workmanship of the poem.

The originality of Ennius will be still more apparent
if we compare the fragments of the Annals, in some
points of detail, with the complete works of the great
epic poet, whom he regarded as his prototype. There
was, in the first place, a marked difference between
Homer and Ennius in their modes of representing hu-

man life and character. The personages of the Iliad
and of the Odyssey are recognised as the most living
and forcible, and, at the same time, transcendent types
of individual character. In Achilles, in Hector, and
in Odysseus,—in Helen, Andromache, and Nausicaa,
human nature is represented in its most permanent
and most varied aspects. They are for all times ;—em-
bodiments the most real, yet the most imaginative, of
the grandeur, the heroism, the enduring courage, and
strong affection of manhood, and of the grace, the gentle
ness, and the sweet vivacity of woman. The work of
Ennius, on the other hand, instead of presenting these
varied types of human nature, appears to have unfolded
a great gallery of national portraits. The fragments of
the poem still afford some glimpses of the 'good Ancus;'
'of the man of the great heart, the wise Ælius Sextus;'
'of the sweet speaking orator,' Cethegus, 'the marrow
of persuasion.' The stamp of magnanimous fortitude is
impressed on the fragmentary words of Appius Claudius
Cæcus ; and sagacity and resolution are depicted in the
lines which have handed down the fame of Fabius
Maximus. This idea of the poem, as unfolding the heroes
of Roman story in regular series, may be gathered also
from the language of Cicero : 'Cato, the ancestor of our
present Cato, is extolled by him to the skies; the honour
of the Roman people is thereby enhanced : finally all
those Maximi, Fulvii, Marcelli, are celebrated with a
glory in which we all participate.'' This portraiture of
the kings and heroes of the early time, of the orators,
soldiers, and statesmen of the Republic, could not have
exhibited the variety, the energy, the passion, and all
the complex human attributes of Homer's personages.
The men who stand prominently out in the annals of
Rome were of a more uniform type. They were men of
one common aim, --the advancement of Rome; animated

¹ Cicero, Arch. 9.

with one sentiment,—devotion to the State. All that
was purely personal in them is lost in the traditional
pictures which express only the fortitude, the dignity
and the sagacity of the Republic.

Ennius also followed Homer in introducing the element
of supernatural agency into his poem. The action of the
Annals, as well as of the Iliad, was partially dependent
on a divine interference with human affairs, though
exercised less directly, and, as it were, from a greater
distance. Yet how great is the difference between the
life-like representation of the eager, capricious, and passionate deities of Homer's Olympus and that outline
which may still be traced in Ennius, and which is seen
filled up in Virgil and Horace, of the gods assembled,
like a grave council of state, to deliberate on the destiny
of Rome. In one fragment, containing the familiar line,—

Unus erit quem tu tolles in cærula cœli
Templa,—

they are introduced as debating, ‘tectis bipatentibus,’ on
the admission of Romulus into heaven. Again, in the
account of the Second Punic War, Jupiter is introduced
as promising to the Romans the destruction of Carthage;
and Juno abandons her resentment against the descendants of the Trojans,—

Romanis cœpit Juno placata favere.

It may be remarked, as a strong proof of the hold
which their mythology had on the minds of the ancients,
that men so sincere as Ennius and Lucretius, while in
open opposition to that system of religious belief, cannot
separate themselves from its influence and associations
in their poetry. But it is not to be supposed that Ennius, in the passages just referred to, was merely using
an artificial machinery to which he attached no meaning.
In this representation of the councils of the gods, he
embodies that faith in the Roman destiny, which was at
the root of the most serious convictions of the Romans,

in the most sceptical as well as the most believing ages
of their history. This, too, is the real belief, which
gives meaning to the supernatural agency in the Æneid.
Æneas is little more than a passive instrument in the
hands of Fate ; Jupiter merely foreknows and pronounces
its decrees ; the part assigned to Juno and Venus, in
thwarting and advancing these decrees, is a mere ornamental addition to this original conception, apparently
suggested by the experience of female intrigues at an
imperial court.

Homer makes his personages known to us in speech
as well as in action. Among epic poets he alone possessed the finest dramatic genius. But over and above
the natural dialogue or soliloquy, in which every feeling
of his various personages is revealed, he has invested his
heroes with the charm of fluent and powerful oratory, in
the council of chiefs and before the assembled people.
The words of his speakers pour on, as he says of the
words of Odysseus,—

νιφάδεσσιν ἐοικότα χειμερίῃσι,[1]

in the rapid vehemence of passion or the subtle fluency
of persuasion. The fragments of Ennius, on the other
hand, do not afford sufficient ground for attributing to
him a genuine dramatic faculty. But, as the citizen of a republic, in which action was first matured in council, and in
which the leaders of the State had to prove their qualities
and vindicate their acts, before senate and people,—

Indu foro lato sanctoque senatu,

it was incumbent on him to embody in ‘ his abstract
and chronicle of the time’ the speech of the orator no
less than the achievement of the soldier. In his estimate
of character the power of speech is honoured as the
fitting accompaniment of the wisdom of the statesman.
The following lines, for instance, uphold the prudence of
debate in contrast with the violence of war :—

    [1] ‘ Like flakes of snow on a winter’s day.’

Pellitur e medio sapientia, vi geritur res :
Spernitur orator bonus, horrida' miles amatur :
Haut doctis dictis certantes, sed maledictis
Miscent inter sese inimicitiam agitantes ;
Non ex jure manu consertum, sed magi' ferro
Rem repetunt, regnumque petunt, vadunt solida vi.[1]

As oratory had much more influence on ancient than
on modern life, the oratorical spirit has pervaded the
poetry and the histories of classical, far more than of
modern literature. Several single lines of the Annals
are evidently fragments of speeches. The most remarkable oratorical fragment is one from a speech of Pyrrhus,
and is characterised by Cicero as expressing ' sentiments
truly regal and worthy of the race of the Æacidæ.'[2]
This fragment, although evincing nothing of the fluency,
the fervid passion, or the argumentative subtlety of
debate, yet suggests the power of a great orator by its
grave and authoritative appeal to the moral dignity of
man :—

Nec mi aurum posco, nec mi pretium dederitis :
Non cauponantes bellum, sed belligerantes,
Ferro non auro vitam cernamus utrique.
Vosne velit an me regnare era quidve ferat Fors,
Virtute experiamur. Et hoc simul accipe dictum :
Quorum virtutei belli fortuna pepercit,
Eorundem libertati me parcere certum est.
Dono ducite, doque volentibu' cum magnis dis.[3]

Of the same grave and lofty tone is that appeal of

---

[1] ' Wisdom is banished from amongst us, violence rules the day : the
good orator is despised, the rough soldier loved ; striving, not with words
of learning, but with words of hate, they get embroiled in feuds, and stir
up enmity one with another. The battle is fought, not according to law,
but with the sword they demand their rights, assail the sovereignty, advance by sheer force.'

[2] Cic. *De Off.* i. 12.

[3] ' Neither do I ask gold for myself, nor offer ye to me a ransom. Let
us wage the war, not like hucksters, but like soldiers—with the sword, not
with gold, putting our lives to the issue. Whether our mistress, Fortune,
wills that you or I should reign, or what her purpose be, by valour let us
prove. And hearken too to this saying,—The brave men, whom the fortune
of battle spares, their liberty I have resolved to spare. Take my offer, as I
grant it, under the favour of the great gods.'

Appius Claudius, blind and in extreme old age, to the
Senate, when wavering in its resolution, and inclined to
make peace with Pyrrhus—

> Quo vobis mentes rectæ quæ stare solebant
> Antehac, dementes sese flexere viai.[1]

There is something in the tone of these rude fragments
which recalls the elevated feeling, the weight, and commanding power of the great speeches in Milton ;—as in
that high debate, when

> Far within,
> And in their own dimensions like themselves,
> The great seraphic lords and cherubim
> In close recess and secret conclave sat,
> A thousand demigods on golden seats.

While Ennius, in his graphic delineation of Roman
statesmen, reproduced the bold, grave, and dignified
spirit of Roman oratory, Milton has idealised and glorified the stately and serious speech of his own time,
in that majestic representation of the

> Powers and Dominions, Deities of heaven.

The great poets of human action and passion have also
been, for the most part, among the greatest poets of ex
ternal nature.   They may not have possessed that strong
personal sympathy with the mysterious life of nature,
which has been manifested chiefly by the poets of the
present century ; but they show, in different ways, that
their sense and imagination were powerfully affected both
by her outward aspect and by her manifold beauty and
energy.   Homer, not so much by direct description of the
various scenes in which the action of his poems is laid,
as by many indirect touches, by vivid imagery and picturesque epithets, reveals the openness of his mind to every
impression from the outward world, and the power and
delight with which his imagination reproduced the spon-

---

[1] ' Whither have your minds, which heretofore were wont to stand firm,
madly swerved from the straight course ?'

taneous activity of his senses. If he has left any
personal characteristic stamped upon his poetry, it is
the trace of adventure and keen sensuous enjoyment
in the open air, among the most stirring sights, and
sounds, and forces of nature. The imagery of Virgil
is of a much more peaceful cast. It seems rather to be
' the harvest of a quiet eye,' gathered in the conscious
contemplation of rural beauty, and stored up for use
along with the products of his study and meditation.
The fragments of Ennius, on the other hand, afford few
indications either of active toil and unconscious enjoyment among the solitudes of nature, or of the luxurious
and pensive susceptibility to beauty by which the poetry
of Virgil is pervaded. He was the poet, not of the woods
and rivers, but, essentially, of the city and the camp.
No sentiment could appear less appropriate to him than
that of Virgil's modest prayer,—

Flumina amem silvasque inglorius.[1]

Yet both in his illustrative imagery and in his narrative,
he occasionally reproduces with lively, if not with much
poetical force, some aspects of the outward world, as well
as many real scenes from the world of action.

His imagery is sometimes borrowed from that of
Homer; as, for instance, the following simile, which is
also imitated by Virgil :—

Et tum sic ut equus, qui de praesepibu' fartus,
Vincla suis magnis animis abrupit, et inde
Fert sese campi per caerula, laetaque prata
Celso pectore, saepe jubam quassat simul altam,
Spiritus ex anima calida spumas agit albas.[2]

Other illustrations are taken from circumstances likely

---

[1] ' Unknown to fame, may I love the rivers and the woods.'

[2] A comparison with the original passage (*Iliad*, vi. 506), will show that
Ennius, while reproducing much, though not all, of the force and life of
Homer's image, has added also some touches of his own :—

ὡς δ' ὅτε τις στατὸς ἵππος, ἀκοστήσας ἐπὶ φάτνῃ
δεσμὸν ἀπορρήξας θείῃ πεδίοιο κροαίνων,

to have been familiar to the men of his own time, but
without any apparent intention of adding poetical beauty
to the object he is representing. Thus, the silent expectation with which the assembled people watch the rival
auspices of Romulus and Remus is brought before the
Romans of his own age, by the following illustration :—

> Exspectant vel uti consul cum mittere signum
> Volt, omnes avidi spectant ad carceris oras,
> Quam mox emittat pictis e faucibu' currus.[1]

There may be noticed also, in fragments of the narrative, occasional expressions and descriptive touches implying some sense of beauty and sublimity in the familiar
aspects of the outward world. The sky, with its starry
host, is poetically presented in that expression, which has
been adopted by Virgil, ' stellis ingentibus aptum ;' and
in the following line,

> Vertitur interea caelum cum ingentibu' signis.

In the description of the auspices of Romulus, the scene
is wonderfully enlivened by this vivid flash, ' simul
aureus exoritur Sol,' following instantaneously upon the
appearance of the first bird of omen. A lively sense of
natural objects is implied in these lines from the dream
of Ilia :—

> Nam me visus homo pulcher per amoena salicta
> Et ripas raptare locosque novos ;—

> εἰωθὼς λαύεσθαι εὔρροιοῖ ποτάμοιο,
> κυδιόων ὑψοῦ δὲ κάρη ἔχει, ἀμφὶ δὲ χαῖται
> ὤμοις ἀίσσονται· ὁ δ' ἀγλαΐηφι πεποιθώς,
> ῥίμφα ἑ γοῦνα φέρει μετά τ' ἤθεα καὶ νομὸν ἵππων.

Cf. Virgil, Æn. xi. 492 :—

> Qualis ubi abruptis fugit praesepia vinclis
> Tandem liber equus, campoque potitus aperto
> Aut ille in pastus armentaque tendit equarum,
> Aut adsuetus aquae perfundi flumine noto
> Emicat, arrectisque fremit cervicibus alte
> Luxurians, luduntque jubae per colla, per armos.

[1] 'They watch, as when the consul is going to give the signal, all look
eagerly to the barrier, to see how soon he may start the chariots from
the painted entrance.'

in this description of a river, afterwards imitated both
by Lucretius and Virgil :—

Quod per amœnam urbem leni fluit agmine flumen ;—

and in these lines which recall a familiar passage in the
Æneid :—

Jupiter hic risit tempestatesque serenæ
Riserunt omnes risu Jovis omnipotentia.[1]

The rhythm and the diction of these fragments suggest
another point of comparison between the father of Greek
and the father of Roman literature. For the old Saturnian verse of the Fauns and Bards, which had been
employed also by Livius Andronicus and Nævius, Ennius
substituted the heroic hexameter, which he moulded
to the use of Roman poetry, with little art and grace,
but with much energy and weight. He is to be regarded
also as the creator of that poetical style which was
brought to high perfection by Lucretius and Virgil.
As he imitated the metre of Homer, he has in several
places (as in a simile already quoted, and, again, in describing the conduct of a brave tribune in the Istrian
war), attempted to reproduce his language. Nothing,
however, can show more clearly the vast original difference between the genius of Greece and of Rome than
the contrast presented between the rhythm and style
of their earliest epic poets. In their regard for law
and civil order, in military and political organisation,
in practical power of understanding, the Romans of
the second century B.C. had made a great and permanent
advance beyond the Greeks of the time of Homer.
But, in the very dawn of their civilisation, the Greeks
possessed a gift, which neither the progress of the
world nor all the subsequent labours of poets and critics
have enabled later generations to surpass. The genius
of poetry has never, since the time of Homer, appeared

[1] Olli subridens hominum sator atque deorum
Vultu, quo cælum tempestatesque serenat.—Æn. i. 254.

in union with a faculty of expression so true and
spontaneous, so faultless in purity, so inexhaustible in
resources. It is difficult to imagine a greater contrast
than that between the varied and harmonious power
of the earliest Greek epic, and the rugged rhythm and
diction of the Annals. Yet the very rudeness of that
work is significant of the energy of a man who had to
accomplish a gigantic task by his own unaided efforts.
His ear had not been passively trained by the musical
echoes from earlier minstrels; nor did he inherit the
fluency and richness of expression which a long line of
poets hands on to their successors. While professing to
imitate the structure of the Homeric verse, he was unable to seize its finer cadences. Nor had he learned the
stricter conditions under which that metre could be
adapted to the powerful and weighty movement of the
Latin language. If he did much to fix the laws of
Latin prosody, yet many points which were regulated
unalterably for Virgil were left quite unsettled by Ennius.
There are found occasionally in these fragments lines
without any cæsura before the fifth foot, as the following,
in one of the longest and least imperfect of his remains—

Corde capessere : semita nulla pedem stabilitat.

And though such marked violations of harmony are rare,
yet there is a large proportion of lines in which the laws
for the cæsura observed by later poets are violated.
Again, it is to be observed that the final 's' is in most
cases not sounded before a word beginning with a con-
sonant, as indeed frequently happens even in Lucretius;
while, on the other hand, the final 'm' is sometimes left
without elision before a vowel, as in the following
line—

Miscent inter sese inimicitiam agitantes.

The quantity of syllables was so far unsettled, that such
lines as the following are read,

Partem fuisset de summis rebu' regredis ;—

and this,

Nequum rumores ponebat ante salutem.

Among the ruder characteristics of his diction, his use of prosaic and technical terms is especially to be noticed. The following line, for instance, reads more like the bald statement of a chronicle, or of a legal document, than an extract from a poetical narrative :—

Cives Romani tunc facti sunt Campani.

Yet, in spite of these imperfections, both his rhythm and language produce the impression of true power and originality. With all the roughness and irregularity of his measure, and notwithstanding the inharmonious structure of continuous passages, his lines often have a weighty and powerful effect, like that produced by some of the most impressive passages in Lucretius and Virgil. It is said of the rhetorician Ælian that he excessively admired in Ennius both 'the greatness of his mind and the grandeur of his metre." Something of this sonorous grandeur may be recognised in a fragment descriptive of the havoc made by woodcutters in a great forest,— a passage in which the language of Ennius again appears as a connecting link between Homer and Virgil :—

Incedunt arbusta per alta, securibu' caedunt,
Percellunt magnas quercus, exciditur ilex,
Fraxinu' frangitur, atque abies consternitur alta.
Pinus proceras pervortunt : omne sonabat
Arbustum fremitu silvai frondosai.[2]

In the longest consecutive passages,—the dream of Ilia, the auspices of Romulus, and that from book

[1] 'Ennius Populum ποιητὴν ἐν Ἀλιαρὸς ἐπαινῶν ἔξιδα φησι .... ἤμων δὲ ἐι ἐπιθήσει τῷ τοιητοῦ τὴν μεγαλδοσαν καὶ τῶν μέτρων τὸ μεγαλεῖον καὶ ἐξιδγασεν.—SUIDAS, vol. I. p. 1258, Ed. Gaisford.

[2] Cf. Iliad, xxiii. 114-120; and also Virgil, Æn. vi. 179 :—
Itur in antiquam silvam, stabula alta ferarum,
Procumbunt piceae, sonat icta securibus ilex,
Fraxineaeque trabes cuneis et fissile robur
Scinditur. advolvunt ingentis montibus ornos.

seventh, already quoted as illustrative of the poet's character,—there is, notwithstanding the roughness of the
lines, something also of Homeric rapidity ;—a quality
which the Latin hexameter never afterwards attained in
elevated poetry.

The diction also of the Annals is everywhere fresh
and forcible, sometimes highly imaginative. But perhaps
the most remarkable quality of its style is a great
earnestness and sincerity of tone. Especially is this
the case in those passages where Ennius gives utterance
to his genuine appreciation of moral grandeur. To
take a well-known instance, the lines on Fabius Maximus owe their lasting effect to this grave and unadorned
simplicity of expression :—

> Unus homo nobis cunctando restituit rem :
> Nonum rumores ponebat ante salutem :
> Ergo plusque magisque viri nunc gloria claret.[1]

This strong, simple, and deep-graven record of sagacious
resolution and momentous services leaves upon the mind
the same impression of august, antique majesty, as is
produced by the epitaphs found in the tombs of the ·
Scipios. In neither case is there any sign of effort to
enhance the simple effect of great and heroic qualities.
A similar power of style is often exhibited by Lucretius,
especially in passages where he gives a voice to the depth
and earnestness of his feeling in contemplating the solemn realities of human life.

III. CHARACTER OF HIS GENIUS.

III.—From a review of the extant fragments both of
the Tragedies and the Annals of Ennius, it appears that
his prominent place in Roman literature, and influence

---

[1] 'One man, by biding his time, restored the commonwealth. He cared
not for what men said of him, as compared with our safety ; therefore now
his fame waxeth brighter day by day.'

over his countrymen, were due much more to a great
productiveness and activity, and to an original force
of mind and character, than to the artistic conception or
execution of his works. A consideration of the spirit
and purpose of his various works has led to the conclusion that they were, in a great measure, inspired by the
genius of Rome,—that they were much more the fresh
beginning of a new literature than the mechanical repro
duction of the literature of the Greeks. It remains
to consider what inference may be formed from these
fragments as to the nature of his genius, national
sentiment, moral sympathies, and power of understanding.

The remarkable force of many of the expressions in
these fragments, and the power with which various
incidents, situations, and characters, are represented,
indicate the presence of a very vivid imagination. A
sense of energy and life-like movement, is perhaps the
chief impression produced by a study of the language
and the longer passages in these remains. Many single
lines and phrases that have been gathered accidentally,
as mere isolated words, disjoined from the context in
which they originally occurred, bear clear traces of the
force and ardour with which they were cast into shape.
In longer passages, the whole heart, sense, and understanding of the writer, seem to be thrown into his narrative. His gift does not seem to have been the fine
contemplative eye of an artist, like Catullus, who ob-
serves, as it were, from a distance, and fixes as in a
picture, some transient phase of passionate feeling or
some beautiful aspect of repose. But he suggests the
idea of a man of practical energy, who has been present
and taken part in the action described, entering with
living interest into every detail, watching it at the same
time with a sagacious judgment and a strong enthusiasm.
His power as a narrative poet is the power of forcibly

reproducing both the movement and the vital meaning
not the mere outward pictorial effect—of an action, and
of identifying himself with the hearts and minds of the
actors on the scene. Several passages, wanting altogether in poetical beauty, yet arrest the attention by
this energy and truth of conception ; as, for example,
this short and rugged fragment, descriptive of a com-
mander in the crisis of a battle,—

> Aspectabat virtutem legioni' mai,
> Expertans, si mussaret, quæ denique pausa
> Pugnandi fieret, aut duri æni' laboria.[1]

Even in the abrupt dislocation from their context these
lines leave on the mind a strong and real impression of
the calm vigilance of a general, and of his confidence,
not unmixed with anxiety, in ' the long-enduring hearts'
of his men.   The same truth and energy of conception,
with more poetical accompaniment, may be recognised
in the longer passages, from Book VII. and Book I.,
already quoted or referred to.

But a still higher imaginative power is revealed by the
suggestive force of many single expressions and by the
delineation of more poetical or passionate situations.
Such expressions as the following, most of which are
discovered shining again with an antique lustre in the
gold of Virgil's diction, are indicative of that power of
the imagination which imparts a new life and meaning
to familiar objects and ideas,—

> Mœsæ quæ pedibus magnum pulsatis Olympum.[2]

> Transmarit cita per teneras caliginis auras.[3]

> Postquam discordia tætra
> Belli ferratos postes portasque refregit.[4]

[1] ' He watched the courage of his men, to see if any murmur should arise for some pause to the long battle, some rest from their weary toil.'
[2] ' Muses, who beat the great Olympus with your tread.'
[3] ' Swiftly she floated through the delicate air of the darkness.'
[4] ' After foul Discord had broken down the iron-cased door-posts and gates of war.'

                    Quem super ingens
Porta tonat cæli.[1]

Spiritus austri imbricitor.   Naves velivolas, etc. etc.[2]

These and similar phrases, some of which have already
been quoted, imply original poetical power as well as
vigour of mind. They tend to justify the estimate of
the genius of Ennius, indicated in the language of high
admiration applied to him by Lucretius,—

> Ennius ut noster cecinit, qui primus amœno
> Detulit ex Helicone perenni fronde coronam,
> Per gentes Italas hominum quæ clara clueret ;[3]

and in the many signs of the careful study of the Annals, which may be traced in the elaborate workmanship
of the Æneid.

The best specimen of imaginative narrative from the
hand of Ennius, is the passage in which the vestal Ilia
relates to her sister the dream that portended her great
and strange destiny :—

> Excita cum tremulis annus attulit artubm' lumen,
> Talia commemorat lacrimans, exterrita somno.
> Euridica prognata, pater quam noster amavit,
> Vires vitaque corpu' meum nunc deserit omne.
> Nam me visus homo pulcher per amœna salicta
> Et ripas raptare locosque novos ; ita sola
> Postilla, germana soror, errare videbar
> Tardaque vestigare et quærere te neque posse
> Corde capessere : semita nulla pedem stabilibat.
> Exin compellare pater me voce videtur
> His verbis : 'O gnata, tibi sunt ante ferendæ
> Ærumnæ, post ex fluvio fortuna resistet.'
> Hæc ecfata' pater, germana, repente recessit
> Nec sese dedit in conspectum, corde cupitus,
> Quanquam multa manus ad cæli cærula templa
> Tendebam lacrimans et blanda voce vocabam :
> Vix ægro cum corde meo me somno' reliquit.[4]

---

[1] 'Over whom the vast portal of heaven is thundering.'

[2] 'Rain-rousing breath of the South.'   'Sail-winged ships,' etc. etc.

[3] 'As sang our Ennius, the first who brought down from pleasant Helicon
a chaplet of unfailing leaf, the fame of which should be bruited loud through
the nations of Italian men.'

[4] 'When the old dame had risen, and with trembling limbs had brought the
light, thus she (Ilia), roused in terror from her sleep, with tears tells her tale:

H

Though these lines are rough and inharmonious as compared with the rhythm of Catullus or Virgil, yet they
flow more smoothly and rapidly than any of the other
fragments preserved from Ennius. The impression of
gentleness and tender affection produced by the speech
of Ilia, implies some dramatic skill in the conception of
character. And there is real imaginative power shown
in the sense of hurry and surprise, of vague awe and
helplessness, produced by the lines—

Nam me visus homo pulcher per amœna salicta, etc.

From this passage Virgil has borrowed one of the most
striking features in his delineation of the passion of
Dido, the sense of horror and desolation haunting the
Carthaginian queen in her dreams—

Agit ipsa furentem
In somnis ferus Æneas : semperque relinqui
Sola sibi, semper longam incomitata videtur
Ire viam, et Tyrios deserta quærere terra.[1]

Another of the most impressive passages in the early
books of the Æneid—the dream in which Hector appears to Æneas[2]—was evidently suggested by the de-

"Daughter of Eurydice, whom our father loved, my strength and life now fail
me through all my frame. For methought that a goodly man was bearing
me off through the pleasant willow-groves, by the river-banks, and places
strange to me. Thereafter, O my sister, I seemed to be wandering all alone,
and with slow steps to track my way, to be seeking thee, and to be unable
to find thee near; no footpath steadied my step. Afterwards methought
I heard my father address me in these words—'Daughter, trouble must
first be borne by thee; afterwards thy fortune shall rise up again from
the river.' With these words, O sister, he suddenly departed, nor gave
himself to my sight, though my heart yearned to him, though I kept eagerly
stretching my hands to the blue vault of heaven, weeping, and calling
on him with loving tones. With pain and weary heart at last sleep left
me."[1]

[1] 'And stern Æneas in her dreams appears,
Disdainful as by day : she seems, alone
To wander in her sleep, through ways unknown,
Guideless, and dark : or, in a desert plain,
To seek her subjects, and to seek in vain.'—DRYDEN.

[2] Æn. ii. 270.

scription which Ennius gave of the appearance of the shade of Homer to himself. Some of his dramatic fragments, also, as for instance the scene between Hecuba and Cassandra already referred to, show a real power of conceiving and representing passionate situations. The imaginative feeling, as well as the imaginative activity, of Ennius is stamped on many striking fragments. His poetry seems to have been immediately inspired by the impulse of patriotism. In the manifestation of this impulse, he shows an affinity to Virgil in ancient, and to Scott, in modern times. He resembles them in their mingled feelings of veneration and affection towards the national heroes of old times, and the great natural features of their country, associated with ancient memories and legendary renown. Such feelings are expressed by Ennius in the lines of tender regret and genuine hero-worship, which represent the sorrow of Senate and people at the death of Romulus—

> Pectora . . . tenet desiderium, simul inter
> Sese sic memorant, O Romule, Romule die
> Qualem te patriae custodem di genuerunt !
> O pater, O genitor, O sanguen dis oriundum !
> Tu produxisti nos intra luminis oras.[1]

The idealising affection of patriotism appears also in the language which he applies to the sacred river of Rome, which had preserved the founder of the city from his untimely fate, and was thus inseparably identified with the national destiny—

> Teque pater Tiberine tuo cum flumine sancto.[2]

The enumeration of the great warlike races in the line

> Marsa manus, Peligna cohors, Vestina virum vis,

may recall the pride and enthusiasm which are kindled

---

[1] 'Regret and sorrow fill their hearts, while thus they say to one another, O Romulus, God-like Romulus, how great a guardian of our country did the gods create in thee ! O father, author of our being, O blood sprung from the gods ! it is thou that hast brought us forth within the realms of light.'

[2] 'And thee, father Tiberinus, with thy hallowed stream.'

in the heart of Virgil by the names of the various tribes of Italy, and of places renowned for their fame in story, or their picturesque environment.[1] This fond use of proper names recalling old associations or the charm of natural scenery, is also among the most familiar characteristics of the poetry of Scott.

It was seen in a former chapter that the Roman mind was peculiarly susceptible of that kind of feeling, which perhaps may best be described as the sense of majesty. This vein of poetical emotion evidently ran through the poem of Ennius. His language may have little grace or beauty, but it is full of the sense of greatness and order, both in the material world and in human affairs. His nature seems to be moved in harmony with the attributes of power, immensity, and long duration, and with the moral qualities analogous to these, such as resolution, magnanimity, and what has been called 'monumental immobility'[2] of character. His genius also feels a sympathy with the commanding attributes and august forms of government. Thus his style appears to have been not only animated by a strong vital force, but to have been pervaded by gravity, dignity, and impressive solemnity. This susceptibility of his genius is clearly seen in single expressions such as the following—

> 'Magnum pulsatis Olympum.'   'Indu mari magno.'
> 'Litora lata sonant.'
> 'Latos per populos terrasque.'
> 'Magnae gentes opulentae.'
> 'Quis potis ingentis oras evolvere belli?'
> 'Vertitur interea caelum cum ingentibu' signis:'

---

[1] E.g., passages such as the following—

> Quique altum Praeneste viri, quique arva Gabinae
> Junonis gelidumque Anienem et roscida rivis
> Hernica saxa colunt, quos dives Anagnia pascit,
> Quos, Amasene pater.—Æn. vii. 682-3.

[2] Applied by De Quincey to Marius.

and again in the following—

'Indu foro lato sanctoque senatu.'
'Augusto augurio postquam incluta condita Roma est.'
'Omnibu' cum viris ater esset induperator;'

and in the epithet which Cicero quotes as applied to cities—

Urbes magnas atque ' imperiosas.'

His imagination appears also to have been impressed by that sense of pomp and magnificence, which exercised a strong spell on the Roman mind in all ages, and obtained its most complete and permanent realisation in the outward state and splendour of the Empire. A short passage from one of his tragedies, the Andromache, may be quoted as illustrative of this influence, even in the writings of Ennius, though naturally it is much more apparent in the style of those poets who witnessed the grandeur of Rome in her later era :—

O pater, O patria, O Priami domus,
Saeptum altisono cardine templum!
Vidi ego te, astante ope barbarica,
Tectis caelatis, lacuatis,
Auro'ebore instructum regifice !'

While his peculiar poetical feeling is present chiefly in the fragments of the Annals, the moral elements of his poetry may be gathered both from his epic and dramatic remains. The strong and dignified qualities of character are those which especially kindle the fervour of his moral sympathy. Yet in delineating the agitation of Ilia, and in other places, he reveals also much tenderness of feeling,—the not unusual accompaniment of the manly genius of Rome. A similar tender-

---

[1] 'O father! O fatherland! O house of Priam, palace, closing on high-sounding hinge, I have seen thee, guarded by a barbaric host, with carved and deep-fretted roof, with ivory and gold royally adorned.'
Cicero (Tusc. Disp. iii. 18) says on this passage :—' O poetam egregium ! quanquam ab his cantoribus Euphorionis contemnitur.'

ness is found in union with the grave and severe tones
of Pacuvius and Attius, and in still greater measure
with the stern fortitude of Lucretius and the stately
majesty of Virgil. But the language of Ennius more
frequently expresses his appreciation of the strong qualities both of character and intellect, such as fortitude,
sincerity, magnanimity, and capacity for affairs. Thus
a latent glow of enthusiasm may be discerned in the
lines which record the brave resolution of the Roman
people during the first hardships of the war with
Pyrrhus :—

> Ast animo superant atque aspera prima
> Volnera belli disperaunt ;[1]

and also in this strong and scornful triumph over natural sorrow, from the Telamon :—

> Ego cum genui tum moritaros scivi, et ei rei sustuli :
> Praeterea ad Trojam cum misi ob defendendam Graeciam,
> Scibam me in mortiferum bellum, non in epulas mittere.[2]

The generosity and courage of a magnanimous nature
are stamped upon the kingly speech which he puts into
the mouth of Pyrrhus. A frank sincerity and simplicity of character reveal themselves in such passages
as the following :—

> Eo ego ingenio natus sum,
> Æque inimicitiam, atque amicitiam in frontem promptam gero.[3]

There is no subtlety nor rhetorical point in the expression of his moral convictions. The very style of the
tragedies, which, as Cicero says,[4] ' does not depart from

[1] 'But they rise superior in spirit, and spurn the first sharp wounds of
war.'

[2] 'When I begat them, I knew that they must die, and to that end I
bred them. Besides, when I sent them to Troy to fight for Greece, I was
well aware that I was sending them, not to a feast, but to a deadly war.'

[3] 'Such is my nature. Enmity and friendship equally I bear stamped
on my forehead.'

[4] 'Ennio delector, ait quispiam, quod non discedit a communi ordine
verborum.'—*Orator*, 11.

the natural order of the words,' is a symbol of frankness
and straightforward honesty.

He shows also, in his delineations of character, high
appreciation of practical wisdom, and of its most powerful
instrument in a free State, the persuasive power of oratory. This appreciation is expressed in the lines so much
admired by Cicero and Aulus Gellius,[1] though ridiculed
by the purism of Seneca :—

> Is dictus 'st ollis popularibus olim
> Qui tum vivebant homines, atque ævum agitabant,
> Flos delibatus populi suadæque medulla.[2]

His admiration appears to have been given more to
the sterling qualities of character and intellect than to
the brilliant manifestations of impulse and genius. He
celebrates the heroism of brave endurance rather than
of chivalrous daring ;[3] the fortitude that, in the long
run, wins success, and saves the State,[4] rather than the
impetuous valour which achieves a barren glory ; the
confidence based on moral strength,[5] rather than the
pride of power ; the sincerity and simplicity which are
stronger than art, yet that know when to speak and
when to be silent ;[6] the sagacity which enables men to
understand their circumstances, and to turn them to
the best account.

Many of his fragments, again, show traces of that
just and vigorous understanding of human life, and that
shrewdness of observation, which constitute a great

---

[1] Cicero, *Brutus*, 15—Aulus Gellius, xii. 2.
[2] ' He was called by those, his fellow-countrymen, who flourished then
and enjoyed their day, the chosen flower of the people, and the marrow
of persuasion.'
[3] Compare his account of the Tribune in the Istrian war :—
> Undique conveniunt, velut imber, tela tribuno, etc.
[4] Cf. Unus homo nobis cunctando restituit rem, etc.
[5] Cf. Ille vir haut magna cum re, sed plenu' fidei.
[6] Cf. Ita sapere opino esse optimum, ut pro viribus
> Tacere ac fabulari tute noveris.

satirist.   The didactic tone of satire appears, for instance,
in the following lines—

> Otioso in otio animus nescit quid velit ;
> Hic itidem est : enim neque domi nunc nos neque militiæ sumus,
> Imus huc, illuc hinc, cum illuc ventum est, ire illinc lubet ;
> Incerte errat animus : præter propter vitam vivitur,[1]—

a fragment which might be compared with certain passages in the Epistles of Horace, that give expression to
the *ennui* experienced as a result of the ease and pros-
perity of the Augustan age.   But a closer parallel will
be found in a passage where Lucretius has assumed
something of the caustic tone of Roman satire—

> Exit sæpe foras magnis ex ædibus ille
> Esse domi quem pertæsum 'st, subitoque revertit,
> Quippe domi nihilo melius qui sentiat esse,' etc.[2]

Ennius, as well as Lucretius, gives scarcely any
indication of humour.   Yet the folly and superstition of
his times could provoke him into tones of contemptuous irony, especially where he has to expose the arts
of false prophets and fortune-tellers.   The men of the
manliest temper and the strongest understanding in
ancient times were most intolerant of this mischievous
form of imposture and credulity.   Thus Thucydides,
in general so reserved in his expression of personal feeling, treats, with a manifest irony, all supernatural pre-
tences to foresee or control the future.   The tone in
which Ennius writes of such professions is something
like the tone of Milton's grim contempt for

> Eremites and friars
> White, black, and grey, with all their trumpery.

Thus, in a fragment of Book XI. of the Annals, the fears
excited by the prophets and diviners, at the commence-

---

[1] ' In idleness the mind knows not what it wants.   This is now our case.
We are neither now at home nor abroad.   We go hither, back again to the
place from which we came,- when we have reached it we desire to leave it
again.   Our mind is all astray—existence goes on outside of real life.'
[2] III. 1060–67.

ment of the war with Antiochus, are encountered with
the pertinent question—

Satin' vates verant ætate in agenda ?[1]

Thus, too, the pretensions and the ignorance of astrologers are exposed in a line of one of the dramas—

Quod est ante pedes nemo spectat : cœli scrutantur plagas.[2]

And the following passage may be quoted as applicable
to charlatans of every kind, in every age and country --

Sed superstitiosi vates, impudentesque arioli,
Aut inertes aut insani, aut quibus egestas imperat,
Qui sibi semitam non sapiunt, alteri monstrant viam,
Quibus divitias pollicentur, ab eis drachmam ipsi petunt.[3]

There are passages of the same spirit still preserved
among the fragments of Pacuvius and Attius.

There is not much indication of speculative thought
or philosophy in any of these fragments. The blunt
sentiment which Ennius puts into the mouth of Neo-
ptolemus was probably applicable to himself—

Philosophari est mihi necesse, at paucis : nam omnino haut placet.[4]

His reflections on life are neither of an imaginative, of a
very abstract, nor of a purely satiric character. Unlike
the thoughts of the Greek dramatists, they show no
attempt to read the divine laws which govern human
destiny ; they want the universality and systematic basis
of philosophical truths ; they are expressed neither with
the pointed wit nor with the ironical humour of satire.
They are the maxims of a strong common sense and the
dictates of a grave rectitude of will. They are practical,
not speculative. They have their origin in a sense of duty

---

[1] ' Are these prophets true men in their own lives ?'

[2] ' No one looks at what is before his feet : but they pry into the skies.'

[3] ' But your superstitious prophets and impudent fortune-tellers, idle fel-
lows, madmen, or the victims of hunger, who cannot discern the path for
themselves, yet point the way out to others, and beg a drachma from the
very persons to whom they are promising wealth.'

[4] ' Philosophy is necessary to me, but in moderation. I don't like it as
a whole.'

rather than of consequences. They express the gravity,
the fortitude, the plain sincerity of the old Republic;
and they show what sterling worth was combined with
the ardent enthusiasm, and how much practical sense
with the strong imagination of the poet.

Such appear to be the chief attributes of genius and
the chief moral and intellectual features in the father of
Roman poetry. It is not indeed possible, from the tenor
of single passages, to judge of the composition of a whole
drama or of a continuous book of the Annals. No single
scene or speech can afford sufficient grounds for inferring
the amount of creative power with which his characters
were conceived and sustained in all their complex relations. Yet enough has appeared in these fragments,
which, from the accidental mode of their preservation,
must be regarded as the ordinary samples and not the
choice beauties of his style, to confirm the ancient belief
in his pre-eminence and to determine the prevailing
characteristics of his genius. There is ample evidence
of the great popularity which he enjoyed among his
countrymen, and of the high estimate which many of
the best Roman writers formed of his power. It is recorded that great crowds (' magna frequentia') attended
the public reading of the Annals. Virgil was said to
have introduced many lines into the Æneid, with the
view of pleasing a public devoted to Ennius (' populus
Ennianus'). The title of Ennianista was assumed by a
public reader of the Annals in the time of Hadrian.[1]
Cicero often speaks of the poet as ' noster Ennius,' and

---

[1] ' And there it is announced to Julianus that a certain public reader, an
accomplished man, with a very well-trained and musical voice, read the
Annals of Ennius publicly in the theatre. Let us go, says he, to hear this
' Ennianista,' whoever he is,—for by that name he chose to be called.'—*Aulus
Gellius*, xviii. 5.

The following line of Martial (v. 10. 7) implies also his popularity under
the Empire—

    Ennius est lectus, salvo tibi, Roma, Marone.

quotes him with all the signs of hearty admiration and affection. The numerous references in his works to the Annals and the Tragedies imply also a thorough familiarity with these poems on the part of the readers for whom his philosophical and rhetorical treatises were written. The criticism of Quintilian, ‘ Ennium sicut sacros vetustate lucos adoremus, in quibus grandia et antiqua robora jam non tantam habent speciem quantam religionem,'[1] expresses a sentiment of traditional reverence as well as of personal appreciation. Aulus Gellius, a writer' of the time of Hadrian, often quotes and comments upon him with hearty and genial sympathy. The greatest among the Roman poets also, directly and indirectly, acknowledge their admiration. The strong testimony of Lucretius, the most imaginative poet and the most powerful thinker whom Rome produced, is alone sufficient to establish the fame of Ennius as a man of remarkable force and genius. The spirit of the Annals still lives in the antique charm and national spirit, which make the epic poem of Virgil the truest representation of Roman feeling which has come down to modern times. By Ovid he is characterised as—

Ennius, ingenio maximus, arte rudis.

Horace, although more reluctant and grudging in his admiration, yet allows the ‘ Calabrian Muse' to be the best preserver of the fame of the great Scipio. Even the disparaging lines—

Ennius et sapiens et fortis et alter Homerus,
Ut critici dicunt, leviter curare videtur
Quo promissa cadant et somnia Pythagorea,[2]

are a strong testimony in favour of the esteem in which

---

[1] ‘ Let us venerate Ennius like the groves, sacred from their antiquity, in which the great and ancient oak-trees are invested not so much with beauty as with sacred associations.'—Inst. Or. x. i. 88.

[2] ‘ Ennius, the wise and strong, and the second Homer, as his critics will have it, seems to care little for the issue of all his promises and Pythagorean dreams.'—Epist. ii. i. 50-2.

the vigour and sagacity of Ennius were held by those who had all his works in their hands. As one of the founders of Roman literature, it was impossible that he could have rivalled the careful and finished style of the Augustan poets ; but, by his rude and energetic labours, he laid the strong ground-work on which later poets built their fame.

He has been exposed to more serious detraction in modern times, as the corrupter of the pure stream of early Roman poetry. It is alleged against him by Niebuhr, that through jealousy he suppressed the ballad and epic poetry of the early bards. The answer to this charge has already been given. There is no sufficient evidence to prove that any such poems were in existence in the time of Ennius. By other modern scholars he is disadvantageously compared with Nævius, who is held up to admiration as the last of the genuine Roman minstrels. Nævius appears indeed to have been a remarkable and original man, yet his very scanty fragments do not afford sufficient evidence to justify the reversal of the verdict of antiquity on the relative greatness and importance of the two poets. The old Roman party, in opposition to whom Ennius and his friends are supposed to have introduced the new taste and suppressed the old, never showed any zeal in favour of poetry of any kind. Cato, their only literary representative, wrote prose treatises on antiquities and agriculture, and in one of his speeches reproached Fulvius Nobilior for the consideration which he showed to Ennius. The evidence of these epic and dramatic fragments which have just been considered, is all in favour of the high verdict of antiquity on the importance and pre-eminence of the author of the Annals. Whatever in the later poets is most truly Roman in sentiment and morality, appears to be conceived in the spirit of Ennius.

He stands out prominently in that early time as a man
of true genius, and of a great and original character.
His lot was not cast, like that of the Augustan poets,
in the midst of a refined and courtly society, with all
the aids and appliances of literary leisure, and in secure
exemption from any harsh collision with the world.
Neither was he a poetical artist, like Catullus, yielding
himself up to the enjoyment of beauty, and reproducing
in his verse the charm which he had found in life, in
nature, and in earlier art. His poetry was the serious
product of a manly and energetic life, and of a vital
interest in the great affairs of his time. Till middle life
he is dimly discerned as an obscure Calabrian soldier,
claiming descent from an old race of kings, but a
stranger to the great city which in after times regarded
him as the father of her literature. In mature manhood,
and in a kindly old age, he is seen exercising a constant
literary industry in manifold ways, living plainly and in
cheerful independence, applauded by his fellow-citizens,
and honoured by the friendship of the greatest among
his contemporaries.

The variety and extent of his works bear witness to
remarkable learning, as well as a strong productive
energy. With a wide knowledge of Greek literature,
he combined the heart and will of a Roman ; and to the
study of the best books, he added a close contact with
men. Expressions in his remains indicate the opposite
religious feelings and convictions of a mystic and a scep-
tic. In his temper and character, a high self-consciousness appears united with a true simplicity and hearty
appreciation of others ; and a great gravity of tone and
purpose with a cheerful and sanguine spirit. His moral
sympathies are most deeply moved by such qualities
as fortitude, magnanimity, integrity, and practical wisdom ; and the transparent sincerity of his words gives
assurance that he himself was formed out of the same

true metal which he recognised in 'the old manners and
men' of his adopted country.

In his poetry, he represented the traditions and the
steady continuous growth of the Roman State, and expressed the confidence which the people reposed in their
destiny, their institutions, and their leading men. His
dramas, although founded on Greek models, and dealing
with Greek legends and personages, yet had a real national air in the sentiments they expressed, and in the
lessons of life they inculcated. His epic poem was in
form, spirit, and substance, inspired by the genius of
his country, and was finished with the strong and massive execution of Roman workmanship. While discard-
ing the native Saturnian measure, as unequal to the
elevated tone of a long narrative poem, he moulded the
Latin language to the conditions of a new metre, which,
in later times, was successfully wrought into the most
expressive organ of the majesty of Rome. In his reproduction of the Homeric mythology, he has embodied
the idea of the national destiny. The characteristic sentiment of his poetry indicates his affinity not to Homer
and Sophocles, but to Lucretius and Virgil. There are
gleams also of true creative power in these fragments.
If wanting in the fine accomplishment and the contemplative faculty of a poetic artist, he seems to have
possessed a strength and energy of conception unsurpassed by any of his successors. He was endowed also
with that living power which gives new meaning to
familiar things; which, without distorting or exagge-
rating the truth, sees and reveals the glory and the
grandeur of human life.

CHAPTER V.

OF the three great forms of poetical composition produced during the first period of Roman literature, the
Tragic Drama, although least original in form and substance, was apparently the most popular. Even before
the time of Livius Andronicus, the Romans had been
used to various kinds of scenic performances; and from
the date of his first representation till the overthrow of
the Republic, both tragedy and comedy continued to be
brought forward and received with general favour. Till
the time of Ennius, comedy had been cultivated with
most activity and success. He gave the first powerful
impulse to the cultivation of Roman tragedy; and the
interest awakened by him in this form of literature was
sustained by his nephew, M. Pacuvius, and after him by
L. Attius. The popularity of the tragic drama at this
period may be estimated from the fact that, of the early
writers of poetry, Lucilius alone contributed nothing to
the Roman stage. The plays of the three tragedians who
have just been mentioned, were not only performed during the lifetime of their authors, but, as appears from
many notices of them in Cicero, they held their place on
the stage with much popular applause, and were read
and admired as literary works till the last days of the
Republic. This popularity implies either some adaptation of Roman tragedy to the time in which it was produced, or some special capacity for awakening new

interests and ideas in a people hitherto unacquainted
with literature. Yet, on the other hand, the want of
permanence, and the want of any power of development
in the Roman drama, would indicate that it was less
adapted to the genius of the nation than either the
epic or the satiric poetry of this era. If the dramatic
art of Pacuvius and Attius had been as true an expression of national character as either the epic poem of
Ennius or the satire of Lucilius, it might have been
expected that it would have flourished in greater perfection in the eras of finer literary accomplishment.
The efforts of Nævius and Ennius were crowned with
the fulfilment of Virgil, and the spirit and manner of
Lucilius still live in the satires of Horace and Juvenal;
but the Roman drama dwindled away till it became a
mere literary exercise of educated men, and remains
only in the artificial and rhetorical compositions attributed to the philosopher Seneca.

From the fact that early Roman tragedy left no literary heir, it is more difficult to discern its original features
and character than those of the epic or satiric poetry of
the period. A further difficulty arises out of the very
nature of dramatic fragments. Isolated passages in a
drama afford no grounds for judging of the conduct of
the action, or the force and consistency with which the
leading characters are represented. There is, moreover,
very slight direct evidence bearing on the dramatic
genius of the early tragic poets. Roman critics seem to
have paid little attention to, or had little perception of
this kind of excellence. They quote with admiration
the fervid sentiment and morality—' the rugged maxims
hewn from life'—expressed on the Roman stage; but
they have not preserved the memory of any great typical
character, or of any dramatic plot creatively conceived
or powerfully sustained.

The Roman drama was confessedly a reproduction or

adaptation of the drama of Athens. The titles of the
great majority of Roman tragedies indicate that they
were translated or copied from Greek originals, or were
at least founded on the legends of Greek poetry and
mythology. The *Medea* of Ennius and the *Antiope* of
Pacuvius are known, on the authority of Cicero, to have
been directly translated from Euripides. Other dramas
were more or less close adaptations from his works, or
from those of the older Attic tragedians. There is, however, distinct evidence that in some cases the Roman
poets departed considerably from their originals. Something of a Roman character was imparted to the Greek
personages who were represented. Many of the extant
fragments breathe the spirit of Rome much more than of
Athens. They are expressed not with the subtlety and
reflective genius of Greece, but in the plain and straightforward tones of the Roman Republic. The long-continued popularity of Roman tragedy implies also that
it was something more than an inartistic copy of the
masterpieces of Athenian genius. Mere imitations of
Æschylus, Sophocles, and Euripides might possibly have
obtained some favour with a few men of literary education, but could never have been listened to with applause,
for more than a century and a half, by miscellaneous
audiences.

The following questions suggest themselves as of most
interest in connexion with the general character of early
Roman tragedy:—How far could it have reproduced,
not the substance and form only, but the spirit of the
Greek drama? What was its bearing on the actual
circumstances of Roman life, and what were the grounds
of the favour with which it was received? What cause
can be assigned for the cessation of this favour with the
fall of the Republic?

(1.) The materials or substance of Roman tragedy
were almost entirely Greek. The stories and characters

I

represented were, except in two or three cases, directly
derived either from the Greek tragedians or from Homer
and the cyclic poets. In point of form and metre also,
Roman tragedy endeavoured to imitate the models on
which it was founded, with probably as little percep
tion of the requirements of dramatic art as of refinement in expression and harmony in rhythm. But while
generally conforming to their models, the early Roman
poets departed, in some important respects, from their
practice. Thus they banished the Chorus from the
orchestra, assigning to it merely a subsidiary part in
the dialogue. Although some simple lyrical metre,
such as the anapaestic, continued to be employed in
the more rapid and impassioned parts of the dialogue,
there was no scope, on the Roman stage, for the
great lyrical poetry of the Greek drama, and for the
nobler functions of the chorus. On the other hand, there
seems to have been more opportunity both for action
and for oratorical declamation. The acting of a Roman play must have been more like that on a modern
stage than the stately movement and the statuesque
repose of the Greek theatre. Again, in imitating the
iambic and trochaic metres of the Greek drama, the
Roman poets were quite indifferent to the laws by which
their finer harmony is produced. Any of the feet ad-
missible in an iambic line might occupy any place in the
line, with the exception of the last. There is thus little
metrical harmony in the fragments of Roman tragedy;
but, on the other hand, it may be remarked that the
order of the words in these fragments appears more
natural and direct than in the more elaborate metres
of the later Roman poets.

But it was as impossible for the Roman drama to
reproduce the inner spirit of Greek tragedy as to rival
its artistic excellence. Greek tragedy, in its mature
glory, was not only a purely Greek creation, but was the

imaginative expression of a remarkable phase through
which the human mind has once passed ;—a phase in
which the vivid fancies and emotions of a primitive age
met and combined with the thought, the art, the social
and political life of the greatest era of ancient civilisation. The Athenian dramatists, like the great dramatists of other times, imparted a new and living interest
to ancient legends ; but this was but one part, perhaps
not the most important part, of their functions. They
represented before the people the destiny and sufferings
of national heroes and demigods, sanctified in the feelings of many generations by long association, still honoured by a vital worship, and appealed to as a present
help in danger. Thus a highly idealised and deeply
religious character was imparted to the tragic representation of human passion and destiny on the Athenian
stage. This view of life, represented and contemplated with a deep solemnity of feeling in the age of
Pericles, would have been altogether unmeaning to a
Roman of the age of Ennius. Such a one might understand the natural heroism of a strong will, but not the
new force and elevation imparted to the will by contemplating the hidden powers and laws by which human
affairs are overruled. He might, perhaps, be moved to
sympathy with the sufferers or actors on the scene ;
but he would be altogether insensible to the higher
consolation which overcomes the natural sorrow for the
mere earthly catastrophe in a great dramatic action.
The inward strength and dignity of a Roman senator
might enable him to appreciate the magnanimity and
kingly nature of Œdipus ; but the deeper interest of the
great dramas founded on the fortunes of the Theban
king, especially the interest arising from his trust in
final righteousness, his sense of communion with higher
powers, and from the thought of his elevation out of the
lowest earthly state into perpetual sanctity and honour,

was widely remote from the tangible objects of a
Roman's desire, and the direct motives of his conduct.
Or perhaps a Roman would have a fellow-feeling with
the proud, soldierly bearing of Ajax ; but he would be
blind to the inward lesson of self-knowledge and self-
mastery, which Sophocles represents as forced upon the
spirit of the Greek hero through the stern visitation of
Athene. Equally remote from the ordinary experience
and emotions of a Roman would be the feeling of awe,
gloom, and mystery, diffused through the great thoughts
and conceptions of Æschylus. Both in Æschylus and
in Sophocles all the light and the gloom are cast over
the human story from a higher region. But in the fragments of the Roman tragedians, though there is often
found the expression of magnanimous and independent
sentiment, and of a very dignified and manly morality,
there is no trace of any sense of dependence upon Divine
power ; and there are some indications not only of a
scorn for common superstition, but also of indifference
to every form of religious faith. The thought of the
insecurity of life, of the vicissitudes of human affairs,
and of the impotence of man to control his fate, which
so deeply affected the Greek poets and historians of the
fifth century B.C., was utterly alien to the natural temperament of Rome, and to the confidence inspired by
uniform success during the long period succeeding the
Second Punic War.

The contemplative and religious thought of Greek tragedy was as remote from the practical spirit of the Romans as the political license and the personal humours of
the old Athenian comedy were from the earnestness of
public life, and the dignity of the governing power in the
great aristocratic Republic. And thus it happened that,
as the comic poets of Rome reproduced the new comedy
of Athens, which portrayed the passions of private not of
political life, and the manners of a cosmopolitan rather

than of a purely Greek civilisation, so the tragic poets
found the art of Euripides more easy to imitate than
that of Æschylus and Sophocles. The interest of tragedy, as treated by Euripides, turns upon the catas-
trophes produced by human passion : the religious
meaning has, in a great measure, passed away : the
characters have dwindled from their heroic stature to
the proportions of ordinary life : his thought is the result of the analysis of motives, and the study of familiar
experience. He is less of a pure Athenian, and has more
affinity with the ordinary thoughts and moods of men
than either of the older poets. The earlier and the later
Greek writers have a nearer relation to the spirit of
other eras of the world's history than those who represent Athenian civilisation in its maturity. It requires
a longer familiarity with the mind and heart of antiquity
to realise and enjoy the full meaning of Sophocles,
Thucydides, or Aristophanes, than of Homer, Euripides,
or Theocritus. Homer is indeed one of the truest, if not
the truest, representative of the genius of Greece,—the
representative also of the ancient world in the same
sense as Shakspeare is of the modern world,—but he is,
at the same time, directly intelligible and interesting
to all countries and times, from his being one of the
most natural and powerful representatives of the ele-
mentary feelings and principles of human nature. The
later poets, on the other hand, such as Euripides and
the writers of the new comedy, were not more truly
human, but were less distinctively Greek than their
immediate predecessors. They had advanced beyond
them in the analytic knowledge of human nature ; but,
with the decay of religious belief and political feeling,
they had lost much of the genius and sentiment by
which the old Athenian life was characterised. Both
their gain and their loss bring them more into harmony with later modes of thought and feeling. Thus

it has happened that, while the influence of Æschylus
and Sophocles, Thucydides and Aristophanes, is scarcely
perceptible in Roman literature, Homer and the early
lyrical poets who flourished before Greek civilisation
exhibited its most special type,—and Euripides (who,
though a contemporary of Sophocles and Aristophanes,
yet belonged in spirit and tone to a younger generation),
—the writers of the new comedy,—and the Alexandrian
poets, who flourished when the purely Greek ideas and
character were being merged in a more general civilisation,—exercised a direct influence on Roman taste
and opinion in every age of their literature. The early
tragic poets of Rome could not rival or imitate the
dramatic art, the pathetic power, the clear and fluent
style, the active and subtle analysis of Euripides ; but
they could approach nearer to him than to any of his
predecessors, by treating the myths and personages of
the heroic time apart from the sacred associations and
ideal majesty of earlier art, and as a vehicle for inculcating the lessons and the experience of familiar life.

(2.) The primary attraction, by means of which the
tragic drama established itself at Rome, must have been
the power of scenic representations to convey a story,
and to produce novel impressions on a people to whom
reading was quite unfamiliar. In Homer, the cyclic poets,
and the Attic dramatists, there existed for the Romans
of the second century B.C. a new world of incident and
human interest quite different from the grave story of
their own annals. This new world was first opened up
to them in the works of their tragic poets. It cannot
be supposed that these poets attempted to reproduce the
antique Hellenic character of the legends on which they
founded their dramas. In this early stage of literary
culture, the harmonious cadences of rhythm, the fine
and delicate shades of expression, the main requirements
of dramatic art, such as the skilful construction of a

plot, the consistent keeping of a character, the evolution
of a tragic catastrophe through the meeting of passion
and outward accident,—would have been altogether lost
upon the unexacting audiences who thronged the temporary theatres on occasional holidays. The fragments
of the lost dramas indicate that the matter was presented in a straightforward style, little differing in sound
and meaning from the tone of serious conversation.
Although little can be known or conjectured as to the
general conduct of the action in a Roman drama, yet
there are indications that in some cases a series of
adventures, instead of one complete action, were represented.[1] But while failing, or not attempting to reproduce the Greek spirit and art of their originals, the
Roman poets seem to have animated the outlines of
their foreign story and of their legendary characters with
something of the spirit of their own time and country.
They imparted to their dramas a didactic purpose and
rhetorical character which directly appealed to Roman
tastes. The fragments quoted from their works, the
testimonies of later Roman writers, and the natural inference to be drawn from the moral and intellectual
characteristics of the people all point to the conclusion
that the long-sustained popularity of tragedy rested on
the satisfaction which it afforded to the ethical and political sympathies, and to the oratorical tastes of the
audience.

The evidence for this popularity is chiefly to be found
in Cicero ; and it is mainly, though not solely, to the
popularity which the tragic drama enjoyed in his own
age that he testifies. The loss of the earlier writings
renders it impossible to adduce contemporary evidence
of the immediate success of this form of literature. But
the activity with which tragedy was cultivated for about
a century, and the favour with which Ennius, Pacuvius,

[1] E.g., the *Dulorestes* of Pacuvius.

and Attius, were regarded by the leading men in the
State, suggest the inference that the popularity of the
drama in the age of Cicero, after the writers themselves
had passed away, and when more exciting spectacles
occupied public attention, was only a continuation of
the general favour which these poets enjoyed in their
lifetime. Cicero in many places mentions the great
applause with which the expression of feeling in different dramas was received, and speaks of the great
crowds ('maximus consessus' or 'magna frequentia'),
including women and children, present at the representation. Varro states that, in his time, 'the heads of
families had gradually gathered within the walls of the
city, having quitted their ploughs and pruning-hooks,
and that they liked to use their hands in the theatres
and circus better than on their crops and vineyards."[1]
The large fortunes amassed by the actors Æsopus and
Roscius, afford further evidence of the favour with
which the representation of tragedy and comedy was
received in the age of Cicero.   .

According to his testimony, these lively demonstra-
tions of popular approbation were chiefly called out by
the moral significance or the political meaning attached
to the words, and by the oratorical fervour and passion
with which the actor enforced them. Thus Laelius is
represented, in the treatise *De Amicitia*, as testifying
to the applause with which the mutual devotion of
Pylades and Orestes, as represented in a play of Pacuvius, was received by the audience :[2] 'What shouts
of applause were heard lately through the whole body
of the house, on the representation of a new play of
my intimate friend, M. Pacuvius, when, the king being
ignorant which of the two was Orestes, Pylades maintained that it was he, while Orestes persisted, as was

[1] *De Re Rustica*, Lib. ii. Praef.   Quoted also by Columella, Praef. 15.
[2] *De Amicit.* 7.

really the case, that he was the man! They stood up, and applauded at this imaginary situation.' Again, in his speech in defence of Sextius,[1] the same author says, 'amid a great variety of opinions uttered, there never was any passage in which anything said by the poet might seem to bear on our time, which either escaped the notice of the people, or to which the actor did not give point.' In a letter to Atticus (II. 19) he states that the actor Diphilus had applied to Pompey the phrase 'Miseria nostra tu es magnus,' and that he was compelled to repeat it a thousand times amid the shouts of the whole theatre. He mentions further, in the speech in defence of Sextius,[2] that the actor Æsopus had applied to Cicero himself a passage from a play of Attius (the Eurysaces), in which the Greeks are reproached for allowing one who had done them great public service to be driven into exile ; and that the same actor, in the Brutus, had referred to him by name in the words, 'Tullius qui libertatem civibus stabiliverat ;' he adds that these words 'were *encored* over and over again,' 'millies revocatum est.' These and similar passages testify primarily to the intense political excitement of the time, but also to the meaning which was looked for by the audience in the words addressed to them on the stage, and which was enforced by the actor.

Besides these and other passages in Cicero, the fragments themselves of Roman tragedy testify to its moral and didactic tone, and its occasional appeal to political passions. The passages quoted above, and others which will be brought forward later, imply also that the audience were easily moved by the dramatic art and the elocution of the actor. We hear of the pains which the best actors took to perfect themselves in their art, and of the success which they attained in it. Cicero

[1] Cic. *Pro P. Sextio*, 65.   [2] Chap. 57.

specifics among the accomplishments of an orator, the
' voice of a tragedian, the gestures and bearing of a
consummate actor.'   The stage may be said to have
been to the Romans partly a school of practical life,
partly a school of oratory.   Spirited declamation, the
expression, by voice and gesture, of vehement passion,
of moral- and political feeling, and of practical wisdom,
would gratify the same tastes that were fostered by the
discussions and harangues of the Forum.

The testimony of later writers points to the conclusion that the early Roman tragedy, like Roman oratory,
was characterised both by great moral weight and dignity, and also by a fervid and impassioned character.
The latter quality is suggested by the line of Horace,

Nam spirat tragicum satis et feliciter audet ;[1]

and also by the epithet ' animosus' applied by Ovid to
the poet Attius.   Quintilian describes the ancient tragedies as superior to those of his own time in the ma-
nagement of their plots (' œconomia '), and adds that
' manliness and solemnity of style ' (' virilitas et sanctitas'),[2] were to be studied in them.   He states also that
Attius and Pacuvius were distinguished, ' gravitate sen-
tentiarum, verborum pondere, auctoritate personarum.'[3]
The fragments of all the tragic poets bear further evidence to the union of these qualities in their thought
and style.

(3.) These considerations may afford some explanation of the fact, that the early Roman tragedy, although
having less claim to originality, and less capacity of
development than any other branch of Roman literature,

---

[1] 'For it has the true tragic passion and a happy boldness of style.'—
Epist. 11. i. 166.

[2] Sanctitas certe, et, ut sio dicam, virilitas, ab iis petenda est, quando non
in omnia deliciarum vitia dicendi quoque ratione defluximus.—QUINTIL. Inst.
Or. i. 8. 9.

[3] ' The earnestness of their thoughts, the weight of their language, the
authoritative bearing of their personages.'- Inst. Or. x. i. 97.

yet exercised a more immediate and more general influence than either the epic, lyrical, or satiric poetry of the Republic. For more than a century new trage-dies were written and represented during the public games—as at the Ludi Apollinares—and afforded the sole kind of serious intellectual stimulus and education to the mass of the people. During the lifetime of the old dramatists, there was no regular theatre, but merely structures of wood raised for each occasion. A magnifi-cent stone theatre was at last built by Pompey after the Mithridatic War; but while the works of the older dra-matists were reproduced with unabated favour, no worthy successor appeared to carry on their art. The composi-tion of tragedy passed from the hands of popular poets, and became a kind of literary and rhetorical exercise of accomplished men. We hear that Quintus Cicero com-posed four tragedies in sixteen days; Varius composed a famous tragedy on the subject of Thyestes, and Ovid one on the subject of Medea; Virgil and Horace eulogise the dramatic talent of their friend and patron Asinius Pollio. The 'Ars Poetica' implies that the composition of tragedy was the most fashionable form of literary pursuit among the young aspirants to poetic honour in the Augustan age. These were, however, futile attempts to impart artificial life to a withered branch; they obtained no popular favour, and left no name or fame behind them. Of all forms of poetry the drama is most dependent on general sympathy. With the loss of contact with public feeling, the Roman drama lost all its vital power. One cause of the change in public taste was the passion for coarser excitement, such as gladiatorial combats and shows of wild beasts, among a soldiery brutalised by constant wars, and the civic masses degraded by idleness and by intermixture from all quarters of the world. Other causes may have acted on the poets themselves, such as the exhaustion of

the mine of ancient stories fit for dramatic purposes,
and the truer sense, acquired through culture, of the
bent of Roman genius.   But another cause was the loss
of mutual sympathy between the poet and the people,
arising from the decay and final extinction of political
life.   In ancient, as perhaps also in modern times, the
contests and interests of politics were the means of
affording the highest intellectual stimulus, of which they
were capable, to the large classes on whom literary
influences act only indirectly.   So long as the old republican sense of citizenship remained, there was a bond
of common feelings, ideas, and sympathies between the
body of the people and some of the foremost and most
highly educated men in Rome.   There was an immediate
sympathy between the political orator and the people;
there was a sympathy, more remote, but still active,
between the poet of the Republic, who had the strong
feelings of a Roman citizen, and the great body of his
countrymen.   With the overthrow of free government,
this bond of union between the educated and the unedu-
cated classes was destroyed.   The former became more
refined and fastidious, but lost something in breadth and
genuine strength by the want of any popular contact.
The latter became more debased, coarser, and more
servile.   Poetic works were more and more addressed to
a small circle of men of rank and education, sharing the
same opinions, tastes, and pleasures.   They thus became
more perfect as works of art, but had less direct bearing
on the passions and great public interests of their time.

The origin and the earliest stage of the Roman drama
have been examined in a previous chapter.   For about
a century after the close of the Second Punic War
new tragedies continued to be represented at Rome with
little interruption, first by Ennius, afterwards by his
nephew Pacuvius and by Attius.   The older poets,
Livius and Nævius, had produced both tragedy and

comedy: Ennius neglected or failed to attain success
in comedy; and his two successors appear to have
devoted themselves more exclusively than any of their
predecessors to the composition of tragedy. While the
fame of Ennius chiefly rested on his epic poem, Pacuvius
and Attius are generally classed together, as representatives of the tragic poetry of the Republic. Though in
point of age there was a difference of fifty years between
them, yet Cicero mentions, on the authority of Attius
himself, that they had brought out plays under the same
Ædiles, when the one was eighty years of age and the
other thirty.

M. Pacuvius, nephew, by the mother's side, of Ennius, was born at Brundusium, in the south of Italy,
about 219 B.C., and died at Tarentum about 129 B.C., at
the age of ninety. He obtained some distinction as a
painter,[1] and he is supposed to have written his tragedies
late in life. The Eusebian Chronicle records of him,
'picturam exercuit et fabulas vendidit.' Cicero represents Lælius as speaking of him as a friend, 'amici et
hospitis mei.' A pleasing anecdote is told by Aulus
Gellius[2] of his intercourse with his younger rival, L.
Attius. When Pacuvius, at a great age, and suffering
from a disease of long standing, had retired from Rome
to Tarentum, Attius, at that time a considerably younger
man, on his journey to Asia, arrived at that town,
and stayed with Pacuvius. And being kindly entertained, and constrained to stay for several days, he read
to him, at his request, his tragedy of Atreus. Then, as
the story goes, Pacuvius said, that what he had written
appeared to him sonorous and elevated but somewhat
harsh and crude. ' It is just as you say,' replied Attius;
' and in truth I am not sorry for it, for I hope that I
shall write better in future. For they say that the same
law holds good in genius as in fruit. Fruits which are

---

[1] PLINY, *Hist. Nat.* xxxv. 7.   [2] xiii. 2.

originally harsh and sour afterwards become mellow and pleasant; but those which have a soft and withered look, and are very juicy at first, become soon rotten without ever becoming ripe. It appears, accordingly, that there should be left something in genius also for the mellowing influence of years and time.' This anecdote, while giving a pleasing impression of the friendly relation subsisting between the older and younger poets, seems to add some corroboration to the opinion that the Romans were moved more by the oratorical style than by the dramatic art of their tragedies. It affords support also to the testimony of Horace and Quintilian in regard to the distinction which the admirers of the old poetry drew between the excellence of Pacuvius and Attius:

> Ambigitur quotiens uter utro sit prior, aufert
> Pacuvius docti famam senis, Attius alti.[1]

Aulus Gellius quotes the epitaph of Pacuvius,—written by himself and left to be inscribed on his tombstone,— with a tribute of admiration to ' its modesty, simplicity, and fine serious spirit :'—' Epigramma Pacuvii verecundissimum et purissimum dignumque ejus elegantissima gravitate.'

> Adolescens, tametsi properas, te hoc saxum rogat,
> Ut se aspicias, deinde quod scriptum est, legas,
> Hic sunt poetae Pacuvi Marci sita
> Ossa. Hoc volebam nescius ne esses, Vale.[2]

With all its quiet and modest dignity this inscription is still significant of that strong self-consciousness which characterised all the early Roman poets, though the feeling was displayed with more self-assertion by Nævius

---

[1] ' When the question is raised which of the two old poets is superior, the palm of learning is awarded to Pacuvius, of elevation to Attius.'—Hor. Epist. ii. l. 63.

[2] ' Young man, though thou art in haste, this stone entreats thee to regard it, and then read what is written :--Here are laid the bones of the poet Marcus Pacuvius. This I desired to be not unknown to thee—farewell.'

and Ennius, and apparently also by Attius and Lucilius, than by Pacuvius.

Among the testimonies to his literary qualities the best known is that of Horace, quoted above. Cicero, in speaking of the age of Lælius as that of the purest Latinity, does not allow this merit to Pacuvius and to the comic poet Cæcilius. He says of them, 'male locutos esse.'[1] Another author[2] contrasts the *sententiæ* of Ennius with the *periodi* of Pacuvius,—a distinction probably connected with the progress of oratory in the interval between the poets. The satirist Persius applies the term ' verrucosa' (an epithet not inapplicable to his own style) to the Antiope of Pacuvius, which, on the other hand, was much admired by Cicero.[3] A manly seriousness of style, combined with high spirit and fervour, is the excellence attributed to him by the best ancient critics, and is that which is most manifest in his remains.

Pacuvius is known to have been the author of about twelve tragedies, founded on Greek subjects; and of one, *Paulus*, founded on Roman history. Among these, the *Antiope* was perhaps the most famous and most admired. It was, like the Medea of Ennius, a translation from Euripides. The principal characters in it were the brothers Zethus and Amphion, the one devoted to hunting, the other to music. Their dispute as to the use of music and philosophy is referred to by Cicero and Horace, and by other authors. The Zethus of Pacuvius is described by Cicero[4] as one who made war on all philosophy; and the author of the treatise addressed to Herennius describes their controversy as beginning about music, and ending about philosophy and the use of virtue. Two

---

[1] *Brutus*, 74.

[2] The writer of the treatise on rhetoric addressed to C. Herennius.

[3] Quis enim tam inimicus pæne nomini Romano est, qui Ennii Medeam aut Antiopam Pacuvii spernat aut rejiciat, quod se eisdem Euripidis fabulis delectari dicit.—Cic. *De Fin.* i. 2.

[4] *De Oratore*, ii. 37.

dramas, the *Dulorestes* and the *Chryses*, the latter being
a continuation of the first, represented the adventures of
Orestes in his wanderings with his friend Pylades, after
the murder of his mother. The former play, in which
Orestes was represented as on the point of being sacrificed by his sister Iphigenia, contained the passage
already referred to, in which Pylades and Orestes contend as to which should suffer for the other. The Chryses
was founded on their subsequent adventures, and the
title of the play was apparently taken from the old Homeric priest of Apollo, Chryses, who bore a prominent
part in it. Another of the plays of Pacuvius, the *Niptra*,
was founded on, though not translated from one of
Sophocles ;[1] and the title seems to have been suggested
by the story of the recognition of Ulysses by his nurse,
Euryclea, told at Odyssey xix. 386, etc. The subjects
of his other dramas may be inferred from the following
titles:—*Armorum Judicium, Atalanta, Hermione, Ilione,
Io, Medus* (son of Medea), *Pentheus, Peribœa, Teucer.*

The fragments of Pacuvius amount to about four
hundred lines. Many of these are single lines, preserved
by grammarians in illustration of old forms and usages
of words, and thus are of little value in the way of
illustrating his force of mind or character. Several of
them, however, are interesting, from the light which
they throw on his mode of thought, his moral spirit, and
his poetical power.

1. A remarkable passage is quoted from the Chryses,
showing the growth of that interest in physical philosophy, which was first expressed in the Epicharmus of
Ennius, and which continued to exercise a great charm
over many of the Roman poets :—

> Hoc vide, circum supraque quod complexu continet
> Terram
> Solisque exorta capessit candorem, occasu nigret,

[1] Cic. *Tusc. Disp.* ii. 21.

Id quod nostri caelum memorant, Graii perhibent aethera :
Quidquid est hoc, omnia animat, format, alit, auget, creat,
Repelit recipitque in sese omnia, omniumque idem est pater,
Indidemque eadem quae oriuntur, de integro aeque eodem incidunt.[1]

The following fragment illustrates the dawning interest
in ethical speculation, which became so much more active in the age of Cicero, under the influence of Greek
studies :—

Fortunam insanam esse et caecam et brutam perhibent philosophi
Saxoque instare in globoso praedicant volubili :
Insanam autem esse aiunt, quia atrox, incerta, instabilisque sit :
Caecam ob eam rem esse iterant, qnia nil cernat quo sese adplicet :
Brutam quia dignum atque indignum nequeat internoscere.
Sunt autem alii philosophi, qui contra fortunam negant
Esse ullam, sed temeritate res regi omnis autumant.
Id magis veri simile esse usus reapse experiundo edocet :
Velut Orestes modo fuit rex, factu'st mendicus modo.[2]

These lines again from the Chryses show that Pacuvius,
like Ennius, exposed and ridiculed the superstition of
his time—

Nam isti qui linguam avium intelligunt
Plusque ex alieno jecore sapiunt quam ex suo,
Magis audiendum quam auscultandum censeo ;[3]

and this is to the same effect—

[1] 'Behold this, which around and above encompasseth the earth, and puts
on brightness at the rising of the sun, becomes dark at his setting; that
which our people call Heaven, and the Greeks Æther. Whatever this is, it
is to all things the source of life, form, nourishment, growth, existence ; it
is the grave and receptacle of all things, and the parent, too, of all things :
all things which arise from it equally lapse into it again.'

[2] 'Philosophers say that Fortune is mad, blind, and senseless, and represent her as set on a round rolling stone. They say that she is mad, because
she is harsh, fickle, untrustworthy ; blind, for this reason, that she can
see nothing to which to attach herself ; senseless, because she cannot distinguish between the worthy and unworthy. Other philosophers again deny
the existence of Fortune, but hold that all things are ruled by chance. That
this is more probable, common experience proves, as Orestes was but the
other day a king, and is now a beggar.'

[3] 'For those men who understand the language of birds, and have more
wisdom from examining the liver of other beings than from their own (i.e.,
understanding), I think should be heard rather than listened to.'

K

Nam si qui, quæ eventura sunt, providerent, æquiparent Jovi.[1]

2. The fragments of Pacuvius show not only the cast of understanding, but also the grave and dignified tone of morality, which was found to be one of the most Roman characteristics of Ennius. They indicate also a similar humanity of feeling. The moral nobleness of the situation, in which Pylades and Orestes contend which should sacrifice himself for the other, has already been noticed : ' stantes plaudebant in re ficta.' Again, in the Tusculan Disputations (II. 21), Cicero commends Pacuvius for deviating from Sophocles, who had represented Ulysses, in the Niptra, as utterly overcome by the power of his wound ; while, in Pacuvius, those who are supporting him, ' personæ gravitatem intuentes,' address this reproof to him, ' leviter gementi :'—

> Tu quoque Ulysses, quanquam graviter
> Cernimus ictum, mis pæne animo es
> Molli, qui consuetu's in armis
> Ævom agere ![2]

The strong tones of Roman fortitude are heard in this grave rebuke ; and the lines in which Ulysses, at the point of death, reproves the lamentations of those around him, have the direct, even bald simplicity that may be supposed to have characterised the serious speech of the time :—

> Conqueri fortunam adversam, non lamentari decet :
> Id viri est officium, fletus muliebri ingenio additus.[3]

The following maxim is quoted by Aulus Gellius, with the remark ' that a Macedonian philosopher, a friend of his, an excellent man, thought it deserving of being written in front of every temple :'—

---

[1] ' For if men could foresee the future, they would be on a level with Jove.'

[2] ' Thou, too, Ulysses, although we see thee sore wounded, art yet almost too much cast down ; thou, who hast been used to pass thy life in arms !'

[3] ' To complain of adverse fortune is well, but not to lament over it. The one is the act of a man ; it is a woman's part to weep.'

Ego odi homines, ignava opera et philosophia sententia.[1]

A careful examination of many single lines, of which it is impossible to ascertain the context, brings out more and more prominently this strong moral tone, combined with vigorous common sense and a direct nervous diction, as the chief characteristic of Pacuvius, in common with the other tragic dramatists of the Republic. Other passages appear to be fragments of spirited dialogue, and well adapted to show the art and the elocution of the actor. Cicero[2] quotes from the Teucer of Pacuvius the reproach of Telamon, couched in much the same terms as those which Teucer himself anticipates in the Ajax of Sophocles :—

> Segregare abs te ausu's aut sine illo Salamina ingredi,
> Neque paternum aspectum es veritus, quom aetate exacta indigvu
> Liberum lacerasti orbasti extinxti, neque fratris necis
> Neque ejus gnati parvi, qui tibi in tutelam est traditus — ?[3]

In commenting on these lines, Cicero speaks of the passion displayed by the actor ('so that even out of his mask the eyes of the actor appeared to me to burn'), and of the sudden change to pathos in his voice as he proceeded. He adds the further comment, 'Do we suppose that Pacuvius, in writing this passage, was in a calm and passionless mood?'—one of many proofs that the 'gravity' of the old tragedians was that of strong and ardent, not of phlegmatic natures, and that their strength was tempered by a pathos and humanity of feeling alien to the old Roman austerity. The language in such passages has not only the straightforward directness which is the general characteristic of the

---

[1] 'I hate men who do nothing, and are always uttering philosophic sentiments.'

[2] *De Orat.* ii. 46.

[3] 'Didst thou venture to let him part from thee, or to enter Salamis without him ; and didst thou not fear to see thy father's face, when in his old age, bereft of his children, thou hast torn him with anguish, robbed, crushed him ; nor didst thou feel for thy brother's death, and his child, who was trusted to thy protection— ?'

early literature, but a force and impetuosity added to
its gravity, recalling the style of some fragments of the
oratory of the period.[1]

3. The fragments of Attius afford the first hint of that
enjoyment of natural beauty which enters largely into
the poetry of a later age ; but one or two fragments of
Pacuvius, like several passages in Ennius, show the
power of observing and describing the sublime and
terrible aspects of Nature. The description of the storm
which overtook the Greek army after sailing from Troy,
is perhaps the best specimen in this style :—

> Profectione laeti judicium lasciviam
> Intuentur, nec tuendi capere satietas potest.
> Interea prope jam occidente sole inhorrescit mare,
> Tenebrae conduplicantur, noctisque et nimbum occaecat nigror,
> Flamma inter nubes coruscat, caelum tonitru contremit,
> Grando mista imbri largifico subita praecipitans cadit,
> Undique omnes venti erumpunt, saevi existunt turbines,
> Fervit aestu pelagus.[2]

There are also, in the same style, these rough, graphic,
and impetuous lines—

> Armamentum stridor, flictus navium,
> Strepitus, fremitus, clamor tonitruum et rudentum sibilus,[3]—

which Virgil must have had in his mind when he wrote
the line—

> Insequitur clamorque virum, stridorque rudentum.

Pacuvius composed one drama on a Roman subject, the
title of which was Paulus. Whether the principal character of the drama was the Æmilius Paulus who fell at

[1] Compare especially the fragments of the speeches of C. Gracchus.
[2] 'Glad at their starting, they watch the play of the fish, and are never
weary of watching them. Meanwhile, nearly at sunset, the sea grows rough,
darkness gathers, the blackness of night and of the storm-clouds hides the
world, the lightning flashes between the clouds, the heaven is shaken with the
thunder, hail mixed with torrents of rain dashes down in sudden showers ;
from all quarters all the winds burst forth, the wild whirlwinds arise, the
sea boils with the surging waters.'—Quoted partly from Cic. De Div. i. 14 ;
partly from De Orat. iii. 39.
[3] 'The groaning of the ships' tackling, the dashing together of the ships,
the uproar, the crash, the rattle of the thunder, and the whistling of the ropes.'

Cannæ, whom Horace commemorates as one of the national heroes in the words—

Animæque magnæ
Prodigum Paulum, superante Pœno,[1]

or his more fortunate son who conquered the Macedonians at Pydna, there is no direct evidence to determine. But it would seem more probable that the poet should celebrate a great triumph of his own time, achieved by one in whom, from his connexion with Scipio, the nephew of Ennius would feel a special interest, than that he should recall a great calamity of a past generation, neither near enough to excite immediate attention, nor sufficiently remote to justify an imaginative treatment. The Fabulæ Prætextatæ, of which this was one, were, as Niebuhr[2] has pointed out, historical plays rather than tragedies. Such a drama would not naturally or necessarily require a tragic catastrophe, but would represent the traditions of the earlier annals, or the great events of current history, in accordance with the dictates of national feeling. No important fragment of this drama has been preserved, but the fact of its having been written by Pacuvius is interesting, as proving that the poetical treatment of the Roman Annals, which Ennius had first commenced, was continued by his successor.

Neither the fragments nor the ancient notices of Pacuvius produce on a modern reader so distinct an impression of his peculiar genius and character as may be formed of Nævius, Ennius, and Lucilius. His remains are chiefly important as throwing light on the general features of the Roman tragic drama; but it would be impossible to determine from internal evidence alone

[1] 'And Paulus, lavish of his mighty life, when the Carthaginian won the day.'
[2] 'It represented the deeds of Roman kings and generals; hence it is evident that at least it wanted the unity of time of the Greek tragedy; that it was a history like Shakspeare's.'—Niebuhr's *Roman History*, vol. i. note 1180.

whether any particular passage came from the lost
works of Pacuvius or of Attius. The fragments of
these poets are insufficient to explain the grounds on
which the critics of the Augustan age awarded the
raise of learning to Pacuvius, and of elevation to Attius. The main points that are known in the life of
Pacuvius are his provincial origin, and his relationship
to Ennius; the fact of his supporting himself, first by
painting, afterwards by the payment he received from
the Ædiles for his plays; his friendship with Lælius,
the centre of the literary circle in Rome during the
latter part of the second century B.C.; his intimacy
with his younger rival Attius; the facts also that, like
Sophocles, he preserved his poetical power unabated
till a great age, and that, like Shakspeare, he retired to
spend his last years in his native district. The language of his epitaph is suggestive of a kindly and
modest temper, and of the calm and serious spirit of
age; while that of many of his dramatic fragments
bears evidence to his moral strength and worth, and
to the manliness and latent fervour of his temperament.

L. Attius (or Accius) was born in the year 170 B.C.,
of parentage similar to that of Horace—'parentibus
libertinis.' He possessed a farm near Pisaurum, in
Umbria, which was afterwards known as 'Fundus At-
tianus.' Like Pacuvius, he lived to a great age, though
the exact date of his death is uncertain. Cicero, who
was born B.C. 106, speaks of the oratorical and literary
accomplishment of D. Junius Brutus—Consul, along with
P. Scipio Nasica, B.C. 138, and one of the most famous
soldiers and chiefs of the senatorian party in that age—
on the authority of what he had himself often heard
from the poet: 'ut ex familiari ejus L. Attio poeta sum
audire solitus.'¹ The meeting of the old tragic poet

¹ *Brutus*, 28.

and of the great orator is remarkable, as a link connecting the two epochs in literature, which stand so
widely apart in the spirit and style by which they are
respectively characterised. Cicero again, in the speech
in defence of Archias, mentions the intimacy subsisting between D. Brutus and the poet.[1] The expressions 'familiari ejus' and 'amicissimi sui,' like that of
'hospitis et amici mei,' applied by Lælius, in Cicero's
dialogue, to Pacuvius, indicate that the relation between the poets (generally men of humble or provincial
origin) and eminent statesmen and soldiers, was in that
age one of familiar intimacy rather than of patronage
and dependence. The earlier poets, Plautus and Naevius, were allied in sympathy with the commonalty ;
and the latter expressed in his writings a direct antagonism to the senatorian power. Ennius and his successors, though not less patriotic and public-spirited,
attached themselves to the most liberal and able representatives of the Roman aristocracy, and show in the
whole tone of their remains a sympathy with the authority and dignity of an aristocratic republic rather than
with the bold freedom of a democracy.

Although Cicero's notice of his own intimacy with
Attius, which is not likely to have existed before the
former assumed the toga virilis, is a proof of the great
age which the poet attained, it is not certain how long
he continued the practice of his art. Seneca, in quoting
from the Atreus of this poet the well-known tyrant's
maxim,—oderint dum metuant[2]—a maxim, according to
Suetonius, constantly in the mouth of Caligula,—adds
the remark that 'any one could see that it was written
in the days of Sulla.' But Aulus Gellius, on the other

---

[1] 'Decimus quidem Brutus, summus ille vir et imperator, Attii, amicissimi sui, carminibus templorum ac monumentorum aditus exornavit suorum.'
—Chap. 11.

[2] 'Let them hate, provided they fear.'

hand, states that the Atreus was the play which had been
read by the poet in his youth to Pacuvius at Tarentum.
The termination of the literary career of Attius may be
fixed about the beginning of the first century B.C., so
that about half a century elapses between the last of
the early poetic works and the appearance of the great
poem of Lucretius. The journey of Attius to Asia, shows
the beginning of that taste for foreign travel, which became prevalent among the most educated men in a
generation later, and grew more and more easy with the
advance of Roman conquest, and more attractive from
the increased cultivation of Greek literature. Attius is
the first of the early poets who possessed a country residence; and some taste for country life, and some observation of the common aspects of nature, first betray
themselves in one or two of his fragments. He possessed
apparently all the self-esteem and high spirit of the earlier
poets. Pliny mentions that though a very little man,
he placed a colossal statue of himself in a temple of the
Muses,[1] and other anecdotes are told indicative of his
consciousness of his own importance, and his boldness
in asserting it.

He was the author of a great number of tragedies
founded on Greek subjects, and of two national dramas,
viz., the Brutus, and one called the Æneadæ or Decius.
The latter is founded on the story of the second Decius,
who devoted himself at the battle of Sentinum, as
may be inferred from one line which has been quoted
from the play—

Patrio exemplo et me dicabo atque animum devoto hostibus.

He is said also to have written poetical annals, and a
critical work or works, in verse, called Didascalica and

---

[1] *Hist. Nat.* xxxiv. 10 :—' Notatum ab auctoribus, et L. Attium poetam
in Camenarum æde maxima forma statuam sibi posuisse, cum brevis admodum
fuisset.'

Pragmatica. The subject of this last work, as well as the subjects of some of the satires of Lucilius, implies that the attention of authors was now directed to the principles of composition.

The qualities most conspicuous in the fragments of Attius, and attributed to him by ancient writers, are, in the main, the same as those which the dramatic fragments of Ennius and Pacuvius exhibit. Cicero testifies to his oratorical force, to his 'gravity,' and to the didactic purpose of his writings. His most important remains illustrate these attributes of his style, along with the shrewd sense and vigorous understanding of the earlier writers, and afford some traces of a new vein of poetical emotion, which is scarcely observable in earlier fragments. Horace applies the epithet 'altus,' Ovid that of 'animosus' to Attius. Cicero characterises him as 'gravis et ingeniosus poeta,' and attests the didactic purpose of a particular passage in the words that follow : ' scripsit gravis et ingeniosus poeta, non ut illos regios pueros, qui jam nusquam erant, sed ut nos et nostros liberos ad laborem et ad laudem excitaret.'[1] The style of a passage from the Atreus of Attius is described by the same author, in the dialogue ' De Oratore,' as 'contentum, vehemens, imminens quadam incitatione gravitatis.'[2] Oratorical fervour, energy, and dignity, seem thus to have been the most distinctive characteristics of his style. Virgil, whose genius made as free use of the diction and sentiment of native as of Greek poets, has cast the ruder language of the old poet into a new mould in some of the greatest speeches of the Æneid, and seems to have drawn from the same source something of the high spirit and lofty pathos with which

---

[1] 'The earnest and thoughtful poet so wrote, not to stimulate those princes, who did not then exist, but to stimulate us and our children to energy and honourable ambition.'—Pro Plancio, 24.

[2] 'Nervous, vehement, impending with a certain impassioned and weighty force.'—De Orat. iii. 53.

he has animated the personages of his story. The famous
address, for instance—

> Disce puer virtutem ex me verumque laborem,
> Fortunam ex aliis,[1]

though originally found in the Ajax of Sophocles, was
yet familiar to Virgil in the line of Attius—

> Virtuti sis par, dispar fortunis patria.

The address of Latinus to Turnus—

> O præstans animi juvenis, quantam ipse feroci
> Virtute exuperas, tanto me impensius æquum est
> Consulere atque omnis metuentem expendere casus,[2]

is quoted by Macrobius as an echo of the strong speech
and manly tenderness of the old tragic poet—

> Quanto magis te istius mali esse intelligo,
> Tanto, Antigona, magis me par est tibi consulere ac parcere.

The same author quotes two other passages, in which
the sentiment and something of the language of Attius
are reproduced in the speeches of the Æneid. The lofty,
vehement, and fervid oratory, which is one of the most
Roman characteristics of that great national poem, and is
quite unlike the debates, the outbursts of passion, or the
natural interchange of speech in Homer, recalls the manner
of the early tragic poets rather than the style of the oratorical fragments in the Annals of Ennius. The following
lines may give some idea of the passionate energy which
may be recognised in many other fragments of Attius—

> Tereus indomito more atque animo barbaro
> Conspexit in eam amore vecors flammeo,
> Depositus: facinus pessimum ex dementia
> Conflagit.[3]

He gives expression also to great strength of will and

---

[1] 'From me learn the lesson of duty and of high enterprise; from others
learn success.'

[2] 'Brave youth! the more your valour has been tried,
The more becomes it us, with due respect,
To weigh the chance of war, which you neglect.'—DRYDEN.

[3] 'Tereus, in his wild mood and savage spirit, gazed upon her, maddened
with burning passion, quite desperate; in his madness, he resolves a cursed
deed.'

true humanity of heart. There is no subtle reflexion in his style, but a plain enunciation of such truths as are suggested by the natural observation of life, and the instincts of a manly nature. He shows a power of directly seizing the real aspects of human life, and setting aside false appearances and beliefs. The following may be quoted as exhibiting something of his moral strength, humanity, and direct force of understanding—

> Scin' ut quem cuique tribuit fortuna ordinem,
> Numquam ulla humilitas ingenium infirmat bonum.[1]
>
> Erat istuc virile, ferre adversam fortunam facul;[2]
>
> Nam si a me regnum fortuna atque opes
> Eripere quivit, at virtutem non quit.[3]
>
> Nullum est ingenium tantum, neque cor tam ferum,
> Quod non labascat lingua, mitiscat malo.[4]

The following, again, like similar passages already quoted from Ennius and Pacuvius, is expressive of the poet's contempt for that form of superstition that had most practical hold over the minds of the Roman people :—

> Nil credo auguribus, qui auris verbis divitant
> Alienas, suas ut auro locupletent domos.[5]

Again, the view of common sense in regard to dreams is expressed by the interpreter, to whom Tarquinius applies, when alarmed by a strange vision—

> Rex, quæ in vita usurpant homines, cogitant, curant, vident,
> Quæque agunt vigilantes agitantque, ea si cui in somno accidunt
> Minus mirum est.[6]

Besides the characteristics already exemplified, one or

---

[1] 'Dost thou not know, that whatever rank fortune has assigned to a man, no meanness of station ever weakens a fine nature?'

[2] 'This was the part of a man, to bear adversity easily.'

[3] 'Though fortune could strip me of kingdom and wealth, it cannot strip me of my virtue.'

[4] 'No nature is so strong, no breast so savage, which is not shaken by words, does not melt at misfortune.'

[5] 'I trust not those augurs, who enrich the ears of others with their words, that they may enrich their own houses with gold.' There is evidently a pun on the *auris* and *auro*.

[6] 'O king, what men usually do in life, what they think about, care about, are,—their pursuits and occupations, when awake,—if these occur to any one in sleep, it is not wonderful.'

two passages may be appealed to, as implying the more
special gifts of a poet—force of imagination, and some
sense of natural beauty. There is considerable descriptive power in the following lines, for instance, in which
a shepherd, who had never before seen a ship, announces
the first appearance of the Argo—

> Tanta moles labitur
> Fremebunda ex alto, ingenti sonitu et spiritu :
> Prae se undas volvit, vortices vi suscitat :
> Ruit prolapsa, pelagus respergit, reflat.[1]

There is a fresh breath of the early morning in these
lines from the Œnomaus—

> Forte ante Auroram, radiorum ardentum indicem,
> Cum e somno in segetem agrestis cornutos cient,
> Ut rorulentas terras ferro rufidas
> Proscindant, glebasque arvo ex molli exsuscitent.[2]

This is perhaps the first instance in Latin poetry of a
descriptive passage which gives any hint of the pleasure
derived from contemplating the common aspects of nature.
Several other short fragments betray the existence of this
new vein of poetic sensibility in Attius. The early
unfolding of this kind of emotion seems to have been
accompanied with some degree of affectation, or unnatural straining after effect, very unlike the frank sincerity
and directness with which the early poets express their
moral convictions. The jingle of these lines, for instance,

> Hac ubi curvo litore latrato
> Unda sub undis labunda sonit,

reminds us of the alliterations and plays on words, which

---

[1] ' No huge a mass is approaching—sounding from the deep with a mighty
rushing noise ; it rolls the waves before it, forces through the eddies, plunges
forward, throws up and dashes back the sea.' — Quoted in Cic. De Nat.
Deor. ii. 35.

[2] ' By chance before the dawn, harbinger of burning rays, when the husbandmen bring forth the oxen from their rest into the fields, that they may
break the red, dew-sprinkled soil with the plough, and turn up the clods
from the soft soil.'

were seen to be among the errors of taste into which Ennius fell in striving to imitate a subtlety of reflexion altogether alien to his genius.

It remains to sum up the most important results which have been obtained from a consideration of ancient testimony in regard to the early tragic drama of Rome, and of the fossil remains of this lost literature, as we find it collected and arranged, by the industry of modern scholars, from the works of ancient critics and grammarians. The Roman tragedies seem to have borne much the same relation to the works of the Attic tragedians as Roman comedy to the new comedy of Athens. Judging from ancient testimony, tragedy appears to have been received with as much favour as comedy. The expression of Quintilian, 'in comœdia maxime claudicamus,'[1] following immediately on the praise which he bestows on Pacuvius and Attius, implies that in his opinion the earlier writers had been more successful in tragedy than in comedy. But a comparison between the fragments of the tragedians and the extant works of Plautus and Terence, proves that, in style at least, Roman comedy was much the most successful; and this superiority is no doubt one main cause of its partial preservation. The style of Roman tragedy appears to have been direct and vigorous, serious, and often animated with oratorical passion, but singularly devoid of harmony, subtlety, poetical refinement and inspiration. There is no testimony in favour of any great dramatic conceptions or impersonations. The poets appear to have aimed at expressing some particular passion oratorically, as Virgil has done so powerfully in his representation of Dido, Mezentius, Turnus, etc., but not to have created any of those great types of human character, such as the world owes to Homer, Sophocles, and Shakspeare. The popularity and the power of Roman tragedy, during the century preceding the downfall of

[1] *Inst. Or.* x. i. 99.

the Republic, are to be attributed chiefly to its moral and
didactic meaning, to the Roman bearing of the persons
represented, to the national, and occasionally the political cast of the sentiments expressed in it, and to the
plain and vigorous style in which they are enunciated.
The works of the tragic poets aided the development
of the Roman language. They communicated new ideas
and experience, and fostered among the mass of the
Roman people the only taste for serious literature of
which they were capable. They must have exercised a
beneficial influence also on the thoughts and lives of
men. They kept the national ideal of duty, the 'manners of the olden time,' the 'fas et antiqua castitudo'
(to use an expression of Attius), before the minds of
the people : they inculcated by precept and by representations great lessons of fortitude and energy : they
taught the wisdom of common sense, and touched the
minds of their audiences with a humanity of feeling
naturally alien to them. No teaching on the stage
could permanently preserve the old Roman virtue, simplicity, and loyalty to the Republic, against the corrupting and disorganising effects of constant wars and
conquests, and of the gross forms of luxury, that suited
the appetite of Rome ; but among the various influences
acting on the mass of the people, none probably was of
more unmixed good than the tendency of the tragic
drama of Ennius, Pacuvius, and Attius.

CHAPTER VI.

POETICAL satire, as a branch of cultivated literature, arose out of the social and political circumstances, and the moral and literary conditions of Roman life in the second century B.C. The tone by which that form of poetry has been distinguished, both in ancient and modern times, is due to the original character of a remarkable man, belonging to that era, and to the spirit in which he regarded the world. C. Lucilius was the inventor of satire, by first imparting a definite purpose to an inartistic kind of metrical composition, in which miscellaneous topics were treated in accordance with the occasional mood or interests of the writer. Although the art of Lucilius appears to have been rude and incomplete, and retained something of the vague general character belonging to the Satura of Ennius, yet he was undoubtedly the first Roman writer who used his materials with the aim and in the manner which poetical satire has permanently assumed. The indigenous Satura existing at Rome before the rise of regular literature had been merged partly in the Latin comedy of Plautus, Cæcilius, etc., partly in the metrical miscellanies of Ennius and Pacuvius, which, though not written for the stage, retained the name of the old scenic medley. The new satire differed from Latin comedy in form and style, and still more in its earnest national purpose. The satire of Lucilius, and even that

of Horace, retained some features in common with the
desultory medley which Ennius had formed out of the
older Saturn. But the latter was the parent of no permanent form of literary art. The miscellanies of Varro,
the most famous work produced on this model, were
composed partly in prose and partly in verse, and were
never ranked by the Romans among their poetical works.
The former, on the other hand, was the parent of the
satire of Horace, of Persius, and of Juvenal, and, through
that, of the poetical satire of modern times. The spirit
of humorous and censorious criticism, in which Lucilius
treated the politics and morals, the literary taste and the
social manners of his age, has become the essential characteristic of that great form of literature which derived
its name from the old Italian Satura.

Of all the forms of Roman poetry, satire was least
indebted to the works of the Greeks. Quintilian claims
it altogether for his countrymen—'satira tota nostra est.'
While the names by which they are known at once
betray the Greek invention of the other great forms of
poetic art, the name of satire alone indicates a Roman
origin. It is true that Lucilius, like every educated
man of his time, was well acquainted with the Greek
language and literature. It is true also that the satiric
spirit of Greece had found vent for itself in the works
both of the early iambic writers, Archilochus, Simonides
of Amorgos, and Hipponax, and of the great authors of
the old political comedy of Athens. But Roman satire
sprang up and flourished independently of either of those
kinds of composition. In national spirit and moral purpose, it was unlike the personal lampoons of the Greek
satirists. It was perhaps not less personal, but was more
earnest; it was animated less by private enmity, and
more by political spirit. It embraced also a much
greater variety of topics. Horace finds a closer parallel
to the satire of Lucilius in the old Athenian comedy.

These two kinds of literature have this in common, that they are the expression of public, not of personal feeling. But though animated by a similar spirit, Roman satire was not imitated from Greek comedy. Each was the independent result of freedom in different ages and countries. Their difference in form arose out of fundamental differences in the character as well as in the genius of the two nations. Although Roman speakers and writers may have exercised a licence of speech and of personal criticism equal to that which prevailed in the Athenian democracy, and beyond what the spirit of personal honour has ever tolerated in modern times, yet the exposure of public men to ridicule on the stage was utterly repugnant to a Roman's sense of dignity. The tendency of the Roman mind to express itself in abstract comments on life, rather than to represent human nature in living forms, also favoured the assumption by Lucilius of this mode of literature, which addressed itself to the understanding of readers, and not to the vivid sympathies of spectators.

In its nature as well as its origin, satire is seen to be an essentially Roman product. The rude germ out of which it was developed was the *Fescennina licentia*, or, as it is called by Dionysius, the ' κέρτομος καὶ σατυρικὴ παιδιά,' native to the Italian people. But in assuming a regular literary form, this native wit of the Italian was tempered by the gravity and vigorous understanding of Rome, and liberalised by the tastes and ideas of a Greek education. The age in which satire arose was one of strong political passions, of rapid intellectual growth, and of great moral disorganisation ; and all these conditions exercised a powerful influence on its character. As addressed not to the imagination but to the practical understanding, it was in a peculiar manner the literature of a people 'rebus natus agendis.' It combined the wisdom of the ' abnormis sapiens,' expressing itself in pro-

L

verbial sayings, anecdotes, and homely illustrations ; the
keen perceptions, intelligence, and wit of an energetic
and educated society ; the earnest purpose of a moral
reformer ; and the practical philosophy, which results
from the mixed study of men and books. Their circumstances, temper, and pursuits, united these various
elements, in different proportions, first in Lucilius,
and after him in Horace. They wrote what interested
themselves, in accordance with their own natural bent,
and in doing so, they appealed to the practical and
social tastes of their countrymen. While the higher
poetical imagination was a rare and exceptional gift
among Roman authors, and was probably appreciated
only by a limited class of readers, there was in Roman
satire a true popular tone, and a real adaptation to the
national character, understanding, and circumstances.
As the most genuine product of actual Roman life, it
was, if not so luxuriant, a more vigorous plant than
any other species of Roman poetry. It is seen growing
up in hardy vigour under the free air of the Republic,
attaining to mature perfection amid the rich intellectual
life of the Augustan age, and still fresh and vital in the
general intellectual languor and corruption of the Empire.

The thoroughly Roman character of satire is attested
also by the fact that other Roman poets and authors,
besides those who professed to follow in the footsteps of
Lucilius, have exhibited the satiric spirit. The shrewd
sense of Ennius, the earnest indignation of Lucretius,
the bold freedom of Catullus, attest their affinity, in
some elements of character, to the Roman satirists.
There may be remarked also in the best modern works
of poetical satire,—such as the Absalom and Ahitophel,
the Prologue to the Satires of Pope, the Vanity of
Human Wishes,—a conscious or unconscious echo of
that vigorous sense and nervous speech, which accompanied the great practical energy of the Romans.

Satire was not only a national product, but it performed originally a public or political function at Rome.
Even under the Empire, when free speech and comment
on the government were no longer possible, the Roman
satirists claimed to perform an office similar in spirit to
that which the Republic in its best days had devolved
on its most honourable magistracy.   But the writings
of Lucilius, while they aimed at performing this important public object, strove at the same time to play
an active part in the politics of the day.   With the
freedom of a tribune and the severity of a consor, he
hold up the men of high and low degree to public
criticism—

Primores populi arripait populumque tributim ;

and assailed the position of politicians and statesmen,
on the grounds either of public delinquency or of personal immorality.   Nor was his satire confined to aggressive criticism : he made it a vehicle also of political
partisanship, and painted the private virtues of Scipio
and Lælius, as well as the vices of their antagonists—

Attamen et justum poteras et scribere fortem
Scipiadem ut sapiens Lucilius.[1]

Lucilius must have thus performed for his contemporaries something of the same kind of public office as is
performed in the present day by the newspaper.

He had, moreover, other public aims, besides that of
political partisanship.   He endeavoured, by moral means,
to effect objects which the Roman State endeavoured to
effect by direct legislation.   The various sumptuary laws
of that age, and the enactments made to repress the study
of Greek rhetoric and philosophy, emanated from the
same spirit which led Lucilius to denounce the increase
of luxury and the affectation of Greek manners among
his contemporaries.   The strong Roman appetites and the

---

[1] ' Yet you might represent him as just and brave, as the wise Lucilius
represented Scipio.'—Hor. Sat. ii. i. 17.

novelty of new studies prevailed over the artificial re
straints of legislative enactments, and over the humorous
and earnest teaching of satire. But satire might act
upon the character with a power beyond that of censors
or sumptuary laws. While it could brand notorious
offenders it was able also to unmask hypocritical pre-
tences—

> Detrahere et pellem, nitidus qua quisque per ora
> Cederet, introrsum turpis.[1]

It could stimulate to virtue as well as denounce fla
grant offences. By directing the activity of intellect,
awakened by the new studies, to the questions of the
day and the interests of the State, it might hope successfully to contend with Greek rhetoric in educating
men for the contests of public life and for their practical
duties as citizens.

Satire has been defined by a Latin grammarian as
'Carmen maledicum et ad carpenda hominum vitia
compositum."[2] But this definition expresses only one
side of its office. It suggests no notion of those familiar writings of Horace, in which he gives a pleasant
account of his habits and mode of life in town and
country, or of that in which he humorously narrates
his various adventures on his journey to Brundusium.
The writings of Horace and Lucilius bore a more varied
and miscellaneous character both in form and substance. Horace expresses his opinions and feelings in
the form sometimes of a dialogue, sometimes of a
familiar epistle, sometimes of a discourse put into the
mouth of another, sometimes of a moral disquisition.
He makes abundant use of fables, anecdotes, personal
portraiture, both real and imaginary, autobiography, and

---

[1] ' To strip off from every one the skin, in which he, base at heart, passed
sleekly before the eyes of the world.'— Hor. Sat. II. i. 64.

[2] ' A poem of a censorious character, and composed for the purpose of assailing the vices of men.'

self-analysis. The fragments of Lucilius, and the notices
about him in ancient authors, prove that in these respects
Horace was following in his footsteps. One of his satires
was evidently written in the form of an epistle to a
friend ; in one he described a journey to the Sicilian
Strait ; in one a discourse on gluttony was put into the
mouth of Lælius. The testimony of Horace, contained
in the lines—

Ille velut fidis arcana sodalibus olim, etc.,

implies that Lucilius used his satire as a natural vehicle
for expressing everything that interested him, in his own
life and in the circumstances of his time. In regard to
the miscellaneous nature of the topics treated by him,
and the frankness of his personal revelations, his parallel
is Montaigne,—the father of the prose essay, which, in
some respects, has performed the function of ancient
satire more completely than even the poetical satire of
modern times.

C. Lucilius, according to the Eusebian Chronicle,
was born at Suessa Auruncorum, B.C. 148, and died
at Naples B.C. 103. The correctness of these dates has
been questioned on several grounds, but the circumstances urged against them are not incompatible with
their accuracy.[1] He served in the Numantine war,[2]
and, as Numantia was taken B.C. 133, he must have
joined the army before the regular military age. But
such service was not uncommon on the part of volun-
teers, and in some cases was compulsory. Horace
applies to him the term ' senex' (' vita senis'), but his
use of the word in that passage cannot be pressed as
proving that the poet reached a greater age than is
attributed to him in the Chronicle. The language of
Cicero (De Orat. i. 16) implies that he was dead some

---

[1] The objections are fully stated and answered in the article on Lucilius,
by Professor Ramsay, in Smith's Dictionary of Ancient Biography.

[2] Vell. Pat. ii. 9.

time before B.C. 91. His birthplace is marked by the
line of Juvenal—

Per quem magnus equos Auruncæ flexit alumnus.[1]

He was a member of the Equestrian order, a fact to
which Horace alludes where he speaks of himself as
being 'infra Lucili censum.' Horace gives a lively and
agreeable picture of the intimacy subsisting between
Scipio, Lælius, and the young poet, who, if the dates of
the Eusebian Chronicle are right, could only have been
about nineteen years of age at the time of Scipio's death.

Quin, ubi se a volgo et scena in secreta remorant
Virtus Scipiadæ et mitis sapientia Læli,
Nugari cum illo et discincti ludere, donec
Decoqueretur olus, soliti.[2]

The circle of Scipio and Lælius embraced the men
most eminent in war and statesmanship, in literature and
philosophy, and was, according to all ancient testimony,
distinguished by a plain but not austere simplicity, by
genuine worth and friendliness among its members, by
intellectual activity and refinement, and by nature and
ease in its enjoyments. The charm of his social wit and
lively temperament may have obtained for Lucilius, when
little more than a boy, his admission into this distinguished circle; and his intimacy with the first soldier
and the most prudent statesman of his time probably
gave that practical and political bent to his satire, which
made it a much more real power than the abstract mora-
lising of a young satirist like Persius, whose mind had

[1] i. 20.
[2] 'When the virtue of Scipio and the mild wisdom of Lælius had withdrawn
into retirement from the throng and stage of life, they used to idle and play
with him in easy undress till their dinner of vegetables was ready.'—Sat.
II. i. 71-4.
    The terms used here, and the comment of the scholiast, who mentions that
on one occasion Lucilius was found chasing Lælius round the room with his
table-napkin, afford a certain corroboration of the dates given by the
Chronicle, by suggesting the idea of the extreme youth of Lucilius at the
time of his intimacy with Scipio.

been fed on the study of books and the conversation of
his teachers. His friendship for these statesmen led him
to oppose the extreme popular party, the friends and
partisans of the Gracchi. Among the public men who
were most vehemently assailed by him were P. Cornelius
Lentulus Lupus, L. Hostilius Tubulus,—notorious for
openly receiving bribes, while presiding at a trial for
murder, and L. Papirius Carbo, the friend of C. Gracchus
and the suspected murderer of Scipio. The more reput-
able name of Metellus[1] is also coupled by Horace with
that of Lupus among the objects of his political satire—

Aut laeso doluere Metello,
Famosisque Lupo cooperto versibus.[2]

Yet that he bore the character of a popular poet, and did
not write for the amusement of an exclusive circle, is
intimated by the fact that he was honoured at his death
by a public funeral, and is implied in a saying of his that
he wished to have neither the most ignorant nor the most
learned men for his readers.[3] He wrote, as he said, for
Tarentines, Consentini, and Sicilians, rather than for
formidable critics, like Scipio and Rutilius.[4] Little is
known of his life with the exception of this early intimacy with Scipio and Laelius. His bold personal attacks
seem to have made him many enemies, and, on one
occasion, he was assailed by name on the stage. The
author of this assault was acquitted, while a writer who
had taken a similar liberty with the tragic poet Attius
was condemned. The account given of Lucilius by
Horace, especially in those characteristic lines quoted in
a former chapter[5]—

Ille velut fidis, etc.,

---

[1] Q. Caecilius Metellus Macedonicus, of whom Cicero says (De Off. i. 25),
'Qualis fuit later P. Africanum et Q. Metellum sine acerbitate dimensio.'
[2] 'Were they pained when Metellus was assailed or Lupus was bespattered
with verses that made him infamous.'— Sat. ii. i. 67.
[3] Cic. De Orat. ii. 6.
[4] Cic. De Fin. i. 3.   [5] Vide supra, page 22.

suggests the notion of an independent, self-reliant life,
which found instruction and enjoyment in study, in
travelling, and in retirement, as well as in society. As
contrasted with the rest of the early poets, he was comparatively a young man when he died at Naples in the
year B.C. 103.

He was the author of thirty books of satires. Most of
these were composed in hexameter verse ; a few of the
later books in iambic and trochaic metres. Nothing is
known in regard to the number of satires contained in
each book. The fragments preserved from them are very
numerous ; but in a large majority of cases, very unimportant. There are only three or four consecutive passages of sufficient length to give a fair idea of his style.
Many single lines have been preserved by grammarians,
as illustrating peculiarities in the use of words. Such
fragments naturally produce the impression of abnormal
difficulty and roughness ; but this impression is produced
much more by the isolated lines, preserved by grammarians, than by the longer passages, found in the works of
Cicero and Lactantius. The plan on which a few of these
satires were constructed may still be faintly traced, along
with clearer vestiges of some of the subjects discussed,
and some of the characters represented in them ; but it
is important to remember that they were of the nature
of miscellaneous compositions, in which various topics,
not closely connected together, were treated as they may
have suggested themselves to the author, rather than
works of art, each constructed with a distinct unity of
purpose. Horace, who had a great admiration of his
genius, as well as a strong sense of his imperfections,
testifies to the haste with which he wrote—

> Nam fuit hoc vitiosus : in hora saepe ducentos,
> Ut magnum, versus dictabat stans pede in uno ; [1]

---

[1] 'For in this he was at fault : he would dictate two hundred verses in
an hour, standing on one foot, as if it were a great matter.'—*Sat.* i. 4.9.

and the impression produced by the collected fragments of any one of the books of satires is, that they were written with great discursiveness, as well as careless rapidity—

Garrulus atque piger scribendi ferre laborem.

The first Book of Satires was dedicated to the contemporary grammarian, L. Ælius Stilo, as may be gathered from the line,

Has res ad te scriptas Luci misimus Æli.

This book represented a council of the gods, assembled to consider how the Roman State might be preserved—

Quo pacto populum atque urbem servare potismet
Ampliu' Romanam ;

and contained the lines quoted by Cicero,[1] in which some of the most notorious public characters were branded with infamy—

Tubulus si Lucius unquam
Si Lupus aut Carbo, Neptuni filiu', Divos
Esse putasset, tam perjurus et impius ille
Fuisset ?[2]

In the third book he gave that account of his journey from Rome to the Sicilian Strait, which is imitated by Horace in the fifth satire of his first book. From the line,

Mantica cauteri costas gravitate premebat,

it is inferred that he made the journey on horseback ; and Horace probably had that line in his mind when he wrote the passage—

Nunc mihi curto
Ire licet mulo, vel, si libet, usque Tarentum,
Mantica cui lumbos onere ulceret, atque eques armos.[3]

The fourth book contained an address of Lælius against

---

[1] De Nat. Deor. I. 23.

[2] 'If ever Lucius Tubulus, if Lupus or Carbo, that son of Neptune, had believed in the existence of the gods, would he have been so perjured and impious?'

[3] 'Now I may go, if I please, even as far as Tarentum, on my humble mule, with the saddle-bags galling his flanks, and the rider his shoulders.'— Sat. i. vi. 104.

the luxury and the gluttony of the time, in which mention was made of the sturgeon, which gained notoriety
for the Præco, Gallonius, and which is introduced also
by Horace in the discourse on the same subject which
he attributes to the rustic Ofella—

> Haud ita pridem
> Galloni præconis erat acipensere mensa
> Infamis.[1]

Both Lucilius and Horace mention, among the favourite
delicacies of their gourmands, sows' teats, fatted fowls,
and a pike caught between the bridges of the Tiber.
Lucilius has the lines,

> Illum sumina ducebant, atque altilium lanx,
> Hunc pontes Tiberino' duo inter capta' catilla.[2]

The last line may be compared with the lines of
Horace—

> Unde datum sentis, lupus hic Tiberinus, an alto
> Captus, hiet? pontesne inter jactatus, an amnis
> Ostia sub Tusci?[3]

The fifth book contained a letter to a friend who had
neglected to visit him during an illness, and began with
the following lines—

> Quo me habeam pacto, tametsi non quaeri', docebo.
> Quando in eo numero mansti, quo in maxima nunc est
> Pars hominum, ut periisse velis, quem visere nolue—
> His cum debueris.   Hoc nol– et debueris, te
> Si minu' delectat, quod ἄτεχνον Isocratium est, 'o—
> χληρώδησρα simul totum ac σομμαιρακιῶδες
> Non operam perdo.[4]

This passage illustrates two characteristics of the satire

[1] *Sat.* II. 2. 46.

[2] ' One yielded to the charm of sow's teats and a dish of fatted fowls;
another, to a glutton of a pike that had been caught between the two bridges.'

[3] ' On what grounds do you know whether this pike, that gapes on the dish,
is a Tiber fish, or has been caught at sea; whether it has been tossed about
between the bridges, or near the mouth of the Tuscan river?'—*Sat.* II. ii. 31.

[4] ' I will tell you how I am, though you don't ask me, since you are
of that kind of which most men now are; who would rather that the man
whom you did not choose to visit, when you ought, had died.   If this nol–
and debueris does not please you, as an instance of the "Isocratic want
of art," of "the tiresome" and the "puerile," I don't waste my time on the
matter.'

of Lucilius,—his habit of mixing up many Greek words
in his style, and the critical attention which he bestowed
on propriety of expression.　The ninth book of the satires
was apparently a dissertation on questions of ortho-
graphy, grammar, and criticism.　In other satires, Lucilius examined and criticised the writings, and especially
the diction, of the earlier Latin poets, as may be inferred
from the lines of Horace—

> Nil comis tragici mutat Lucilius Atti?
> Non ridet versus Enni gravitate minores?[1]

and from an expression of Aulus Gellius (after mentioning Pacuvius and Attius)—'Clariorque tunc in poematis
eorum obtrectandis Lucilius fuit.'[2]

The traces of the outline of these and of the other
books of satires are necessarily very faint.　More certainty, however, may be attained in regard to the subjects treated in some of them.　The fragments in which
these subjects are indicated are especially interesting,
from the fact that the vices and peculiarities assailed by
Lucilius re-appear in the pages of the later satirists, and
are, indeed, the chief modes of excess to which the
Roman temperament was prone.　The ordinary Roman
character was liable to fall into one of two extremes—
either a coarse sensuality and vulgar ostentation, or extreme meanness and avarice.　These were the opposite
results of the sudden acquisition of enormous wealth by
a people of strong physical organisation, adapted and
trained to practical pursuits, long accustomed to an
austere frugality, and endowed with little natural taste
for the refined pleasures of life.　The intensity of the
Roman temper tended also to produce those one-sided
types of character which have been the favourite subjects

---

[1] 'Does the polite Lucilius refrain from correcting the style of the tragic
poet Attius?　Does he not laugh at the verses of Ennius, as wanting in
dignity?'—Sat. i. x. 54.

[2] 'And Lucilius at that time was more famous by his censures on their
poems.'—XVII. 21.

of comic and satiric portraiture. The gluttons and the misers of Horace—his Maenius, for instance, and his Avidienus—are amongst his most strongly marked personal sketches. Lucilius witnessed the same vices in his time, and exposed them to ridicule with even greater freedom. It is certain that Horace has used the names, which Lucilius first transferred to his pages from real life, as typical representatives of the vices which he satirises. Among these are the names of Nomentanus, Maenius, and Gallonius, all gluttons and men of profligate character. In the discourse against luxury, supposed to be spoken by Laelius, the following lines occur—

> O Publi, O gurges, Galloni! es homo miser, inquit,
> Consasti in vita nunquam bene, quom omnia in ista
> Consumis squilla atque acipensere quom decumano.[1]

A line from another satire is directed against this form of sensuality, which grew up into still more gigantic proportions from the decay of the higher energies under the Empire—

> Vivite lurcones, comedones, vivite ventres.[2]

A line which Horace has imitated[3]—

> Purpureo tersit tunc latas gausape mensas,[4]

marks the beginning of that luxury and love of show which vulgarised the Roman character in the times of Horace and Juvenal.

Money-making and usury formed a natural outlet for the practical energy of the Romans, when the accumulated treasures of the world were thrown open to their enterprise, and when war and politics no longer absorbed their attention. The restless discontent of the

---

[1] 'O Publius Gallonius, thou whirlpool of excess; thou art a miserable man (he says); never in thy life hast thou supped well, since thou spendest all thy substance in that lobster and that monstrous sturgeon.'
[2] 'Long live ye gluttons, gourmands, belly-gods.'
[3] Gausape purpureo mensam pertersit.—Sat. ii. viii. 11.
[4] 'Then he wiped the ample table with a purple cloth.'

merchant, the sedulous pains of the usurer, the meanness and self-inflicted penance of the miser, are painted
by Horace, as different types assumed by the love of
money in his day. The same disposition appears in the
fragments of Lucilius, sometimes in contrast with the
rational happiness of simple living. The lines—

> Denique uti stulto nihil est satis, omnia cum sint ;[1]
> Rugosi passique senes eadem omnia quaerunt ;[2]
> Sic tu illos fructus quaeras adversa hieme olim
> Queis uti possis ;[3]

and others of like import, remind the reader of passages
where Horace exposes the folly and meanness of avarice,
or inculcates the lessons of good sense and moderation
in the use of money.

From several of the fragments, it is obvious that
Lucilius satirised other modes of licentiousness besides
the excess of gluttony. One book appears to have been
directed against the character and manners of women,
and there are several passages expressive of the objections against marriage, which prevailed among the most
educated and wealthy Romans during the last ages of
the Republic. Aulus Gellius quotes a passage to the same
effect from a speech of Q. Metellus :[4] 'Si sine uxore pos-
semus, Quirites, esse, omnes ea molestia careremus; sed
quoniam ita natura tradidit ut nec cum illis satis com-
mode, nec sine illis ullo modo vivi possit, saluti per-
petuae potius quam brevi voluptati consulendum.'[5] This
recommendation of marriage as an evil to be encountered

---

[1] 'As the fool finds nothing sufficient, however much he may have.'
[2] 'Wrinkled and withered old men all are intent on the same objects.'
[3] 'Seek you those gains which you may hereafter put to use when the
storms of adversity come.'
[4] This was the Q. Metellus Macedonicus, already mentioned, though the
words are attributed by Aulus Gellius to Q. Metellus Numidicus.
[5] 'If, Quirites, we could do without wives, we should all keep clear of
that plague ; but since, in the way of nature, we cannot live with them
comfortably, nor without them in any way, we should provide rather for
the continued good of the world, than for our own brief gratification.'

only under a sense of duty and necessity, implies the
same estimate of the character of women, which is hinted
in several passages of Lucilius, as, for instance, this passage from Book xxvi.—

> Homines ipsi hanc sibi molestiam ultro atque aerumnam offerunt,
> Ducunt uxores, producunt quibus haec faciant liberos.[1]

The intellectual peculiarities, as well as the social and
moral evils of the time, were also assailed in his satire.
The following passage, directed against the credulity of
the age, is a continuous specimen of his style, and is an
instance of that vigorous protest against superstition
which was made by all the earlier writers—

> Terriculas Lamias, Fauni quas Pompiliique
> Instituere Numae, tremit has, hic omnia ponit,
> Ut pueri infantes credunt signa omnia ahena
> Vivere, et esse homines; et sic isti omnia ficta
> Vera putant, credunt signis cor inesse in ahenis.
> Pergula pictorum, veri nihil, omnia ficta.[2]

Another remarkable passage, which is quoted below, in
illustration of the author's style, reprobates the growing
taste for public speaking, and the insincerity of character
thereby produced. The pretensions of the kind of philosopher, who is a favourite subject of ridicule to Horace,
are exposed in the following lines—

> Paenula, si quaeris, cantariu', servo', segestre
> Utilior mihi, quam sapiens;[3]

And in these—

> Mundo nondum etiam omnia habebit qui sapiens, si
> Formosus, dives, liber, rex solu' videtur.[4]

[1] 'Men voluntarily bring this plague and vexation on themselves; they marry wives, they beget children, to whom they may act in the same way.'

[2] 'These bugbears and goblins from the days of the Fauni and of Numa Pompilius fill him with terror; he believes anything of them. As children suppose that brazen statues are alive and are real men, so they fancy all these delusions to be real; they believe that images of brass have a heart; mere painter's blocks, no reality, all a delusion.'

[3] 'A great-coat, if you ask me, a nag, a slave, a wrapper, is of more use to me than your philosopher.'

[4] 'The philosopher will not yet have everything in the world, though he alone is supposed to be handsome, rich, free, a king.'

Men of the world, among Roman writers, like Lucilius, Catullus, Horace, and Juvenal, were especially intolerant of all kinds of pedantry and affectation, whether displayed by the professors of an austere and artificial system of life, or by the poetasters against whom Catullus waged his warfare. The affectation of Greek manners and tastes by Titus Albutius, is ridiculed in a passage described by Cicero,[1] as being written 'cum multa venustate et omni sale.' Lucilius, as may be learned both from his own fragments, and from the testimony of Horace, was himself fond of mixing Greek words and phrases with his Latin style. This practice, though continued in familiar epistles, was condemned by the good sense of Horace, as unsuited for writings addressed to the public. But it came not unnaturally to Lucilius, who wrote with careless ease in the familiar and conversational style of men educated in the new learning, and powerfully attracted by the interest and novelty of the Greek language and literature.

To judge of the style of Lucilius solely from the fragments preserved by grammarians, as illustrating peculiarities of language, would probably be to exaggerate the harshness and difficulty of his ordinary manner. The terms applied to him by Cicero and even Horace, such as 'comes,' 'perurbanus,' and the like, imply that his mode of expression was that natural to refined and educated men of his age. The value which he attached to education appears from a saying of his quoted with approval by Cicero, that he considered no one could be an orator, who was not a man of liberal education, 'neminem esse in oratorum numero habendum, qui non sit omnibus iis artibus quae sunt libero homine dignae, perpolitus.'[2] Among the few continuous passages that have been preserved from his works, the two following may be quoted as specimens of his style. The first

1 *De Fin.* 1. 3.   2 *De Orat.* 1. 16.

exemplifies the serious moral spirit with which ancient
satire was animated ; the second vividly represents and
rebukes one of the most prevalent pursuits of the age

Virtus, Albine, est pretium persolvere verum,
Queis in versamur, queis vivimu' rebu', potesse :
Virtus est hominis, scire id, quod quaeque habeat res.
Virtus scire homini rectum, utile, quid sit honestum ;
Quae bona, que mala item, quid inutile, turpe, inhonestum ;
Virtus quaerenda rei finem scire modumque :
Virtus divitiis pretium persolvere posse ;
Virtus id dare quod re ipsa debetur honori :
Hostem esse atque inimicum hominum morumque malorum,
Contra defensorem hominum morumque bonorum,
Hos magnifacere, his bene velle, his vivere amicum ;
Commoda praeterea patriae sibi prima putare,
Deinde parentum, tertia jam postremaque nostra.[1]

There is neither poetical grace nor rhetorical artifice in
the expression of these sentiments ; but the language is
clear, natural, and serious, with a tone both earnest and
dignified, befitting the practical sense and the healthy
morality of the thoughts.   The next passage, written in
language equally plain and forcible, gives a graphic picture of the growing taste for forensic oratory—

Nunc vero a mane ad noctem, festo atque profesto,
Toto itidem pariterque die, populusque patresque
Jactare indu foro se omnes, decedere nusquam,
Uni se atque eidem studio omnes dedere et arti,
Verba dare ut caute possint, pugnare doloso,
Blanditia certare, bonum simulare virum se ;
Insidias facere, ut si hostes sint omnibus omnes.[1]

Much is said by ancient writers of his learning and

[1] 'Virtue, Albinus, consists in being able to give their true worth to
the things on which we are engaged, among which we live.   The virtue
of a man is to understand the real meaning of each thing : to understand what
is right, useful, honourable for him ; what things are good, what bad, what
is unprofitable, base, dishonourable ; to know the due limit and measure in
making money ; to give its proper worth to wealth ; to assign what is really
due to honour ; to be a foe and enemy of bad men and bad principles ; to
stand by good men and good principles ; to extol the good, to wish them
well, to be their friend through life.   Lastly, it is true worth to look on
our country's weal as the chief good ; next to that, the weal of our parents ;
third and last, our own weal.'

[1] 'But now from morning till night, on holiday and week-day, the whole

wit ('antiquæ et vernaculæ festivitatis'), and of the boldness and vehemence of his invective--

Secuit Lucilius urbem,
Te, Lupe, te, Muci, et genuinum fregit in illis.[1]

But no particle of imaginative power or poetical susceptibility has been attributed to him. His satires were not
the result of imitation nor of mere literary taste, but of
his force of character, his practical sense, and his ardent,
impetuous love of virtue. That impetuosity of temperament ran through his whole style. Horace applies to
him the phrase 'fluere lutulentum,'[2] as characteristic of
the force and haste with which he threw off his two
hundred lines before and as many after supper. Yet he
admits that he was more polished than the earlier poets.
He seems at least to have paid more attention to gram-
matical and idiomatic purity of speech. As in the case
of most ancient and modern humorists, previous to the
present century, the freedom of his language appears
occasionally to have passed into coarseness. His remains, however, do not enable us to judge fairly of the
character and quality of the wit for which he was
admired by his countrymen. Sincerity and force are
the most striking characteristics of his style, so far as
the remaining fragments allow of any criticism on the
subject.

The satire of Lucilius, like that of Horace which was
founded upon it, fulfilled two offices of literature—
that of representing the manners and characters of the
time, and especially the tastes and pursuits of the author

day alike, common people and senators are bustling about within the Forum,
never quitting it—all devoting themselves to the same practice and trick
of wary word-fencing, fighting craftily, vying with each other in polite-
ness, assuming airs of virtue, plotting against each other as if all were
enemies.'

[1] 'Lucilius scourged the city—you, Lupus ; you, Mucius—and broke his
grinders upon them.'. Persius, i. 115.

[2] 'Flowing on, in a muddy stream.'

himself; and that of a teacher, a censor, and a critic.
A frank and bold temper, a keen and vigorous understanding, enabled him to succeed in both offices of satiric writing. His portraiture of living men may have
been coloured by public feeling and political partisanship; but there is no ground for attributing to him
anything of personal envy and vindictiveness, or of mere
rhetorical indignation. The line in which Horace sums
up his character—

Scilicet uni æquus virtuti atque ejus amicis,[1]

is a fine tribute to the sterling worth of his writings.
He was vehement in invective, because he was thoroughly earnest in his purpose to expose vice and baseness among the high and low with impartial severity.
Although probably few writers of verse have had less
poetical faculty, yet by his originality and force of character he became the favourite of his own time and country, and he alone among Roman writers has introduced
a new and permanent form of poetry into the world.

---

[1] ‘Always on the side of virtue only, and of virtue's friends.’

CHAPTER VII.

THE authors whose fragments have been examined in the last four chapters were, with the exception of the writers of comedy, the only poets of eminence who adorned the two centuries from the end of the First Punic War till the last age of the Republic. We hear, indeed, of the names of a few other poets who flourished about the beginning of the first century B.C. A poem on the Istrian War was written by Hostius ; and the name of Porcius Licinus is known as the author of a critical work on Roman poetry, from which the two following lines are preserved—

> Ponico bello secundo Musa pinnato grada
> Intulit se bellicosam in Romoli gentem feram.[1]

The same author is quoted by Aulus Gellius,[2] along with Valerius Ædituus and Q. Catulus (the colleague of Marius in his consulship, B.C. 102), as the writer of short amatory epigrams. But there is no reason to suppose that any of these poets exercised a great influence on Roman literature. The satires of Lucilius must be regarded as the last of the important works which were produced in this period. Half a century elapsed before the appearance of the poems of Lucre-

---

[1] 'In the Second Punic War, the Muse, with winged speed, entered the fierce, warlike nation of Romulus.'

[2] XIX. N.

tius and Catullus, which come next to be considered.
But before passing on to this more familiar ground, a
few pages may be devoted to a rapid review of the
general features, powers, and attainments which marked
the few original men by whom Roman feeling and
thought were first expressed in verse, and by whom the
rude speech of Latium was first moulded into a literary
language.

With striking individual varieties of character, these
poets present something of a common aspect, distinct
from that of the literary men of later times. They were
placed in different circumstances, and lived in a different
manner from the poets who adorned the last days of the
Republic and the Augustan age. The spirit and culture
of their time tended also to produce marked peculiarities
in the form and substance of their poetry.

Like nearly all the literary men of later times, they
were of provincial birth and origin. They were thus
born under circumstances more favourable to, or at least
less likely to repress, the expansion of individual genius,
than the public life and private discipline of Rome.
Their minds were thus also more open to the reception
of new influences; and their position as aliens, by cut-
ting them off from an active public career, may have led
them to turn their energies to literature. Their provincial birth and Greek education did not, however, check
their Roman sympathies, or prevent them from stamp-
ing on their writings the impress of a Roman character.

While, in common with many of the later poets, they
had come originally as strangers to Rome, unlike them,
they seem to have, in later years, resided habitually
within the city. The taste for country life prevailing in
the days of Cicero and of Horace was not manifest to any
great extent in the times of Ennius and Lucilius. The
great Scipio, indeed, retired to spend the last years of his
life at Liternum; and Cicero mentions the boyish delight

of Lælius and the younger Africanus in escaping from the public business and the crowded streets of Rome to the pleasant sea-shore of Caieta.[1] But the early poets, with the exception of Lucilius, were men of moderate means and station ; nor had any Mæcenas then appeared to bestow farms or country-houses on his literary friends. By their circumstances, as well as the general taste of their time, they were thus brought almost exclusively into contact with the life and interests of the city ; and this, no doubt, was among the causes why their works were more distinguished by their strong sense and understanding than by any fine poetic susceptibility.

It is remarkable that nearly all the early poets lived to a great age, and maintained their intellectual vigour unabated to their latest years ; while of their successors none reached the natural term of human life, and some among them, like many great modern poets, were cut off prematurely before their promise was fulfilled. The finer sensibility and more passionate agitation of the poetic temperament appear, in some cases, to exhaust prematurely the springs of life ; while, in natures more happily balanced, or formed by more favourable circumstances, the gifts of genius seem to be accompanied by stronger powers of life, and to maintain the freshness of youth unimpaired till the last. The length of time during which Nævius, Ennius, Pacuvius, and Attius exercised their art suggests the inference, either that they were men of firmer fibre than their successors, or that they were tempered to a more enduring strength by the action of their age. As the work of men writing in the fulness of their years, their poetry was founded on the mature interests of manhood, and was addressed to the more serious and practical sympathies of their countrymen.

But perhaps the most important condition determin-

[1] *De Orat.* ii. 6.

ing the original scope of Roman poetry, was the predominance in that era of public over personal interests.
Like Virgil and Horace, most of the early poets were
men of moderate station, who by their genius and character forced their way to eminence, and became the
familiar friends of the foremost men in the State.   But
while the poets of the Augustan age owed the charm of
their existence to the patronage of the Court, the earlier
poets depended for their success mainly on popular
favour.   The intimacy subsisting between the leaders of
action and of literature during the second century B.C.
arose from the mutual attraction of greatness in different
spheres.   The chief men in the Republic obtained their
position by active service to the State, and by the display
of capacity and character in a great and open career.
The personal attachment of men of literature to eminent
statesmen was also a bond connecting them with the
public interests.   The poets of that age, while united,
by tastes and sympathies, to the men of highest social
station, became neither the flatterers nor the favourites
of a class, but employed their powers to foster public
spirit, and to uphold the national character and dignity.

The forms of poetry first adopted at Rome are those
in which the great subjects of human interest, that do
not immediately affect the individual, are best represented.   The passions and pursuits of private life were
embodied in the lyrical and elegiacal poetry of a later
age.   But the poetry of the second century B.C. was
founded on those moral and national sources of interest
which men feel independently of their own fortunes.
In this era alone the poetry of Rome was, like that of
Greece in every era, addressed to popular sympathy.
The crowds that witnessed and applauded the representations of tragedy, afford a sufficient proof that the reproduction of Greek subjects and personages could be
appreciated without the accomplishment of a Greek

education. The popularity of the poem of Eunius is attested by his own language, as well as by the evidence of later writers. The honour of a public funeral awarded to Lucilius, implies the general appreciation with which his contemporaries enjoyed the wit, sense, and moral worth which secured for his satire the favour of a more refined and critical age.

This general popularity is a strong argument in favour of the originality of this early literature. It implies the power of embodying some sentiment or idea of national or public interest. Thus Roman tragedy appears to have been received with favour, chiefly in consequence of the grave Roman tone of its maxims, and the Roman bearing of its personages. The spectators saw, under the outward guise of ancient Greek heroes or demigods, an embodiment of the gravity of speech and demeanour, the fortitude and dignity of character, that formed their highest ideal. The epic poetry of the age did not, like the Odyssey, relate a story of personal adventure, but unfolded the annals of the State in continuous order, and appealed to the pride which men felt, as Romans, in their history and destiny. The satire of Lucilius was not intended merely to afford amusement by ridiculing the follies of social life, but played a part in public affairs by political partisanship and antagonism, and maintained the traditional standard of manners and opinions against the inroads of foreign influences. The national tones, both of the serious and satiric poetry of the age, appealed directly to the citizens of a free, powerful, and orderly Republic, in which popular boldness was tempered by patrician dignity, and the conflicting passions of the present were moderated by the steadfast memories of the past.

The national character of this poetry is attested also by the kind of feeling which it embodied, and the spirit which it breathed. While the tragic and satiric

poetry of the time expressed the moral and prac
tical energy of the Republic, the poem of Ennius first
gave a voice to the imaginative susceptibility latent
in the Roman temperament. Their earlier institutions
and their later art prove that the Romans, although a
grave and a practical people, and not gifted with creative
genius, were yet open to the influence of a certain class
of high and powerful emotions. Thus it was through
the silent impulse of imaginative enthusiasm that they
were moved in early times to commemorate their great
men by statues, public monuments, and ancestral images.
This impulse was something quite different from the
hero-worship of the Greeks, which arose out of their
tendency to attribute supernatural power both to the
mythical personages of ancient legend, and to historical
personages who, in their life or by their death, had powerfully impressed their imagination. The Roman feeling,
on the other hand, had its root in the admiration of commanding character, and gratitude for services which had
magnified the State. Such a feeling was liable to change
or violent revulsion when directed towards living men,
who were either too honest 'to serve the hour,' or who
were not preserved by greatness in one sphere from
faults or errors in another. But the lapse of time acting through the reconciling power of the imagination,
brought out the image of past greatness in stronger relief
and more harmonious proportions. So too the effect of
time acting through the imagination upon their character, is seen in the tenacity with which the Romans
clung to ancient memories, and in their sense of the
vital connexion of their past career with the grander
destiny awaiting them. The Greeks cherished their
genealogies, professing to extend in unbroken series to
the Olympian gods; and, in the ripest epoch of their civilisation, they looked back upon their heroic age through
the richly-blended colours of poetry and religion. But

the past was to them altogether ideal, undefined by accurate limits of time, and separated by an untraversed gulf from actual realities. The Romans, on the other hand, both in the epoch of their most vigorous growth, and of their established empire, looked back upon their past, not as a time of mythical brightness, but as the real morning of the long day through which they were acting the foremost part in human affairs.

Their institutions again were in a peculiar manner impressed with the stamp of majesty. Many passages in the Attic dramatists show that the highest minds of Greece were deeply moved in spirit and imagination by ideas of law and authority. But the actual administration of affairs was not surrounded with the same august associations at Athens as at Rome. The ancient forms and attributes of English government appealed to a feeling analogous to the Roman sense of majesty, and thus it is easier to find a parallel to this characteristic of Roman poetry in English than in Greek literature. Milton especially, whose republicanism was in harmony not so much with the equality and changeful energy of Greek democracy, as with the orderly and commanding spirit of Rome, is, in modern times, the most powerful exponent of that form of imaginative feeling, which, in Ennius, expressed itself in loyalty to the Commonwealth, and which, in another age, when freedom was no longer possible, moved Virgil to become the sincere panegyrist of the imperial government.

The Roman mind was also in all ages powerfully affected by outward pomp and ceremonial. This tendency appeared even in early times before the plainness of private living was lost in the luxury of the Empire. The glory which Pericles claims for his countrymen— 'φιλοκαλοῦμεν μετ' εὐτελείας' · · would have had no attraction for the natural temper or the acquired tastes of Rome. Thus, for example, the pride of the old Republic pro-

claimed itself in the long triumphal procession by which
a great military success was celebrated, while the simple
taste of the Greeks is seen in the plain trophy, erected
as a memorial of the rout of the enemy, on the field
of battle.   A similar contrast between the two races is
suggested by the difference in their architecture.   While
the genius of Greece expressed itself in works of delicate and graceful proportion, the Roman temperament
sought its satisfaction in works of colossal design and
of massive execution, and such as bore the promise of
great duration.   These native characteristics of feeling,
sympathy, and taste, are all recognised in the fragments
of the poetry of Ennius, and prove that his genius,
though moulded by the master-spirit of Greece, drew its
deepest nourishment from those powerful emotions which
in early times helped to form the men, manners, and institutions of Rome, and which were so congenial to her
temper, that they long survived even the decay of her
political virtue and moral purity.

   This vein of imaginative feeling running through the
national epic poem of the Republic scarcely betrays itself in the fragments of the early dramatic or satiric
poetry.   Moral fervour is the most general and predominant characteristic which is recognised in the remains
of the other writers.   It may be observed, that the literature of every age and country which is inspired by the
sense of greatness in practical affairs—whether it takes
the form of poetry, history, oratory, or philosophy—has
exhibited this ardour of dignified emotion, sometimes
glowing openly in the style, sometimes betrayed by an
ironical restraint.   In Roman literature the force of
moral emotion is felt in its immediate, rather than in its
subtler effects, and nowhere with more simple directness
than in the fragments of the early writers.   The qualities in human nature which call out in them this glow
of moral sympathy may be summed up in the word

virilitas,—the manlier instincts, obedient to the sense of public duty. The strong reality of their feeling is implied in the characteristic word *gravitas*,—expressive of the constancy of an ardent, as opposed to the transient excitement of a passionate nature.

The serious purpose of the early poets appears to have been independent of any belief in the religious traditions of Rome, and of any adherence to the schools of philosophy. The relation of the visible life of man to an invisible order,— the thought of which dominates over the mere human interest of the Greek drama,—finds scarcely any voice in the earlier Roman poetry. Ennius, indeed, in whom the imaginative was curiously blended with the sceptical spirit, had proclaimed the mystical faith of Pythagoras in the transmigration of the soul; but he was also the first to introduce to his countrymen the negative and prosaic rationalism of Euhemerus. The other poets of the time attacked the credulity and superstition of their age, apparently without any sense of the need of a more rational belief. On the other hand, the morality which they inculcate appears to have rested on natural strength of character and the sense of public duty, without any direct support from philosophic rules and tenets. Indirectly, indeed, at this time, the easy doctrines of Epicurus had been partially diffused through life by the pleasant unsystematic teaching of the new comedy; and perhaps the grave moral tone and magnanimous maxims of Roman tragedy may have owed some indirect debt to the spirit of Stoicism, which was beginning to find its congenial sphere of action in Roman energy. But neither of these systems was at that time generally professed and applied to life with that logical intensity which marked the later Stoics and Epicureans.

There is no ground for believing that the early poets were men of subtle or comprehensive thought. Their

fragments contain no original speculation on human
affairs; they afford more evidence of the attraction
exercised by physical than by ethical inquiries. Their
understanding was more practical than reflective. The
intellectual excellence which is most clearly stamped on
all their minds is common sense. Roman critics speak
with admiration of the *urbanitas* of Lucilius, but they
have preserved few favourable specimens of his wit or
irony. The humour of the Romans was not accompanied
with any play of imagination. It seems to have been
rather the other side of their strong perception of decorum, utility, and rectitude. The 'home-bred humour'
of Lucilius appears, from all ancient testimony, to have
been of this direct and practical kind, and to have been
used in aid of his earnest moral purpose in assailing
the follies and vices of his contemporaries.

In passing from the substance of the early literature to its merits and defects in point of form and
style, the first point to observe is its apparent rudeness in proportion and design. The fragments of
the narrative poems of the age afford clear evidence
of the inartistic conception and workmanship of the
original poems. It is more difficult to determine the
plan on which the lost dramas were constructed; but
the fragments of all the early tragic poets produce the
impression of careless, unfinished execution. The satire
of Lucilius retained much of the character of the original
satura, and continued to treat the most miscellaneous
topics in a free and discursive manner. In contrasting
the consciousness of their art expressed by all the
Augustan poets, with the evident neglect of form and
style in the early literature, it is natural to infer that
the Roman mind was slowly educated by imitative effort
to literary accomplishment. The refined works of later
times show a careful and elaborate workmanship, not,
like the masterpieces of Greek poetry, the spontaneous

evolution of nature. The early poets, on the other hand, express what they have got to say in a direct and natural manner; but their indifference to form and style, or their failure in attaining these accomplishments, is the cause why their complete works only supplied materials for more careful artists, instead of remaining as the living witness of the most interesting epoch in Roman history.

The careless ease with which they wrote conduced, however, to their great literary productiveness. Among the later poets, Ovid alone can be compared to them in regard to the extent and variety of his compositions. The labours of his predecessors had made his path comparatively smooth and easy. But the early poets were like the settlers in a new country who are spared the pains of careful cultivation, from the absence of previous occupation, and the large extent of ground thus open to their industry. The first tragedians were also writers of comedy. Nævius enjoyed great reputation in epic as well as dramatic poetry. Pacuvius obtained fame as a painter before he was distinguished as a poet. Attius was the author of annals and critical works, as well as of a great number of dramas. The energy and versatility of Ennius, exercised in many fields of literature, would have been remarkable in any age and amongst any people. He was the type of one phase of Roman genius, Catullus the type of the other. They have little in common except the qualities of vigour and sincerity. The greatest contrast, both in their careers and their poetic gifts, is forced upon the mind when one compares the rude fragments of the lost works of Ennius, which embodied the results of a long, active, hearty, and serious life, with the one small volume which still preserves the flower of a few passionate years, as fresh as when the young poet first sent it forth :

Arida modo pumice expolitum.

The style of the early poets was marked by haste, harshness, and redundance, occasionally by verbal conceits and similar errors of taste. That of the writers of comedy, on the other hand, is easy, natural, and elegant. The Latin language seems thus to have adapted itself to the needs of ordinary social life more readily than to the expression of elevated feeling. Though many phrases in these fragments are boldly and vigorously conceived, few passages are written with continuous ease and smoothness, and the language constantly halts, as if inadequate to the emotion which labours under it. The style has, in general, the merits of directness and sincerity, often of freshness and vigour, but wants altogether the depth and richness of colour, combined out of many ancient memories and feelings in the language of a more imaginative people. Their merits of style, such as the simple force with which they go directly to the heart of a matter, and the grave earnestness of their tone, are qualities characteristic rather of oratory than of poetry. But this colouring of their style is very different from the artificial rhetoric of the literature of the Empire. The oratorical style of the early poets was the natural result of a sympathy with the most practical intellectual instrument of their age. The rhetoric of the Empire was the expression of an artificial life, in which literature was cultivated to beguile the tedium of compulsory inaction, and the highest form of public speaking had sunk from its proud office as the organ of political freedom into a mere exercise of pedants and schoolboys.[1]

The same impulse in this age which gave birth to the forms of serious poetry, stimulated also the growth of oratory, history, and comedy. While these different modes of mental accomplishment all acted and reacted on one another, oratory appears to have exercised the

[1] Cf. Ut pueris placeas et declamatio fias.—Juv. x. 167.

most influence on the others. Roman literature is alto gether more pervaded by oratorical feeling than that of any other nation, ancient or modern. From the na- tural deficiency of the Romans in dramatic and specu- lative genius, the rhetorical element entered largely into their poetry, their history, and their ethical discussions. Cicero identifies the faculties of the orator with those of the historian and the philosopher. His treatise *De Claris Oratoribus* bears witness to the energy with which this art was cultivated for more than a century before his own time ; and the remains of Ennius and Lucilius confirm this testimony. It was from the im- passioned speech of the forum that the Roman language first acquired its capacity of expressing great emotions. All the serious poetry of the age bears traces of this in- fluence. Roman tragedy shows its affinity to oratory in its grave and didactic tone. This affinity is further im- plied in the political meaning which the audience at- tached to the sentiments expressed, and which the actor enforced by his voice and manner. It is also attested by the fact that in the time of Cicero, famous actors were employed in teaching the external graces of public speaking. The theatre was a school of elocu- tion as much as a place of dramatic entertainment. Cicero specifies among the qualifications of a speaker, ' Vox tragœdorum, gestus præno summorum actorum.' Although the epic poetry of the time mainly appealed to a different class of sympathies, yet the fragments of speeches in Ennius indicate that kind of rhetorical power which moves an audience by the weight and au- thority of the speaker. Roman satire could wield other weapons of oratory, such as the fierce invective, the lashing ridicule, the vehement indignation which have often proved the most powerful instruments of debate in modern as well as ancient times.

Historical composition also took its rise at Rome at

this period. Although the earliest Roman annalists composed their works in the Greek language, it was not from the desire of imitating the historic art of Greece that this art was first cultivated at Rome. The origin of Roman history may be referred rather to the same impulse which gave birth to the epic poems of Nævius and Ennius. The early annalists were men of action and eminent station, who desired to record the important events in which they themselves had taken part, and to fix them for ever in the annals of their country. History originated at Rome in the impulse to keep alive the record of national life, not, as among the Greeks, in the spell which human story and the wonder of distant lands exercised over the imagination. It was essentially commemorative, with little dramatic colouring or philosophical reflection. Its office was not to teach lessons of political wisdom, but to satisfy a Roman's pride in the past and his trust in the future of his country. The word *annales* suggests a different idea of history from that entertained and exemplified by Herodotus and Thucydides. The purpose of building up the record of unbroken national life was present to, though probably not realised by, the earliest annalists who preserved the line of magistrates, and kept account of the religious observances in the State : in the time of the expansion of Roman power, this purpose directed the attention of men of action to the composition of prose annals, and stimulated the productive genius of Nævius and Ennius; and when, in the Augustan age, the national destiny seemed to be fulfilled, the same purpose inspired the great epic of Virgil and the 'colossal master-work of Livy.'

This was also the flourishing era of Latin comedy. Plautus was the contemporary of Nævius and Ennius : Terence as well as Lucilius lived in the circle of Lælius and the younger Africanus. Other writers of comedy,

such as Cæcilius and Afranius, were ranked by their
countrymen as equal to those whose plays have come
down to modern times. Owing to our imperfect knowledge of the social manners of the time, and to our want
of any specimen of the Attic new comedy on which
that of Rome was built, it is impossible to say what
amount of originality there was in Roman comedy. It
is probable that Roman tragedy deviated more from the
original type which it imitated, and assumed more of a
national character, than Roman comedy. It is easier to
modify the representation of ideal types of man than the
representation of the social life of any particular age.
There was apparently little in common between the Athenian manners and life in the days of Menander, and those
of the Romans in the days of the great Scipio or of Tibe-
rius Gracchus. Roman satire dealt with the humours
of private life with more freedom than Roman comedy,
but there is not much in the fragments of Lucilius that
directly reminds the reader of the characters brought on
the stage by Plautus and Terence. Of the early forms
of literature, comedy had the least bearing on public or
national life, yet it must have aided in awakening an
intellectual interest among a rude and untutored people,
and also in modifying the Roman temper and ways of
thought. Its tendency must have been to break up the
old Roman cast of character into a more cosmopolitan
type, to accustom the minds of men to the idea of an
easy life of pleasure in opposition to the austere virtue
enforced by ancient discipline, and to some extent to
bring the national religion into contempt. The same
causes contributed to the decline of tragedy as of comedy at Rome, especially the separation in taste between an educated class and the mass of the people,
who, under the stimulus of wars and sensual indulgence,
craved for a coarser excitement than what is afforded by
the liveliest form of intellectual pleasure.

N

The fragments of this early literature, originally scattered through the works of many later authors, and
collected together and arranged by the industry of
modern scholars, are thus seen to possess great and
varied interest. They recall the features of the remarkable men by whom the foundations of Roman literature
were laid, and the Latin language was first shaped into
a powerful and symmetric organ. They present the
Roman mind in its earliest contact with the genius of
Greece; and they are almost the sole contemporary
witnesses of national character and public feeling in the
most vigorous and interesting age of the Republic.
They throw also much light on the national sources of
inspiration in the later Roman literature. The poets
whose remains have been examined are seen to be men
living the life of citizens in a Republic, appealing to
popular taste, not to the sympathies of a refined and
limited society; men of mature years and understanding, animated by a serious purpose and with a strong
interest in the affairs of their time; rude and negligent
but direct and vigorous in speech,—more remarkable for
energy, industry, and common sense, than for the finer
gifts and susceptibility of genius. Their poetry springing from their sympathy with national and political life,
and from the impulses of the will and the manlier energies, was less rich, varied, and refined than that which
flows out of the religious spirit of man, out of his passions and affections, or of his imaginative sense of the
life and grandeur of nature. But in these respects the
early poetry was of essentially a Roman spirit, in harmony with the direct strength, the plain sagacity, the
severity, fortitude, and dignity of Rome. The accomplished art of the Augustan age, and of the
age immediately preceding the overthrow of the Re-
public, owed much of its national and moral nourishment
to the vigorous life of this early literature. The earnest

enthusiasm of Ennius was caught up and repeated by Lucretius,—his patriotic tones by Virgil. The lofty oratory of the Æneid was an echo of the grave and ardent style of early tragedy. The strong sense and knowledge of the world, the frank communicativeness and lively portraiture of Lucilius reappeared in the familiar writings of Horace, while his fierce vehemence and bold invective were reproduced by the great satirist of the Empire.

SECOND PERIOD.

LUCRETIUS AND CATULLUS.

CHAPTER VIII.

It is in keeping with the isolated and independent position which Lucretius occupies in literature, that scarcely anything is known of the circumstances of his life. As in the most civilised epochs of antiquity, there was little inclination for personal adventure apart from public action, so there was slight interest felt in personal biography when unconnected with the main stream of political history. It was only after the decay of creative genius, when the place of poets and philosophers was filled by rhetoricians and grammarians, and when public spirit had been extinguished with the loss of liberty and national life, that curiosity began to be directed to the lives of men eminent in thought and literature. But this curiosity was combined with little disposition to criticise the evidence of the statements by which it was satisfied. A kind of spurious mythology gathered round the names of the early poets and philosophers, in some cases shaping itself out of a vague tradition of real events, often the mere creation of an idle fancy. It is thus natural to regard with suspicion any very remarkable statements concerning the personal history of an· cient writers, which are unsupported by contemporary evidence.

Although the name of Lucretius is mentioned in the literature of his own age,[1] the sole account of his life

[1] Cicero, *Epist. ad Quint. Fratr.* ii. 11 ; Corn. Nep. *Atticus*, 12.

which has reached modern times cannot be traced to
any source near his own time. This account rests on
the authority of Hieronymus, who, in the Eusebian
Chronicle, mentions that the poet Titus Lucretius was
born in the year B.C. 95 (according to the common
reading) ;[1] that after having been driven mad by a
love-potion, and having composed several books in
his lucid intervals, which were corrected by Cicero,
he committed suicide in the forty-fourth year of his
age. Donatus, in his life of Virgil, mentions that
Lucretius died on the same day on which Virgil assumed the *toga virilis*, in the year B.C. 55 ; but he
says nothing of his having committed suicide. The
contemporaries of the poet, and the later writers by
whom he is mentioned, are entirely silent about this
remarkable history ; nor is it corroborated by any allusion in literature anterior to the Eusebian Chronicle.
It is perhaps fanciful to look for any internal evidence
in the poem, either to strengthen or shake the probability of the story. One great modern critic[2] sees
in the unrelieved intensity of the work a symptom of
that morbid strain of mind which readily passes into
insanity. But it might be urged, on the other hand,
that the power of sustained feeling and consistent
thought which the work manifests in a remarkable degree, is rather the evidence of sanity of genius and
strength of understanding.

Besides the doubts arising from the silence of the
contemporaries and immediate successors of the poet,
there is something in the aspect of this story which
excites suspicion. It has the air of being the invention of a late era, to which the name of Lucretius was

---

[1] B.C. 98, according to Lachmann ; B.C. 96, according to C. Fr. Hermann.
*Disputatio de Scriptoribus Illustribus, quorum tempora Hieronymus ad Eusebii
Chronicon quadraverit.*

[2] De Quincey.

probably known merely by a vague reputation. The poem on which his fame rested is not likely to have been popular at any time, nor was it easily understood by general readers.[1] His supposed atheism, and his denial of at least one of the cardinal points in all religions, might, in an age little gifted with the faculty of literary criticism, but just awakening to the paramount importance of religious truth, invest his name with that kind of mysterious horror which clings to the memory of eminent men who are believed to stand apart from the common hopes and faith of mankind. The traditions which float about in connexion with the destinies, and especially with the dying hours of such men, shape themselves in accordance with the faith and feelings of those who receive them ; and a doom so mysterious and calamitous as that of madness and suicide might well appear to the minds of Christians in the third or fourth centuries to be the fitting consequence of what seemed to them a daring impiety and unbelief. It might be urged further against the probability of the story, that it is but a vulgar credulity which ascribes a mysterious potency to a love-philtre. It would be strange if so remarkable a poem had been written in the lucid intervals of insanity. It would be not less strange if it could be shown that any drug was known to the ancients capable of producing so terrible an effect on the human mind.

Whether, indeed, this vague story of love, madness, and suicide be an unsubstantial myth of a late age, like the myths that gathered round the name of Plato, or a meagre and distorted account of real facts, is beyond the reach of our knowledge. And it is perhaps better to dismiss it altogether from our minds, not only on the ground of its uncertainty, but as being too bare and slight, even if it were accepted, to make the poet's life

[1] Cf. QUISTIL. Inst. Or. x. i. 87.

and genius more intelligible. It is more favourable to
a candid estimate of the work that it should be read
in a frame of mind undisturbed by any doubts of its
author's sanity. No new light is thrown on the meaning of the poem, either by accepting or rejecting this
account of the author's personal history.

One part, however, of the statement in the Chronicle
derives apparent confirmation from internal evidence.
A careful examination of the structure of the poem first
led Lachmann—the most eminent and original of all
the later critics on Lucretius—to the conclusion that it
must have been left in an unfinished state at the author's
death. In this conclusion the more recent editors[1] of
Lucretius agree. From the state in which the poem
has reached us, especially from the occasional want of
arrangement in the argument of the later books,[2] it may
fairly be inferred that before it was given to the world
it passed through the hands of some editor, who has not
performed his task very skilfully. But there is considerable difficulty in accepting the statement that this
editor was Cicero. His own silence on the subject of
his editorial labours, when contrasted with the general
communicativeness of his epistles, suggests some doubt
of the truth of the story. This doubt is increased by
the slight notice of the poem in a letter to his brother
Quintus :—' The poem of Lucretius is just, as you say,
a work not of much genius, but of great art.   But, when
you come here, if you can read the Empedocleu of Sallustius, I'll think you really a man, though hardly a
human being.'[3]   The strong opposition of Cicero to the
doctrines of Epicurus—a feeling which he has expressed

[1] Bernays and Mr. Munro.

[2] This point is discussed in the next chapter.

[3] Lucretii poemata, ut scribis, ita sunt, non multis luminibus ingenii, multæ
tamen artis. Sed quum veneris, virum te putabo, si Sallustii Empedoclea
legeris, hominem non putabo.—Cic. Epist. ad Q. Frat. II. 11.

with some contempt, and with probable allusion to this poem, in the Tusculan Disputations[1]—suggests a further doubt as to his having taken upon himself the task of editing the work of so ardent a partisan and polemic as Lucretius. The tendency of the imagination to find some bond of connexion between eminent literary contemporaries, or to invest some popular author with the whole glories of his age—a tendency exemplified in the present day by the fancy that has attributed the composition of the plays of Shakspeare to the genius of Bacon —may account for the origin and reception of this belief during the four centuries which elapsed between the age of Lucretius and that of Hieronymus.

The difficulties in connexion with the statement that the poem was corrected or edited by Cicero have led Lachmann and Bernays[2] to the opinion that the person referred to was Quintus, and not Marcus Cicero. This opinion gains some confirmation from the fact that Q. Cicero was himself both a writer of poetry and a student of philosophy. But, on the other hand, it seems impossible that a writer in the fourth century A.D. should apply the familiar name of Cicero, not to the famous orator and philosophic writer, but to his comparatively obscure brother. No hint, moreover, to justify this opinion, is conveyed in the passage in which the poem is spoken of. Nothing more is implied in that passage than that Quintus had recently read the poem, and had, in a letter to his brother, expressed an opinion on its merits similar to that contained in the reply to

[1] *Tusc. Disp.* l. 21.
The whole chapter is applicable to Lucretius; and the sentence,—' Quae quidem cogitans soleo saepe mirari nonnullorum insolentiam philosophorum, qui naturae cognitionem admirantur, ejusque inventori et principi gratias exsultantes agunt eumque venerantur ut deum,' pointedly refers to him.

[2] Mr. Munro, in the preface to his edition of the text of Lucretius, intimates his dissent from them on this point, and adheres to the belief that the poem was really edited by M. Cicero.

his letter. The words of Cicero are to this effect, " I
agree with you about the merits of Lucretius, but I shall
be much surprised if you can read through another work
of the kind—the Empedocles of Sallustius.' This slight
and cursory notice of the poem, the absence of all allusion to their editorial labours, and the juxtaposition in
which the two philosophical works are mentioned, all
seem to favour the conclusion that neither M. Cicero nor
his brother had any more connexion with the one work
than with the other.

The only really trustworthy inference which can be
drawn from this notice of the poem is, that it had been
read by both the brothers, shortly before the date of the
letter, that is, about the end of the year B.C. 55, or the
beginning of B.C. 54. Some expressions in the introduction to the poem itself appear to indicate that Lucretius was engaged in its composition a few years before
this date. It has been conjectured,[1] with much probability, that the pointed lines—

> Nam neque nos agere hoc patriai tempore iniquo
> Possumus aequo animo nec Memmi clara propago
> Talibus in rebus communi desse saluti,[2]

refer to the time when Memmius was Praetor, B.C. 58,
and distinguished himself by his opposition to Julius
Caesar and his partisan Clodius. The term, *patriai
tempore iniquo*, might well apply to any time in that
period of restless intrigues and conspiracies, which preceded the outbreak of the great civil war. From the
nature of the work, and from several expressions in it,
it may be inferred that Lucretius had been a long time
engaged upon his task. It may accordingly fairly be
concluded that the poem was written some time be-

[1] By Mr. Munro, in the *Journal of Classical and Sacred Philology*, vol. I,
page 38.

[2] ' For I cannot devote myself to this task with a quiet mind in the evil
days of my country, nor can the noble scion of the line of Memmius, at
such a time, fail in his duty to the commonwealth.'—i. 41-3.

tween the years B.C. 60 and B.C. 55. On the supposi
tion that it was published after the author's death, the
date assigned by Donatus for that event may be ac
cepted as resting on very probable, if not certain evidence.

It may well, indeed, have happened that Lucretius
attracted little notice during his lifetime. His philosophy, which was not merely a speculative system, but
a practical rule of conduct, preached the wisdom of
withdrawing altogether from the passions and the business
of the world. The tastes which the poem indicates are
those of a man who had sincerely accepted his master's
motto, 'λάθε βιώσας,'—'pass through life unknown.' There
is no ground for believing that he had written or done
anything to acquire distinction before his work appeared.
There is no expression in the writings of any of his
literary contemporaries which implies any personal in
timacy with him. It is, however, a curious coincidence,
that the one friend whom Lucretius is known to have
possessed, C. Memmius, to whom the poem is dedicated,
is the object of intense hatred and scorn to the contemporary poet Catullus. Virgil, a great admirer and
diligent student of Lucretius, makes no allusion to his
personal fortunes ; but the language in which he evidently refers to him in the second Georgic would cer
tainly appear strange, if written by one who had any
knowledge of the tragical history with which the name
of the older poet was associated in a later age.[1]

Lucretius is thus known to us solely as the author of
a great didactic poem, as the poetical exponent of the
ancient atomic philosophy, and as the fervent teacher
of the moral doctrines of Epicurus. The poem, which is

[1] Felix, qui potuit rerum cognoscere causas,
Atque metus omnes et inexorabile fatum
Subjecit pedibus, strepitumque Acherontis avari.—
Georg. ii. 490.

entitled *De Rerum Natura*,—a translation of the title,
'περὶ φύσεως,' which the earlier Greek philosophic poets
gave to their works,—is the sole result of his life, the sole
witness of his circumstances and personal characteristics. But it throws scarcely the faintest light upon his
history. Nothing is known, either from the poem or
from any other source, of the author's birthplace, parentage, and connexions ; of his education, of his ordinary
place of residence, of his career in life, of his good or
evil fortune. But from an attentive study of the work,
there may be discerned some traces of his temper and
disposition, of his inner life and occupations, of the
aspect which the world presented to him. Great reliance may be placed on these indirect personal revelations, from the extreme sincerity of his language. No
writer, ancient or modern, uses words more truthfully,
or shows a greater contempt for all rhetorical artifices.
The language in which he expresses this contempt[1] reminds us of the terms in which Thucydides characterises the writings of the early logographers.[2] Of
Lucretius it may confidently be affirmed that his words
are the clear mirror of his thoughts. And as he throws
his whole heart into his subject, and seems to have
concentrated upon it the whole experience of his life,
the poem possesses much of the interest of a personal
revelation, as well as of a great philosophical argument.

In his personal relations he is known only from the
dedication of the work to C. Memmius, a man of some
distinction in politics and literature. The terms in which
Lucretius addresses him,

[1] Omnia enim stolidi magis admirantar amantque,
Invenia quæ sub verbis latitantia cernont,
Veraque constituunt, quæ belle tangere possunt
Aurea et lepido quæ sunt focata sonore.—i. 643-6.

[2] ἀτε ὡς λογογράφοι ξυνέθεσαν ἐπὶ τὸ προσαγωγότερον τῇ ἀκροάσει ἢ ἀληθέστερον.
—THUC. i. 21.

Sed tua me virtus tamen et sperata voluptas
Suavis amicitiæ,[1]

have the air of being written by one who was addressing
not a patron but an equal friend. It may be inferred,
therefore, that the poet, like his friend, belonged to the
higher and wealthier class of Romans, to which class,
indeed, literary distinction appears to have been confined at that time. Memmius bore a prominent part in
the politics of the day, and, like many of his contemporaries, combined the characters of a politician, a man
of letters, and a man of pleasure. Both his public and
private character were bad, and his career ended in dis-
grace. As a literary man, he was known as the author
of amatory poems, more remarkable for their immorality than their elegance. The graceful compliment of
Lucretius,

Memmiadæ nostro quem tu, dea, tempore in omni
Omnibus ornatum voluisti excellere rebus,[2]

contrasts strangely with the words of bitter scorn in
which Memmius is characterised by Catullus. From
time to time in the course of his poem, Lucretius appeals
by name to his friend, sometimes expressing an anxious
fear lest he should relapse into the errors of the popular
belief. But it is to be remembered that in giving to his
argument the form of a personal address, Lucretius
was following the example of the oldest didactic and
philosophic poems. The frequent introduction of the
name of Memmius into the poem is not therefore to be
pressed as implying a desire to produce conviction on
his mind exclusively. Like the address of Hesiod to
'foolish Perses,' and of Empedocles to 'the son of An-
chitus,' these personal appeals add vivacity to the
poem. They enable the reader to feel that he is not so

[1] 'Thy worth, and my hope of enjoyment in thy sweet friendship.'—i. 140.
[2] 'To my own Memmius, who by thy will, O goddess, at all times excels
in all accomplishments.'—i. 26.

much following a written argument, as listening to the
eloquent voice of a living man, who is earnestly enden-
vouring to produce conviction upon his mind. But they
can hardly be taken as throwing any real light on the
author's sympathies and affections, apart from his feeling
for the truths which he is inculcating.

The spirit and purpose with which Lucretius ex-
pounds the philosophy of nature, are clearly revealed
throughout the poem, and can be understood without
any collateral knowledge of his history. The animating
impulse of his philosophy and his poetry is the wish to
raise human life out of the ignorance of superstition,
and above the weakness and the passions of our natural
condition. It is the constant presence of this practical
purpose which imparts to his words that peculiar tone
of impassioned earnestness to which there is no parallel
in ancient literature. The poetical power to which the
work owes its immortality was seemingly valued by the
author at a much lower rate than the physical and ethical
doctrines which it taught. He speaks of his art, as a
pleasing means of instilling the unpalatable medicine of
his philosophy into the minds and hearts of unwilling
hearers.[1] The great mass of the poem is devoted to the
systematic exposition and copious illustration of the
argument. The finest poetry appears in those special
passages where he pauses in the main course of his discussion to interpret the energy or the beauty of nature,
and to give utterance to the solemn import of human
life. But his whole general conception both of the
natural and the moral world is thoroughly imaginative.
Even the driest details of abstract thought, and the most
fanciful results of the Epicurean physics, are quickened
into new life by the active conception and feeling of a
poet. The human interest and the poetical beauty of
the work are seen to be no adventitious ornaments, but

[1] i. 933-50.

to stand in vital relation to the great speculative ideas
on which the argument is ultimately based.

Of his personal characteristics, none is more prominent
than the strong sense which he entertained of the greatness of the work in which he was engaged. This was
found to be one of the points of resemblance between
him and his countryman Ennius; it is also one of those
features in which he reminds a modern reader of Milton.
The lines in which Lucretius expresses his sense of the
novelty and importance of his task—

> Avia Pieridum peragro loca nullius ante
> Trita solo ;[1]

and—

> Insignemque meo capiti petere inde coronam
> Unde prius nulli velarint tempora musae,[2]

were probably in the mind of the English poet when he
wrote his great invocation—

> I thence
> Invoke thy aid to my adventurous song,
> That with no middle flight intends to soar
> Above the Aonian mount, while it pursues
> Things unattempted yet in prose and rhyme.

Lucretius is conscious of the difficulty, as well as of the
greatness and the novelty of his undertaking—

> Nec me animi fallit quam sint obscura.[3]

His words bear witness also to the passionate delight
which he took in the exercise of his art. He speaks of
'his great hope of fame,' and of 'the sweet love of the
muses' which inspired and supported him.[4] The idea
of a long, ardent, and joyful devotion to his subject, as
the great work of his life, is gathered from lines such as
the following—

---

[1] 'I wander over the lonely haunts of the Pierides, where no foot of man
hath ever trod before.'— i. 926-7.

[2] 'To gather for my head a famous chaplet from haunts from which the
muses have never decked the brows of any poet of old.'— i. 929-30.

[3] 'Well too I know how dark these matters are.'— i. 922.

[4] i. 924-5.

o

> Conquisita diu dulcique reperta labore
> Digna tua pergam disponere carmina cura.[1]

And this also—

> Nunc age dicta meo dulci quaesita labore
> Percipe.[2]

The conscientious thoroughness with which he carried on his work, appears from such expressions as 'studio disposta fideli.' The passionate devotion of a student breaks forth in those lines in the opening of the poem—

> Suadet et inducit noctes vigilare serenas, etc. ;[3]

and in those forming part of the praise of Epicurus--

> Tuisque ex, inclute, chartis,
> Floriferis ut apes in saltibus omnia libant,
> Omnia nos itidem depascimur aurea dicta,
> Aurea, perpetua semper dignissima vita.[4]

The absorbing passion with which he carried on the works of inquiry and of composition, is revealed in passages of his poem where he illustrates his argument by reference to his own pursuits. Thus, for instance, in explaining the phenomena of dreams, after mentioning how, in their sleep, lawyers fancy themselves pleading a cause, generals fancy that they are fighting a battle, sailors that they are struggling with the elements, he adds—

> Nos agere hoc autem et naturam quaerere rerum
> Semper et inventam patriis exponere chartis.[5]

His feeling is something more than the delight which a poet or artist takes in his art, a scholar in his books, a philosopher in his abstract thought, a man of science

---

[1] 'My strains long since gathered together, and gained in happy toil, I shall now unfold in order, so as to be worthy of thy care.'—III. 419-20.

[2] 'Come now give ear to the words gained by my happy toil.'—II. 730.

[3] I. 142, etc.

[4] 'As bees sip all the sweets in flowery glades, so, great master, we too feed on all the golden words in thy writings; golden words most worthy of immortal life.' —III. 10-13.

[5] 'While I seem to be ever plying this task, ever searching into Nature, and setting forth my discoveries in my native strains.'—IV. 969-70.

in the observation of nature. It combines all these
phases of emotion, and even goes beyond them. It
is the passion of his whole being, moral as well as
intellectual, concentrated on the greatest subject of contemplation, 'majestas cognita rerum,' for the greatest
practical object, the reformation of the world. The kind
of life of which the poem gives evidence is one purely
contemplative, but it is the contemplative life of a man
not yielding to indolent, passive musing, but seeking the
truth through active and arduous inquiry. It is a life
of study, varied and braced by original observation of
outward things. Above all, it is the life of a poet, who,
with his great love of nature, and his great enjoyment
in his poetical gift, did not forget

'The human heart by which we live.'

From many indications in the poem, it may be gathered
that Lucretius, while leading the life of a contemplative
student, lived also much in the open air, and among
many varied scenes of nature. This appears indirectly
from his clear representation of the aspects of outward
things,—a faculty in which he is equalled or surpassed
by Homer alone among all the writers of antiquity,
—and, directly, from the frequent use of expressions[1]
implying that the objects which he is describing had
passed before his own eyes. Some of his illustrations
were undoubtedly drawn from the physics of Epicurus;[2]
but the vividness of his descriptions implies that they
had all been verified in his personal observation. The
variety as well as the distinctness of his illustrations
from outward things shows that he possessed the clear
eye and scientific curiosity of a naturalist, not less
than imaginative susceptibility to the life and grandeur of nature. The experience indicated in most of
these passages is that of a man more familiar with

[1] Such, for instance, as vidi, iv. 577.
[2] E.g. iv. 353.

the sights and sounds of the outward world, in remote
and solitary places, than with the life of cities.   Many
such passages bear witness to hours of minute observation
and keen interest spent on the sea-shore,—as, for instance,
those in which his argument is drawn from the slow
effect of the exhalations of the sea in wearing away
rocks and walls, or from the variety of shells paving the
shore,— his description of a sudden storm passing over
the deep (vi. 256),—his notice of the salt taste produced
by the sea air (iv. 222), and the like.   Other arguments
and illustrations of his philosophy are drawn from his
recollection of wandering among mountain solitudes ; as,
for instance—

> Palantis comites cum montis inter opacos
> Quærimus et magna dispersos voce ciemus ; [1]

and in another place he uses the words,

> Montis cum ascendimus altos.[2]

The first of these passages speaks of the presence of
others ; and, in one of his most familiar descriptions,
the charm of pleasant companionship is introduced as
enhancing the enjoyment of a simple natural life—

> Cum tamen inter se prostrati in gramine molli
> Propter aquæ rivum sub ramis arboris altæ
> Non magnis opibus jucunde corpora curant.[3]

The evidence of such passages suggests the inference
that his lonely isolation as a thinker, and his genuine
love of nature, while making him independent of the
artificial wants and tastes of his time, were not the
results of any unsocial austerity.   In other illustrations
of his philosophy, he recalls the sensation of sailing,[4] the

[1] 'When we seek companions lost among the gloom of the mountains,
and call upon the stragglers with loud voice.'—iv. 575-6.
[2] vi. 469.
[3] 'When, however, all together, stretched at length on the soft grass, by
the bank of a river, under the branches of a lofty tree, with simple fare
they joyously regale themselves.'—ii. 29-31.
[4] iv. 572.

appearance presented in riding through a rapid stream,[1]
and in several passages he speaks of dogs tracking their
game among woods and mountains. In other places,
although these are less frequent, he draws his facts from
the recollection of some of the pursuits and pleasures of
the city, as, for instance, his description of the state of
mental tension produced by witnessing public games
and spectacles for several days in succession.[2] The lines
in which he speaks of the wonders of Sicily[3] might
suggest the inference that he had been a traveller; and
other passages,[4] that he had been an eye-witness, not,
indeed of actual warfare, but of the pomp and pageantry
of great armies. But while the general traits and even
habits of the author seem undoubtedly to be traceable
among the store of facts by which his argument is
copiously illustrated, it would be unsafe to infer special
experience from the activity of his mind in outward
observation or in inward analysis. He does not conceal
himself and his own experience in the impersonal representations of art; yet, at the same time, he entirely
forgets himself in the absorbing interest of his subject.
The impression of his personal presence is indeed stamped
visibly and permanently on the poem, but this has been
done quite unconsciously. He does not care to call the
attention of the world to himself and his fortunes; but
by his single-minded devotion to his work, and by the
direct use which he has made of his own opportunities
for observation, some light is indirectly cast, not only
on his own inner nature, but also on his own ways of
living.

More certainty, however, may be attained in reading
the indication of his intellectual sympathies than in
tracing the signs of his outward life. No trait, perhaps,
is more characteristic of him than the dogmatic confidence with which he maintains his own views, and the

[1] iv. 420.   [2] iv. 973-83.   [3] i. 726.   [4] ii. 40; ii. 323-32.

enthusiastic admiration which he expresses for the philosophers and poets who had exercised the chief influence
over his mind. His high trust in the masters of his
own school is combined with an intolerant contempt
of the doctrines of that school which was the chief
antagonist of Epicureanism at Rome. The polemical
spirit in which he conducts his argument, appears in
the frequent use of expressions such as 'vinco,' 'dede
manus,' and the like, addressed to an imaginary opponent.
His tone in combating philosophic scepticism or error,
betrays the one-sided earnestness and scorn, though not
the deeper irony and more passionate indignation of his
grand protests against superstition. In applying the
test of common sense to the fancies of his opponents,
he makes use of such expressions as, 'ut quidam fin-
gunt,' 'perdelirum esse videtur' (i. 692), and others of
the same import. Heraclitus, whom modern students of
philosophy have discovered to be the subtlest and most
suggestive thinker before the time of Plato, is described
by him in much the same terms as might be applied by
a modern positivist to a great metaphysician —

> Clarus ob obscuram linguam magis inter inanis
> Quamde gravis inter Graios qui vera requirunt.[1]

The traditional opposition between Democritus and Heraclitus lived after them. The tenets of 'the laughing'
and of 'the weeping' philosophers passed into the more
modern systems of Epicureanism and Stoicism. The
believers in the atoms and the believers in the pure fiery
element of Heraclitus, became thus still more widely
separated by a real and radical variance in their whole
theory of human life.

The scorn which the Stoics entertained for his master,
is repaid in full measure by Lucretius, but he does not
mention either them or their founder by name, nor do

---

[1] 'Famous rather amongst fools by reason of his obscurity, than amongst
those earnest Greeks who seek the truth.'—i. 639-40.

the greater names of Socrates, Plato, and Aristotle
appear in the poem. It seems certain, however, that he
was not unacquainted with the writings of Plato. Thus,
for example, the well-known lines,

> Inque brevi spatio mutantur secla animantum
> Et quasi cursores vitai lampada tradunt.[1]

are obviously suggested by a passage in the Laws—

> γεννῶντάς τε καὶ ἐκτρέφοντας παῖδας, καθάπερ λαμπάδα τὸν βίον παραδιδόντας
> ἄλλοις ἐξ ἄλλων.[2]

Though very ardent and intense, his philosophical sympathies, like his doctrines, were one-sided and limited.
The whole enthusiasm of his nature breaks forth in his
admiration for Epicurus. He is 'the true interpreter
of nature,' the 'purifier of the human heart,' the 'guide
out of the storms and darkness of life into clear light
and perfect peace,' 'the sun, who at his rising extinguished all the lesser stars.' 'He is to be ranked even
as a god by reason of his great services to man'—

> Deus ille fuit, deus, inclyte Memmi,
> Qui princeps vitæ rationem invenit eam quæ
> Nunc appellatur sapientia, quique per artem
> Fluctibus e tantis vitam tantisque tenebris
> In tam tranquilla et tam clara luce locavit.[3]

He is celebrated in the introductions to Books i. iii. v.
and vi. as 'the Greek who first dared to lift his eyes
against the phantom of superstition,' as 'the ornament
of the Greek race, who makes clear the blessings of life,'
as 'more deserving to be ranked among the gods than
Ceres, Liber, or Hercules, inasmuch as a pure heart is
more needful than corn or wine, and as the conquest
over the passions is more needful than over the monsters

---

[1] 'And in a brief space the generations of living things are changing, and
like runners in a race, they hand on the torch of life.'—ii. 78.

[2] 'Begetting and rearing children, handing on life like a torch, from one
generation to another.'

[3] 'A god he was, a god, noble Memmius, who first discovered that way
of life which is now called philosophy, and who, by his art, hath raised life
out of such a stormy sea and such darkness, and established it in such peace
and in such a clear light.'—v. 8-12.

of the material world.' The language in which Lucretius
speaks of his master combines the affection of a disciple
towards a living teacher[1] with something of the ecstatic
delight and awe of a devotee.[2] This sincere but excessive admiration for one of the least godlike of philosophers, looks more like the one-sided enthusiasm of
youth, than the calm convictions of riper age. The
poet attributes his own passionate interest in the investigation of nature, to a philosopher who sought in
physical speculation only a basis for his denial of all
religious doctrines. He throws all his own deep human
feeling into a moral system which professed to secure
the happiness of man by escaping from all that was
deepest and most earnest in human life.

There was a much more real affinity of nature between
Lucretius and another philosopher whom he names with
the warmest feelings of love and veneration—Empedocles of Agrigentum—the most famous of the early
poetical philosophers of Greece. He flourished during
the fifth century B.C., and was the author of a didactic
poem on Nature, of which some fragments still remain,
sufficient to indicate the nature of the work and the
character of the man. These fragments prove that Lucretius had carefully studied the older poem, and adopted
it as his model in using a poetical form and diction to
expound his philosophical system. He declares, indeed,
his opposition to the doctrine of Empedocles, which
traced the origin of all things to four original elements ;
but he adopted into his own system many both of his
expressions and of his philosophical ideas. The line in
which the Roman poet enunciates his first principle—

Nullam rem e nilo gigni divinitus unquam.[3]

[1] Non ita certandi cupidus quam propter amorem
Quod te imitari aveo.—III. 5-6.
[2] His ibi me rebus quaedam divina voluptas
Percipit atque horror.—III. 28-29.
[3] 'No thing is ever produced out of nothing by divine agency.'—I. 150.

was obviously taken from the lines of the old poem περὶ
φύσεως—

ἐκ τοῦ γὰρ μὴ ἐόντος ἀμήχανόν ἐστι γενέσθαι
τό τ' ἐὸν ἐξόλλυσθαι ἀνήνυστον καὶ ἄπρηκτον.

Speaking of Sicily as a land of wonder and richness,
Lucretius thus pays his tribute of love and admiration
to its great imaginative thinker—

Nil tamen hoc habuisse viro praeclarius in se
Nec sanctum magis et mirum carumque videtur.
Carmina quin etiam divini pectoris ejus
Vociferantur et exponunt praeclara reperta,
Ut vix humana videatur stirpe creatus.[1]

There is a close agreement between the two poetical
philosophers in their imaginative conceptions of nature.
They both represented the beauty and life of the universe under the symbol of the Goddess of Love—' Κύπρι
βασίλεια ;' 'alma Venus, genetrix.' They both explain
the unceasing process of decay and renovation in the
world by an image drawn from the most impressive
spectacle of human life—a constant battle between opposing forces. The burden and the mystery of the
world seem to weigh heavily on each of them, and to
mould their very language to a deep, monotonous solemnity of tone. But along with this affinity of temperament there is also a marked difference in their
modes of thought and feeling. The view of nature in
the philosophy of Empedocles appears to be just emerg-
ing out of the anthropomorphic fancies of an earlier
time : the first rays of knowledge are seen trying to
pierce through the clouds of the early dawn of inquiry ;
the dreams and sorrows of religious mysticism accompany the awakened energies of the reason. His mournful tone is the voice of the intellectual spirit lamenting

[1] ' But nought greater than this man does it seem to have possessed, nor
aught more holy, more wonderful, or more dear. Yea, too, strains of
divine genius proclaim aloud and make known his great discoveries, so that
he seems scarcely to be of mortal race.'—i. 729-33,

its former home, and baffled in its eager desire to comprehend 'the whole.' Lucretius, on the other hand, saw the outward world, not glorified by the mystic colours of religion, nor concealed by the shadowy shapes of mythology, but in the clear light of day. He was moved neither by the passionate longing of the soul, nor by the 'divine despair' of the intellect; but he felt profoundly the real sorrows of the heart, and was weighed down by the ever-present consciousness of the misery and wretchedness in the world. The complaint of the first is one which may have been uttered from time to time by some solitary thinker in modern as well as ancient days :—

> ταῦρα δὲ ξωῆς ἀβίου μέρος ἀθρήσαντες
> ὠκύμοροι, καπνοῖο δίκην ἀρθέντες ἀνέσταν
> αὐτὸ μόνον πεισθέντι, ὅτῳ προσέκυρσεν ἕκαστος,
> παντοσ' ἐλαυνόμενοι· τὸ δ' ὅλον πευσέχεται τόμοῖς
> αὐτῶν· οὔτ' ἐπιδερκτὰ τάδ' ἀνδράσιν οὔτ' ἐπακουστὰ
> οὔτε νόῳ περιληπτά.[1]

The other gives a real and startling utterance to that 'thought of inexhaustible melancholy,' which has weighed on every human heart :—

> Miscetur funere vagor
> Quem pueri tollunt visentis luminis oras;
> Nec nox ulla diem neque noctem aurora secutast
> Quae non audierit mixtos vagitibus aegris
> Ploratus mortis comites et funeris atri.[2]

Other philosophers and poets are mentioned in the poem in terms of admiration similar to those which are

[1] 'When they have gazed for a few years of a life that is indeed no life, speedily fulfilling their doom, they vanish away like a smoke, convinced of that only which each hath met in his own experience, as they were buffeted about to and fro. Vainly doth each boast to have discovered the whole. The eye cannot behold it, nor the ear hear it, nor the mind of man comprehend it.'

[2] 'With death there is ever blending the wail of infants newly born into the light. And no night hath ever followed day, no morning dawned on night, but hath heard the mingled sounds of feeble infant wailings and of lamentations that follow the dead and the black funeral train.'—ii. 576-80.

applied to Epicurus and Empedocles. In common with
all great imaginative thinkers, Lucretius was profoundly
moved by the impulse of reverence. But this feeling
was in him absolutely divorced from a belief in the religious traditions of his country. The feelings of awe
and veneration which the ideas and symbols of religion
awaken in others were called forth in him by the contemplation of the majesty of Nature, and of the great
minds by which her secrets had been revealed. Thus
he characterises a doctrine of Democritus as 'sancta viri
sententia,' 'the holy thought of the man.'[1] Those philosophers even to whom he is opposed he extols as
'discovering many things well and by divine inspiration,' and as 'uttering their responses from the shrine
of their own hearts, with more holiness and truth than
the Pythia from the tripod and the laurel of Apollo.'[4]
The faculty by which truth is discovered is that which
he regards as the divinest faculty in man. The highest
office of poetry is not to create and shape divine or
human story, but to add the charm of graceful expression and of musical verse to the discoveries of thought.[3]
But he speaks also of some of the poets of former days,
especially of Homer and of Ennius, in the language of
fervent enthusiasm. To the first he assigns a high pre-
eminence above all other poets—

Adde repertores doctrinarum atque leporum,
Adde Heliconiadum comites ; quorum unus Homerus
Sceptra potitus eadem aliis sopito' quiertert.[4]

But he is introduced into his poem, not as the poet of
war and national glory, but as the interpreter of nature.
As Horace made his study of Homer yield to him lessons
of practical wisdom, Lucretius seems to have found in that

[1] II. 371 ; v. 020.   [2] I. 737.   [3] I. 943-50.
[4] 'Consider, too, the discoverers in knowledge and in art ; consider the
companions of the Muses, among whom the peerless Homer held the sceptre ;
yet he too sleeps the sleep of all the rest.'—III. 1036-38.

poet an aid to his contemplative study of the outward
world, and of the inward strength and dignity of man.
Other poets of Greece are alluded to, although not
named, sometimes in tones of indifference or contempt,
as having, in common with the painters of former times,
given shape and form to the superstitious terrors and
fancies of mankind.[1] It is clear that his taste and understanding were cultivated and formed by the earlier
writers of Greece, not by the later school of Alexandria. There are traces in his poem of the careful study
both of Æschylus and of Thucydides ; to the former of
whom he bears some resemblance in poetic genius, to
the latter in philosophic thought and vigour of understanding.

The language and rhythm of the poem imply also
that he was an admiring student of Ennius, to whom he
bore a still more decided affinity in temper and character.   Many of his lines, expressions, and archaic
words, as, for instance—

> ' Per gentis Italas hominum quæ clara clueret.'
>
> ' Lumina sis oculis etiam bonus Ancu' reliquit.'
>
> ' Multa munita virum vi'—' cæli templa '—' luminis oras '—' famul
> infimus '—' induperator,' etc.,

come back upon the reader like echoes from the older
poet.   The few allusions to Roman history in the poem,
as, for instance—

> Scipiadas, belli fulmen, Carthaginis horror ;

the introduction of elephants in his pictures of the pomp
and circumstance of war ;[2] and again, the passage
beginning—

> Ad confligendum venientibus undique Pœnis[3]—

might suggest the idea that, just as English history used
to be known, even to educated men, from the historical

plays of Shakspeare, so the past history of his country
was familiar to Lucretius, solely or chiefly, in the Annals
of Ennius. He betrays scarcely any trace of national
pride or patriotic sympathies. He seems to stand almost
as much aloof from his country as from his age. The
only feeling approaching to patriotism which he displays
is in the introduction to his poem, where he speaks of
' the evil days of his country' as disturbing the calm
spirit in which he wished to devote himself to his great
argument. The poem is illustrated as frequently by
allusion to Greek as to Roman history, to the wonders
of distant lands, as to the beauty of Italian scenes. The
Georgics of Virgil often remind us of single expressions
and long passages in Lucretius ; but the finer episodes
of that poem, in which Virgil pours forth all his Roman
feeling and his love of Italy, are conceived in a spirit
altogether alien to that of the older poet. The philosophic height from which Lucretius contemplated all
human history, as a process of ' nation succeeding nation
and handing on the torch of life in succession to one
another,'[1] was far apart from the position from which
Virgil beheld all the nations of the world doing homage
to the greatness of Rome. The poem of Lucretius
breathes the spirit of a man altogether indifferent to
the ordinary sources of pleasure and pride among his
contemporaries. Living in one of the most momentous
eras of antiquity, he was only repelled by its energetic
and turbulent activity. His sense of the infinity, the
eternity, and the fixed order of nature, made the issues
of that age and the glories of his country appear to him
as transient as the events of the Trojan war. He regarded both alike, as merely accidents—

Corporis atque loci, res in quo quaeque geruntur.[2]

To him, as to the modern poet who most resembles him,
the contemplation of more enduring realities had—

1 ii. 77. 2 i. 483.

' Power to make
Our noisy years seem moments in the being
Of the eternal silence.'

But while the sympathies expressed in the poem of
Lucretius are not those naturally to be expected in a Roman writer, and while he, alone among his countrymen,
inherited some of the old speculative genius of Greece, yet,
more than most Romans, he possessed the moral temper
and heart of the great Republic. He is a truer type of the
virtue of Rome than Virgil, Horace, and the other Augus
tan poets. He was made of the same strong metal as
Ennius and his contemporaries. Like Ennius he was a
poet more by native force and sincerity than by artistic
accomplishment. No extant Roman writer, with the
exception perhaps of Tacitus, represents with so much
power the gravity, dignity, and fortitude of his race.
But he is much more than a type of even the greatest
Roman qualities. While he regards all weakness with
mixed pity and scorn, he has a depth of human sympathy and pathos, equalled by perhaps no ancient writer
except by Homer. He reveals indeed a wonderful
freshness of feeling, and, as one might think, a strong
capacity for natural enjoyment ; but, at the same time,
few writers of any age have been so constantly haunted
by the remembrance of the deep sources of melancholy
in human life. In this respect also Homer alone among
ancient writers has sounded as deeply ; but the poet of
the heroic age of Greece was gifted with infinitely more
of the buoyancy of spirit, and of the joy and energy of
life, to raise him above the occasional gloom and sadness
of his thought.

It is, however, in his devotion to truth, perhaps more
than in any other quality, that Lucretius rises clearly
above the level both of his countrymen and of his age.
He thus seems to combine in himself what was greatest
in the Greek and in the Roman mind—the Greek ardour

of inquiry; the Roman manliness of heart. He is a
Roman poet of the time of Julius Cæsar, animated with
the spirit of one of the early Greek philosophers. He
unites the speculative passion of the dawn of ancient
inquiry with the real observation of its meridian; and
he has brought the imaginative conceptions of nature
that gave birth to the earliest philosophy into harmony
with the Italian love of the living beauty in the world.

CHAPTER IX.

THE poem of Lucretius brings him before us in three different aspects :

I. As the exponent, in Latin verse, of a philosophical argument based on the atomic theory of Democritus, and on certain physical doctrines of Epicurus :

II. As the earnest advocate of the moral doctrines of Epicurus, and the earnest antagonist of the popular religion :

III. As a great contemplative poet of nature and of human life.

In making his proud and confident assertion of his genius, he himself professes to fulfil these three distinct offices of a philosophical teacher, a moral reformer, and a poet—

> Primum quod magnis doceo de rebus et artis
> Religionum animum nodis exsolvere pergo,
> Deinde quod obscura de re tam lucida pango
> Carmina, musaeo contingens cuncta lepore.[1]

It is chiefly as a poet and as a moralist that he has been admired in modern times ; and it has so happened to him, more perhaps than to any other great writer, that his work is more popular when read in extracts than when studied as a whole. But, on many grounds, it is desirable to examine the philosophical argument,

[1] 'First, by reason of the greatness of my argument, and because I set the mind free from the close-drawn bonds of superstition ; and next because, on so dark a theme, I weave such lucid verse, touching every point with the grace of poesy.'—i. 931-4.

which forms, as it were, the skeleton of the whole work, before considering his thoughts on human life, and his art and genius as a poet.

In the first place, it is only after a survey of the poem as a whole that it is possible to estimate its completeness or incompleteness as a work of art. Again, it is in the regular course of the argument, and in those passages which express his varied observation of nature, quite as much as in his highest poetry, that his personal tastes and pursuits are revealed to us. It is impossible to understand the main passion and labour of the poet's life, without a fair appreciation of that system of philosophy on which his convictions were based. It will be seen also that the full meaning of his human philosophy and the full power of his poetry stand in a close relation to his abstract doctrines. Moreover, the study of the argument is interesting on its own account. In no other work are the strength and the weakness of ancient physical philosophy so apparent. If the poem of Lucretius adds nothing to the knowledge of scientific facts, it throws a powerful light on one phase of the ancient mind. It is a witness of the eager imagination, and of the searching thought of that early time, which endeavoured, by the force of individual inquirers and the intuitions of genius, to solve a problem probably beyond the reach of the human faculties, and to explain, at a single glance, secrets of nature which have only slowly been revealed to the patient labours of many generations of inquirers.

I.—EXAMINATION OF THE ARGUMENT.

I. The philosophical theory expounded in the poem is the atomic system, originally advanced by Leucippus and Democritus, afterwards adopted by Epicurus as the physical basis of his moral and religious doctrines.

P

Lucretius lays no claim to original discovery as a philosopher ; it is sufficient for him to explain, in his native
language, 'Graiorum obscura reperta.' Along with the
first principles of the atomic philosophy, he discusses
in the poem some special applications of that doctrine,
which formed part of the physical system of Epicurus.
But the extent to which he carries these discussions is
limited by the practical purpose of raising human life
above the terrors of superstition. The source of these
terrors is traced to the general ignorance of certain facts
in nature,—ignorance, namely, of the constitution and
condition of our souls and bodies, of the means by
which the world came into existence and is still maintained, and lastly, of the causes of many natural phenomena, which are attributed to the direct agency of the gods.
In order to shake the strong hold which superstition has
over the mind, it is necessary to establish clear knowledge
in room of ignorance on these points; and this can only
be accomplished after a complete examination of the first
principles of being. In the first two books of the poem,
accordingly, the ultimate principles of the atomic philosophy are systematically unfolded and copiously illustrated. In the third and fourth books, the positions
thus established are used to explain the nature of the
soul, to prove its non-existence after death, and to
account for the belief in a future state. In the fifth and
sixth books an attempt is made to show that the creation
and preservation of the universe, and that the phenomena
of thunder, tempests, volcanoes, and the like, are the
results of natural laws, without Divine intervention.
Although the treatment of his subject may sometimes
carry him into greater detail than is necessary for his
purpose, yet the key-note to the whole poem is his
conviction of the irreconcilable opposition between the
truth of nature and the falsehood of the ancient mythology. This thought determines the course of the

argument. The following lines, for example, are repeated
as a kind of prelude to the argument, where it is taken
up at the beginning of the first, the second, and the
third books :—

Hunc igitur terrorem animi tenebrasque necessest
Non radii solis neque lucida tela diei
Discutiant, sed naturae species ratioque.[1]

His conviction of the absolute opposition between a
true knowledge of nature and an ignorant and base
superstition, is openly expressed in many passages of
deep feeling and powerful poetry. The action of the
poem might be described as the gradual defeat of the
ancient dominion of superstition by the new power of
knowledge. This meaning seems to be symbolised in its
magnificent introduction, where the genial, all-pervading
power of nature,—the source of order, beauty, and delight,—and the grim phantom of superstition—

Horribili super aspectu mortalibus instans,[2]

the cause of ignorance, degradation, and misery,—are
vividly personified and presented in close contrast with
one another. It is this thought which gives its full meaning and earnestness to the poem. The whole processes
of nature are explained not merely or chiefly from the
love of knowledge, but as the only means of establishing
light in the room of darkness, peace in the room of
terror, certain faith in the laws and the facts of nature
in the room of blind dependence on capricious, and
tyrannical powers.

What then was this philosophy, which satisfied the
reason of Lucretius, and supplied him with an answer to
all the perplexities of existence ? The object which
the early systems of ontology placed before them was to
discover the original substance or substances from which

---

[1] 'This terror of the soul, therefore, and this darkness must be dispelled,
not by the rays of the sun or the bright shafts of day, but by the outward
aspect and harmonious plan of nature.'—i. 146-8.
[2] 'With awful aspect impending over mortals from on high.'—i. 65.

all existing things were formed, and which alone remained permanent among the changing aspects of the
world.   Various systems, of a semi-physical, semi-meta
physical character, were founded on the answers given
by the earliest inquirers to this question.   In the first
book of the poem several of these theories are discussed.
Lucretius following Epicurus, adopts the answer of
Democritus to this question, that the original substances
were the 'atoms and the void'—ἄτομα καὶ κενόν.   After
the invocation to the spirit of nature, and the represen
tation of the tyranny which superstition exercised over
the world, until it was vanquished by Epicurus, he lays
down this principle as the starting-point of his argument,
—that no existing thing is formed out of nothing by
divine agency—

Nullam rem e nilo gigni divinitus unquam.

Numerous facts are appealed to, as establishing universal
order and causation, in opposition to the notion that
existence is either arbitrarily produced out of nothing,
or can again be resolved into nothing.   The original
substances out of which all things are produced, and
into which they are ultimately resolved, are next stated
to be certain primordial particles of matter or atoms,
which are called by various names—'materies,' 'genitalia
corpora,' 'semina rerum,' 'corpora prima;'—some of
these names, it may be observed, expressive not only of
their primordial character, but also of their germinative
or productive power.   These atoms are admitted to be
invisible to our senses, but by many instances it is
shown that there must be numerous invisible bodies
acting in nature—

Corporibus caecis igitur natura gerit res.

In addition to these primordial atoms there is vacuum
or space; otherwise there could be no motion in the
universe.   But besides these there is no other original
or absolute substance—

Ergo præter inane et corpora tertia per se
Nulla potest rerum in numero natura relinqui.[1]

All existing things result from the combination of these primary existences. They alone absolutely exist, and are absolutely distinct from one another. The atoms alone contain no void within them ; they alone are solid and indivisible. Their existence through all eternity is shown to be a necessary consequence of the first principle of this philosophy, that existing things cannot arise out of nothing, or be resolved into nothing :—

Sunt igitur solida primordia simplicitate
Quæ minimis stipata cohærent partibus arte,
Non ex illarum conventu conciliata,
Sed magis æterna pollentis simplicitate,
Unde neque avelli quicquam neque deminui jam
Concedit natura reservans semina rebus.[2]

The atoms and space are thus conceived of as a kind of resting-place in nature ;—as the permanent substances underlying all the changes of phenomena. At this point, from line 635 to 920 of Book I., the first principles of other philosophers, and particularly of the systems of Heraclitus, Empedocles, and Anaxagoras, are discussed and refuted at considerable length.

It is next shown that the atoms must be infinite in number, and space infinite in extent ;—the contrary supposition being both inconceivable and incompatible with the origin, preservation, and renewal of all existing things.

In the second book, after the ornate introduction concerning the vanity of ambition, the argument proceeds to explain the process by which these atoms, primordial, indestructible, and infinite in number, combine

---

[1] i. 445-6.

[2] 'The original atoms are, therefore, of solid singleness, composed of the smallest particles in close and compact union, not kept together by any meeting of these particles, but rather powerful by their eternal singleness, from which nature allows no loss by violence or decay, storing them as the seeds of all things.'—i. 609-14.

together in infinite space, so as to carry on the birth,
growth, and decay of all things. While the sum of
things always remains the same, there is constant change
in all phenomena. This is explicable only on the supposition of the original elements being in eternal motion.
The atoms are borne through space, either by their own
weight, or by contact with one another, with a rapidity
of motion far beyond that of any visible bodies. All
motion is naturally in a straight direction, but to account
for the contact of the atoms with one another, it must
be supposed that in their movements they make a slight
declension from the straight line at certain intervals.
This power of declension is the sole thing to break the
chain of necessity—' quod fati foedera rumpat.' It is a
power in the primal elements corresponding to, and the
cause of, volition in living beings.

All things therefore are in ceaseless motion, although
they may present to our senses the appearance of perfect rest.

It is necessary further to assume the existence of other
properties in the atoms, in order to account for the
variety of nature, and the individuality of existing things.
They have original differences in form ; some are smooth,
others round, others rough, others hooked, etc. These
varieties in form are not infinite, but limited in number.

As the variety of nature depends on the variety of
these forms, the order and regularity of nature imply
that there is a limit to these varieties. But while they
are limited, the individuals of each kind are infinite,
otherwise the primordial atoms would be finite in number, and there could be no cohesion among those atoms of
the same kind, in the vast and chaotic sea of matter—

> Unde ubi qua vi et quo pacto congressa coibant
> Materia tanto in pelago turbaque aliena ?[1]

The motions which tend to the support and the de-

[1] ii. 549.

struction of created things are balanced by one another ; there must be an equilibrium in these opposing forces—

Sic æquo geritur certamine principiorum
Ex infinito contractum tempore bellum.[1]

Further, the great variety in nature is to be accounted for by variety, not only in the original forms of matter, but also in their modes of combination. No existing thing is composed solely of one kind of atoms. The greater the variety of forces and powers in anything, the greater is the variety of the elements out of which it was originally composed. There is, however, a limit to the combinations of the atoms, and it is only by some secret affinities that they are capable of combining with one another. The different modes of combination give rise to many of the secondary properties of matter, which are not in the original elements. Colour, for instance, is not one of the original properties of atoms ; for all colour is changeable, and all change implies the death of what previously existed. Moreover, colour depends on light, and the atoms never come into the light. The atoms are also devoid of heat and cold, of sound, taste, and smell. All these properties must be kept distinct from the original elements—

Immortalia si volumus subjungere rebus
Fundamenta quibus nitatur summa salutis ;
Ne tibi res redeant ad nilum funditus omnes.[2]

Further, although they are the origin of all living and sentient things, the atoms themselves are devoid of sense and life, otherwise they would be liable to death. All living things are merely results of the constant changes in the primordial elements contained in the heavens and the earth.

[1] II. 575-6.
[2] ‘ If we are to suppose the existence of an eternal substance, at the basis of all things, on which the safety of the whole universe rests, lest you find creation resolved into nonentity.’—II. 802-4.

Finally, from the infinity of space and matter, it may be inferred that there are infinite other worlds and systems beside our own. Many elements were added from the infinite universe to our system before it reached maturity; and many indications prove that the period of growth is now past, and that we are living in the old age of the world.

The sum of the first two books, in which the first principles of the atomic philosophy are methodically unfolded and illustrated, is, accordingly, to this effect :— that all things have their origin in, and are sustained by, the various combinations and motions of solid elemental atoms, infinite in number, various in form, but not infinite in the variety of their forms,—not perceptible to our senses, and themselves devoid of sense, of colour, and of all the secondary properties of matter. These atoms, by virtue of their ultimate conditions, are capable only of certain combinations with one another. These combinations have been brought about by perpetual motion, through infinite space and through all eternity. As the order of things now existing has come into being, so it must one day perish. Only the atoms will permanently remain, moving unceasingly through space, and forming new combinations with one another.

These first principles being established, the way is made clear for the true explanation, according to natural laws, of those phenomena which give rise to and maintain the terrors of superstition.

The third book treats of the nature of the mind, and of the vital principle. As it is by the fear of death, and of eternal torment after death, that human life is most disturbed, it is necessary to explain the nature of the soul, and to show that it perishes in death along with the body.

The mind and the vital principle are parts of the man, as much as the hands, feet, or any other members. The mind is the directing principle, and is seated in the centre of the breast. The vital principle is diffused over the whole body, obedient to and in close sympathy with the mind. The power which the mind has in moving the body proves its own corporeal nature, as motion cannot take place without touch, nor touch without the presence of a bodily substance.

The soul (including both the mind and vital principle) is, therefore, material, formed of the finest or minutest atoms, as is proved by the extreme rapidity of its movement, and by the fact that there is nothing lost in appearance or weight immediately after death :—

> Quod simul atque hominem laeti socura quies est
> Indepta atque animi natura animusque recessit,
> Nil ibi libatum de toto corpore cernas
> Ad speciem, nil ad pondus: mors omnia praestat
> Vitalem praeter sensum calidumque vaporem.[1]

Four distinct elements enter into the composition of the soul—heat, wind, calm air, and a finer essence 'quasi anima animai.' The variety of disposition in men and animals depends on the proportion in which these elements are mixed.

The soul is the guardian of the body, and inseparably united with it, as the odour is with frankincense ; nor can the soul be disconnected from the body without its own destruction. This intimate union of soul and body is proved by many facts. They are born, they grow, and they decay together. The mind is liable to disease, like the body. Its affections are often dependent on bodily conditions. The difficulties of imagining the state of the soul existing independently of the body are next urged ; and the book concludes with a long passage of sustained

[1] ' So soon as the deep rest of death hath fallen upon a man, and the mind and the life have departed from him, there is no loss in his whole frame to be perceived, either in appearance or in weight. Death still presents everything that was before, except the vital sense and the warm heat.'—III. 211-15.

clevation of feeling, in which the folly and the weakness
of fearing death are passionately insisted upon.

The fourth book, which treats of the images which
all objects cast off from themselves, and, in connexion
with that subject, of the senses generally, and of the
passion of love, is intimately connected with the preceding book. If there is no life after death, what is
the origin of the universal belief in the existence of the
souls of the departed? The images cast off from the
surface of bodies, and borne incessantly through space
without force or feeling, appearing to the living sometimes in sleep and sometimes in waking visions, have
suggested the belief in the ghosts of the dead, and in
many of the portents of ancient mythology. The rapid
formation and motion of these images and their great
number are explained by various analogies. Some apparent deceptions of the senses are next mentioned and
explained. These deceptions are shown to be not in the
senses, but in our minds not rightly interpreting their
intimations. There is no error in the action of the
senses. They are our 'prima fides'—the foundation of
all knowledge and of all human conduct—

> Non modo enim ratio ruat omnis, vita quoque ipsa
> Concidat extemplo, nisi credere sensibus ausis.[1]

Images that are too fine to act on the senses, sometimes directly affect the soul itself. Discordant images
unite together in the air, and present the appearance
of Centaurs, Scyllas, and the like. In sleep, images
of the dead—

> Morte obita quorum tellus amplectitur ossa,[2]

appear, and give rise to the belief in the existence of
ghosts. The mind sees in dreams the objects in which
it is most interested, because, although all kinds of

---

[1] 'For, not only would all reason come to nought, even life itself would
immediately be overthrown, unless you dare to trust the senses.'—iv. 507-8.
[2] i. 135.

images are present, it can discern only those of which
it is expectant.

Several other questions are discussed in connexion
with the doctrine of the 'simulacrm.' The final cause
of the senses and the appetites is denied, and, by impli-
cation, the argument from design founded on the belief
in final causes. The use of everything is discovered
through experience. We do not receive the sense of
sight in order that we may see, but having got the
sense of sight, we use it—

> Nil ideo quoniam natumst in corpore ut uti
> Possemus, sed quod natumst id procreat usum.[1]

There follows an account of sleep, and of the condition of the mind during that state ; and the book concludes with a physical account of the passion of love,
which is dependent on the action of the simulacra on
the mind. Love is shown also to arise from natural
causes, and not to be engendered by divine influence.
The fatal consequences of yielding to the passion are
then enforced with much poetical and satirical power.

The object of the fifth book is to explain the formation of our system—of earth, sea, sky, sun, and moon,
—the origin of life upon the earth, and the advance of
human nature from its savage state to the arts and
usages of civilisation. The purpose of these discussions
is to show that all our system was produced and is
maintained by natural agency, that it is neither itself
divine nor created by divine power, and that, as it has
come into existence, so it must one day perish.

As the parts of our system,—earth, water, air, and
heat,—are perishable, and constantly passing through
processes of decay and renovation, the system must
have had a beginning, and will have an end. There

---

[1] 'Since nothing in our body has been produced in order that we might
be able to put it to use, but what has been produced creates its own use.'—
IV. 834-5.

must at last be an end of the long war between the
contending elements.

The world came into existence as the result not of
design, but of every variety of combination in the elemental atoms through infinite time. Originally they
were all confused together. Gradually those that had
mutual affinities combined and separated themselves
from the rest. The earthy particles sunk to the centre.
The elemental particles of the empyrean (æther ignifer)
formed the ' mœnia mundi.' The sun and moon were
formed out of the particles that were neither heavy
enough to combine with the earth, nor light enough to
ascend to the highest heaven. Finally, the liquid particles separated from the earth and formed the sea.
Highest above all is the empyrean, entirely separated
from the storms of the lower air, and moving round
with its stars by its own impetus. The earth is at rest
in the centre of our system, supported by the air, as
our body is by the vital principle. The movements of
the stars and of the sun and moon through the heavens
are next explained ; then the origin of vegetable and
animal life on the earth, and of the progress of human
society.

First plants and trees, afterwards men and animals,
were produced from the earth in the early and vigorous
prime of the world. Many of the animals originally
produced afterwards became extinct. Those only were
capable of continuation which had either some faculty
of self-preservation against others, or were useful to
man, and so shared his protection. The existence of
monsters such as Scylla, the Centaurs, the Chimæra, is
shown to be impossible according to the natural laws
of production.

The earliest condition of man was one of savage
vigour and power of endurance, but liable to danger and
destruction from many causes. The first humanising

influence is traced to domestic union and the affection inspired by children.

> Et Venus inminuit viris moorique parentum
> Blanditiis facile ingenium fregere superbum.[1]

The origin of language is next explained, then that of civil society, of religion, and of the arts,—the general conclusion being that all progress is the result of natural experience, not of divine guidance.

The last source of superstition is our ignorance of the causes of natural phenomena—

> Praesertim rebus in illis
> Quae supera caput aetheriis cernuntur in oris.[2]

Hence the sixth book is devoted to the explanation of thunderstorms, tempests, volcanoes, earthquakes, and the like,—phenomena which are generally attributed to the direct agency of the gods. The whole work terminates with an account of the Plague at Athens, closely borrowed from Thucydides.

The first question that arises after a review of the whole argument of the poem, is one suggested by the statement in the Eusebian Chronicle, and brought into prominence since the publication of Lachmann's edition of Lucretius, viz., whether there is reason to believe that the poem was left by the author in a finished state. In giving an answer to this question, it is to be remarked, in the first place, that the argument appears to be quite complete for the practical purpose which the author contemplated. He announces, at Book i. 54, etc., and again, at i. 127, etc., the design of the poem as embracing the first principles of natural philosophy, and the application of these principles to cer-

---

[1] 'And love impaired their strength, and children, by their gentle ways, easily broke down the proud temper of their fathers.'—v. 1017-8.

[2] Especially in those things which are seen in the heaven above our head.—vi. 60-1.

tain special subjects, viz., the nature of the soul and
body, the origin of the belief in ghosts, the natural
causes of creation, and the meaning of certain celestial
phenomena.

The practical purpose of the poem, viz., the overthrow
of superstition, limits the argument to these subjects of
discussion. They are severally mentioned where the
argument is resumed, in Books iii. iv. v. and vi., as
those matters which demand a clear explanation from
the poet. All the topics enunciated in the opening
sketch of the plan of the work are discussed with the
utmost fulness. The great strongholds of superstition
are attacked and overthrown in regular succession. No
further exposition of natural phenomena was demanded
for the purpose of the poem. Further, it is to be observed that a passage in the introduction to the sixth
book—

> Tu mihi supremae praescribta ad candida calcis
> Currenti spatium praemonstra, callida musa
> Calliopa, requies hominum divomque voluptas,
> Te duce ut insigni capiam cum laude coronam,[1]

clearly implies that the poet was approaching the end of
his argument.

But, on the other hand, an examination of the poem
in detail, leads to the conclusion that it did not receive
its author's final touch. The continuity of the argument is occasionally broken in all the books except the
first. In the fourth, fifth, and sixth books especially,
it is obvious that the mass of materials which the author
was constantly accumulating had not finally been reduced into harmony with the whole plan of the work.
The poem everywhere produces a sense of great fulness
of matter, and of the delight which the author took in

---

[1] 'Do thou be my guide over the course, as I hurry on to the white mark
of my goal, O wise muse, Calliope, who givest rest to men and joy to gods,
that, under thy guidance, I may gain a crown of high renown.'—vi. 92-5.

adding to his stores of knowledge. Thus we read in one passage—

Usque adeo largos hanstus e fontibu' magnis
Lingua meo suavis diti de pectore fundet.[1]

In many places, also, he indicates the importance which he attached to the systematic arrangement of his subject. In the general conduct of the argument, and especially in the first two books, he proves himself to be a thorough master of methodical exposition, so that the occasional breaks in the continuity of the later books must be attributed rather to want of time than want of skill. The conclusion accordingly to which all his most recent editors have come, is, that many passages were left by the poet, at the time of his death, which had not been finally brought into their proper connexion, and that these were fitted to their present position, not always very judiciously, by the hands of some editor, whom, on the authority of the Eusebian chronicle, they suppose to be one or other of the two Ciceros.

It was also part of the author's general design to enunciate his deepest thoughts on the gods, on nature, and on human life, in more highly-finished digressions or episodes. Such passages are, in general, introduced at the beginning and the end of the different books. They are like rich and quiet resting-places in the toilsome march of the argument. They serve to bring out the deeper meaning and more catholic interest which underlie the special subject of the poem. Some of these passages are very highly finished, and were evidently fixed by the poet in the places which he designed them to occupy. This is the case especially with the introductions to the first, second, and third books, and with the concluding passages in the second, third, and fourth books. But, on the other hand, there are occasional repetitions of

---

[1] 'With such force shall my sweet-speaking tongue from the depths of my rich heart pour forth floods drawn from copious sources.'—L. 412-3.

these episodical passages, as for instance, at ii. 177, and
v. 195 ; and one fine passage—

Avia Pieridum peragro loca, etc.

comes in near the end of the first book,—after the discussion of the systems of Heraclitus, Empedocles, and
Anaxagoras,—and again as the introduction to Book iv.
A short passage at ii. 167, is an anticipation of a longer
passage at v. 110, to the same effect; and neither of these
is closely connected with the course of the argument
at the particular points where they are introduced.
Again, at v. 155, there is an instance of an unfulfilled
promise. In speaking of the nature of the gods, and of
their dwelling-places, the poet passes from the subject
with this announcement, which is never fulfilled—

Quae tibi posterius largo sermone probabo.[1]

Considered also as a work of art, the poem bears
the mark of incompleteness. The whole of the first
book has the appearance of finished execution ; so also
have the introductory and concluding passages in the
second and third books. But there are other passages
of considerable power which are seen to be wanting in
poetic finish, as well as harmonious adaptation to the
course of the argument. The elaborate introduction
shows how carefully and artistically the whole work was
planned ; but the poem terminates in a mere episode
having no close bearing on the general subject of which
it treats.

The conclusions, accordingly, to which we are led,
are, in the first place, that the main purpose of the
poem is fully satisfied. The announcements of the first
book are fulfilled. The author shows his thorough grasp
of the subject as a whole, and his power of complete
and consistent exposition. But, on the other hand, besides accomplishing his practical object, he desired to
communicate all the stores of his knowledge in an

[1] 'Which I shall afterwards prove to thee in copious language.'—v. 155.

ordered harmony, to enforce the bearing of his doctrines on human life in passages of more impressive
solemnity, and to secure immortality for his poem by
giving to it the fine proportions and the careful execution of a work of art. He has given abundant proof of
possessing both the power and the taste necessary for
the accomplishment of his task, but he failed to impart
to it the master's final touch, and so to produce either
a perfectly continuous argument, or a perfectly finished
poem. There is no reason for suspecting that any long
passages have been lost, or have been interpolated by
another hand. But it must remain a matter of doubt
whether the poem has reached us substantially as it was
left by the author, or whether the present arrangement
of the materials is partially due to one of the Ciceros,
or to some other editor.

The poem, however, though incomplete in regard to
the arrangement of its materials, presents a full and
clear view of the philosophy which satisfied the mind of
Lucretius. What, then, is the interest and value of the
work, considered as a great argument, in which the
plan of nature is explained, and the position of man
in relation to that plan is determined? Is it true, as
an eminent modern critic[1] has said, that 'the greatest
didactic poem in any language was written in defence
of the silliest and meanest of all systems of natural and
moral philosophy?' Is this work a mere maze of in-
geniously woven error, enriched with a few brilliant
colours which have not yet faded with the lapse of time;
or is it a true monument of the ancient mind, marking
indeed its limitations, but at the same time perpetuating
the memory of its native strength and greatness? Has
all the meaning of this controversy between science in
its infancy and the pagan mythology in its decrepitude
passed away, as from the vantage-ground of nineteen

[1] Macanley.

Q

centuries the blindness and the ignorance of both com-
batants are apparent? Or, may we not rather discern
that amid all the confusion of this dim νυκτομαχία a
great cause was at issue; that truths the most vital to
human wellbeing were involved on both sides; and that
the strife was one which called out high energies both
of heart and mind?

The system expounded by Lucretius exhibits both the
weakness and the greatness of ancient physical philosophy. That philosophy was false or inadequate in its
aim, method, and results. Its greatness consisted in the
stimulus and discipline which it gave to the faculties
of the mind, and in the speculative ideas which it embraced. All the ancient systems of physics were one-
sided, built on mere assumption, and, owing to their
defective methods of inquiry, incapable of giving a certain
explanation of any single phenomenon. They were radi-
cally at fault in the problem which they proposed to solve.
They endeavoured to explain, by some simple hypothesis, all physical, all moral, all divine existence. This
explanation was supposed to be within the reach of the
intuitive sagacity of the mind, acting upon the obvious
sensible appearances of things. The knowledge of the
whole was supposed to precede the knowledge of the
parts. There was no notion of applying experiment
in aid of natural observation, or of advancing slowly
from one set of established facts to another. The atomic
system proposed to itself the same ambitious problem
as the other systems—those, for instance, of Heraclitus,
of Empedocles, and of Anaxagoras, which are condemned
by Lucretius—and with as inadequate resources for solv-
ing it. The original hypothesis of the atoms and the
void, is a happy guess, suggested by a few superficial
analogies, and supported by many arbitrary assumptions.
A vast number and variety of physical facts, observed
with great clearness, vivacity, and accuracy, are ad-

duced as proofs and illustrations of the argument, but
there is no real attempt to verify the connexion between the facts adduced and their supposed causes.
Lucretius seems to have no feeling of the inadequacy
of deductive processes, founded on arbitrary conceptions
of the understanding, to explain the complex and obscure phenomena of nature. The falsest conclusions are
thus asserted with dogmatic certainty. Nor did any of
the ancient inquirers into nature seem to be aware of
how little was really known by them, as compared with
the vast region of which they were ignorant.

It might be said, generally, that the argument of
Lucretius was an attempt to give a philosophical description of nature before the advent of physical science.
But as a means of throwing light on the inadequacy of
such speculations, it may be well to consider in detail
some of those points where the argument most obviously
fails in premises, method, and results.

The ancient as well as the modern inquirer was met
at starting with this question, On what faculty or faculties is the foundation of our knowledge built? Is knowledge obtained originally through the exercise of the
reason or the senses, or through their combined and in-
separable action? To this question Lucretius distinctly
answers, that the senses are the foundation of all our
knowledge.[1] They are our 'prima fides;' the basis not
only of all sound inference, but of all human conduct.
The very conception of the meaning of true and false is
derived from the senses :—

> Invenies primis ab sensibus esse creatam
> Notitiem veri neque sensus posse refelli.[2]

One of his strongest objections to Heraclitus is thus
expressed—

[1] E.g. t. 694.
[2] 'You will find that the notion of what is true arises primarily from
the senses, and that the senses cannot be rebutted.'— IV. 478-9.

Nam contra sensus ab sensibus ipsa repugnat
Et labefactat eos, unde omnia credita pendent.[1]

Yet the data of his own philosophy are not ascertainable through this original source of all our knowledge. The atoms are represented as lying far below the reach of our senses—

Omnis enim longe nostris ab sensibus infra
Primorum natura jacet.[2]

It was thus impossible for Lucretius, on his own principles, to have any certain warrant for their existence, or to determine their original properties of form and consistency, their motion, or their modes of combination with one another. It is not the direct intimations of sense, but only certain superficial analogies from sensible things, which supplied the first principles of this philosophy. The starting-point of Lucretius is really as remote from the certain data of modern science, as the starting-point of the systems of Thales, or Heraclitus, or Anaxagoras. Their clear and vivid observation supplied these inquirers with a great accumulation of facts; but they had not the means of ascertaining the whole nature of their facts. Their minds were active in the formation of hypotheses, but they were unable to establish a true connexion between the facts and the hypotheses. The doctrine of the primordial atoms, and of their motions and combinations, is a creation of the imagination, first suggested by the analogy of sensible things, as, for instance, the motes in the sunbeam, and completed by arbitrary assumptions (e.g., ii. 216, etc.), by à priori reasoning from ideas (as the conception of body, vacuum, the infinite, etc.), and by a kind of spurious induction, i.e., by attributing the properties of many known phenomena to those unknown and imaginary

[1] 'For, starting from the intimations of sense, he himself contradicts the sense, and thus undermines the very foundations of all belief.'—i. 693-4.
[2] 'For the whole nature of these first elements lies far below the reach of our senses.'—ii. 312-13.

existences which are conceived to be analogous to them.
What Lucretius says about other systems applies with
equal truth to his own—

> Quamquam multa bene ac divinitus invenientes
> .   .   .   .
> Principiis tamen in rerum fecere ruinas
> Et graviter magni magno cecidere ibi casu.[1]

The first principles of this philosophy are thus seen to
be either *à priori* assumptions, or immediate inferences
from outward appearance. But even on the supposition
that the existence and properties of the atoms had been
satisfactorily established, they are entirely inadequate as
an explanation of the facts of creation. The same difficulty is encountered at the outset of this as of all other
ancient systems of ontology, viz., how to pass from the
abstract to the concrete,—from the eternal forms of the
atoms to the variety and transitory nature of sensible
objects. This is the very difficulty which Lucretius
himself urges against the system of Heraclitus,—

> Nam cur tam variae res possint esse requiro,
> Ex uno si sunt igni puroque creatae.[2]

The order of nature now subsisting is declared to be the
result of the manifold combination of the atoms through
infinite time and space, but the intermediate steps by
which this process was effected are conceived only in the
most vague and shadowy way. The question still remains how the mere varieties in form and size of atoms
devoid of life, colour, sense, etc., can by any combination
produce one single object in nature, much more the perfect order and manifold life of our system. There is no
power of passing over this wide chasm by the help of
the atoms of Democritus, any more than by the watery

---

[1] ' Although discovering many things well and by divine inspiration . . .
yet in their very first principles they have suffered overthrow, and, mighty as
they are, have fallen heavily there with a mighty fall.'— i. 736-41.

[2] ' For I ask how there can ever be such variety in the world if all things
are produced from the single and pure element of fire?'   i. 645-6.

element of Thales or the fiery element of Heraclitus.
But in Lucretius this difficulty is partially concealed, by
means of a tacit assumption, really inconsistent with the
blind and dead materialism on which his philosophy professes to be based. It is to be observed that while the
Greek word ἄτομα implies merely the notion of individual existences, the words used by Lucretius, ' semina,'
' genitalia corpora,' really indicate a creative capacity in
these existences. In conceiving their power of carrying
on and sustaining the order of nature, his imagination is
thus aided by the analogy of the growth of plants and
living beings. With unconscious inconsistency, he assumes the presence of a secret faculty in the atoms distinct
from their other properties. Thus he says—

> At primordia gigantadis in rebus oportet
> Naturam clandestinam curamque adhibere.[1]

In his statement of the doctrine of the *Clinamen*, or slight
declension in the motion of the atoms, so as ' to break the
chain of fate,' he attributes to them a power analogous to
volition in living beings. It is only on the assumption
of a creative power that any meaning or coherence can
be given to his explanation of the mode in which the
earth and heavens, plants, and all living things, have been
formed out of the concourse of lifeless and senseless
elements.

The hypothesis of the atoms is thus seen to be, in the
first place, a mere guess, and, in the second place, a
guess which explains little or nothing. It cannot be
shown either how they succeeded in arranging themselves in order, or how from their negative properties
all positive life has been produced. The physical doctrines expressed in the four last books, as to the nature
of our bodies and souls,—as to the senses,—the origin
and existence of the sun, moon, the earth and the living

[1] ' But it is necessary that the atoms, in the act of creation, should exercise
some secret, invisible faculty.'—t. 778 9.

beings upon it, etc., although professedly deduced from the principles established in the first two books are really reached independently. They are either immediate inferences from the obvious intimations of sense, or they are the suggestions of analogy.

The weakness as well as the power of ancient science lay in its perception of analogies. The eager and far-reaching eye of early inquiry was quick to mark ' those same footsteps of nature treading on diverse subjects or matter,' but trusted too implicitly to their guidance, and to its own keen intuition in following them. The mind of Lucretius was obviously under the influence of many of the old analogical modes of reasoning, and he also shows great boldness and originality in the novel application of analogy. He is most happy in applying this form of thought to illustrate the details of his subject ; and his use of poetical analogies implies a force and penetration of imaginative insight unsurpassed by any ancient writer. But, in common with the earlier inquirers of Greece, he trusts too implicitly to this ' lux sublustris' to guide him through all his daring adventure. He seems to believe that the properties of invisible things were as clearly revealed in this uncertain light as if they had been laid bare by the ' lucida tela diei.' —

To take one prominent point, it is remarkable how, in his explanation of our mundane system, he is both consciously and unconsciously guided by the analogy of the human body. In Lucretius even, as well as in Empedocles, it may be seen how difficult it was for ancient physical philosophy to escape from the conceptions of mythology. Lucretius is indeed conscious of the inconsistency of attributing life and sense to the earth ; yet not only does he speak poetically of Earth being the creative mother, Æther the fructifying father of all things, but his whole conception of creation is derived from a supposed likeness between the properties of our terrestrial and celestial systems, and those of living beings. Thus we read—

> Undique quandoquidem per canlas ætheris omnis
> Et quasi per magni circam spiracula mundi
> Exitus intraituaque elementis redditus extat.[1]

Of the growth of plants and herbage it is said—

> Ut plama atque pili primam setæque creantur
> Quadrijiedum membris et corpore pennipotentum,
> Sic nova tum tellus herbas virgultaque primum
> Sustulit, inde loci mortalia æcla creavit.[2]

From v. 535 to 563 the power of the air in supporting the earth 'in media mundi regione' is compared with the power which the delicate vital principle has in supporting the human body.

Again, the gathering together of the waters of the sea is thus represented—

> Tam magis expressens minus de corpore sudor
> Augebat mare manaado camposque natantia.[3]

And finally, though it would be easy to multiply such quotations, the striking account, at the end of the second book, of the growth and the decay of our world is drawn directly from the obvious appearances of the growth and decay of the human body ; e.g.—

> Quoniam nec venæ perpetiuntur
> Quod satis est neque quantum opus est natura ministrat.[4]

As a necessary result of a system of natural philosophy based on imaginary assumptions, largely illustrated, indeed, but not corroborated by the observation

[1] 'Since on all sides, through all the pores of the Æther, and, as it were, all round through the breathing - places of the mighty world, a free exit and entrance is given to the atoms.'—VI. 492-4.

[2] 'As feathers, and hair, and bristles are first formed on the limbs of beasts and the bodies of birds, so the young earth then first bore herbs and plants, afterwards gave birth to the generations of living things.'—v. 788-91.

[3] 'So more and more, the sweat oozing from the salt body, increased the sea and the moving watery plains by its flow.'—v. 487-8.

[4] 'Since neither its veins can support adequate nourishment, nor does Nature supply what is needful.'—II. 1141-2.

of phenomena, with no verification of experiment or ascertainment of special laws, there is throughout the poem the utmost hardihood of assertion and inference on many points, in which modern science clearly proves this system to have been as much in error as it was possible to be. It is strange to note how little idea Lucretius had of the vastness and complexity of the problem which he professed to solve. He has no real conception of the progressive advance of knowledge, and of the necessity of patiently building on humble foundations. The striking lines—

> Namque alid ex alio clarescet nec tibi caeca
> Nox iter eripiet quin ultima naturai
> Pervideas : ita res accendent lumina rebus.[1]

look rather like an unconscious prophecy of the future progress of knowledge than an account of the process of inquiry exhibited in the book.

A few out of many dogmatic assertions about physical facts beyond the knowledge of that time, and some probably altogether beyond human knowledge, may be noticed. Thus, at i. 1052, the existence of the Antipodes is denied. Again, in book iii. the mind is stated to be a material substance, seated in the centre of the breast, composed of very minute particles, the relative proportions of which determine the characters both of men and animals. Lucretius shows a very close and subtle observation of the interdependence of mind and body, but no suspicion of that interdependence being in any way connected with the functions of the brain. His whole account of the *mundus*, of the earth at rest in the centre, and of the rolling vault of heaven, with its sun and moon and stars—'trembling fires in the vault'— all no larger than they appear to our eyes, is given

---

[1] 'For one thing will grow clear after another : nor shall the darkness of night make thee lose thy way, before thou seest, to the full, the furthest secrets of nature ; so shall all things throw light one on the other.'—i. 1115-7.

without any notion of the inadequacy of his data
to bear out his conclusions. While enlarging on the
variety and subtlety in the combinations of his imaginary atoms, he appears to have no idea of the variety
and subtlety in the real forces of nature. His observation of the outward and visible appearances of things
is accurate and careful : there is often great ingenuity
as well as a true apprehension of logical conditions in
his processes of reasoning both from ideas and from
phenomena ; yet most of his conclusions as to the facts
of nature, which are not immediately perceptible to the
senses, are mere fanciful explanations, indicating, indeed, a lively curiosity, but no real understanding of
the true conditions of the inquiry. The root of his
error lies in his not feeling how little can be known
of the processes and facts of nature by ordinary observation, without the resources of experiment and of
scientific method built upon experiment.

The weak points of this philosophy, the mistaken aim
and incomplete method of inquiry, the real ignorance of
facts disguised under an appearance of systematic treatment, the unproductiveness of the results for any practical accession to man's power over nature, are quite
obvious to any modern reader, who, without any special
study of physical science, cannot help being familiar
with information now universally diffused, and yet beyond the reach of the most ardent inquirers and original
thinkers of antiquity. But the amount of information
possessed by different ages, or by different men, is no
criterion of their relative intellectual power. The men
tal force of a great and adventurous thinker may be
recognised struggling through these mists of error. The
weakness of this system, interpreted by Lucretius, is
the necessary weakness of the childhood of knowledge.
But along with the weakness and the ignorance there
are also the strong feeling, the clear eye, and the buoy-

aut fancies of early years,—the germs and the promise
of a strong maturity.

The full light in which ancient poetry, politics, and
mental philosophy are read, makes us apt to forget that
a great part even of the intellectual life of antiquity is
only revealed to us in uncertain twilight or in rare
gleams of sunshine. In no other ancient writer is this
light so full and clear as in Lucretius. If for nothing
else his poem would thus be valuable as a witness to the
ardent and disinterested curiosity, felt long ago, to penetrate the secrets of nature, and as affording examples of
the clear, varied, and minute power of observation which
ministered to this curiosity. The Greek masters, whom
he followed, are preserved only in fragments. It is
something to realise, by the light of this poem, the impression which they produced on the mind of one who
tried to follow in their footsteps. The genius of Plato
and Aristotle may be estimated, perhaps, as justly in
modern as in ancient times. But the great intellectual
life of Democritus, Empedocles, or Anaxagoras, escapes
our notice in the more familiar studies of classical literature. The work of Lucretius is especially valuable on
this ground, that we are reminded in it of the amount
of thought and feeling that was lavished upon the earliest inquiries into nature. In some respects the general ignorance of the times enhances our sense of the
greatness of individual philosophers. Each new attempt
to understand the world was an original act of creative
power. The intellectual strength of the poet himself
must also be taken into account as some measure of
the strength of his masters, whose opinions he adopted,
and who filled his mind with affection and astonishment.

The history of the physical science of the ancients is
not indeed so interesting or important as that of their
metaphysical philosophy. And this is so, not only on
account of the comparative scantiness of their real ac-

quisitions in the one as compared with the great ideas
which they have contributed to the other, and with the
masterpieces which they have added to its literature ; but
still more on this account, that in physical knowledge new
discovery supplants the place of previous error or ignorance, and can be understood without reference to what
has been supplanted : whereas the power and meaning of
philosophical ideas are unintelligible, apart from the knowledge of their origin and development. The history of
physical science in ancient times affords satisfaction to
a natural curiosity, but is not an indispensable branch
of scientific study. The history of ancient mental philosophy, on the other hand,—the source not only of most
of our metaphysical ideas and terms, but of many of
the most familiar thoughts and words in daily use,—is
the basis of our highest speculation. Yet among the
various kinds of interest which this poem has for different classes of modern readers this is not to be forgotten, that it enables a student of science to estimate
the actual discoveries, and, still more, the prognostica-
tions of discovery attained by the irregular methods of
early inquiry. It is interesting, while contemplating
the rich, well-defined, and highly-cultivated region of
modern science, to mark the few and scattered points
occupied by the first wanderers in search of knowledge.
The school of philosophy to which Lucretius belonged
was distinguished above other schools for the attention
which it gave to the facts of nature. If he was not himself an original inquirer, as indeed he does not claim to
be, he yet shows a philosophical comprehension of the
whole system which he adopted, and a rigorous study of
its details. He does not, like Virgil, merely reproduce
some general aspects or results of ancient physics, which
enhance the poetical conception of nature : as he is not
satisfied with those general results about human life and
the origin of man, which amused a meditative poet and

practical epicurean like Horace. He was a real student both of nature and of man, not a mere poet, casting the interesting results of thought into graceful language. Out of the stores of his abundant information the modern student may best learn not only the errors but also the happy guesses and pregnant suggestions of ancient science. Thus, for instance, the doctrines concerning the elemental atoms and their censeless motion, explained in the first two books, and of the 'simulacra,' or images reflected from all objects, in the fourth book, although in themselves arbitrary assumptions, and fancifully and erroneously applied to the explanation of phenomena, yet have a real relation to the more substantial theories of modern times, and imply some finer and subtler gift than even the clear and vivid observation which belonged to the ancient mind.

To the general reader there is another aspect, in which it is interesting to compare these germs of physical knowledge with some tendencies of scientific inquiry in modern times. The questions, vitally affecting the position of man in the world, which are discussed or suggested by Lucretius in the course of his argument, are parallel to certain questions which have risen into prominence in connexion with the increasing study of nature. Most conspicuous among these is the relation of physical inquiry to religious belief. Objections were urged against such inquiry in ancient times, on the ground of its impiety and unbelief, as we gather from such passages as this—

Impia te rationis inire elementa viamque
Indugredi scelcris.[1]

Just as there are found in modern times those who reprobate the insufficiency and audacity of human reason,

so there were, in the time of Lucretius, those who de-
nounced the inquirers into natural phenomena, as—

Immortalia mortali sermone notantes.[1]

The views of Lucretius as to the natural origin of life,
and the progressive advance of man from the rudest condition, by the exercise of his senses and accumulated experience,—his denial of final causes universally, and spe-
cially in the human faculties,—his resolution of all our
knowledge into the intimations of sense,—his materialism
and consequent denial of immortality,—and his utilita-
rianism in morals,—all present striking parallels to the
opinions of one of the great schools of modern thought.
At Book v. 875, there is a passage concerning the preservation and destruction of species, which looks like
a faint poetical anticipation of a theory which has attracted much notice in the present day.   It is there
observed that those species alone have escaped destruction which possess some natural weapon of defence, or
which are useful to man.   Of other species that could
neither live by themselves nor were maintained by
human protection, it is said—

Scilicet haec aliis praedae lucrumque jacebant
Indepedita suis fatalibus omnia vinclis,
Donec ad interitum genus id natura redegit.[2]

It would be more unjust to compare ancient and modern
religion than even ancient and modern science.   Yet it
is not uninteresting or useless to observe certain tendencies that are brought to light in modern controversy,
already anticipated under totally different conditions.
More tolerance may perhaps be felt for the denial of
Lucretius, in an age when a corrupt and decaying superstition, with its unworthy views of the nature of God
and man, was opposed to the intimations of natural

[1] 'Dishonouring immortal things by mortal words.'—v. 121.
[2] 'They, doubtless, became the prey and the gain of others, unable to
break through the bonds of fate by which they were confined, until Nature
caused that species to disappear.'—v. 875-7.

reason and a true sense of human dignity, than for the
dogmatism of extreme partisans in the present day,
who, from a spirit of irreverence or a spirit of un-
truthfulness, still endeavour to make the apparent
divergence between true religion and true science irreconcilable.

But altogether apart from the truth and falsehood,
the right and wrong tendencies of this system of philosophy, a genuine source of interest is found in tracing
the power of reasoning, observation, and expression put
forth by the poet through the whole course of his argument. The pervading characteristic of Lucretius is the
'vivida vis animi.' Power, energy, vividness are stamped
on every line of his work. The words which he applies
to himself—

Mente vigenti
Avia Pieridum peragro loca.

truly characterise him. This freshness and force are the
qualities of his understanding, and of his whole nature, as
much as of his poetic faculty. There is the same intensity of belief and eagerness to produce conviction in the
enunciation of his physical as of his moral doctrines.
He shows a strength of passion and energy of conception
in treating of the laws and phenomena of nature, different
indeed in kind from his feeling and imagination as a poet,
but not less powerful in intensity. Though there may be
some unconscious inconsistency in the development of his
argument, and though he may, as was natural, have failed
in adequately conceiving the transition from the fortuitous
concourse of lifeless atoms to the exuberant life and
perfect order of the world, yet he has a strong command
over his whole subject. He shows the capacity of unfolding it, and marshalling all his arguments in sym-
metrical order, and of arranging in due subordination
vast masses of details. Fulness and richness of mind,
implying vigour in acquiring and in retaining the know-

ledge of facts, are combined with the highest organising faculty of the understanding. He shows also, beyond any other Roman writer, a power of analysing and understanding abstract ideas, such as that of the infinite, of space and time, of causation and the like, and of keeping the consequences involved in these ideas present to his mind through long-sustained processes of reasoning. He alone among his countrymen possessed, if not the faculty of original speculation, the genuine philosophic impulse, and the powers of reason demanded for abstruse and systematic thinking.

This vigour of understanding is displayed in many processes of reasoning, in the analogies by which the argument is illustrated and elucidated, in the clearness and variety of his observation of natural phenomena, and in the cogency and distinctness of his language. While his argument absolutely fails as a whole, there is much sound and ingenious reasoning in the parts. The reasoning in the first book, for example (Book i. 298-328), in which the existence of invisible bodies is established, shows his faculty of seeing a common principle involved in a great number and variety of phenomena. The argument also at i. 338-397, where he establishes the existence of vacuum, and that also in which he shows the infinity of space, imply the higher power of following abstract ideas into the consequences involved in them. He confutes his adversaries both by reference to his own first principles, and also by appeal to the evidence of facts. It is characteristic of a follower of Epicurus, that he neither enunciates nor employs any regular logic. His system is neither purely deductive nor purely inductive ; but he displays very vigorous faculties of reasoning, both from facts to other facts and to general principles, and from general principles to their consequences. It is the absence of experiment and the insufficiency of his scientific method, not any natural

defect in reasoning power, which give rise to his erro-
neous results.

The vigour of his reasoning faculty may be judged
most fairly by his arguments on the progress of society,
in Book v., where he is more on an equality with modern
speculation. It is characteristic of his positive tendencies that he discards altogether the fancies concerning a
heroic or a golden age, and assumes as his data the facts
of human nature as observed in his own day. The
grounds from which he starts, his method of reasoning, and the nature of his conclusions, remind a
reader more of Thucydides, in the introduction to his
history, than of any other ancient writer. The importance of personal qualities, such as beauty, strength, and
powers of mind, in the earliest stage of civil society, the
influence of accumulated wealth at a later period, the
causes of the establishment and overthrow of tyrannies,
and of the rise of commonwealths in their room, are all
set forth with a degree of strong sense and historical
sagacity, which few ancient writers, with the exception
of the great Greek historian, have exhibited. He is
as unlike Thucydides as possible in his indifference to
the actual events of his time ; but he is more like him
than any other Roman writer in his apprehension of the
philosophy of history. On such topics, where the data
were accessible to the natural faculties of observation
and inference, and where conclusions were sought which,
without aiming at definite accuracy, should yet be true
in the main, the reader of Lucretius has no sense of that
wasted ingenuity which he often feels in following the
investigations into the primary conditions of the atoms,
the component elements of the soul, the process by which
the world was formed, or the causes of electric or vol-
canic phenomena.

Lucretius makes a copious, and often a very happy use,
of analogies, both in the illustration of his philosophy,

R

and in passages of the highest poetical power. Some of the
most striking of the former kind have already been noticed
as sources of error, or at least of disguising ignorance, in his
reasoning, viz., those founded on the supposed parallel
between the world and the human body ; others again
are employed with great force and ingenuity in support
of various positions in his argument. Among these may
be mentioned his comparison of the effect of various
combinations of the same letters in forming different
words, with that of the various combinations of similar
atoms forming different objects in nature. There is
something striking in the analogy of the human body
immediately after death to wine 'cum Bacchi flos evanu-
uit,' and again, in that of the relation of body and soul
to the relation of frankincense and its odour- -

> E thuris glæbis evellere odorem
> Haud facile est quin intereat natura quoque ejus.[1]

Many other instances might be given of his power and
originality of mind in seeing resemblances between remote and seemingly unconnected objects ; but it is not
perhaps easy to illustrate this faculty of understanding
in him as distinct from his poetical imagination and
feeling.

So also it is difficult to separate his faculty of clear,
accurate, and vivid observation from his poetical interpretation of the life and beauty of nature. His powers
of observation were, however, stimulated and directed by
scientific as well as poetic interest in phenomena. From
the wide scope of his philosophy he was led to examine
the greatest variety of facts, physical as well as moral.
His sense of the immensity of the universe led him to
contemplate the largest and widest operations of nature,
—such as the movements of the heavenly bodies, the re-
currence of the seasons, the forces of great storms, volcanoes, etc. ; while, again, the theory of the invisible

[1] III. 327 8.

atoms drew his attention to the minutest processes of
nature, in so far as they can be perceived or inferred
without the appliances of modern science. Thus, for
instance, in a long passage beginning—

Denique fluctifrago suspensa in litore vestes,[1]

he shows by an accumulation of instances that there are
many invisible bodies, the existence of which is inferred
from visible effects. Again, at Book v. 247, etc., he
notices the insensible diminution of bodies : the facts
of rivers slowly wearing away their banks,—of walls
on the sea-shore mouldering from the long-continued
effects of the exhalations from the sea,—the gradual
decay of towers, temples, images of the gods, and
the like.

In describing the ordinary appearances of outward
nature, he comes nearer to the truth and clearness of
Homer than any ancient writer. There is indeed a
peculiar charm in Homer's descriptions, from their constant suggestion of activity or personal adventure in
the open air ; while Lucretius makes himself known to
us solely or chiefly as the contemplative observer of the
forms and changes of outward things. In some respects
he appears at an advantage, even as compared with
Homer. His sense of the ordinary aspects of things is
wonderfully enlarged by his perception of their connexion with the whole power and meaning of nature.
He possessed the distinctness and accuracy of a scientific
observer, as well as the deep insight of a poetical interpreter of nature.

Again, the argument is frequently illustrated by observation of the habits of various animals. Lucretius shows
the tastes of a naturalist, as well as of a poet in these
passages. He sketches the outward appearance and
habits of birds and beasts, and also seems to enter into
their inner nature by a kind of poetical sympathy. How

[1] i. 305.

graphic, for instance, is his description of dogs following
up the scent of their game—

> Errant saepe canes itaque et vestigia quaerunt.[1]

How happily their characteristics are struck off in the
line—

> At levisomna canum fido cum pectore corda.[2]

The various cries and habits of birds are often observed
and described, as—

> Et validis cycni torrentibus ex Heliconis
> Cum liquidam tollunt lugubri voce querellam;[3]

and again—

> Parvus ut est cycni melior canor ille gruum quam
> Clamor in aetheriis dispersus nubibus austri.[4]

The description of the sea-birds,

> Mergique marinis
> Fluctibus in salso victum vitamque petentes,[5]

recalls the vivid and natural life of those that haunted
the isle of Calypso—

> τανύγλωσσοί τε κορῶναι
> εἰνάλιαι, τῇσίν τε θαλάσσια ἔργα μέμηλεν.[6]

His lively personal observation and active interest in the
casual objects presented to his eyes in the course of his
walks, are seen in such passages as—

> Cum lubrica serpens
> Exuit in spinis vestem; nam saepe videmus
> Illorum spoliis vepres volitantibus auctas.[7]

There is also great truth and liveliness of observation
in his notices of psychological and physiological facts;

[1] iv. 705.

[2] 'Dogs, lightly sleeping, with faithful heart.'—v. 864.

[3] 'When from the strong torrents of Helicon the swans raise their liquid
wailing with doleful voice.'—iv. 547-8.

[4] 'As the low note of the swan is sweeter than the cry of the cranes,
far-scattered among the south-wind's skiey clouds.'—iv. 181-2.

[5] 'And gulls among the sea-waves, seeking their food and pastime in the
brine.'—v. 1079-80.

[6] Od. vi. 66.

[7] 'And likewise, when the lithe serpent casts its skin among the thorns;
for often we notice the briers, with their light airy spoils, hanging to them.'—
iv. 60-2.

as in those passages where he establishes the connexion
between mind and body, and in his account of the senses.
With what a graphic touch does he point the outward
effects of death,[1] the decay of the faculties with age, and
the madness that overtakes the mind—

> Adde furorem animi proprium atque oblivia rerum,
> Adde quod in nigras lethargi mergitur undas ;[2]

the bodily waste, produced by long-continuous speaking—

> Perpetuus sermo nigrai noctis ad umbram
> Aurorae perductus ab exoriente nitore ;[3]

the reflex action of the senses, produced by the nervous
strain of witnessing games and spectacles for many
days in succession ; the insensibility to the pain of
the severest wounds in the excitement of battle. The
wide and varied range of facts contained in the poem
does not seem to exhaust his stores of observation. He
professes to furnish only those that are wanted to make
clear the principles he is enunciating. The universality
of his philosophic system directs and gives unity to his
active and many-sided interest in things. The least
and the greatest, the most familiar and the rarest phenomena, all appear to him invested with new life and
wonder, imparted to them both by his poetical sensibility and his scientific curiosity.

The strength of his understanding may be still further
seen in the clearness and consecutiveness of his philosophical style. His complaint of 'the poverty of his
native tongue' is directed against the capacities of the
Latin language for scientific, not for poetical expres-
sion--

---

[1] III. 213-15.

[2] 'Consider, too, the special madness of the mind, and forgetfulness of
things ; consider its sinking into the black waves of lethargy.'— III. 828-9.

[3] 'Unbroken speech prolonged from the first light of dawn till the shadows of the dark night.'— IV. 537-8.

Nunc et Anaxagoræ scrutemur Homœomerian
Quam Grai memorant nec nostra dicere lingua
Concedit nobis patrii sermonis egestas.[1]

That language, which is emphatically the language of
common sense, is ill adapted both for the expression of
abstract ideas and for maintaining a long process of connected argument. Lucretius has occasionally to meet
the first difficulty by the adoption of Græcisms, and
the second by some sacrifice of artistic elegance. Thus
he uses *omne* for τὸ πᾶν (II. 1108), *esse*, again, for τὸ
εἶναι, and the like. He frequently avails himself of the
tmesis of prepositions, in imitation of the Greek usage ;
as, for instance, 'disjectis disque supatis.' There is some
awkwardness and want of variety in the links of his
argument, as in his use of certain connecting particles,
such as the 'etenim,' 'quippe ubi,' 'quod genus,' 'am-
plius hoc,' 'huc accedit,' and the like. Virgil has retained some of the most striking of these connecting
formulæ, such as 'contemplator item ;' but, as was natural in a poem setting forth precepts and not proofs, he
uses them much more sparingly and with happier selec-
tion. As used by Lucretius, they add to our sense of
the vividness of the book, of the constant personal address of the author, and of his ardent polemical tone.
They also keep the framework of the argument more compact and distinct ; but they seem to bring into greater
prominence the artistic mistake of conducting an abstract
discussion in verse. The very merits of the work considered as an argument,—its clearness, fulness, and consecutiveness,— detract somewhat from the pleasure which
a work of art naturally produces. But the style cannot
be too highly praised, in respect both of the logical
power, by which the whole subject is articulated, and

[1] 'Now, too, let us examine the "Homœomeria" of Anaxagoras, as the
Greeks call it, though the poverty of our native speech does not admit of its
being named in our language.'— 1. 830-2.

the bearing of every detail on the general design, is
brought out, and in respect of the clearness and lucidity
of the illustrations. The meaning of Lucretius can never
be mistaken from any ambiguity in his language. There
are difficulties arising from the uncertainty of the text,
difficulties also from our unfamiliarity with his method
and principles, or with the objects he describes, but none
from confusion in his ideas or his reasoning, or from a
vague or trite use of words.

II.—THE SPECULATIVE IDEAS IN LUCRETIUS.

There is, however, a higher side to the philosophy of
Lucretius, from which point of view his abstract doctrines are seen to be in harmony with his deepest convictions on human life and with his most impassioned
poetry. It is in his thorough grasp of great ideas, and
in his application of them to the living world, in its
moral and its natural aspects, that the speculative greatness of Lucretius consists. The substantial truth of
all the ancient philosophies lay in the ideas which they
attempted to express and embody, not in the casual
shapes which successively rose up and assumed form to
represent these ideas. Above the transitory and delu-
sive symbols of contending systems ancient inquirers
attained to certain high eminences of thought, from
which they saw things in a truer and clearer light than
through the logical conclusions of their understanding.
The few adventurous thinkers of antiquity were thus
not only raised immeasurably above the great mass of
their contemporaries, but in many of their general conceptions of nature and of human life they had reached
the higher levels of modern thought. And there came
to them, naturally, that which is so rare and difficult to
modern inquiry, the fresh and poetical sense of surprise
and vivid interest, as at the first discovery of a new

world, which has now, for a long time, been familiar not only in its general outlines, but through many of its most interesting provinces.

1. The philosophy of the poem ultimately rests upon the most certain of all our conceptions, that of universal order or law in nature. The starting-point of the system---

> Nullam rem e nilo gigni divinitus unquam,

is itself an inference from the recognition of this condition. And the validity of the whole argument rests on the assumption of its certainty. This fact of universal order is indeed supposed to result from the eternal immutable properties of the atoms and from the original limitation in their varieties ; but the idea of law is prior to, and the condition of, all the principles enunciated in the first two books, in regard to the nature and properties of matter. In no ancient writer do we find the certainty and universality of law so frequently, so strongly, and so unmistakably expressed as in Lucretius. The superiority of Epicurus is proclaimed on the ground of his having revealed the fixed and certain limitations of all existence—

> Unde refert nobis victor quid possit oriri,
> Quid nequeat, finita potestas denique cuique
> Quanam sit ratione atque alte terminus haerens.[1]

Following on his steps the poet himself professes to teach—

> Quo quaeque creata
> Foedere sint, in eo quam sit durare necessum,
> Nec validae valeant aevi rescindere leges.[2]

In another place he says---

---

[1] ' Whence returning victorious he brings back to us tidings of what may and what may not come into existence : according to what plan, in fine, the power of each thing is determined and the deeply-fixed limit of its being.'— i. 75-7.

[2] ' According to what condition all things have been created, what necessity there is that they abide by it, and how they may not annul the mighty laws of the ages.'—v. 56-8.

Et quid quæque queant per fœdera naturai
Quid porro nequeant, sancitum quandoquidem extat.[1]

All knowledge and speculative confidence are declared
to rest on this truth—

Certum ac dispositumst ubi quicquit crescat et insit.[2]

Superstition is said to be the result of ignorance

Quid queat esse,
Quid nequeat.[3]

It is needless to bring forward further expressions of
that thought which underlies and gives cogency to the
whole argument. The subject of the poem is 'majestas
cognita rerum,'— the discovered majesty or order of the
universe. The cardinal truth which Lucretius proclaimed
was that creation was no result of chance or of a capricious exercise of power, but arose out of certain regular
and orderly processes, dependent upon certain primal conditions, of which no further account can be given. His
idea of these ultimate conditions seems to involve some
unconscious or half-felt inconsistency. But this idea, if
less strictly logical, is broader and more vital than a
belief either in blind chance or in an iron fatalism. A
secret power or force, analogous to volition in man, is
conceived to be inherent in the primal atoms, by means
of which creation is able to break from the chains of
fate into a more free development (II. 254). The *fœdera
naturai* are opposed to the *fœdera fati*. Only on the
assumption of this original force is creation conceived to
be possible. The idea of law in nature, as understood
by Lucretius, is not the same as that of invariable
sequence or concomitance of phenomena. It implies at
least the further idea of power. It leads up necessarily,
although this is not consciously realised by him, to the

---

[1] 'Since it is absolutely decreed, what each thing can and what it cannot
do, by the conditions of nature.'—i. 586.
[2] 'It is fixed and ordered where each thing may grow and exist.'—
iii. 787.
[3] v. 88-9.

wider and higher idea of will. His conviction of the
universality and certainty of law, although antagonistic
to the popular religions of antiquity, is in no way incompatible with the convictions of modern Theism. It is
from an ancient rather than from a modern point of view,
that the ultimate principles of the philosophy of Lucretius can be called atheistic.

The idea of law, moreover, not only supports the whole
fabric of his physical philosophy, but moulds his convictions on human life and imparts to his poetry that
contemplative majesty by which it is pervaded. It is
from this ground that he makes his most powerful assault on the belief in the arbitrary and capricious agency
of the gods. Nature is thus declared to be free—

> Libera continuo dominis privata superbis,[1]

through obedience to the universal order. Man also is
under the same law, and is made free by his knowledge
and acceptance of this condition. A sense of security
is thus gained for human life ; a sense of elevation above
its weakness and passions, and the courage to bear its
inevitable evils.[2] This absolute reliance on law does not
act upon his mind with the depressing influence of
fatalism. Although the fortunes of life and the phases
of individual character are said to be the results of the
infinite combinations of blind atoms, yet man is made
free by knowledge and the use of his reason. Notwithstanding the original constitution of his nature, arising
out of influences over which there is no control, he still
has it in his power to live a life worthy of the gods :—

> Illud in his rebus videor firmare potesse,
> Usque adeo naturarum vestigia linqui
> Parvola, quae nequeat ratio depellere nobis
> Ut nil impediat dignam dis degere vitam.[3]

[1] II. 1091.   [2] VI 32.
[3] 'This, in these circumstances, I think I can establish, that such faint
traces of our native elements are left beyond the powers of our reason to
dispel, that nothing prevents us from leading a life worthy of the gods.'—
III. 319-22.

From these high places of his philosophy,

Edita doctrina sapientum templa serena,[1]

the poet derives not only a sense of certainty in thought
and security in life, but also his wide contemplative
view, and his profound sense of the grandeur and the
majesty of the universe. The idea of absolute universal
law imparts much of its peculiar character to his poetical
feelings, informs his language, and seems to mould even
the very rhythm of his verse. It is this idea which
gives its unity of tone to the whole poem, and which
enables him to apprehend in all the processes of nature
a greater presence than what is suggested by the outward
appearances of things.

2. But a nearer view brings another aspect of the world
into light ; viz., the subtle interdependence of all things
on one another. There is not only fixed order, but there
is also infinite mobility in nature. The sum of all things
remains unchanged, but all individual existences decay
and perish. There is no rest anywhere ; all things are
continually changing and passing into one another ;
decay and renovation form the very life and being of all
things. Nothing is ever lost. 'Nature repairs one
thing from another, and allows of no birth except
through the death of something else': —

Haud igitur penitus pereunt quæcumque videntur,
Quando alid ex alio reficit natura nec ullam
Rem gigni patitur nisi morte adjuta aliena?[2]

As the 'ever-during peace' at the heart of all things is
supposed to result from the eternal and immutable properties of the atoms, this 'endless agitation' arises out of
their unceasing motion through infinite space. There
are two kinds of motion,—the one tending to the renewal,—the other, to the destruction of things as they
now exist. The maintenance of our whole system depends
on the equilibrium of these opposing forces —

[1] ii. 8.   [2] i. 202-4.

> Sic aequo geritur certamine principiorum
> Ex infinito contractam tempore bellum.[1]

The destruction of our system and of all visible things,
—that day on which,

> Sustentata ruet moles et machina mundi,[2]

will come suddenly through the termination of the long-balanced warfare—

> Denique tantopere inter se cum maxima mundi
> Pugnent membra, pio nequaquam concita bello,
> Nonne vides aliquam longi certaminis ollis
> Posse dari finem? vel cum sol et vapor omnis
> Omnibus epotis umoribus exsuperarint;
> Quod facere intendant, neque adhuc conata patrantur.[3]

There is thus seen to be not only absolute order, but also infinite change in the processes of nature. Decay and renovation, death and life, support the existing creation in unceasing harmony. The imagination represents this condition under the impressive symbol of an endless battle, in which now one side now the other gains some position, but neither can become master of the field —

> Nunc hic nunc illic superant vitalia rerum,
> Et superantur item.[4]

This symbol is the poetical form of the old philosophical distinction of αὔξησις and φθορά; it is another form of the ἔρις and φιλία which to the imagination of Empedocles appeared to pervade the universe. The symbol of a constant battle invests the infinite and all-pervading subtlety of nature with the interest and the life of human passion on the grandest and widest sphere of action.

[1] 'So in equal battle, the war of elements that hath been waged from infinite time still is carried on.'—II. 573-4.

[2] 'The mass and fabric of the world, long upheld, shall fall to pieces.'—v. 96.

[3] 'Finally, since the vast members of the world, engaged in no holy warfare, so mightily contend with one another, see'st thou not that some end may be assigned to their long conflict, either when the sun and every male of heat, having drunk up all the moisture, shall have gained the day, which they are ever tending to do, but do not yet accomplish,' etc.—v. 380-5.

[4] II. 573-6.

The greatness of the thought makes each particular
object in nature pregnant with a deeper meaning, imparts a poetic interest to trivial and ordinary phenomena,
and throws an august solemnity around the familiar
aspects of human life. The passage in which this principle is most powerfully announced—

Nunc hic nunc illic superant vitalia rerum,[1]

swells into deeper and grander tones, as the poet is
borne on to declare the real human pathos involved in
this strife of elements. This struggle of life and decay
is no mere war of abstractions; it is the daily and
hourly reality of existence. Birth and death are the fulfilment of this law. 'The old order changeth, yielding
place to new'—

Cedit enim rerum novitate extrusa vetustas,[2]

'New nations wax strong, while the old are waning away ;
the generations of living things are changed within a
brief space, and, like the runners in a race, pass on the
torch of life'—

Augescunt aliæ gentes, aliæ minuuntur,
Inque brevi spatio mutantur sæcla animantum
Et quasi cursores vitai lampada tradunt.[3]

Man also must resign himself to the universal law, and
accept his life not as a thing to be possessed for ever,
but only to be used for a time --

Sic alid ex alio nunquam desistet oriri
Vitaque mancipio nulli datur, omnibus usu.[4]

The contemplation of this law deepens his poetic sense
of the power and wonder of nature, while it adds
solemnity and elevation to his thoughts on human
destiny. Under this law of universal decay and restoration, he sees the rains of heaven lost in the earth, but

---

[1] II. 575.   [2] III. 964.   [3] II. 77-9.
[4] 'So one thing shall never cease being born from another, and life is
given to no man as a possession, to all for use.'- III. 970-1.

passing into new life in the fruits from which all living
things are supported—

> Hinc alitur porro nostrum genus atque ferarum,
> Hinc lætas urbes pueris florere videmus
> Frondiferasque novis avibus canere undique silvas.[1]

Or he sees the waters of a stream lost to outward appearance, but passing again through the earth, and so
returning to their original source—

> Inde super terras fluit agmine dulci
> Qua via secta semel liquido pede detulit undas.[2]

Under the same law, the temples of the gods, even the sun,
the moon, and the earth, which are themselves believed
to be divine, all appear liable to decay. He can call up
before his imagination the sublime and awful vision of
that ' single day,' in which the whole ' mass and fabric '
of our world shall pass away, leaving only void space
and the viewless atoms in their room—

> Tria talia texta
> Una dies dabit exitio, multosque per annos
> Sustentata ruet moles et machina mundi.[3]

3. It is to be observed, also, how vividly Lucretius
realises and how steadfastly he keeps before his mind the
thought of the eternity and infinity of the primordial
atoms and of space. These conceptions support him in
his antagonism to the popular religion, and deepen the
feeling with which he contemplates human life and
nature. Our world of earth, sea, and sky is only one among
infinite other systems. It stands to the universe in
much the same proportion as any single man to the
whole earth—

---

[1] ' Hence, moreover, the race of man and the beasts of the forest are fed ;
hence we see cities glad with the flower of their children, and the leafy
woods on all sides loud with the song of young birds.'—i. 254-6.

[2] ' Thence flows over the earth in a fresh stream, by the channel which
first bore its waters down in their limpid race.'—v. 271-2.

[3] ' These three fabrics one day shall bring to destruction, and the mass
and framework of the world, that hath endured through many years, shall
crumble in ruins.'—v. 94-6.

Et videas cælum summai totius unum
Quam sit parvula pars et quam multesima constet
Nec tota pars, homo terrai quota totius unus.[1]

It is the glory of Epicurus that he first passed beyond the empyrean that bounds our world—

Atque omne immensum peragravit mente animoque.[2]

This immensity of the universe is declared to be incompatible with the constant agency and interference of the gods—

Quis regere immensi summam, quis habere profundi
Indu manu validas potis est moderanter habenas.[3]

In this opposition of Lucretius to the belief in the gods of mythology is really involved a latent sense of the attribute of Omnipotence. This negative idea is, at least, a step in advance towards a higher and truer conception of the attributes of Deity. The infinity and complexity of the universe are incompatible with the limited and divided powers of the gods,—as the natural feelings of human nature are incompatible with the moral qualities attributed to them.

The power of these conceptions is also seen in the poet's deep sense of the littleness of human life. Such pathetic expressions of the shortness and triviality of each man's mortal span, as that,

Degitur hoc ævi quodcunquest,[4]

are called forth by the ever-present thought of the Infinite and the Eternal. But this thought, if associated with a feeling of the pathos of human life, does not pass with Lucretius into cynicism or despair. It rather elevates him and fortifies him to suppress all personal complaint in the presence of ideas so great and awful. His —

[1] 'And that you may see how very small a part one firmament is of the whole sum of things, how small a fraction it is, and not so much in proportion as a single man is to the whole earth.'—VI. 650-2.

[2] 'And traversed the whole boundless region of space, in mind and spirit.' — I. 74.

[3] 'Who can order the infinite mass? who can hold with a guiding hand the mighty reins of immensity?'—II. 1095-6.

[4] II. 16.

imagination expands in contemplating the objects either
of thought or of sight, which produce the impression
of immensity or of vast duration. Thus, as much of
the majesty of his poetry may be connected with his
contemplative sense of law, much of its pervading life
with his sense of the mobility of nature, so the element
of sublimity, which he displays above any other Roman,
and almost above any Greek poet, may be traced to
the influence of the ideas of immensity on his imagination. For the negative notions of infinity in space and
time his imagination substitutes the positive conceptions
of vastness and of long duration, and thus strives to
represent the continued action of the great masses and
forces of nature through all the ages and over the vast
spaces of the universe.

4. Again, it was in the atomic philosophy, that the
thought of 'the individual' first rose into prominence.
The meaning of the word 'atom' is simply 'individual.'
The sense of each separate existence is not merged in
the conception of law or of the immensity of the universe.
The atoms are not only infinite in number, they are
also varied in kind and powerful in solid singleness,—
'solida pollentia simplicitate.' From their variety and
individuality, the variety and individuality in nature
emerge. No two classes and no two single objects are
exactly alike. Between any two of the birds that gladden
the sea-shore, or the river banks, or the woods, there
is some difference in outward appearance—

invenies tamen inter se differre figuris.[1]

Each individual of a flock is different from every other,
and by this difference only can the mother recognise her
offspring. This sense of individuality intensifies the
pathos of many passages in the poem. Through sympathy with the feeling of a single heart, the poet realises
the feeling of all living things,—of dumb animals as well

[1] ii. 346.

as of human creatures. So, too, the distinctness and reality with which his imagination represents single objects, come from an eye trained by his philosophy to see each thing not only as part of the life of nature, but as existing in and for itself.

5. The abstract properties of the atoms, which, at first sight, appear to be arbitrary assumptions, without any relation to actual existence, are thus seen to be deductions from the orderly, ever-changing, vast, and infinitely varied aspect of the world. Law, change, infinity, individuality, are the substantial truths of which the primary doctrines of the atomic philosophy are the shadows. These conceptions, which to the poet's reason and imagination bridge over the gulf between the infinite particles of lifeless matter and the living world, are united, but not merged or lost, in the general conception of Nature. The actual visible result of the original properties, forces, and combinations of these invisible atoms, is this great whole, in which all things live, move, and have their being. The sum of the philosophy of Lucretius is a recognition of the unity, the diversity, the order, and the life of nature. The purpose of the poem is to interpret the meaning and explain the operations of this power in those spheres of action that most directly affect human welfare. The poem might be fancifully regarded as a great epic, the action of which was the defeat of the old 'Principalities and Powers' of superstition by the clear and calm majesty of this newly-discovered principle.

What then is involved in this idea which imparts unity to the philosophical and poetical conceptions in the poem? Something more than the union of the notions of law, interdependence, infinity, and individuality. There is further all that is involved in the idea of an organic whole. But to this whole new attributes are attached, independent of, and ultimately inconsistent

s

with the principles of the atomic philosophy. In emancipating himself from the religious traditions of antiquity, Lucretius did not escape from the power of an idea, rooted not only in all past thought, but in the depths of the human consciousness. It is against the limitations which the imagination of former times attached to the idea of God rather than to the truth of the idea itself that his philosophy is opposed. The higher conception of God was neither consciously accepted nor consciously denied by him. But in his idea of Nature there is implied the idea of a 'concealed omnipotence' pervading the world. As there is in the feeling with which Nature inspires him a truer reverence and piety than in the feelings with which the gods of the ancient Pantheon were regarded, so there is in his denial of the popular faith the latent germ of a higher and more rational belief. To this Nature he attributes not only life but power,—creative power in many passages; a governing power, and even something like an active interference with human affairs, in other places. In many places, too, the imagination endows the great forces of this mysterious power with personal and human qualities. This is done with the license, indeed, of poetry, but yet with an unconscious acknowledgment of some attribute analogous to will, in a power independent of and superior to man. There would be more truth in calling this conception pantheistic than atheistic. But the sense of will, active force, and individual life ever present in the poem comes nearer to an unconscious, half-realised Theism than to the pantheistic conception of Nature and of human life.

The conception of Nature in Lucretius is as much a religious as a speculative and poetical idea. It rises above the old mythological modes of thought, establishes itself as a new principle in their room, but yet is not entirely independent of them. More than any other

ancient writer Lucretius was free from the direct
influences of religious tradition, yet indirectly his
thoughts are shaped by imaginative impressions of the
same nature as gave birth to the old mythologies. He
rejects with his whole heart and understanding, and
explains away the fables concerning the gods and
goddesses of the old Olympian dynasty. To some of
these fables he applies the principles of Euhemerus,
which Ennius had made familiar to his countrymen.
Thus, in the beginning of the fifth book, Ceres, Liber,
and Hercules are spoken of among those human bene
factors with whom Epicurus is compared. Other fables
of mythology are explained as creations of the imagination out of physical phenomena or moral ideas. Thus,
the poetical stories of the music of Pan are traced to
the many echoes heard among lonely mountains. The
stories of the sufferings of Tantalus, the Danaides, and
Sisyphus in hell are resolved into the elemental passions
of our being. Other forms of belief again are traced
back to an older phase of the human mind. The fable
of Phaethon is a symbol of the fact that the power of fire
was at one time more felt and more widely spread ; and
other fables are shown to be the memorials of a time
when the waters overspread the earth. The worship of
Cybele is resolved into the natural sense of the great
productiveness of the earth : her crown of towers is the
symbol of the cities which she supports : the wild beasts
drawing her chariot are symbolical of the civilising in
fluence of parental care on the most savage offspring.
It is to be observed that while his understanding rejects
all those fables, the zeal and indignation of Lucretius are
aroused only by the cruel terrors of mythology. It is
against the tyranny of superstition over natural human
feeling that he rebels. You may speak, he says, of the
sea as Neptunus, of the earth as the Magna Mater, of
the fruits of the earth under the name of Ceres, and the

like, while the mind yet holds clearly that all these
objects are not only not divine, but are altogether devoid of will and feeling.

This license he himself assumes to address the vital
power of Nature under the title of—

> Æneadum genetrix, hominum divomque voluptas,
> Alma Venus.[1]

In his recognition of this power he is still to some extent under the influence of associations derived from the
early mythology. Although he has a stronger grasp of
realities than the early Greek philosophers, who lived
in the twilight between mythology and science, yet he
still interprets the world by analogies and illustrations
founded on a sense of the personality and human attributes of Nature. Thus he speaks of Æther as the fructifying father, of the Earth,. as the great mother of all
created things—

> Denique cælesti sumus omnes semine oriundi ;
> Omnibus ille idem pater est, unde alma liquentis
> Umoris guttas mater cum terra recepit,
> Feta parit nitidas fruges arbustaque læta
> Et genus humanum, parit omnia sæcla ferarum.[2]

His account of the creation and of the support of life in
the earth is taken, as has already been seen, from the
analogy of the human body. In Empedocles, and the
older writers of the kind, the ideas of philosophy and
the fancies of mythology appear still to be identified or
confused in thought. In Lucretius, while there is a
clear logical recognition of the falsehood of the early
fables, yet the old impressions and the fanciful thoughts
and analogies, out of which some of these fables were
originally formed, force themselves back on the mature
convictions of the educated understanding : as, in the

[1] i. 1-2.
[2] 'In fine, we are all born of the seed of heaven : that heaven is the common father of all, from which our bounteous mother earth receives the liquid
drops of rain, and, conceiving, bears fair fruits and luxuriant groves, and the
race of man, and all the generations of wild beasts.'—ii. 991-95.

individual, the first indelible images of scenes familiar
to childhood will recur to the imagination in later
life, and force themselves into the picture which the
mind forms of some ideal or actual scene, which
by a remote association recalls these earliest impressions.

The mysterious power of Nature is most clearly acknowledged in the invocation to the poem, when that
principle is identified with the Goddess of Love, and
the mythical ancestress of the Roman people. The
expression ' rerum natura' is sometimes in the poem
used for the inert matter which elsewhere is called
' rerum summa,' but often also for this power,—the all-
pervading source of life, the creator and sustainer of all
order, beauty, and delight. This power, as the source of
all life in the world, and of all grace and accomplishment
in man, the poet invokes to aid him in his task, and to
give eternal beauty to his words—

> Quo magis æternum da dictis, diva, leporem.[1]

Here, as in the older invocations to the Muse, there is a
recognition of the truth that the feeling, the fancy, and
the words of the poet, come to him, in a way which he
does not understand—

> ἡμεῖς δὲ κλέος οἶον ἀκούομεν, οὐδέ τι ἴδμεν—

and by the gift of a power which he cannot control.
Lucretius among the ancients, as Goethe among the
moderns, identifies his own inspiration with the active
and mysterious energy of nature, from which all life,
beauty, and order, are silently emanating. The thoughts
and feelings of the poet seem to fill his mind, and to
assume form and beauty there, as the vital power of
nature in early spring fills the world with new life and
beauty. The invocation passes into a prayer that the
Goddess may prevail on the God of War to grant peace
over all the world -

Effice ut interea fera moenera militiai
Per maria ac terras omnis sopita quiescant.[1]

If this prayer for peace must be looked on merely as a poetical expression of the heart-felt weariness of war, experienced by a mind which contrasted the alarm and the duties of a time of trouble with the peaceful energies of philosophy, yet the association of Venus with Mars in this passage is something more than poetical ornament. It is a symbolical representation of the philosophical idea of Nature, as creating and sustaining the harmonious process of life, by destruction and dissolution in union with a productive and restoring principle. In this invocation there is a combination of poetical illustration, of symbolical representation, and of sincere conviction. This power, addressed and invoked with so deep a sense of its mystery and reality, is not a mere creation of imitative art, or even a mere philosophical abstraction. There is in this passage at least an acknowledgment of a living power, independent of and superior to man, to whose sway, whether harsh or benignant, man, in common with all other creatures, is subject. In the room of the many phantoms of superstition a new power has arisen, greater and more orderly, if not more beneficent to man, which speaks to him not indeed with the voice of terror, but sometimes in the tones of stern and just reproof—

Denique si vocem rerum natura repente, etc.[2]

This power does not exist to minister to his pleasure or wellbeing. She is the common parent of gods and men and all living things. The gods receive all things at her hands

Omnia suppeditat porro natura neque ulla
Res animi pacem delibat tempore in ullo.[3]

[1] 'Grant meanwhile that the wild work of warfare may sink to sleep through all lands and seas.'—i. 29.
[2] ii. 931.
[3] 'Nature, moreover, provides all things for them, nor does aught impair the peace of their soul through all time.'— iii. 23-4.

And the wants of the lower animals, who do not 'wage a foolish strife with her,' are amply satisfied—

> Quando omnibus omnia large
> Tellus ipsa parit naturaque daedala rerum.[1]

But to man she is the cause both of the good and the evil of his lot ;—of shipwrecks, earthquakes, pestilence, and untimely death, as well as of all beauty and delight. To the imagination of Lucretius, Nature was the task-mistress not the servant of man. He sees her trampling, with secret irony, like the old Nemesis of Greek religious thought, on the pride and pomp of human affairs—

> Usque adeo res humanas vis abdita quaedam
> Opterit et pulchros fascis saevasque secures
> Proculcare ac ludibrio sibi habere videtur.[2]

In presence of her power he feels that the only security for happiness consists in knowing and bowing to her will.

It is this conception of Nature which brings the abstract philosophical system of Lucretius into complete harmony with his poetical feelings and his moral convictions. The poetry of the living world is thus breathed into the 'dry bones' of the atomic system of Democritus. The unity which the mind strains to grasp in contemplating the universe is thus made compatible with the perception of individual life in everything. The sense of the feebleness and the pathos of human life, the conviction of what becomes our dignity and secures our peace, arise from our recognition of the relation in which we stand to this power above and around us. The contemplation of Nature satisfies the imagination of Lucretius by her aspects of power and life, order, immensity, and beauty. But with his poetical emotion there is a deeper feeling interfused. There is through all his poem a pervading solemnity of

---

[1] 'Since to all the earth itself and all-shaping nature bounteously provides all things.' v. 233.

[2] 'So doth some secret power ever trample on human affairs, and appears to tread under foot, and make a mockery of their glorious fasces and cruel axes.'—v. 1231.

tone, as of one awakening to the consciousness of a
great invisible Power in the world. Not only is the
feeling of Lucretius more poetical, but his spirit is far
more religious than that of his master Epicurus. His
language in many places implies a latent sense of a truth
inconsistent with the negative principles of his philosophy. This inconsistency between the doctrines and the
spirit of Lucretius is, to some extent, to be accounted
for by the fact that he often leaves the beaten road of
Epicureanism for the higher but less definite paths over
which the adventurous genius and religious enthusiasm
of Empedocles had borne him. But this inconsistency
may be accounted for on other grounds. Though the
mechanical view of the universe may be accepted by the
understanding, it has never been acquiesced in by the
higher speculative faculty which combines the feeling of
the imagination with the insight of the reason. The
imagination, which recognises the presence of infinite
life and harmony in the world, rises to the recognition
of a creative and governing Power, which it cannot help
endowing with consciousness and will. The acknowledgment of this Power was at least an advance on the
superstition and idolatry of the popular religion. It
enabled the poet to contemplate human life with some
sense of security and elevation, while it imparted a
deeper and more earnest feeling to his enjoyment of
the beauty of the world. His belief is not atheistic
nor pantheistic ; it is not definite enough to be theistic.
It is rather the twilight between an old and a new
faith—

ἦμος δ᾽ οὔτ᾽ ἄρ πω ἠώς, ἔτι δ᾽ ἀμφιλύκη νύξ.

CHAPTER X.

LUCRETIUS does not enforce his moral teaching on the
systematic plan on which his physical philosophy is discussed. His view of human life is sometimes indeed presented as it arises in the regular march of the argument,
but at other times in highly finished digressions, inter-
spersed throughout the work with the view apparently of
breaking its severe monotony. These passages may be
compared to the lyrical odes in a Greek drama. They
afford relief to the strained attention, and constantly
suggest the close and permanent human interest involved in what is apparently special, abstract, and
remote. There is no necessary connexion between
the atomic theory of philosophy, and that view of the
end and objects of life which Lucretius derived from
Epicurus. Epicureanism really started from independent sources, viz., from the later development of the
ethical teaching of Socrates, and from the personal circumstances and disposition of Epicurus. By the ordinary
Epicurean his philosophy was valued chiefly as afford
ing a basis for the denial of the doctrines of Divine
Providence and of the immortality of the soul. But
there is a wide difference between ordinary Epicureanism
and that serious and solemn view of human life which
was first given to the world in the poem of Lucretius.
The power which his speculative philosophy exercised over
his mind was one cause of this difference. Although

there is no necessary connexion between his philoso
phical convictions and his ethical doctrines, yet the
depth and intensity which he imparted to the most one-
sided and the meanest of all moral systems may be, in
some measure at least, traced to the influence which the
partial grandeur of the philosophy of Democritus exercised over his imagination.

Epicureanism, in its original form, was the expression
of a character as unlike as possible to that of Lucretius.
It arose in a state of society and under circumstances
widely different from the social and political condition
of the last stage of the Roman Republic.   It was a doctrine suited to the easy social and literary life which
succeeded to the great political career, the energetic
ambition, and the creative genius which ennobled the
older Athenian life.   It was essentially the philosophy
of the ῥᾷα ζώοντες, who found in refined and equable
pleasure, in friendliness and sociability, a compensation
for the loss of political existence, and of the sacred associations and ideal glories of their ancestral religion.
Human life, while stripped of all its solemnity, mystery,
and high practical interest, was supposed to be understood and realised, and brought under the control of a
comfortable and intelligible philosophy.   Pleasure was
the obvious end of existence ; the highest aim of knowledge was to ascertain the conditions under which most
enjoyment could be secured ; the triumph of the will
was to conform to these conditions.   All violent emotion, all care and anxiety, whatever impaired the capacity of enjoyment or fostered artificial desire, was to be
controlled or resisted, as inimical to the tranquillity of
the soul.   The philosophers of the garden taught and
acted on the practical truth, that pleasure depended on
the mind more than on external things ; that a simple
life tended more to happiness than luxury ; that excess of every kind was recompensed by reaction.

They inculcated political quiescence as well as the abnegation of personal ambition. As death was 'the end of all,' life ought to be temperately enjoyed while it lasted, and resigned, when necessary, with cheerful composure.

Such a philosophy would scarcely be thought capable of having given birth to any form of serious and elevated poetry. Its natural fruit was the refined, cheerful, and witty new comedy of Athens. Yet the genius of Lucretius and of Horace expressed these doctrines in tones of dignity and beauty, which have been denied to more ennobling truths. The philosophy of pleasure has thus made its appeal to the poetical susceptibility of finer natures, as well as to the ordinary temperament of men. It might have been thought also that no philosophy would have been less attractive to the dignity of the nobler type, or to the coarser texture of the common type of Roman character. Yet among the Romans of the last age of the Republic, Epicureanism was a formidable rival to the more congenial system of Stoicism, and was professed by many men of pure character and intellectual tastes. These two systems, although antagonistic in their view and aim, yet had this common adaptation to the Roman character, that they held out a definite plan of life, and laid down rules by which that life might be attained. The strength of will and singleness of aim, characteristic of the Romans, their love of rule and impatience of speculative suspense, inclined and enabled them to embrace the teaching of those schools whose tenets were most definite and most readily applicable to human conduct. To a Greek philosopher the interest of conforming his life to any system arose in a great measure from the freedom and exercise thereby afforded to his intellect. Thus Epicurus, in denying the power of luxury to give happiness, says, 'These are not the things which form the life of pleasure,' — 'ἀλλὰ νήφων λογισμὸς καὶ τὰς αἰτίας ἐξερευνῶν πάσης αἱρέσεως καὶ φυγῆς καὶ τὰς δοξὰς ἐξελαύνων, ἀφ' ὧν πλεῖστος τὰς ψυχὰς καταλαμβάνει θόρυβος.'[1] To a Roman, on the other hand, such a scheme of life was recom mended by the new power which was thus imparted to the will. Greek philosophy has sometimes been reproached as the cause of the corruption of Roman character and the decay of Roman religion. But it would be more true to say that, to the higher natures at least, philosophy supplied the place of the ancient principles of duty, which had perished from other causes. The idea of regulating life by an ideal standard afforded a broader aim and a more humane and liberal sphere of action to that self-control and persistence out of which, in combination with absolute devotion to the State, the ancient Roman virtue had been formed. But still it is true that the principles of Epicureanism were incompatible with some of the conditions, both good and bad, of Roman character. While fostering the gentler feelings and more social tastes, and so softening the primi tive rudeness and austerity, these doctrines discouraged all national and political spirit, and withdrew the energies of the will from outward activity to the regulation of the inner life. The attitude both of Stoicism and Epicureanism was one of resistance on the part of the will to outward influences ;—the one system striving to attain entire independence of circumstances, the other to regulate life in accordance with them, so as to secure the utmost positive enjoyment, and the utmost exemption from pain. The political passions of the last age of the Republic inclined men of thought and literary taste to that philosophy which seemed best fitted to meet and satisfy—

---

[1] 'But the sober exercise of reason, investigating the causes why we choose or avoid anything, and banishing those opinions which cause the greatest trouble in the soul.'

'The longing for confirmed tranquillity
inward and outward.'

But while Epicureanism was a natural refuge from the
passions of a revolutionary era, Stoicism was a fortress
of inward strength to the few who, at the fall of the
Republic, resisted the inevitable tendency of things, and,
in a later age, to those who strove to maintain the feelings of Roman citizens even under the degradation of
the Empire.

The moral doctrines of Epicurus leavened the thoughts
of many who did not profess to have studied or adopted
them systematically. Thus the spirit of Catullus is
epicurean, although his life and poetry were altogether
unreflective. Nor was the profession of Epicureanism
confined to men like Atticus and Lucretius, who stood
aloof from political life. The stoical spirit often manifested by Lucretius has been remarked as a proof of the
inward identity of those apparently opposite systems.[1]
The real affinity between them may also be perceived
in the fact that Cassius, who acted and suffered for the
same cause as the Stoic Cato, was a professed Epicurean.
The profession of that philosophy at Rome must thus
have been consistent with a practical departure from
some of its tenets. Political apathy at least was not
essential to the character of a Roman Epicurean. Lucretius, although animated by an ardent spirit of prosely-
tism, does not desire that Memmius should forget his
duties as a citizen and a statesman. The Roman Epicureans of that age were distinguished rather by their systematic denial of the divine interference in human affairs,
and of the doctrine of a future state, than by an essential
agreement in political opinion or action. The religious
unsettlement of the age assumed in them a more positive
form. They were the Sadducees of Rome, who escaped
from the perplexity as well as from the most elevating

[1] By Mr. Munro, *Journal of Classical and Sacred Philology*, vol. i. p. 22.

influences of life, by moulding their feelings and conduct on the firm conviction, that while man was master of his happiness in this world, he had nothing either to hope or fear hereafter.

It is a strange sign of the moral confusion of that time to find the ethical doctrines of Lucretius emanating from this denial of the highest hopes of mankind. Few writers of antiquity have presented a purer or more solemn idea of human life : no one was more profoundly impressed by the serious import and the mystery of our being. Yet he appears as the consistent and unhesitating advocate of all the tenets of this philosophy, and denies the foundations of religious belief with a zeal more like religious earnestness than the spirit of any other writer of antiquity. Without conscious deviation from the teaching of his master, he reproduces the calm unimpassioned doctrines of Epicurus, in a new type,— earnest, austere, and ennobled ; enforcing them not for the sake of ease or for the love of pleasure, but in the cause of truth and human dignity. Pleasure is indeed recognised by him as the universal law or condition of existence—' dux vitae dia voluptas,'—the great instrument of nature through which all life is created and maintained. But to attain peace and 'a pure heart' is the real object of his teaching. Life, he says, may go on without corn or wine, but not without a pure heart—

> At bene non poterat sine puro pectore vivi.

All that nature craves is that the body should be free from actual pain ; the mind undisturbed by fear and anxiety, should be open to the influence of natural enjoyment—

> Nonne videre
> Nil aliud sibi naturam latrare, nisi ut, cui
> Corpore sejunctus dolor absit, mente fruatur
> Jucundo sensu cura semotu' metuque.[1]

In many places he expresses or implies his indifference

[1] ii. 16-19.

to all the adventitious stimulants to enjoyment. The sole worthy and adequate pleasure is that which Nature herself bestows on a mind free from cares, passions, and violent emotions, from restless discontent and slothful apathy.

Although no new principle or maxim of conduct appears in his teaching, the view of human life presented by Lucretius was really something new in the world. A strong and deep flood of serious thought and feeling was for the first time poured into the shallow channel of Epicureanism. The spirit in which Lucretius contemplated the world was different from that of any other man of antiquity; especially different from that of his master in philosophy. To the one, life was a pleasant scene, to be temperately enjoyed and gracefully quitted at the appointed time; to the other, it was the sad and tragic side of the august spectacle which all nature presented to the contemplative mind. Moderation in enjoyment was the practical lesson of the one; superhuman fortitude and resignation were the demands which the other made of all who wished to live a worthy life.

This difference in the spirit rather than the letter of their philosophy, is to be attributed in some degree to this, that Lucretius was a Roman of the antique type of Ennius, inheriting the natural force and fervour of the older poets, and the brave endurance of the Roman Republic. Partly too, as was said before, the effect of the speculative philosophy which he embraced, was to deepen and strengthen that mood of imaginative contemplation, which he shares, not with any of his countrymen, but with a few great thinkers of every age. It is this power of philosophical thought which distinguishes the teaching of Lucretius from the meditative and practical wisdom which has made Horace the favourite epicurean teacher and companion of modern times. Partly too, this new aspect of Epicureanism in Lucretius, may be attributed to the reaction of his nature from the confusion of the times in which he lived. Although he does not record, and perhaps does not directly refer to any contemporaneous events, yet he shows, in many places, how the general features of his age repelled him. Thus, in the opening of the poem, he betrays his sense of the insecurity of the time, and his weariness with the wars from which his country was then enjoying a short breathing-time. In speaking of the miseries of the savage state of man, he adds as a great compensation of their lot—

> At non multa virum sub signis milia ducta
> Una dies dabat exitio.[1]

While the pomp of armies impressed his imagination, he entertained a deep sense of the inhumanity of war, strange in a Roman of that or of any age. He balances the miseries arising from the excesses and crimes of his own age against those proceeding from the ignorance and the wants of man's earliest condition on the earth.[2] The strife of political ambition, with its anxieties and disappointments, its crimes, and bloodshed, especially repels him—

> Sanguine civili rem conflant divitiasque
> Conduplicant avidi, cædem cæde accumulantes.[3]

Once or twice he seems to preach the doctrine of political quiescence, as if in foreboding of the fate which within a few years overtook the world—

> Ut satius multo jam sit parere quietum
> Quam regere imperio res velle et regna tenere.[4]

It is not indeed possible to learn whether the passions of

---

[1] 'But a single day did not then consign to death many thousands of men ranged under their banners.'—v. 909-1000.

[2] v. 1007-10.

[3] 'By civil bloodshed they amass riches, and greedily double their wealth, by heaping carnage upon carnage.'—III. 71-75.

[4] 'So that it is now much better to acquiesce in submission, than to wish for command over affairs and imperial sway.'—v. 1129-30.

his age first drove him to Epicureanism, or whether
the doctrines of that philosophy, adopted on speculative
grounds, may not rather have led him to regard his age
in the spirit of contemplative isolation, which he has described in the well-known passage—

Suave, mari magno turbantibus æquora ventis, etc.

His philosophy may have been forced on him by experience, or the intimations of experience may have assumed
their form and colour from the nature of his philosophy.
But the impressions from his age did undoubtedly largely
enter into his thoughts and feelings on human life.
Some of the most marked forms of evil against which
he makes war had never been so prominently displayed
in any former time. Yet all these considerations afford
only a partial explanation of the character of his practical
philosophy. There were other Roman Epicureans, contemporary with him and later, and none were in any way
like him. Although his nature was made of the strong
Roman fibre; although his mind had been deeply imbued
with the philosophy of Greece; although, like all great
thinkers, he was not free from the influence of his times;
yet, above all these considerations, this is predominant,
that he was one of the most conspicuously original men
whom Rome produced,—the man who, in strength of
thought and feeling, rose most clearly above the range
of his age and country. Hence it is that he is least of
all to be explained by his relation to other men or to the
circumstances in which he was placed.

The moral teaching of the poem may be described
rather as an active protest against various forms of evil
than as the proclamation of any positive good. The
happiness which the philosophic life promised is described in shadowy outline, like the delineation in
the poem of the calm and passionless existence of the
gods. Epicureanism appears here in antagonism to the
prejudice and ignorance, the weakness and the passions

T

of human nature, rather than in its hold of any positive
good. Hence it is that the tones of Lucretius might in
many places be mistaken for those of a Stoic rather
than an Epicurean. In their resistance to the common
forms of evil these systems were at one. Perhaps, too,
in the positive good at which he aimed, the spirit of
Lucretius was more that of a Stoic than he imagined.
His sense of human dignity was much more powerful
than his regard for human enjoyment. Yet his philosophy enabled him, along with the strength of Stoicism,
to cherish humaner and more genial sympathies with
life. While his earnest temper, his scorn of weakness,
and his superiority to pleasure, were in harmony with
the militant rather than the quiescent attitude of each
of these philosophies, his humanity and tenderness of
feeling, his simplicity and poetry of nature, were more
in harmony with the better side of Epicureanism than
with the rigid and formal teaching of the Porch.

The evils of life, against which Lucretius considers his
philosophy available, appeared to him to spring not out
of man's relation to nature, but out of the weakness and
corruption of his own heart. The great service of Epicurus consisted not only in revealing the laws of nature, but
in laying his finger on the secret cause of man's unhappiness. Observing the insufficiency of all external goods
to bestow peace and contentment, he saw that the evil lay
in the vessel into which these blessings were poured :—

> Intellegit ibi vitium vas efficere ipsum
> Omniaque illius vitio corrumpier intus,
> Quae conlata foris et commoda cumque venirent :
> Partim quod fluxum pertusumque esse videbat,
> Ut nulla posset ratione explerier umquam ;
> Partim quod taetro quasi conspurcare sapore
> Omnia cernebat, quaecumque receperat, intus.[1]

[1] 'Thereupon he perceived that the vessel itself caused the evil, and that
all external gains and blessings were vitiated within through its fault, partly
because he saw that it was so unsound and leaky that it could never be filled
in any way, partly that it tainted inwardly everything which it had received
as it were with a nauseous flavour.'—VI. 17-23.

The most real, and at the same time the most remediable forms of evil are the cowardice which dares not accept the blessings of life, the weakness which repines at what is inevitable, the restless, unsatisfied desires, which cannot enjoy the present, and crave for what is beyond their reach, and, lastly, the apathy and insensibility to natural enjoyment, arising out of luxurious indulgence. Thus the end of his philosophy was to purify the heart from superstition, from the fear of death, from the passions of ambition and of love, from all artificial pleasures and desires.

Of these the great curse of life is superstition. This is what surrounds life with the gloom of death—

> Omnis suffundens mortis nigrore.[1]

All the passions and all the crimes of the world are shown to be dependent on the secret ever-present fear of an arbitrary and cruel power exercised by the gods. The ruling impulse of Lucretius is his hatred of this influence, not as a restraint on natural inclinations, but as a base and intolerable burden, unworthy of gods and men, degrading human life, confounding all genuine feeling, corrupting our conception of what is holiest and most divine. He has expressed, with the whole force of his feeling and genius, the antagonism between the exactions of the popular creed and the most sacred affections of human nature. The pathetic story of the sacrifice of Iphigenia is told to enforce the moral—

> Tantum religio potuit suadere malorum.[2]

The real impiety of this violation of human feeling is contrasted with the imaginary impiety attributed by ignorance and superstition to philosophical inquiry. Every line of the poem is indirectly a protest against the religious errors of antiquity. At occasional intervals this protest is directly uttered, sometimes with indignant irony, at other times with deep, almost religious pathos.

[1] ii. 39.   [2] i. 101.

The former feeling breaks forth, with great power, in the passage at VI. 380, etc., where the poet argues against the fancies which attribute the thunder to the capricious anger of the gods. ' Why is it,' he asks, ' that the bolts pass over the guilty and often strike the innocent ? Why are they idly spent on desert places ? Is this done by the gods merely in the way of practice and exercise for their arms ? Why is it that Jupiter never hurls his bolts in a clear sky ? Does he descend into the clouds in order that he may take a closer aim ? Why does he cast his bolts into the sea ? What charge has he against the waters ?—

> Quid undas
> Arguit et liquidam molem camposque natantis.[1]

Why is it that he often destroys and disfigures his own temples and images ?'

In other passages, however, a feeling is betrayed by Lucretius deeper than scorn,—a feeling which seems to flow out of a true reverence and recognition of what appeared to him most holy and divine in the world. There is no passage in the poem in which he speaks more from the depth of his heart than in the lines—

> O genus infelix humanum, talia divis
> Cum tribuit facta atque iras adjunxit acerbas !
> Quantos tum gemitus ipsi sibi, quantaque nobis
> Volnera, quas lacrimas peperere minoribu' nostris !
> Nec pietas ullast volatum saepe videri
> Vertier ad lapidem atque omnis accedere ad aras
> Nec procumbere humi prostratum et pandere palmas
> Ante deum delubra neu aras sanguine multo
> Spargere quadrupedum nec votis nectere vota,
> Sed mage pacata posse omnia mente tueri.[2]

---

[1] VI. 404-5.

[2] ' O miserable race of man when they imputed to the gods such acts as these, and made them the slaves of angry passion. How great sorrow did they then prepare for themselves, what deep wounds for us, what tears for our descendants. For there is no holiness in being often seen, with head veiled, bowing before a stone, and in drawing nigh to every altar; nor in lying prostrate in the dust, and uplifting the hands before the temples of the gods ; nor in sprinkling altars with the blood of beasts, and in stringing vows to vows, but rather in being able to look at all things with a mind at peace.'—v. 1194-1203.

He denounces the terrors of the popular mythology as a violation of the majesty of the gods, and as the cause of infinite evil to ourselves,—not indeed from the power of any thought or act of ours to rouse the divine anger, but from the effect that these terrors have on our own minds. ' No longer can we approach the temples of the gods with a quiet heart, nor receive into our heart the intimation of the divine nature in peace—'

> Nec delubra deum placido cum pectore adibis,
> Nec de corpore quae sancto simulacra feruntur
> In mentes hominum divino nuntia formae
> Suscipere hae animi tranquilla pace valebis.[1]

This passage and others in the poem imply that Lucretius both believed in the existence of the gods, and conceived their calm influence as filling the mind with solemn awe and peace. But the account which he gives of their eternal existence is vague and poetical, and may almost be regarded as a symbolical expression of what is most holy and divine in man. The highest aim of man is to 'lead a life worthy of the gods:' the essential attribute of the divine life is 'peace.' The gods are said to consist of the finest and purest essence, to be exempt from death, decay, and wasting passions, to be supplied with all things by the liberal bounty of nature, and to dwell for ever in untroubled serenity above the darkness and the storms of our world. Their abode is described in words almost literally translated from the description of the Heaven of the Odyssey—

> Apparet divam numen sedesque quietae
> Quas neque concutiunt venti nec nubila nimbis
> Aspergunt neque nix acri concreta pruina
> Cana cadens violat semperque innubilus aether
> Integit, et large diffuso lumine ridcnt.[2]

[1] vi. 75-78.

[2] ' The presence of the gods becomes visible, and their peaceful dwelling-places, which neither the winds beat upon, nor the clouds bedew with rain ; nor does snow, gathered in flakes by keen frost, and falling white, invade them ; ever the cloudless ether enfolds them, and they are radiant with far-spread light.'   iii. 18-22.

Their being has been revealed by the appearance in dreams and waking visions of images of ampler size and more august aspect than that of our mortal condition. The fears and ignorance of man have invested these unchanging forms with the attributes of creators and lords of the world, and hence there have arisen all over the earth temples and altars, along with the festivals and the solemn rites of superstition. But the gods are neither the arbitrary tyrants nor the beneficent guardians of the world. Why should they have done anything for the benefit of man? How can be add to or detract from their eternal happiness? Shall we suppose them weary of their existence, and infected with a human passion for change?—

> At, credo, in tenebris vita ac mœrore jacebat,
> Donec diluxit rerum genitalis origo.[1]

Whence could they have obtained the idea of creation, whence gathered the secret powers of matter—

> Si non ipsa dedit specimen natura creandi.[2]

He meets the old argument from final causes, by dwelling on the imperfections of the world, such as the waste of nature's resources on vast tracts of mountain and forest, desolate marshes, rocks, and seas,—the enmity to man of other occupants of the earth,—the malign influences of climate and the seasons,—the feebleness of infancy—the devastations of disease,—the untimeliness of early death.[3]

While his belief in the gods is thus expressed in shadowy outline, and poetical symbolism, yet it is clear that he recognised both a mysterious, orderly, and all-pervading power in nature, and also the ideal of a purer and serener life, than that of earthly existence. These were the elements of his unconscious re-

---

[1] 'Forsooth their life lay in gloom and misery, till the creation of the world dawned upon them.'—v. 170-71.
[2] 'Unless Nature herself had given the sample of creation.'—v. 186.
[3] v. 145-223.

ligion ;—an absolute recognition of the omnipotence
and order of nature ;—a vague sense of a diviner life,
with which man might, in this world, have some communion. His denial extended not only to all the fables
and false conceptions of ancient mythology, but to the
doctrine of a Divine Providence recompensing men,
either here or hereafter, according to their actions. The
intensity of his nature perhaps led him to identify all
religion with the cruel or childish fables of the popular
faith. The certainty with which he grasped the truth
of the laws and order of nature, was incompatible with
the only conception he could form of a divine action on
the world. His deep sense of human rights, and deep
sympathy with human feeling, rebelled against a belief
in powers who exercised a capricious tyranny over the
world, and who had to be propitiated by human sacrifice.
His reverence for truth, and for the real power and
mystery of nature, led him to scorn the virtue attributed
to an idolatrous and formal worship. This attitude
of religious isolation, not from his own time only, but
from all the ages, in a man of unusual earnestness and
reverence of feeling, is certainly among the most impressive phenomena of ancient literature. The denial of
Lucretius is not to be judged of in the spirit in which
the denial of a personal God would be judged in modern
times. In elevation of feeling, and in truth of conception, Lucretius, with all his one-sided incompleteness
of view, rises not only above the popular theology,
but, in some way, above all, except the very loftiest
minds of antiquity. As the scepticism of Thucydides
is allied with more truth and justice of thought and
character, and more nobleness of sentiment than the
credulity of Xenophon, so the stern consistency and
desolate grandeur of Lucretius produce the impression
of depth of feeling and reality of conviction, far more
than the pious acquiescence of Virgil in the forms of

his composite theology. It is his intensity of feeling
which chiefly distinguishes the denial of Lucretius from
that of his master Epicurus. The spirit in which he
opposes the faith of centuries is far from resembling the
triumph of a cold philosophy over the religious associations of mankind. His imagination appears to be even
moved to a kind of poetical sympathy with some of the
ceremonies and symbols of Paganism. A deep sense of
religious awe is expressed, for instance, in the lines which
describe the procession of Cybele through the great cities
and nations of the world. His mind, while guarding itself
against the pollution of a base idolatry, yet acknowledges
the power of the truths symbolised in that worship ;
viz., the majesty of nature, and the duties arising from
the elemental affections to parents and country. In
regard to all his religious impressions, the intensity of
his nature and the strength of his poetical imagination,
place him on a solitary height, nearly as far apart from
the followers of his own school as from their adversaries.

The same qualities of heart and mind characterise
that passage of sustained and impassioned feeling, in
which Lucretius encounters the thought of eternal
death. The vast superiority of the Roman poet over the
Greek philosopher in point of human sympathy, is most
strongly brought out by contrasting the cold, unreal
language of the epistle to Menœceus with the fervent and profoundly mournful tones of the third book
of the poem of Lucretius. Epicurus seems to escape
from the fear of death through a placid indifference of
feeling, an easy contentment with the comforts of this
life ; a sense of relief in getting rid of 'the longing for
immortality' (τὸν τῆς ἀθανασίας πόθον). The passionate
heart of Lucretius, on the other hand, realises the full
pathos and solemnity of the thought of eternal death ;
while he preaches acquiescence in the inexorable majesty

of Nature with a stern and steady consistency, and a
proud, desperate fortitude.

The whole of the third book is devoted to this part of
his subject, and the argument of the fourth is to a great
extent supplementary to that of the third book. The
physical doctrine enunciated and illustrated in the first
half of the third book is the materiality of the soul, and
its indissoluble connexion with the body. The practical
consequences of this doctrine are then enforced in a long
passage[1] of more sustained power and solemnity of feeling than perhaps any other in the poem. The poet urges
first the entire unconsciousness in death throughout all
eternity. As it was before we were born, so shall it be
hereafter. As we felt no trouble in the past at the clash
of conflict between Roman and Carthaginian, when all
the world shook with alarm, so nothing can touch us or
move us then—

> Non si terra mari miscebitur et mare cælo.[2]

It is merely the trick of our fancy which suggests the
thought of any kind of suffering after all consciousness
has ceased—

> Nec radicitus e vita se tollit et eicit,
> Sed facit esse sui quiddam super inscius ipse.[3]

Men feel that the sadness of death lies in the separation from wife, and children, and home ; in the extinction which a single day has brought to all the blessings
and the gains of a lifetime. But they forget that along
with these blessings is extinguished all desire and longing for them. Thus, too, men 'spice their fair banquets'
with the thought of death. They say, 'our joy is but
for a season ; it will soon be past, nor ever again be
recalled,'—as if forsooth any feeling or any desire can
haunt that sleep from which there is no awaking—

<hr/>

[1] From 830 till the end.
[2] iii. 842.   [3] iii. 877-8.

Nec quisquam expergitus extat,
Frigida quem semel est vitai pansa scenta.[1]

Nature herself might utter this reproof to all weak complaining : 'Thou fool, if thy life hath given thee joy,
and all its blessings have not been poured into a leaky
vessel, why dost thou not leave the feast like a satisfied
guest, and take thy rest contentedly ? But if all has
hitherto been to thee vanity and vexation of spirit,
why seek to add to thy trouble ? I can devise or frame
no new pleasure for thee. "There is no new thing
under the sun"—eadem sunt omnia semper.' To the
weak complaint of age, Nature would speak with sterner
voice : 'Away hence with thy tears and thy complain-
ings. It is because, unable to enjoy the present, thou
art ever weakly longing for what is absent, that death
has come on thee unsatisfied.' This would be, indeed,
a just charge and reproof. For the old order is ever
yielding place to new ; and life is given to no man in
possession, to all men for use. The time before we were
born is a mirror to us of what the future shall be. Is
there any gloom or horror there ? Is there not a deeper
rest than any sleep ?

The terrors of the unseen world are but the hell
which fools make for themselves out of the passions
of this life.[2] The torments of Tantalus, of Tityus, of
Sisyphus, and the Danaides, are but symbols of the
blind cowardice and superstition, of the craving pas
sions, of the ever-foiled and ever-renewed ambition, of
the thankless discontent with the natural joy and beauty
of the world, which curse and degrade our mortal existence. The stories of Cerberus and the Furies, and
the tortures of the damned, are formed out of the fears
of a guilty conscience and out of the experiences of
earthly punishment.

Other consolations are suggested by the thoughts of

[1] III. 920-30.   •   [2] Hic Acherusia fit stultorum denique vita.

those who have gone before us. Echoing the terrible
irony of Achilles—

> ἀλλά, φίλος, θάνε καὶ σύ· τίη ὀλοφύρεαι οὕτως;
> κάτθανε καὶ Πάτροκλος, ὅπερ σέο πολλὸν ἀμείνων [1]—

he reminds us that better and greater men have died
before us,—kings and soldiers, poets and philosophers,
the mightiest equally with the humblest. In the spirit,
and partly too in the words of Ennius, he recalls the
thought that 'Scipio, the thunderbolt of war, the terror
of Carthage, gave his bones to the earth as if he were
the meanest slave.' Why, then, should one whose life
is half a sleep, the prey of weak fears and restless discontent, complain that he too is subject to the common
law? What is this wretched love of life, which makes
us tremble at every danger? Death cannot be avoided ;
no new pleasure can be forged out by longer living.
This evil of our lot is not inflicted by Nature, but by
our own craving hearts, which cannot enjoy, and are yet
ever thirsting for longer life. [2]

The power of the whole of this passage depends partly
on the vividness of feeling and conception with which
the thought is realised, partly on the august and solemn
associations with which it is surrounded. Such graphic
touches as the following—

> Frigida quem semel est vitai pausa secuta ; [3]
>
> Cum summo gelidi cubat aequore saxi ; [4]
>
> Urgerive superne obtritum pondere terrae, [5]

and again, the life, truth, and tenderness of the picture
presented in the lines—

---

[1] 'But, my friend, die also thou : why art thou thus bewailing thyself ?
Patroclus too died—a far better man than thou.'—*Iliad*, xxi. 106-7.

[2] iii. 830-1094.

[3] 'On whom, once for all, cold obstruction hath fallen.'—iii. 930.

[4] 'When he lieth on the surface of a cold stone.'—iii. 892.

[5] 'To be pressed and crushed down from above by a weight of earth.'—
iii. 893.

Jam jam non domus accipiet te læta, neque uxor
Optima nec dulces occurrent oscula nati
Praeripere et tacita pectus dulcedine tangent,[1]

bring home to the mind, in startling distinctness, the
old familiar contrast between the ' cold obstruction' of
the grave and ' the warm precincts of the cheerful day.'
But the mere horror and pain of the thought of death
are lost in a feeling of august resignation to the universal law. The fact is made present to our minds in
its sternest reality, but yet encompassed with the pomp
and majesty of great memories and associations. It
suggests the thought of the most momentous crisis in
history—

Ad confligendum venientibus undique Poenis ;[2]

of the regal state of kings and emperors—

Inde alii multi reges rerumque potentes
Occiderunt, magnis qui gentibus imperitarunt ;[3]

of the simpler and more real grandeur of great men,
like the ' good Ancus' or Scipio, or Homer, Democritus, and Epicurus ; lastly, of the great law of
nature—

Sic alid ex alio nunquam desistet oriri.[4]

From this conviction, the most depressing of all possible beliefs to human hopes, and the most paralysing to
human endeavours, the poet draws a higher lesson than
the maxim of ' Eat and drink, for to-morrow we die.'
He understands the epicurean precept of ' carpe diem'
in a sense more befitting to human dignity. The lesson
which he learns and teaches is the need of conquering
all weakness, sloth, and irresolution in life. This life is
all that we have through eternity ; let it not be wasted
through folly and ignorance ; let us understand our-

---

[1] 'Soon shall thy happy home and thy true wife no longer welcome thee ;
nor thy dear children run to snatch thy first him, touching thy heart with
silent gladness.'—III. 894-6.
[2] III. 833.   [3] III. 1027-8.
[4] 'No one thing shall never cease to arise out of another.'—III. 970.

selves and our position here, bear and enjoy whatever is allotted to us during our few years of existence. We are masters of ourselves and of our fortunes, so far at least as to rise clearly above the degradation of ignorance and misery.

The practical use of philosophy, according to Lucretius, is, first, to inspire confidence in the room of an ignorant and superstitious fear of the course of nature; and, second, to show what human nature really needs, and so to clear the heart from all artificial desires and passions. A mind free from error, and a heart neither incapable of natural enjoyment (fluxum pertusumque) nor vitiated by false appetite,[1] are the objects which man needs, and which it is in the power of philosophy to bestow. It is knowledge which must enable us to overcome the natural fear of the gods and of death, and also the passions of our own heart. Superstition and the fear of death are the most deeply seated of evils. They infect the whole human race; they are the secret parents of the most destructive modes of passion and desire. The other passions, which had assumed the largest dimensions, and dominated over human happiness in the age of Lucretius, were ambition and the lust of wealth. In the opening lines of the second book, the strife of ambition, the rivalries of rank and intellect, are contrasted with the serene life of philosophy, as darkness, error, and danger with light, certainty, and peace -

Sed nil dulcius est, bene quam munita tenere
Edita doctrina sapientum templa serena,
Despicere unde queas alios passimque videre
Errare atque viam palantis quaerere vitae,
Certare ingenio, contendere nobilitate,
Noctes atque dies niti praestante labore
Ad summas emergere opes rerumque potiri.[2]

[1] Compare the metaphorical expressions at VI. 20-4.

[2] 'But there is no greater joy than to hold well guarded the tranquil heights, upraised by the learning of the wise, whence thou mayest look down on other men, and see them wandering every way, and lost in error,

Yet to be the master of armies and of navies, or to be
clothed in gold and purple, gives not that exemption
from the real terrors and anxieties of life which the
power of reason only can bestow —

> Quod si ridicula hæc ludibriaque esse videmus,
> Re veraque metus hominum curæque sequaces
> Nec metuunt sonitus armorum nec fera tela,
> Audacterque inter reges rerumque potentis
> Versantur neque fulgorem reverentur ab auro
> Nec clarum vestis splendorem purpureai,
> Quid dubitas quin omni' sit hæc rationi' potestas ?
> Omnis cum in tenebris præsertim vita laboret.[1]

The desire of power and station leads to the shame and
misery of baffled hopes, of which the toil of Sisyphus is
the type, and also to the guilt which deluges the world
in blood, and violates the most sacred ties of nature.[2]
While to fail is degradation, to succeed is often the
prelude to the most sudden downfall.   Weary with
bloodshed, and with forcing their way up the hostile and
narrow road of ambition,[3] they reach the summit of
their hopes only to be hurled down by envy as by a
thunderbolt.[4]   Men are slaves to ambition, merely because they cannot distinguish the true from the false,
because they cannot judge of things as they really are,
apart from the estimate which the world puts upon
them —

> Quandoquidem sapiunt alieno ex ore petuntque
> Res ex auditis potius quam sensibus ipsis.[5]

seeking the road of life ; mayest mark the strife of genius, the rivalries of
rank, the struggle night and day with surpassing effort to reach the highest
place, and be master of the State.'—II. 48-54.

[1] 'But if we see that all this is but folly and a mockery, and, in real truth,
the fears of men and their dogging cares dread not the clash of arms nor
the fierce weapons of warfare, and boldly mix with kings and the lords of
the earth, nor fear the splendour of gold or the bright glare of purple robes,
canst thou doubt that it is the force of reason on which all this depends,
especially since all our life is in darkness and tribulation ?'—II. 48-55.

[2] III. 70.   [3] v. 1131.   [4] v. 1123.

[5] 'Since their wisdom is drawn from the lips of others, and they pursue
their object in accordance rather with what they hear than with what they
really feel.'—v. 1133-4.

The lust of riches and the passion for luxurious living,
which had begun to corrupt the Roman character even
in the age of Lucilius, had increased to gigantic dimensions, although they had scarcely yet culminated in the
last age of the Republic. By no aspect of his age was
Lucretius more repelled than by this. No doctrine is
enforced in the poem with more sincerity of conviction
than that of the happiness and dignity of plain and
natural living, the vanity of all the appliances of wealth,
and their inability to give real enjoyment either to body
or mind. In a well-known passage at the beginning of
the second book he adapts an ideal description from
Homer's account of the palace of Alcinous, to the costly
magnificence and the glare and splendour of Roman
banquets, with which he contrasts the pleasure of grati-
fying simple tastes, in fine weather, among the beauties
of nature—

> Praesertim cum tempestas adridet et anni
> Tempora conspergunt viridantis floribus herbas.[1]

With real fervour and simplicity, very unlike the com-
monplaces of many comfortable and delicate moralists,
he declares, that ' to the man who would govern his life
by reason, plain living and a contented spirit are great
riches'—

> Quod aliquis vera vitam ratione gubernet,
> Divitiae grandes homini sunt vivere parce
> Æquo animo.[2]

Moderation, independence, and self-control, are the virtues
of Horace. His doctrine is to enjoy both the luxury
of the city and the simple fare of the country. Lucretius
is more active in his resistance to the dangers of pam-
pering the body and enervating the mind. He shows a
more real superiority to the common forms of indulgence ; more truly simple tastes, fresher capacity of
natural enjoyment. He is vividly sensible of the apathy,

<hr/>

[1] ii. 33.   [2] v. 1117-19.

sloth, and *ennui*, produced by the luxury and inaction
of his age. Others among the Roman poets, with more
or less sincerity and consistency, appear to long for a
return to more natural ways, and paint their ideals of
the purity and simplicity of country life. But no writer
of antiquity is less of an idealist than Lucretius: there
is no writer, ancient or modern, whose words are more
truthful and unvarnished; and no one has shown a more
real independence of external things, a more real scorn
of the pomps and pleasures of the world.

A new form of passion had assumed great prominence
in Roman life in the age of Lucretius. With the decay
of the ancient interest in the State, the pursuits and
pleasures of private life assumed a new importance.
The poetry of Catullus in that age, and of Horace and
the Elegiac poets in the succeeding age, prove how large
a part was now played by the passion of love, especially
in the lives of young men of rank, wealth, and literary
accomplishment. Extreme license was indulged by the
men most eminent both in action and in literature; but
over and above this, Roman poetry affords evidence that,
in the case of many, the passion of love had assumed the
form of an absorbing sentiment and pursuit. The Elegiac
poets of the Augustan age exhibit a view of the duties
and interests of life, the only parallel to which must be
sought in the modern novelists of France. With this
phase of life, apparently quite alien to the dignity and
independence of the Roman character, Lucretius felt no
kind of sympathy. No Roman writer has shown a pro-
founder reverence for the affections; but no one has
treated the claims of passion and sentiment with more
austere indifference. His strong sympathy with human
affection is proved by many passages and casual expressions in the poem. The crowning guilt of superstition
consisted in the cruel violation of the strongest ties of
natural piety; the chief bitterness of death arises from

the thought of eternal separation from wife and children; the first civilising influence on human nature is traced to the power of the blandishments of children over the savage pride of strength. The pathos of the famous passage, at Book ii. 350, proceeds from the poet's sympathy with the sorrow which arises from the disruption of natural ties, even in the lower animals. Other casual expressions, as in that line of profound feeling—

Æternumque daret matri sub pectore volnus;[1]

or such pictures as that at iii. 469, of friends and relatives surrounding the bed of one who has sunk into a deep lethargy—

Ad vitam qui revocantur
Circumstant lacrimis rorantes ora genasque,[2]

show how deep and real was his regard for the great elemental affections of human nature. But, on the other hand, he has no toleration for the follies or the idealising fancies of lovers. With satirical and not fastidious realism he strips passion of all romance, and exhibits it as a bondage fatal alike to character and independence, to peace of mind and to self-respect. But it is the weakness and unmanliness, not the immorality of licentious passion which he condemns. And it would be altogether an anachronism to attribute to a writer of that age sentiments on this subject in harmony either with the virtuous family life of the primitive Romans, or with the moral standard of modern times. It is not the need of greater purity, but the need of greater strength which Lucretius enforces. It is not the indulgence of inclination, but its elevation into an absorbing passion — placing the happiness and dignity of life in the power of another's capricious will—which he condemns.

It is easy to see how one-sided and incomplete is that philosophy of human nature, which Lucretius entertained

[1] ii. 638.   [2] iii. 468 9.

U

and endeavoured to establish. The chief interest which
attaches to his moral teaching arises from his intensity
of feeling, sincerity of conviction, and independence of
view. A modern reader may admire and sympathise
with much of his spirit without resting in any of his
conclusions. He may recognise in him a rare courage
and consistency of thought, a real superiority to the
weakness and the vanity of life, and a firm faith in
the law and the order of the universe. In his protest
against the popular religion he may see the undeveloped
capacity of a better belief, and he will acknowledge the
limitations on any further advance in thought which
the conditions of that age imposed.

The truths of human nature which Lucretius saw,
were held by him with the intensest fervour of conviction.
He has the strongest sense of human dignity, of the
claims of affection, of the infinite superiority of the
natural over the conventional life. There is no romance
nor self-deception in what he aims at. His longing for
a life according to nature is too fresh and too real to be
mistaken for the morbid reaction of an exhausted age
towards an ideal of primitive simplicity. There may be
some anticipation of the spirit of Rousseau in Virgil,[1] and
still more in Tibullus, but none whatever in Lucretius.
The rudeness and misery of savage life are painted in as
stern and real colours as the luxury and unhappiness
of his own age. It would not be easy to mention any
writer, ancient or modern, by whom the lesson of 'plain
living and high thinking' was more worthily and forcibly
inculcated.

But, in his philosophy, there is no thought of progress,
no sense of duty, no sympathy with human activity.
The chief forms of activity in his age, as in most energetic ages, were war, politics, and commerce, but all
were pursued under no other motive or principle except

[1] Cf. Eclogue i

the lust of personal aggrandisement. Lucretius saw only the worst types of human evil, the most manifest causes of human suffering, in the active pursuits and interests of the world around him. A life of peace not of energy became his ideal. To contemplate all things with a mind at peace is the true religion of man ; in eternal peace consists the supreme happiness of the gods ; the deep uncomplaining peace of the grave reconciles him to the thought of everlasting death. The inadequacy and limitation of his philosophy may thus be partially traced to his defective sympathy with the active principles of human nature. Partly too the bent of his mind to material observation and inquiry—to dwell on what is actual, visible, and tangible, and so to realise vividly all outward appearances of decay and death—had some influence in determining his convictions. In dwelling on the material conditions of life, he loses sight of the inward and spiritual conditions which are the witnesses of immortality. His demand also for logical consistency of thought rendered it difficult for him to conceive of a God apart from human limitations ; and hence, although unconsciously recognising some attributes of a personal agency in the order of nature, he passes on to the positive denial of a divine creator and governor of the world.

The definite results at which he arrived, although they cannot possibly influence modern opinion on these subjects, are yet of great interest, as showing the independent conclusions, on the most vital questions, which the course of ancient thought and life forced on one of the most earnest men and consistent thinkers of antiquity. There is also a critical interest in observing the power of mind exercised by him on these questions.

The same 'vivida vis animi,' which Lucretius exercises in the exposition of his physical philosophy, is displayed in all his thoughts and observations on human life. In

contemplating the passions and characters of men, he
has shown at least an equal truth of insight, and an
equal intensity of feeling, as in observing the processes
of nature; but by no means the same range and variety
of view. In his reasonings on human life he appears to
be too much under the influence of one idea. He seems
to exaggerate the power of superstition on the one hand,
and of philosophy on the other. He certainly pushes
his argument too far, when he resolves all forms of evil
into the fear of death, and that again into the fear of
eternal torment. But when he is not under the influence
of this dominant idea, as in his argument concerning the
social and political progress of man, the origin and
growth of the arts, etc., he reasons with vigorous sense
and with much force and ingenuity, in the sober spirit
of a political historian, rather than with the vague fanci-
fulness of a poetical idealist.

There is great truth also in his observation and delineation of certain conditions of human nature. He
penetrates below outward circumstance to the most permanent types of character and passion, and records the
results of his observation in such strong and deeply-
graven characters, that they may be applied to the same
conditions of human nature in every age and country.
His knowledge of character is not shown by dramatic
versatility, nor by individual portraiture; nor does it
appear to be, like the wisdom of Horace, the result of
social sympathy and experience. But he has the intuitive insight of genius into the common heart of
man; — an insight quickened partly by his poetical
sense of the wonder and mystery of life, partly by his
sympathy with the suffering condition of ordinary men,
partly by the spirit of satire, in which he regards the
weakness and the vanity of the great.

His power as a truthful moral painter is clearly dis-
closed in such passages as that where he describes the

pains and vicissitudes of passion, and the 'amari aliquid'
amongst the very flowers of love—

> Aut cum conscius ipse animus se forte remordet
> Desidiose agere ætatem lustrisque perire,
> Aut quod in ambiguo verbum jaculata reliquit
> Quod cupido affixum cordi vivescit ut ignis,
> Aut nimium jactare oculos aliosve tueri
> Quod putat in voltuque videt vestigia risus.[1]

The weariness, restlessness, and satiety which punish
a rich and luxurious age, are forcibly represented in the
following lines—

> Exit sæpe foras magnis ex ædibus ille,
> Esse domi quem pertæsumst, subitoque revertit,
> Quippe foris nilo melius qui sentiat esse.
> Currit agens mannos ad villam præcipitanter,
> Auxilium tectis quasi ferre ardentibus instans;
> Oscitat extemplo, tetigit cum limina villæ,
> Aut abit in somnum gravis atque oblivia quærit,
> Aut etiam properans urbem petit atque revisit.[2]

The worth of Lucretius considered as a moral writer
(independently of his power as a philosophical and
imaginative poet) is greatly enhanced by his clearness
and directness of expression. The writings of Horace
supply familiar quotations on a greater variety of topics
connected with the philosophy of human life. But
although his observations are equally just, they do not
sink so deeply, nor do they bring out in such startling distinctness great truths or vital characteristics of

[1] 'Either when his mind is stung with the consciousness that he is wasting
his life in sloth, and ruining himself in wantonness; or because from the
shafts of her wit she has left in him some word of double meaning, which
seizes on his passionate heart and burns there like a fire; or because he
fancies that she rolls her eyes too much or gazes at another, and marks the
traces of a smile on her countenance.'—IV. 1133-40.

[2] 'Thoroughly weary of being at home, the lord of some spacious mansion
issues forth from it oftentimes abroad, and suddenly returns, feeling that it
is no better with him abroad. Driving his steeds, he hurries in hot haste
to his country house, as if speeding to bring aid to a house on fire. Straightway he begins to yawn, so soon as he has reached his threshold, or sinks
heavily into sleep and seeks forgetfulness, or even with all haste returns to
the city.' III. 1060-7.

our being. The following lines and expressions, for instance, may often be quoted with a sense that they
express for all time certain thoughts or experience of
perpetual recurrence--

> Tantam religio potuit suadere malorum.[1]
> Cur non ut plenus vitae conviva recedis.[2]
> Vitaque mancipio nulli datur, omnibus usu.[3]
> Surgit amari aliquid quod in ipsis floribus angat.[4]
> Nam verae voces tum demum pectore ab imo
> Eiciuntur et eripitur persona, manet res.[5]

Many other lines and expressions of similar force will
occur to every reader familiar with Lucretius. As his
ordinary style brings the outward aspects of the world
vividly before the mind, so the language in which he
enforces his moral teaching, or expresses the result of
his moral observation, stamps powerfully on the mind
important and permanent truths of human nature. His
thoughts are uttered sometimes with the impressive
dignity of Roman oratory, sometimes with the nervous
energy, not without some flashes of the vigorous wit of
Roman satire. There are occasionally to be heard also
higher and deeper tones than those familiar to his countrymen. His burning zeal and indignation against idolatry, and the scorn with which he exposes the impotence
of false gods—

> Cur etiam lora sola petunt frustraque laborant?
> An tum bracchia consuescunt firmantque lacertos?[6]

show some affinity of spirit to the inspired men of an-

---

[1] 'To so much evil could religion prompt.'—i. 101.
[2] 'Why dost thou not retire like a guest satisfied at the banquet of life?'
—iii. 938.
[3] 'Life is given to no man as a possession, to all men for their use.'—
iii. 971.
[4] 'There ever arises some bitter thought to sting even amid the very
flowers of love.' - iv. 1134.
[5] 'Words of truth are then uttered from the depths of the heart, the mask
is withdrawn, the reality remains.'—iii. 57-8.
[6] vi. 396.

other race and an earlier time.   The 'grandeur of desolation' uttered in the reproof of nature,

Nam tibi praeterea quod machiner inveniamque,
Quod placeat, nil est : eadem sunt omnia semper.[1]

recalls the old words of the Preacher—'The thing that hath been, it is that which shall be ; and that which is done, is that which shall be done : and there is no new thing under the sun.'

[1] III. 044-5.

CHAPTER XI.

IT remains to consider Lucretius as a great and original poet. Much indeed of what may be said on this part of the subject has necessarily been anticipated in the two preceding chapters. His poetry is inseparably united with his philosophy and his moral teaching. The feeling with which he contemplates nature and human life was seen to be, in a great measure, the reflex of his speculative ideas. The moral teaching of the poem was seen to derive much of its force from the poetical power with which that teaching is expressed. The passages which serve to illustrate the greatness of his philosophy, and the intensity of his ethical convictions, are in many cases those best fitted to illustrate the varied exercise of his poetical faculty.

It is probably owing to this triple combination of characteristics that Lucretius received scarcely fair appreciation in ancient times. The high rank which he now holds among the writers of antiquity seems to have been conceded to him in the present century more freely than at any former time; and this rank was awarded to him by poets of kindred genius, such as Goethe, Wordsworth, and Shelley, earlier than by scholars. He attracts modern sympathies by his affinity to the thoughts and feelings of a time of change and movement, by the truth with which he has realised the wonder and the grandeur in the familiar aspects of the world, and by the spirit in which he bears the common burden of human nature.

But among his countrymen, Virgil alone gives indication of having carefully studied him, and of having felt his pre-eminence. Yet it was apparently his power of expression rather than of thought of which Virgil was really emulous. Although he vaguely aspired to reach that philosophical eminence from which Lucretius

Metus omnis et inexorabile fatum
Subjecit pedibus, strepitumque Acherontis avari ;[1]

yet he is really repelled rather than attracted by the consistency of thought and intensity of conviction in the older poet.[1] The words in which Cicero criticises the poem on its first appearance are slight and disparaging, and not even discriminating in their disparagement. Horace does not mention his name, nor, although he shows familiarity with his diction, does he seem to allude to him anywhere. The language of no Roman writer, except perhaps a single line of Statius, appears to do justice to his merit, or to show an intelligent appreciation of his genius.[2] He is indeed named by some ancient critics, along with Catullus, as one of the two great poets of the age ; but there is reason to think that he was less known and valued by his countrymen than either the earlier poets or those of the Augustan age.

The poet himself suggests a reason, which may account for the comparative indifference with which the poem was received—

Quoniam haec ratio plerumque videtur
Tristior esse quibus non est tractata, retroque
Volgus abhorret ab hac.[3]

<hr>

[1] Georg. II. 491.
[2] Cf. the article 'Lucretius,' in Smith's Dictionary of Greek and Roman Biography.
[3] ' Since, for the most part, this method appears too austere to those who have never studied it, and the vulgar shrink away from it.'—I. 943-5.

The systematic treatment of the subject selected by him was not only uncongenial to the Roman taste, but is scarcely compatible with pure poetical art. The greatness and completeness of the work, considered as an exposition of a system of philosophy, produce a different effect upon the mind from the pleasure which is generally afforded by poetry. The models which Lucretius followed in the treatment of his subject, and the construction of his work, were not the purely didactic poems of Alexandria, but the older philosophical poems of Xenophanes, Parmenides, and Empedocles;—men whose imagination was moved by the enthusiasm of discovery rather than by the impulse of artistic genius. The purpose of Lucretius was the same as theirs, to use all his faculty of construction, imagination, and expression, not for the illustration of a topic, selected with a view to poetic treatment, but for the purpose of communicating truth. The vastness of his subject is difficult to reconcile with the compass or the harmony of a work of art. The physical exposition and the moral teaching do not always naturally fit into one another. Many of the details, with which the poem is filled, are not ordinarily associated with poetical feeling. They have been selected to illustrate the scientific argument, not the beauty or sublimity of nature. Nor does the author care to invest ordinary matter of fact with the alien ornament of poetic associations. It is to be remembered also that the mind, in reading or listening to poetry, acts intuitively or contemplatively, recognising sensuous images or complete ideas, not discursive or logical processes. The connecting links of argument suggest the idea of the labour of the workman, not of the finished perfection of the work. Poetry, like all other art, aims at presenting to the mind the completeness of an act of creation. While some of the results of science may be suited for poetic treatment, the slow processes of investigation have been generally banished from the province of verse.

There is, moreover, much roughness and inequality in the artistic execution of the poem. A few passages, indeed, show the very finest sense of harmony, and are finished in a style scarcely, if at all, inferior to that of Virgil. Such, for instance, are the opening lines—

Æneadum genetrix, hominum divomque voluptas, etc. ;

and again, the lines in the introduction to Book iii., at line 18--

Apparet divum numen sedesque quietæ, etc.

But long passages in the poem approach almost as near to the roughness of Ennius as to the harmonious smoothness and elegance of Virgil. Even the greatest passages are characterised by a monotony of cadence, implying inferior skill in rhythm to that of his greatest successor. The style, which in the poetry of individual expressions is far more powerful than that of Virgil, yet often overflows to prosaic redundance, or displays the excellencies of scientific precision and consecutiveness, instead of that of poetical grace and accomplishment. His era in literature coincided with that stage in the development of language, when words are most full of life and meaning, but have not yet fallen into their most harmonious combinations; when the perception of beauty and melody is present as a strong impulse, but is not yet united to the power of perfect execution. All these causes—the vast and miscellaneous range, the abstruse, scientific nature of his subject, the dryness and the unsubstantial character of many of his details, the earnest practical purpose of the work, and, again, the 'patrii sermonis egestas,' or the inadequacy of the Latin language as a vehicle of thought, and its imperfect development as a harmonious organ for the expression of poetical

feeling,—have tended to interfere with the full appreciation of the poem in ancient times, and to render it
more acceptable in parts than as a whole to the majority
of modern readers.

Yet it is only after the poem is understood in all its
details, and in its vital relation to the philosophical ideas
of Lucretius, that its full excellence, even as a work of
art, can be perceived. It is only then that the unity of
purpose and sentiment by which it is pervaded, and the
greatness of design by which the arguments and illustrations are massed, arranged, and made to move in
orderly succession and subordination, can be adequately
recognised. A fresher interest is given to many of the
most familiar beauties in the poem, when we perceive
how they arise in the regular march of the argument ; and a fuller image of the author is formed by
recognising the harmonious co-operation of his clear
faculty of observation, and of his poetical sense of the
power and mysterious agency of nature. In expressing
the speculative thought of a philosopher, the vivid and
faithful observation of a naturalist, or the earnest convictions of a moralist, he is never altogether deserted
by the deep feeling, the suggestive fancy, the subtle
perception of imaginative genius.

The poem when read consecutively, notwithstanding
the unpoetical nature of much of the details, produces
the impression of a pervading passion and inspiration.
Through all the processes of observation, analysis, and reasoning, the poet is borne along by a strong enthusiasm
— the philosophical ἔρως of Plato—akin to the impulse
of poetry. That intensity and marvellous depth of feeling, in conjunction with the operations of the intellect,
which the Greeks regarded as a kind of divine possession, and which Lucretius himself ascribes to the earliest
thinkers, in applying to them such expressions as ' divinitus invenicutes,' animates all his interpretation of the

facts and laws of nature. The passion of speculative inquiry appears stronger in Lucretius than in any extant ancient writer, with the exception of Plato. It gives life to the driest details of the argument, and adds an intenser and more fervent glow to the contemplative representation of nature and of human life.

There is, further, a kind of grandeur and dignity even in the monotony of the verse, varied as it is by occasionally deeper and more majestic tones, or falling into a softer and more harmonious cadence, as the argument sweeps through the sublimer or the serener and more beautiful phases of his subject. There is always a sense of life and onward movement in the flow of his verse. Although the ear is not satisfied in the same manner as by the more intricate and varied harmony of Virgil, yet it recognises an original and characteristic music in the lines of Lucretius. There is often a kind of cumulative force in their sound, as of wave upon wave breaking upon the shore, revealing a more powerful movement of his spirit, as his arguments and objects are pressed one upon another in close and ordered sequence. Thus, for instance, the effect of the following passage, which represents the religious impressions produced upon the early inhabitants of the world by the grander and more awful aspects of nature, depends not solely on the individual lines, but upon the swelling and culminating power with which the whole passage breaks upon the ear—

> In caeloque deum sedes et templa locarunt,
> Per coelum volvi quia nox et luna videtur,
> Luna dies et nox et noctis signa severa
> Noctivagaeque faces caeli flammaeque volantes,
> Nubila sol imbres nix venti fulmina grando
> Et rapidi fremitus et murmura magna minarum.[1]

[1] 'And they placed the dwelling-places and mansions of the gods in the heavens, because it is through the heavens that the night and the moon are seen to sweep—the moon, the day, and night, and the earnest[a] constellations

[a] Compare—'Tall oaks, branch-charmed by the earnest stars.'

KEATS, *Hyperion.*

Although the periodic structure of Virgil's verse, the
more studied variation of his constructions, the more
harmonious combination of rhythm and expression, imply
a finer sense of art and finer power of execution than
can be attributed to this mere massing of arguments, ob
jects, and lines in Lucretius, yet the rhythmical effect
both of such single passages as the above and of the
whole poem is peculiarly fitted to the character of his
subject, and to the pervading solemnity and intensity
of his feeling. In many places it may be noticed how
much is added to the metrical effect by the force or
weight of the concluding line ; as, for instance, in the
passage at iii. 870-93, by the rugged grandeur of this—

Urgerive superne obtritam poudere terra ;[1]

and again, at ii. 569-80, by the sad and solemn movement in this

Floratas mortis comites et funeris atri.[2]

That Lucretius had, to a remarkable degree, the original
gift of using the grandeur of sound as a true symbol of
feeling must be at once recognised by any one who com
pares the rhythmical effect of his noblest passages either
with the earlier fragments of Ennius, or with the contemporary verses of Cicero.

The poetical style of Lucretius is chiefly marked by
freshness and fulness of meaning, and by a daring energy
in the use of metaphorical expressions. Along with all
the force and gravity characteristic of Ennius, he combines a grace and subtle suggestiveness altogether unknown to the earlier poet.

While his art is less refined and elaborate than that of
Virgil, he shows much more natural power of terse and
vigorous speech, and greater creative energy in novel com-

of night, the torches of heaven wandering through the night, and flying
meteors, the clouds, the sun, the rains, the snow, the winds, lightning,
hail, the rapid rattle, the threatening peals and murmurs of the thunder.'
v. 1188-93.
[1] III. 893.   [2] II. 580.

binations of language. Many of his expressions seem to have been too full of poetical life to be retained in common use. They appear more like the creation of modern than of ancient imagination. The good taste and sense of Virgil softened down the poetical diction of Lucretius to suit his own tamer subject, calmer spirit, and less impassioned conceptions. Later poets fashioned their phraseology after the Virgilian model, so that the language of Lucretius has come down to the present time fresh and unhackneyed, with no medium of after associations interposed between his mind and that of a modern reader.

Few poets convey so much meaning by the use of simple words, expressive of the full and literal truth of things. It is by this use of words in their natural sense that he endows the familiar aspects of nature and of human life with the wonder and 'freshness of the early world.' It is more natural to speak of this freshness and sincerity of expression as the pervading characteristic of his style, than to illustrate it by special examples. A few expressions, however, such as the following, may be noticed, as especially full of life, and as bringing before us immediately the truth of nature in her outward aspect or more secret meaning,—equally removed from an abstract or mechanical and from an over-fanciful view of the world :—

> Quæ mare navigerum, quæ terras frugiferentis
> Concelebras : [1]

> Denique per maria ac montis fluviosque rapacis
> Frondiferasque domos avium camposque virentis : [2]

> Quam fluitans circum magnis anfractibus æquor
> Ionium glaucis aspergit virus ab undis : [3]

[1] 'Who makest thy presence felt all through the sea, with its sailing ships, and the fruitful earth.'—i. 3.

[2] 'In fine, through seas, and mountains, and whirling rivers, and the leafy homes of birds, and the green plains.'—i. 17-18.

[3] 'And all around it the Ionian sea, breaking with mighty sweeps, dashes up the briny spray from its blue waves.'— i. 717-18.

Nec tenerae salices atque herbae rore vigentes
Fluminaque illa queunt summis labentia ripis : [1]

Severa silentia noctis
Undique cum constent. [2]

So too, he conveys a deep and solemn sense of human
life by the grave and almost literal fidelity of his
language. No subtlety of reflection, nor any illustrative
imagery could affect the mind more powerfully than the
plain unvarnished grandeur of the following line, for
instance—

Morte obita quorum tellus amplectitur ossa. [3]

No pomp of description could produce a deeper sense
of religious solemnity than the lines in which the influence of the procession of Cybele upon the imagination
is represented—

Ergo cum primum magnas invecta per urbis
Munificat tacita mortalis muta salute. [4]

The strength of natural grief is vividly conveyed in the
line—

Æternumque daret matri sub pectore volnus, [5]

and the mingled blessedness and pathos of affection in
the words—

Tacita pectus dulcedine tangent, [6]

Again, to take a different class of emotions, the delight,
not unmixed with awe, of intellectual discovery, is thus
conveyed with marvellous force—

His ibi me rebus quaedam divina voluptas
Percipit atque horror. [7]

Scarcely any writer brings so clearly into the light
the poetical side of actual existence by the use of the

[1] 'Nor the tender willows, and the grass fresh with dew, and those rivers,
gliding with brimming stream past their banks.'—II. 361-2.
[2] 'When all around there is the stern silence of the night.'
[3] 'Whose bones, after death, the earth holds in its embrace.'—I. 135.
[4] 'When first, borne through great cities, she, mute herself, uplifts the
hearts of men with a silent blessing.'—II. 624-5.
[5] II. 639.   [6] III. 896.
[7] 'By reason of these things a divine ecstasy and awe possess me.'—
III. 28-9.

most direct and truthful language.   One great element
of his power as a poet is thus seen to flow out of his
singleness of eye, and his intense sincerity of character.

His language has the further power of producing the
vague sense of sublimity, where the cause of the feeling
is too vast or undefined to be distinctly conceived or
visibly presented to the mind.   The very sound of his
words seems sometimes to be a kind of echo of the voices
by which nature produces a strange awe upon the
imagination.   Such, for instance, are these lines and
expressions—

> Altitonans Volturnus et auster fulmine pollens.[1]
>
> Nec fulmina nec minitanti
> Murmure compremit caelum.[2]
> Murmura magna minarum,[3] etc.

The sublimity, both of vagueness and of magnitude, is
present in the language of these lines—

> Impendent atrae formidinis ora superne.[4]
> Sustentata ruet moles et machina mundi.[5]
> Aut cecidisse urbis magno vexamine mundi.[6]
> Non si terra mari miscebitur et mare caelo.[7]

He thus conveys with greater force than any other
Roman poet not only the fresh sense of life, and the
solemn meaning of familiar things, but also the vague
suggestion of a secret, mysterious, and awful power in
the universe.

The active power of imagination that gives new life
to words and thoughts, is also present in many vivid
and picturesque expressions, either scattered through the
main argument, or shining in brilliant combinations in
the more elaborate parts of the work.   By this more
imaginative use of language, the poet can illustrate his
ideas and objects by subtle analogies, or embody them
in visible symbols, or endow them with the personal

[1] v. 745.   [2] i. 68-9.   [3] v. 1193.   [4] vi. 251.
[5] v. 96.   [6] v. 340.   [7] iii. 842.

X

attributes of will and energy. Thus, for instance, the
subtlety of the mind in exploring the secrets of nature
is illustrated and made visible by the curious felicity
of the expression (t. 408), 'crecasque latebras insinuare
omnis.' The freedom, originality, and boundless range
of the imagination is suggested with picturesque effect
in the familiar expression—

> Avia Pieridum peragro loca nullius ante
> Trita solo.[1]

The calm serenity of the contemplative mind is symbolised in such figurative expressions as 'sapientum templa
serena;' 'humanum in pectus templaque mentis.' And
again the tumult of the passions is almost visibly represented in this line—

> Volvere curarum tristis in pectore fluctus.[2]

How much life and energy again are imparted to external things by such expressions as these:—'flammai
flore coorto;' 'avido complexu quem tenet æther;' 'cœli
tegit impetus ingens;' 'circum tremere æthera signis;'
'vagos imbris tempestatesque volantes;' 'concussæque
cadunt urbes dubiæque minantur;' 'simulacraque fessa
fatisci;' 'sol lumine conserit arva;' 'lucida tela diei;'
'vivant labentes ætheris ignes,' etc.

A similar power of imagination is displayed in his use
of analogies, in his symbolical representation of ideas,
and in his power of painting scenes from nature and
from human life. Few great poets have indeed been more
sparing in the use of mere poetical ornament. The
grandest imagery which he strikes out, and the finest
pictures which he paints, arise naturally out of his subject. The earnestness of his speculative and practical
purpose restrains all exuberance of fancy. Thus his
imaginative analogies are more often latent in single
expressions than drawn out at length. But the few
which he has elaborated, unlike much of the transient

and fanciful imagery of poetry, ' stand out with the
solidity of the finest sculpture,'[1] to embody some deep
or powerful thought for all time. They are evidently
suggested not by outward resemblance, but by an identity in the innermost meaning of the objects compared
with one another. The strong emotion attending on the
presence of some great thought calls up before the imagination some scene or action, which, if actually witnessed,
would produce a similar effect upon the mind. Thus the
thought of the chaotic confusion which the universe
would present, on the supposition that the original
atoms were limited in number, calls up the image of
the most impressive and awful devastation, wrought by
Nature upon the works of man.

> Sed quasi naufragiis magnis multisque coortis
> Disjectare solet magnum mare transtra gubernaa
> Antemnas proram malos tonsasque natantia,
> Per terrarum omnis oras fluitantia aplustra
> Ut videantur et indicium mortalibus edant,
> Infidi maris insidias viriasque dolumque
> Ut vitare velint, neve ullo tempore credant,
> Subdola cum ridet placidi pellacia ponti,
> Sic ubi si finita semel primordia quaedam
> Constitues, aevum debebunt sparsa per omnem
> Disjectare aetas diversi materiai,
> Numquam in concilium ut possint compulsa coire
> Nec remorari in concilio nec crescere adaucta.[2]

It is through the penetrating power of his imagination
into the deepest meaning of the two phenomena, and
his sensibility to the pathos and the strangeness involved

---

[1] Prevost Paradol, *Nouveaux Essais de Politique et de Littérature.*

[2] ' But, as when there have been great and many shipwrecks, it is the way
of the sea to drive in all directions the rowers' benches, rudders, sail-yards,
prows, masts, and floating oars, so that along all the coasts of land there
may be seen the tossing flag-posts of ships, to warn mortals that they shun
the wiles, and force, and craft of the faithless sea, nor ever trust the
treacherous alluring smile of the calm deep ; so if once you will suppose
any finite number of elements, you will find that the many surging forces
of matter must disperse and drive them apart through all time, so that they
never can meet and gather into union, nor stay in union and wax in
increase.'—II. 552-564.

in each of them, that he sees the birth of each child into
the world under the well-known image of the ship-
wrecked sailor—' saevis projectus ab undis.' Other analogies, suggested rather than elaborately drawn out, are
seen also to express an inward or spiritual, not an outward or bodily resemblance. Or rather the object illustrated is a thought or a mental act, the illustration a
scene or action, visible to the eye, suggestive of the
same power in Nature, and calculated to rouse the same
emotions in the mind. Thus he compares the life transmitted in succession through the nations of the world to
the torch passed on by the runners in the torch-race;
or again, he illustrates his calm contemplation of the
struggles of life from the heights of his Epicurean
philosophy, by the vision of the dangers of the sea, as
seen from the security of the shore.

Although his subject, being the interpretation of the
laws and facts of nature, did not afford much scope for
the exercise of the idealising faculty of a poetical artist,
yet there are some passages in the poem conceived with
the finest plastic and pictorial power. Such, for instance,
is that beautiful picture of the sacrifice of Iphigenia,
suggested indeed by an earlier poet, but executed under
a new and original inspiration. There are also one or
two pictures from the ancient mythology, as that of
Venus and Mars, in the invocation to the poem, and that
of Pan —

Pinea semiferi capitis velamina quassans,[1]

showing that he might have ranked highly among poets
of creative fancy, had he not felt more powerfully the
passion for the discovery and interpretation of the actual
facts of existence. By this power of imagination he
presents that superstition against which all the weight
of his argument is directed, not as an abstraction, but
as a real palpably existing power of evil—

[1] iv. 587.

Qua caput a cœli regionibus ostendelat
Horribili super aspectu mortalibus instans.[1]

So too, in his vivid account of the orderly procession
of the seasons, he invests the freshness and the beauty
of spring with the charm of personal and human as-
·sociations—

It ver et Venus, et veris praenuntius ante
Pennatus graditur zephyrus, vestigia propter
Flora quibus mater praespargens ante viai
Cuncta coloribus egregiis et oloribus opplet.[2]

But, as has been said, it is as the interpreter of nature,
and of the familiar aspects of human life, that Lucretius
has mainly used his power of poetical feeling and expression.   More than any ancient, and perhaps than any
modern poet, he has given a true and great utterance to
the majesty and the power of nature.   He contemplates
the system of creation with emotions similar to those
which the idea of the deep foundations and the authoritative state of Roman institutions calls up in the minds
of Ennius and Virgil.   This kind of feeling, which finds
expression in such phrases as these—

Majestas cognita rerum :[3]
Nec validas valeant ævi rescindere leges,[4] etc. etc.

pervades his whole conception of the creation and support of the universe.

But the life of the world excites in him another class
of emotions, more in harmony with the genius both of
Greek and of modern poetry.   Nature does not appear
to him as an abstraction, or as a vast system of forces
and laws, but as a living power, whose processes are on
an infinitely grander scale, but are yet analogous to the
active and moral energies of man.   He shows the same

---

[1] i. 64-5.
[2] 'Spring advances and Venus, and before them goes the harbinger of
Spring, the winged Zephyr : and near their path, Mother Flora, scattering
her treasures before her, fills all the way with glorious colours and fragrance.'
—v. 737-40.   [3] v. 7.   [4] v. 56.

sympathy with this life of Nature, the same vivid sense
of wonder and delight in her familiar aspects, the same
imaginative perception of her innermost meaning, which
led the early Greek mind to people the world with the
living forms of the old mythology, and which have been
felt anew by the great poets of the present century. All
natural life is thus endowed with a poetical interest, as
being a new manifestation of the creative energy, which
is the fountain of all beauty and delight in the world.

The minutest phenomena and the most gigantic forces
of nature, the changes of decay and renovation in all
outward things, the growth of plants and trees, the habits
of beasts rioting in a wild liberty over the mountains,

> Quod in magnis bacchatar montibu' passim,[1]

or tended by the care and ministering to the wants of
man ; the life and enjoyment of the birds that gladden
the early morning with their song by woods and river-
banks, or that seek their food and pastime among the
sea-waves ;—these, and numberless other phenomena,
are all contemplated and described by an eye quickened
by the poetical sense of an ever-new energy in the world.
No poet was ever more profoundly impressed by the
sense both of the majesty and of the subtle, all-pene-
trating, and all-pervading life of this power—

> Cæli subter labentia signa
> Quæ mare navigerum, quæ terras frugiferentis
> Concelebras, per te quoniam genus omne animantum
> Concipitur, visitque exortum lumina solis ![2]

In describing outward things, he selects those aspects
of the world which reveal the power or the freshness
of nature, or which derive a further interest from their
relation to the deeper meaning of his philosophy. It
is not so much the beauty of form and colour, as
the appearance of force and life which he reproduces.

He does not show, like Catullus, the passion or delight
of a painter of natural scenes. He does not express,
like Virgil, the charm of old associations attaching to
famous places. It is the association of great ideas,
not of great memories, which he recognises in the outward world. Neither has he invested any particular
place with the attraction which Horace has given to
Tibur and his Sabine home, and Catullus to the cape
of Sirmio. But no ancient or modern poet has expressed more happily the natural enjoyment in behold-
ing the changing life and familiar charm of the world.
No other writer makes us feel with more reality the
quickening of the spirit, which is caused by the sunrise
or the early spring, by fine weather or fair and peaceful
landscapes. The freshness of this feeling is one of the
great charms of the poem, especially as a relief to the
gloom and sadness of his thought on human life. A
sense of real enjoyment in the actual presence of nature, not of ideal longings nor of vague meditativeness,
is thus produced on the mind. Although there are in
his poem none of those traces of romantic and adventurous activity which blend with Homer's vivid pictures of
earth, sea, and sky, yet he sees the world with the clear
eye, and feels its force with the strong, healthy heart of
the old epic poet. No morbid or distempered fancies
coloured the natural aspect which the world presented
to his eyes and mind.

It is rather a reflection than a picture of outward
nature which we find in Lucretius. He does not select
and combine his materials with the purpose of satis-
fying the imagination with some perfect landscape, or
some features of exceptional grace or beauty; but
he seizes and reproduces the most vital and impressive characteristics of some actual phase of nature.
In his descriptions, as in those of Homer, there is
always some active movement and change represented

as passing before the eye.   What force and energy
there are, for instance, in the description of a river-
flood—

> Nec validi possunt pontes venientis aquai
> Vim subitam tolerare : ita magno turbidus imbri
> Molibus incurrit validis cum viribus amnis.[1]

The whole passage may be compared with a similar forcible and truthful description, reproduced immediately
from nature, in Burns's 'Brigs of Ayr.'   How naturally
is the fresh and sparkling life of brooks and springs
brought before the mind in the passage at v. 271 already
quoted—and again, in these lines—

> Denique nota vagi silvestria templa tenebant
> Nympharum, quibus e scibant umori' fluenta
> Lubrica proluvie larga lavere umida saxa,
> Umida saxa, super viridi stillantia musco,
> Et partim plano scatere atque erumpere campo.[2]

In the following representation of the sea-shore—

> Concharumque genus parili ratione videmus
> Pingere telluris gremium, qua mollibus undis
> Litoris incurvi bibulam pavit aequor harenam,[3]—

there is the same suggestion of quiet ceaseless movement,
as in a line of the Odyssey representing the same phase
of nature—

> λάγγαι τότε χέρσω ἀνερλίσσοσι θάλασσα.

There is the same sense of active life in all his pictures of the early morning ; as, for instance—

> Primum aurora novo cum spargit lumine terras
> Et variæ volucres nemora avia pervolitantes

---

[1] 'Nor can the strong bridges endure the sudden force of the rushing
water : in such wise, swollen by heavy rain, the stream with mighty force
dashes upon the piles.'—i. 285-7.

[2] 'Finally, in their wandering they made their dwelling in the familiar
woodland grottoes of the nymphs, from which they marked the rills of water
laving the dripping rocks, made slippery with their abundant flow,—dripping
rocks, with drops oozing from the green moss over them,—and bursting
forth and forcing their way over the level plain.'—v. 948-52.

[3] 'And in like manner we see shells paint the lap of the earth, where with
soft waves the sea beats on the porous sand of the winding shore.'—ii. 374-6

Aera per tenerum liquidis loca vocibus opplent,
Quam subito solent sol ortus tempore tali
Convestire sua perfundens omnia luce,
Omnibus in promptu manifestamque esse videmus.[1]

Two passages (at iv. 136 and vi. 190), in which the
movements and changing shapes of the clouds are described, may be compared with one of the finest passages
in the Excursion, in which Wordsworth has represented
similar aspects of outward nature.

Nowhere does he seem to present pictures of pure
repose. His philosophical idea of ceaseless motion animates to his eye every aspect of the world. Every
separate description in the poem possesses the charms
of freshness and faithfulness, and of relevance to the
great ideas of his philosophy. The poetry of these passages is no alien ornament, but the very bloom and beauty
of life. It is a result of the complex harmony of the
poet's nature. His living enjoyment in the world, and
sympathy with all existence, both fed and were fed by
his trust in speculative ideas. The poetical descriptions
of nature which adorn and illustrate his argument are
like the sublime and beautiful scenes which refresh and
reward the adventurous discoverer of distant lands.

Some passages, illustrative of philosophical principles,
blend the movements of animal and human life with
descriptions of natural scenery. The well-known lines
at ii. 352-366, describing the cow searching for her
calf, which has been sacrificed at the altar, may be referred to as combining many of the poetical characteristics of Lucretius. There is the literal—almost too
minute faithfulness of reproduction—as in the line—

Noscit humi pedibus vestigia pressa bisulcis;[1]

[1] 'When the dawn first sheds its new light over the earth, and birds of
every kind, flying over the pathless woods through the delicate air, fill all
the land with their liquid notes, how suddenly the risen sun then clothes
and steeps the world in his light, is clear and obvious to all men.'—
ii. 144 ?.   [1] ii. 356.

the active life of the whole representation, too full of
movement for a picture, yet flashing the objects on the
inward eye with graphic pictorial power;[1] the fresh
sense of nature expressed in the lines—

Nec teneræ salices atque herbæ rore vigentes
Fluminaque illa queunt summis labentia ripis;[2]

the pathos and respect for every mode of natural feeling
denoted in such expressions as 'desiderio perfixa juvenci;'
and, lastly, the power of investing the most familiar
things with the majesty of the laws which they express
and illustrate. This passage is adduced as a proof and
illustration of the varieties in form of the primordial
atoms. In a passage, immediately preceding, the perpetual motion of the atoms, while all things appear to
be at rest, is illustrated by two pictures, one taken from
the jubilant life of the animal creation—

Nam sæpe in colli tondentes pabula læta,[3] etc. :

the other taken from the pomp of human affairs, and the
gay pageantry of armies —

Præterea magnæ legiones cum loca cursu
Camporum complent belli simulacra cientes,
Fulgor ibi ad cælum se tollit totaque circum
Ære renidescit tellus supterque virum vi
Excitur pedibus sonitus clamoreque montes
Icti rejectant voces ad sidera mundi
Et circumvolitant equites mediisque repente
Tramittunt valido quatientes impete campos.[4]

The truth and fulness of life in this passage are immediately perceived, but the element of sublimity is added
by the thought in the two lines with which the passage

[1] This is enhanced by adopting Mr. Munro's suggestion, and reading
'almistens' at line 359.
[2] ii. 361-2.   [3] ii. 317.
[4] 'Besides when mighty legions fill the plains with their rapid movement,
raising the pageantry of warfare, the splendour rises up to heaven, and all
the land around is bright with the glitter of brass, and beneath the mighty
host of men the sound of their tramp arises, and the mountains, struck by
their shouting, re-echo their voices to the stars of the world, and the horse-
men hurry to and fro on either flank, and suddenly charge across the plains,
shaking them with their impetuous onset.'—ii. 323-30.

concludes, which reduces the whole of this moving and
sounding pageant to deep stillness and silence—

> Et tamen est quidam locus altis montibus unde
> Stare videntur et in campis consistere fulgor.[1]

As the contemplative poet of human life, Lucretius
displays a power of feeling and of penetration equally
deep and original, but infinitely less buoyancy and
freshness of spirit.   In dealing with the problem of
human destiny, he has sounded a deeper and more
'perilous way' than any of the other ancient poets
of Italy ; but others have seen and passed through a
greater variety of the moods of life, and have allowed
its many lights and shadows to play more easily over
their poetry.   Lucretius is deeply impressed with the
thought both of the dignity and the littleness of our
mortal state.   His imagination is involuntarily moved
by the pomp and grandeur of affairs, while his strong
sense of reality keeps ever present to his mind the conviction of the vanity of outward state, the weariness of
luxurious living, and the miseries of ambition.   Thus,
for instance, his imaginative recognition of the pomp
and circumstances of war brings out by the force of contrast his deeper conviction of the littleness and impotence
of man in the presence of the great forces of nature—

> Summa etiam cum vis violenti per mare venti
> Induperatorem classis super aequora verrit
> Cum validis pariter legionibus atque elephantis,
> Non divom pacem votis adit ac prece quaerit
> Ventorum pavidus paces animasque secundas,[2] etc.

While his reason acknowledges only inward strength as
the attribute of human dignity, his imagination seems

---

[1] 'And yet there is some place in the lofty mountains whence they
appear to be all still, and a splendour seems to rest upon the plains.'—ii.
331-32.

[2] 'When, too, the utmost force of a violent gale is sweeping the admiral
of some fleet over the seas, along with his mighty legions and elephants,
does he not court the protection of the gods with vows, and in his terror
pray for a calm to the storm, and for favouring breezes?'—v. 1226-30.

to feel the outward spell that swayed the Roman genius, in the symbols of power and authority, in great spectacles, and in impressive ceremonials.

But it is with much more heart-felt sympathy, and with not less imaginative emotion, that he recognises the deep wonder and the infinite pathos of human life. There is perhaps no passage in any poet which reveals more truthfully that union of feelings in meditating on the strangeness and sadness of our mortal destiny than the well-known passage describing the birth of every infant into the world—

> Tum porro puer, ut saevis projectus ab undis
> Navita, nudus humi jacet, infans, indigus omni
> Vitali auxilio, cum primum in luminis oras
> Nixibus ex alvo matris natura profudit,
> Vagituque locum lugubri complet, ut aequum est
> Cui tantum in vita restet transire malorum.[1]

With what truth, applicable to every age, is the complaint of the husbandman over his ineffectual labour and scanty returns echoed—

> Jamque caput quassans grandis suspirat arator
> Crebrius, incassum manuum cecidisse labores,
> Et cum tempora temporibus praesentia confert
> Praeteritis, laudat fortunas saepe parentis
> Et crepat, antiquum genus ut pietate repletum
> Perfacile angustis tolerarit finibus aevom,
> Cum minor esset agri multo modus ante viritim.[2]

The infinite pathos of the passage—

> Jam jam non domus accipiet te laeta,[3] etc.

has already been remarked. ⸮His feeling is also pro-

---

[1] 'Moreover, the babe, like a sailor cast forth by the cruel waves, lies naked on the ground, speechless, in need of every aid to life, when first nature has cast him forth by great throes from his mother's womb ; and he fills the air with his piteous wail, as befits one who has to undergo so much of misery in life.'—v. 222-7.

[2] 'And now, shaking his head, the huge-limbed peasant often laments, with a sigh, that the toil of his hands has come to naught ; and, comparing the present with the past time, he extols the fortune of his father, and complains how the good old race, full of piety, bore the burden of their life very easily within narrow bounds, when the portion of land for each man was far less than now.'—ii. 1164-70.   [3] iii. 894.

foundly solemn, as well as infinitely tender. Above all
the tumult of life, he hears incessantly the funeral dirge
over some one departed, and the infant wail of a new-
comer into the stormy sea of life—

Mixtos vagitibus ægris
Ploratus mortis comites et funeris atri.[1]

His feeling can, indeed, be stern and indignant, as well
as tender and melancholy ; but it is never either morbid
or effeminate.   His tenderness is that of a thoroughly
strong nature.   Some signs of the same mood may be
discovered in the fragments of Ennius ; but the feeling
of Lucretius is the result of a much more meditative
intellect.   It is connected with the vividness with which
he realises all that is involved in the thought of life
and death, and with the sympathies of a contemplative
mind united to a strong and passionate heart.

His imagination, which depicts so forcibly the intimations of experience, is able to bear him also beyond
the known and familiar regions of life.   As it enables
him to pass

Extra flammantia muodi moenia.

and to behold the dawn of creation, and even the blank
desolation which will follow on the overthrow of our
system, so it has enabled him to realise with vivid feeling the primeval condition of man upon the world.   Yet
even in these daring enterprises of his fancy he adheres
strictly to the conclusions of his philosophical system,
and shows that sincerity and truthful adherence to fact
are as genuine attributes of his poetic faculty as of his
understanding and moral nature.

His poem shows, both in its substance and expression,
that he was a diligent student of the great works of
earlier times, as well as a most original thinker and
poet.   In addition to the direct debt which he owed in
philosophy to Democritus and Epicurus, he betrays in

[1] ii. 569-70.

thought, sentiment, and expression many traces of the
study of Homer, of Empedocles, and of Ennius. His
description of the sacrifice of Iphigenia recalls some
features in the picture of the same event from the
Agamemnon of Æschylus ; and the account in Book vi.
of the plague at Athens is closely adapted from Thucydides. There can be no doubt that all these writers
helped to educate and to mould his mind ; but their
influence was to quicken kindred powers and sympathies
in himself, not to overmaster his genius. He has, in
common with Homer, the clear and varied observation of
the outward aspects of nature, and something also of his
deep and true insight into the heart and mind of man.
He recalls the daring thought, the vivid and condensed
energy of imaginative language, and the solemn feeling
of Æschylus. In the Prometheus Vinctus especially the
affinity of the bold and earnest speculation of Æschylus
to that of Lucretius may be traced, as well as an affinity
in their poetical view of the primeval state of man,
of the unknown and remote regions of the world, and of
the whole wonder of creation. The accurate observation of facts as the groundwork of historical and political
reflection, the masculine sense, the contempt for superstition, by which this poem is distinguished, remind the
reader of some of the most marked characteristics of
Thucydides. The parallel and the contrast between
the temper and thought of Lucretius, and those indicated in the fragments of Empedocles and of Ennius,
have already been considered. There can be little doubt
that in the perception and feeling of the realities of life
and the facts of nature, the Roman poet was immeasurably superior to the mystic of Agrigentum ; while his
great speculative power and contemplative interests, as
well as his finer accomplishment in language, rhythm,
and artistic design, separate him widely from the father
of Roman poetry.

His excellencies are so different from those of Virgil
and of Horace that the question need not be entertained,
whether the rank of the greatest of Roman poets is or is
not to be awarded to him.   He certainly stands alone
as the great contemplative poet of antiquity.   He has
proclaimed with more power than any other the majesty
of Nature's laws, and has interpreted with a truer and
deeper insight the meaning of her manifold life.   Few
have felt so strongly the mystery of man's being, or have
indicated so passionate a sympathy with the real sorrows
of life, and so ardent a desire to raise man to his proper
dignity, and to support him in bearing his inevitable
burden.   With all his affinities to some of the greatest
men of earlier times he has much also in common with
the spirit and genius of modern times.   In his contemplation of human life he combines the profound feeling
of Pascal with the speculative elevation of Spinoza.
The loftier tones of his poetry may be compared with
the sustained dignity and majesty of Milton.   His sympathy with nature, at once fresh and imaginative, is
more like the feeling of the great poets of the present
century than the general sentiment of ancient poetry.
In the union of poetical feeling and scientific passion he
seems to anticipate the most elevated mode of the study
of nature, of which the world has seen a few great examples in modern times.   Few writers of any age have
exercised such various faculties in such harmonious
combination.   His powers of perception, thought, feeling, and imagination, are characterised by a remarkable
vitality and sincerity.   His strong intellectual and
poetical faculty is united with some of the rarest and
noblest moral qualities,--with great fortitude, earnestness of feeling, unswerving love of truth, a manly and
genuine tenderness of heart.   And while, on the other
hand, it is not to be forgotten that he used his great
powers of heart, understanding, and genius, in support

of a cause which is now seen to be most fatal to human
happiness and advancement ; it is also to be remembered
that he lived at a time when the most truthful mind
might have despaired of the Divine government of the
world, and might have honestly felt that it was well to
escape, at any cost, from the burden of Pagan superstition.

CHAPTER XII.

CATULLUS.

LUCRETIUS and Catullus were regarded by ancient critics as the greatest poets of the last age of the Republic. They alone represent the poetry of that period to modern times. Although they were exposed to the same outward influences, it would be difficult to mention any two authors of a more distinct type of genius and character. The first has left to us only the record of his lofty contemplation ; the other has stamped upon his pages the lasting impression not only of the deepest joy and pain of his heart, but even of the lighter cares and fancies that occupied the passing hour. He is essentially the poet of passion and enjoyment ; but his passion, if not ennobled by its purity, is redeemed by its sincerity ; and his love of beauty and simplicity of nature impart a charm to all his enjoyment. The idea of him which comes naturally to the mind in reading his poetry is that of 'the young Catullus,' as he is described by Ovid, in his lines on the death of Tibullus—

> Obvius huic venias, hedera juvenilia cinctus
> Tempora, cum Calvo, docte Catulle, tuo.[1]

Although there is some uncertainty about the age at which he died, the peculiar character of his poetry affords the clearest indication that he never passed from the social pleasures, the freedom and the easy efforts of

[1] *Amor.* III. 9, 61.

Y

youth, to the mature interests, the reflective habit, and
the steady labours of riper years.

Some light is thrown upon the nature of his art by
the knowledge which we possess of the other authors
who were contemporary with him. Lucretius and Catullus, although the greatest, were by no means the only
poets who flourished in that age. The mention by
Cicero of the Empedocles of Sallustius implies that an
interest in the old poetical philosophers of Greece was
felt by others as well as by Lucretius. The name of
Catullus is united with that of his friend Calvus, the
orator, both by Horace[1] and by Ovid. The poetry of
the two intimate friends was evidently of the same character. They are named together by Aulus Gellius[2] as
the only Roman poets who were allowed by the Greeks
of his time to have written anything good in the style
of Anacreon. Lævius,[3] Hortensius the orator, Helvidius
Cinna a friend of Catullus, and Memmius, to whom the
poem of Lucretius is dedicated, are mentioned in the
same passage as being also authors of amatory poetry,
but of much inferior merit. Calvus is mentioned by
Suetonius as the author of a satire on Julius Cæsar ;
and the poems of Catullus are coupled by Tacitus[4]
with those of Bibaculus, as being 'referta contumeliis
Cæsarum.' From these and similar notices it may be
inferred that the forms of literature most popular among
the young men of pleasure and literary taste, contemporary with Lucretius and Catullus, were amatory poems
and personal lampoons, the latter being directed chiefly
against Julius Cæsar and his partisans. Catullus also
mentions a poem, by his friend Cæcilius, on Cybele—a
fact which perhaps throws some light on his own selec-

---

[1] *Sat.* i. 10. 17. [2] xix. 9.
[3] There is some uncertainty as to the date of Lævius ; probably he was
somewhat earlier than Calvus and Catullus. The work attributed to him
was known by the name of Protopaignion. [4] *Ann.* iv. 34.

tion of the subject of Atys. He speaks also with humorous horror of the swarms of poetasters—

> Sæcli incommoda, pessimi poetæ,[1]

which the literary culture of the time brought out along
with its few men of true genius and accomplishment.

It may be observed that several of those who have
been mentioned as writers of poetry were also eminent
as orators. The greatest of all the Roman orators attempted, but only with indifferent success, to gain distinction as a poet. His brother Quintus was an aspirant
to similar honours. Asinius Pollio appears from the
eulogies of Virgil and Horace to have been more successful. As compared with any previous age of Roman
literature, the last years of the Republic may be looked
upon as the beginning of that phase of eager but not
always profitable activity, which Horace afterwards characterised in the line—

> Scribimus indocti doctique poemata passim.

Catullus was little, if at all, indebted to the Roman
poets who preceded him. He shows the spirit of the
old Republic only in the boldness and license of his
satire. One or two of the writers of a previous generation—such as Valerius Ædituus, Q. Catulus, and perhaps Lævius, though his date is uncertain—may have
been before him in the field of amatory poetry; but
there is no reason to suppose that his genius was in any
way influenced by them. He drew his materials from
the fresh sources of his own life, and from a constant,
sympathetic study of Greek poetry. It is strange to
find a poet of so much nature and originality striving
to imitate the laboured efforts of the courtly pedants of
Alexandria. The admiration of Catullus for Callimachus
might be compared with the aspiration which Burns has
expressed for 'Shenstone's art.' It is the admiration of
youthful genius, not sure of its own powers, for estab-

lished reputation, learning, and artistic skill. But Catullus found a higher ideal by which to mould his genius
and noble simplicity of expression in the old passion
and melody of Lesbos and Ionia.

Scarcely anything is known of the life of Catullus,
except what may be gathered from his own poems.
There is some uncertainty even in regard to his name,--
one authority giving it as C. Valerius, another as Q.
Valerius Catullus. The statement of the Eusebian
Chronicle that he was born at Verona may be accepted,
as it is confirmed by expressions in earlier authorities.[1]
But the dates of his birth and death, given in the
Chronicle, are contradicted by the evidence of his remains. The statement of Hieronymus is, that he was
born in the year B.C. 87, and that he died in the thirtieth
year of his age, in the year B.C. 57. These dates are
contradicted by several allusions in the poems to events
later than the date assigned for his death, and especially
by the evidence of the poem numbered LII., which clearly
establishes the fact that Catullus witnessed the consulship of Vatinius in B.C. 47. It has been conjectured,[2]
with great probability, that this mistake arose from a
confusion between the consulships of Cn. Octavius, who
held that office along with L. Cornelius Cinna in B.C. 87,
and of another Cn. Octavius, who was consul in B.C. 76
along with C. Scribonius Curio. If we assume this latter
year as the date of the birth of Catullus, as there is no
allusion in his poems to any event later than the consulship of Vatinius, there is no further difficulty in accepting the statement that he died in the thirtieth year of
his age, i.e., in B.C. 46. It is suggested by Haupt[3] that
the words of poem LII.—

Quid est, Catulle ? quid moraris emori ?
Sella in curuli Struma Nonius sedet,

[1] Ovid, Amor. III. 15. 7 ; Martial, xiv. 195 ; and others.
[2] By Lachmann. His conjecture is adopted by Haupt and C. F. Hermann.
[3] Quaestiones Catullinae.

Per consulatum pejerat Vatinius :
Quid est, Catulle ? quid moraris emori ?'

look as if they had been dictated by a presentiment or
consciousness of approaching death. It may not be safe
to found much on this argument; still it may be received
as tending to confirm, so far as it goes, the inference
which may be drawn from the fact that there is no
allusion in any of the poems of Catullus to any event
later than B.C. 47. It can, at all events, scarcely be
doubted, that Catullus had passed away before even the
beginning of the brilliant Augustan era.

The only other information derived from external
sources in regard to his life, is contained in the anecdote
told by Suetonius,* that Julius Cæsar, 'although deeply
feeling the stigma of his lampoons, yet accepted his
apology, and received him at his table on the same day,
and continued his own intimate relations with the father
of Catullus as of old.' This story seems to imply what
is clearly indicated in many of his poems, that Catullus
was born in and habitually lived in the highest and
most cultivated circle of the Roman society of his time.

The volume of the poems of Catullus, which has come
down to modern times, consists of 116 pieces, written
in various metres, and on a great variety of subjects.
They were evidently composed at different times, but
they have not been arranged according either to the time
when they were written, or the subjects of which they
treat. The only principle which seems to have deter-

1 'Why, O Catullus, why
Dost thou delay to die !
See Strama Nonius there
Sits in the curule chair !
Vatinius too, that wretch forsworn,
The Consul's office makes a butt for scorn.
When such men are in power
Why shouldst thou live an hour ?'—MARTIN'S* Catullus.

* Julius Cæsar, 73.

* All the translations from Catullus in this chapter are by Mr. Martin.

mined the order in which they now appear, is that the
longer and more artistic poems occupy the middle of the
work, and that all those written in the elegiac metre
are placed at the end. The dedication of the volume
to Cornelius Nepos, which stands first in the series,
implies that one edition must have been published in the
lifetime of the poet ; but it is quite possible that some
of his later writings may have been included after his
death, in the work as it now stands.

A few of the more artistic of these poems are pure
works of creative fancy, but by far the greater number
of them are founded on the life, interests, and feelings
of the poet himself. They reveal him in many different
moods : in happiness and sorrow,—in the ecstasy and
the despair of passion,—in the frank outpouring of warm
affection and the genial enjoyment of social intercourse,
—in the bitterness of his scorn and animosity,—in the
license of his coarser indulgences. They enable us to
accompany him on his travels, and to see him in his
home, happy in the beauty of nature and the charm of
earlier poetry. Some of these poems indeed might well
have been spared ; others of them might have been expected to have perished with the occasion which called
them forth ; but there is a wonderful sincerity in all of
them, by means of which the whole nature of the poet,
in its better and worse features, is revealed to us as if
he were our contemporary.

From his own words it may be learned that he entered
on the pleasures of life and the practice of his art at a
very early age—

> Tempore quo primum vestis mihi tradita pura est.
> Jocundum cum aetas florida ver ageret.
> Multa satis lusi : non est dea nescia nostri
> Quae dulcem curis miscet amaritiem.[1]

[1] LXVIII. 15-19—

'Ever since, when life to gladsome spring had grown,
And first I donn'd the robe of spotless white,

He went in the train of the Praetor Memmius to
Bithynia, probably in the year B.C. 58, when, according
to the supposition of Lachmann as to the date of his
birth, he must have been about the age of eighteen.
Several of his shorter poems refer to this period of his
life, and express his disgust with the meanness and
rapacity of his chief,[1] —his warm affection for his young
companions in the Praetor's train—

> O dulces comitum valete coetus,
> Longe quos simul a domo profectas
> Diverse varie viæ reportant,[2]—

the enthusiasm of a traveller in visiting the famous cities
of Asia,—

> Ad claras Asiæ volemus urbes,—

his affectionate pride in the yacht which bore its master
safe through the perils of the Euxine, the Ægean, and
the Adriatic,[3]—his deep happiness on his return to the
rest and security of his beautiful Sirmio.[4] The pleasures
of travel and the society of his friends were the chief
rewards of his adventure, as, owing to the selfishness of
Memmius, and the poverty of the province, he returned
home, according to his own statement, a poorer man
than he went.[5] His life seems from this time forward
to have been spent partly at Rome,[6] with occasional
visits to his villa in the neighbourhood of Tivoli,[7] and
partly in his native district, at Verona[8] or Sirmio. He

> Gaily I've lived, not unto Her unknown,
>> Who blends with pain our bitter-sweet delight.'
>>> MARTIN'S *Catullus*.

The words 'multa satis lusi,' like those in Horace (Od. IV. 9. 9)—
>> Nec si quid olim lusit Anacreon,

refer rather to his art than to his life.

[1] X. 12; XXVIII. 9.
[2] XLVI. 9-11 –
>> ' And you, ye band of comrades tried and true,
>>> Who side by side went forth from home, farewell !
>> How far apart the paths shall carry you
>>> Back to your native shore, ah, who can tell ?'
[3] IV. [4] XXXI. [5] XXVIII. 8. [6] LXVIII. 34. [7] XLIV. [8] LXVIII. 27.

indulged freely and ardently in the pleasures of youth ;
but he never lost his warm affection for his friends, and
his passionate delight in the exercise of his art and in
the study of the poets of Greece. He enjoyed the
pleasantest social intercourse with some of the most
witty and cultivated among his contemporaries, such as
Licinius Calvus, Alphenus Varus, Asinius Pollio, and
Helvidius Cinna. He addresses Cicero and Cornelius
Nepos—to the latter of whom his volume is dedicated—
with a mixture of modesty, respect, and frank cordiality,
which might be expected to characterise the feelings of
a generous youth like Catullus, when admitted to the
friendship of older men of established reputation. His
antipathies were as strong as his affections. Besides his
many private enmities towards men of meaner note, he
denounces Memmius and Piso, Mamurra, Vatinius, and
Julius Cæsar, in the language not so much of moral indignation as of the bitterest personal animosity. While
living away from Rome he appears to have taken a
lively interest in the gossip and in the simple pleasures
of the people of his native province.[1] He was a keen
and critical observer of the folly, the meanness, the
affectation, or the pedantry of his less intimate associates. He was peculiarly sensitive to any slight or want
of courtesy; and he felt, with unusual bitterness, any
change in the feelings of his friends. His standard of
conduct seems to have been founded on a strong regard
for the duties of honour and of affection.[2] One great
passion, lavished on an unworthy object, and one heart-
felt sorrow for the death of a dearly loved and valued
brother, were the deepest experiences in his kindly and
genial, but aimless and somewhat tainted life.

[1] Compare especially the poem numbered XVII.—

    O Colonia, quæ cupis ponte ludere magno, etc.

[2] Cf. LXXVI. 3-4—

    Nec sanctam violasse fidem, nec fœdere in ullo
    Divum ad fallendos numine abusum homines.

By none of his poems is Catullus so well known as by
those which record the various phases of his passion for
Lesbia. It is mentioned by Appuleius that her real
name was Clodia. In the same passage it is stated that
the name of the Cynthia of Propertius was Hostia, and
that of the Delia of Tibullus, Plania. This statement,
however, by no means justifies the conclusion that the
Lesbia of Catullus was the same person as the Clodia
whose debaucheries are described with such terrible
power by Cicero in his defence of Cælius. The name
would only suggest the inference that she was a Roman
lady. The language of Catullus clearly proves that she
was a married woman,[1] that she was as faithless to her
lover as she had been to her husband, and that her
fascination was as great as her profligacy. She is the
subject of some of the most beautiful of the short poems
in the earlier part of the volume, and of several of the
elegiac poems, most of which seem to be of a later date.
The poems, which appear to have been written in the
earlier stage of his passion—those especially numbered
ii. iii. v. vii.,—express all the rapture of ardent devotion, combined with the secure sense of requited love.
In some of the later poems he speaks of Lesbia as having
been at this time dearer to him than his own life. He
declares that his affection for her was much more true
and tender than the mere passion of a lover for his
mistress—

> Dilexi tam te non tantum ut vulgus amicam,
> Sed pater ut gnatos diligit et generos.[2]

The two poems on the ' Sparrow of Lesbia' were evi
dently composed at this time, before his eyes were
opened to the unworthiness of his mistress. Both of

[1] LXIX., LXXXIII.

[2] ' I loved you then with love beyond
The transient flash of passion wild ;
Ay, with a tenderness as fond
As binds the parent to the child.' LXXII. 3-4

these poems are written in a style of exquisite grace
and simplicity. The first is expressed in tones of
playful tenderness, not without some touch of that
luxury of melancholy which accompanies and enhances
passion. These words, for instance—

Et solatiolum sui doloris,

and again—

Cum gravis acquiescet ardor,[1]—

describe the pain of the over-strained heart, felt even
at the moment when it is most conscious of its happiness. His lament on the death of the sparrow is perhaps the most famous of all his shorter poems. It
displays all his ease and grace in expression, his love of
all beautiful things—

At vobis male sit, malæ tenebræ
Orci, quæ omnia bella devoratis ;
Tam bellum mihi passerem abstulistis,[2]

some movement, also, half-playful, half-serious, of that
strong power of feeling, which was stirred to its depths,
a few years later, by a more real sorrow. The poems
numbered v. and vii.—

Vivamus, mea Lesbia, atque amemus ;[3]

and

Quæris, quot mihi basiationes,[4]

both addressed to Lesbia, express with even more sincerity the tumult and ecstasy of his passion. Yet from
the very intensity of his happiness the sense of its insecurity is awakened. 'The dust of death' spices the
enjoyment of his love. The thought of the eternal night
enhances, for the moment, the brightness of his brief
day—

[1] II. 7 8.

[2] ' Out upon you, and your power,
Which all fairest things devour !
Orcus' gloomy shades, that e'er
Ye should take my bird so fair !'— III. 13-15

[3] v. 1.

[4] VII. 1.

Soles occidere et redire possunt :
Nobis, cum semel occidit brevis lux,
Nox est perpetua una dormienda.[1]

It is this thought which, to the Epicurean of every age,
according to his mood, either enhances or eclipses all his
enjoyment—

Hoc etiam faciunt ubi discubuere tenentque
Pocula sæpe homines et inumbrant ora coronis,
Ex animo ut dicant 'brevis hic est fructus homullis ;
Jam fuerit neque post unquam revocare licebit.'[2]

It is in the songs, which proclaim most loudly the
freedom and the outward gaiety of his life ; in the passionate love in which he seems to live most strongly ; in
every phase of existence, in which he is most conscious
of his being and his power, that the heart of man most
vividly realises the thought, 'our joy is but for a season,'
—'brevis hic est fructus homullia.'

The vicissitudes of passion, which Lucretius describes,[3]
are remarkably illustrated by the record which Catullus
has given of his own experience. The rapturous happiness described in these early poems was suddenly ter-
minated, not by death, but by the faithlessness of Lesbia.
In poem viii., written in a different metre, expressive of
a calmer but sadder mood, the poet recalls his past happiness, and chides himself for still loving and regretting
one whose unworthiness he had proved. He consoles
himself with the thought, that ' he had had his day '—

Fulsere quondam candidi tibi soles ;[4]

he claims to have loved as he never could love again—

Amata nobis quantum amabitur nulla ;[5]

---

[1] ' When the sun sets, 'tis to rise
    Brighter in the morning skies ;
    But when sets our little light,   •
    We must sleep in endless night.'—v. 4-8.
[2] ' This too is the case oftentimes with men when they recline at the
feast, and grasp the wine-cup, and shade their faces with wreaths, that they
say from their hearts, "our joy is but for a season—it will soon be past
nor may it henceforth ever be recalled." '—LUCRET. III. 912-15.
[3] In the latter part of Book IV.   [4] VIII 3.   [5] VIII. 5.

he tries to steel himself against the folly of unavailing regret, in bidding her a sorrowful and reproachful farewell—

> Vale, puella, jam Catullus obdurat,
> Nec te requiret nec rogabit invitam:
> At tu dolebis, cum rogaberis nulla.[1]

In a poem, written apparently somewhat later, he uses harsher and coarser reproaches, and speaks of his own love as having fallen away irrevocably—

> Velut prati
> Ultimi flos, praetereunte postquam
> Tactus aratro est.[2]

Several of the poems in the elegiac metre, at the end of the series, prove that his passion still underwent various changes, and that having once loved with all his heart, he could not relapse into settled scorn or indifference. Some of these poems represent him as reconciled to his mistress, and half believing in her future constancy; in others he describes himself as torn between opposite feelings of love and hatred—

> Odi et amo. Quare id faciam, fortasse requiris.
> Nescio sed fieri sentio et excrucior,[3]—

in others again he prays, with something almost of pious earnestness, to be delivered from his passion as from a foul disease—

> O dii, si vestrum est misereri, aut si quibus usquam
>   Extremam jam ipsa morte tulistis opem,
> Me miserum aspicite (et, si vitam puriter egi,
>   Eripite hanc pestem perniciemque mihi),
> Hei mihi surrepens imos ut torpor in artus
>   Expulit ex omni pectore laetitias.
> Non jam illud quaero, contra ut me diligat illa,
>   Aut, quod non potis est, esse pudica velit:
> Ipse valere opto et tetrum hunc deponere morbum.
>   O dii, reddite mi hoc pro pietate mea.[4]

[1] VIII. 12-14.

[2]   ' Even like the meadow's border flower,
        Which, by the passing ploughshare torn,
        Lies withering in the dust forlorn.'--XI. 22-24.

[3] LXXXV.

[4] LXXVI. 17-24—

      ' O ye great gods! if you can pity feel,
        If e'er to dying wretch your aid was given,

The fame of Catullus, as, with the exception perhaps of Sappho, the greatest and the truest of all the ancient poets of love, does not rest merely on those poems which record the vicissitudes of his own experience. His longer and more artistic pieces show that the phase of life which he most delighted to paint was either the ardour of youthful passion, or the secure happiness of mutual affection. Thus he selects from Greek legend and poetry, the desertion of Ariadne, the brief union of Protesilaus and Laodamia, the calm, god-like blessedness of Peleus and Thetis, as subjects for his art. Others again of his poems show his deep unselfish sympathy with the happiness and affection of his friends. The most charming of all his greater poems is the Epithalamium, which celebrates the union of his friend Manlius Torquatus with his bride. No ancient poet has presented so true an image of the passionate devotion and ecstasy of lovers, as that which is contained in the playful and tender, and yet burning lines of the 'Acme and Septimius.' His own fate did not teach him the lessons of cynicism. His heart believes in the constancy of love, and his imagination paints the union of passion with a deep affection as the most real source of human happiness. The lines in which he comforts his friend Calvus for the loss of his mistress Quintilia, bear witness to the strength and the delicacy of his friendship, and make us feel that the life of pleasure in that age might be redeemed not

See me in agony before you kneel,
  To beg this curse may from me far be driven,

' Which creeps in drowsy horror through each vein,
  Leaves me no thought from bitter anguish free ;
I do not ask she may be kind again,
  No, nor be chaste, for that may never be !

' I ask for peace of mind—a spirit clear
  From the dark taint that now upon it rests.
Give then, O give, ye gods, this boon so dear
  To one who ever hath revered your hests.'

only by genius and culture, but by a true heart and
unselfish sympathy—

> Si quicquam mutis gratum acceptumque sepulcris
> Accidere a nostro, Calve, dolore potest,
> Quo desiderio veteres renovamus amores
> Atque olim missas flemus amicitias,
> Certe non tanto mors immatura dolori est
> Quintiliae, quantum gaudet amore tuo.[1]

The great charm of the character of Catullus is the
truth and warmth of his affection. Many poets have
sung the praises of love, but few, if any, have left so
pleasant a record of the kindly intercourse of friendship.
Some of the most beautiful among his shorter poems are
serious or playful addresses to the companions of his
youth, or to those with whom he was united by their
common love of literature. In his gayest hours, and in
his greatest sorrow, in his pleasures and in his studies,
he shows his thoughtful consideration for others, and
the value which he attached to hearty sympathy. He
seems to have possessed, in no ordinary measure, the
gift of being made happy, by feeling another's happiness.
He expresses very honest and delicate, but in no way
over-strained, appreciation of the works, and of the wit,
taste, and genius of his friends. The dedication of his
volume to Cornelius Nepos combines a courteous, half-
playful tribute to the labours of that historian, along with
a very modest expression of his own worth—

> Quoi dono lepidum novum libellum
> Arida modo pumice expolitum ?
> Corneli, tibi : namque tu solebas
> Meas esse aliquid putare nugas

---

[1] 'Calvus, if those now silent in the tomb
    Can feel the touch of pleasure in our tears,
For those we loved, who perished in their bloom,
    And the departed friends of former years ;

'Oh, then, full surely thy Quintilia's woe,
    For the untimely fate that bade ye part,
Will fade before the bliss she feels to know,
    How very dear she is unto thy heart.'—XCVI.

Jam tum cum ausus es unus Italorum
Omne ævum tribus explicare chartis
Doctis, Jupiter, et laboriosis ! [1]

His lines addressed to Cicero—

Disertissime Romuli nepotum,
Quot sunt quotque fuere, Marce Tulli, etc. ; [2]

his invitation to his friend and brother poet, Cæcilius—

Poetæ tenero, meo sodali
Velim Cæcilio, papyre, dicas ; [3]

the lines in which he recalls to Licinius Calvus a day
which they had passed together in witty talk and the
interchange of verses over their wine—

Scribens versiculos uterque nostrum
Ludebat numero modo hoc modo illoc
Reddens mutua per jocum atque vinum ; [4]

the humorous contrast which he draws between the
probable fate of ' the Annals of Volusius' and of the
long-delayed poem of his friend Helvidius Cinna ; [5]—
all show that, though fastidious in his literary judg
ments, he was not only without a single touch of envy
in his nature, but that he felt a generous pride and
pleasure in the fame and the accomplishments of his
associates. [6] His affection does not seem to have been
limited by literary sympathy. His friends Veranuius
and Fabullus appear to have been simply young men of

[1] ' My little volume is complete,
And with the pumice made as neat
As tome need wish to be ;
And now what patron shall I choose
For these gay sallies of my muse ?
Cornelius, whom but thee ?

' For though they are but trifles, then
Some value didst to them allow,
And that from thee is fame,
Who darest, in thy three volumes' space,
Alone of all Italians, trace
Our history and name.'—i. 1-7.

[1] XLIX. 1-2. [3] XXXV. 1-2. [4] L. 4-6. [5] XCV. 5-9.
[6] Compare also his humorous account of the compliment paid to the
speech of Calvus against Vatinius—

Dii magni, salaputium disertum.—LIII. 5.

pleasure, who had tried, like Catullus himself, unsuccessfully to better their fortunes by accompanying one of the praetors to his province. The language of affection has never been uttered with more warmth, simplicity, and grace, than in the poem of ten or eleven lines, called forth by the return of Verannius from Spain—

> Venistine domum ad tuos Penates
> Fratresque unanimos anumque matrem ?
> Venisti. O mihi nuntii beati ! [1]

The 'Invitation to Fabullus'[2] is in a much lighter strain. It shows us the freedom and humour which were united with the delicacy and the kindliness of his nature. It speaks of the common enjoyment of wine and pleasure, wit and laughter, which, if not the most noble and enduring, is yet one of the most natural among the many ties which bind men to one another in friendly intimacy. His warm heart, moreover, shows itself even through his playful banter, in the expression, ' venuste noster,' and in those lines of true feeling—

> Sed contra accipies meras amores
> Seu quid suavius elegantiusve.[3]

His regard for these friends appears also incidentally in his half-angry remonstrance with Marrucinus Asinius, the brother of Asinius Pollio, for having filched his napkin during some festive meeting,—'in joco atque vino.' He does not, he says, care for its value, but he treasures it as a keepsake of his friends—

> Quod me non movet aestimatione,
> Verum est mnemosynon mei sodalis ;
> Nam sudaria Saetaba ex Hiberis
> Miserunt mihi muneri Fabullus
> Et Verannius ; haec amem necesse est
> Et Veraniolum meum et Fabullum.[4]

---

[1] IX. 3-5.　　　　[2] XIII.　　　　[3] XIII. 9-10.

[4] ' 'Tis not for its value I prize it—don't sneer !—
But as a momento of friends who are dear.
'Tis one of a set that Fabullus from Spain
And Veranius sent me, a gift from the twain ;

Some of his poems express the pain and disappointment of a sensitive heart, which perhaps expected more from the constancy and disinterestedness of friendship than is commonly found among men. Of this nature are his almost tearful complaint to Cornificius,

Malest, Cornifici, tuo Catullo ; [1]

and the sorrowful and affectionate reproach which he addresses to Alphenus Varus—

Certe tute jubebas animam tradere, Inique, me
Inducens in amorem, quasi tuta omnia mi forent.
Inde nunc retrahis te ac tua dicta omnia factaque
Ventos irrita ferre ac nebulas aërias sinis.[2]

In these lines, and in other poems,[2] we see Catullus to have been a man very sensitive and quick to take offence, and also very dependent for his happiness on the affection of his friends. The tone here employed is, however, very different from the savage bitterness which he pours out against those whose more active unkindness and treachery he had experienced. There is a touch of natural piety in the two lines with which this poem ends—

Si tu oblitus es, at dii meminerunt, meminit Fides :
Quæ te ut pæniteat postmodo facti faciet tui.[4]

Perfidy and falsehood are the sins which are believed to call down the vengeance of heaven. When Catullus, in a later poem,[5] lays claim to a good conscience and the character of a ' pious ' man, he rests this claim on his consciousness of never having violated his word of honour, or abused his oath, in any of his dealings. As peaceful contemplation was the religious ideal of Lucre-

So the napkins, of course, are as dear to Catullus
As the givers, Veranaius himself and Fabullus.'—XII. 12-17.
[1] XXXVIII.
[2] ' Thou bad'st me yield thee up, my love, thou didst,
Wooing my heart in thee its peace to find ;
And now thou turn'st away my grief amidst
Thy works, thy deeds, all scatter'd to the wind.'—XXX. 7-10.
[3] E.g., LXXIII. [4] XXX. 11-12. [5] LXXVI.

Z

tius, good faith between man and man was the one duty
of piety which Catullus acknowledged and observed.

The warm heart of Catullus was doomed to feel a
still more bitter pang than even that occasioned by
the desertion or the unkindness of friends. The great
sorrow of his life was caused by the death of a dearly
loved brother. He died in the Troad—

> Quem nunc tam longe non inter nota sepulchra
> Nec prope cognatos compositum cineres,
> Sed Troja obscena, Troja infelice sepultum
> Detinet extremo terra aliena solo,[1]—

and Catullus paid a pious pilgrimage to his tomb, to
offer upon it the customary funeral gifts, and to bid a
last farewell to his silent ashes. All the poems in which
he speaks of this great grief, breathe a spirit of deep
human feeling and unaffected sorrow. He expresses no
hope of any future meeting after their earthly separation, yet he resolves that his love shall still live, though
severed for ever from its object.[?] Yet while yielding to
this affliction, so far as to become for the time indifferent both to the passion which had swayed his life, and
to the delight which he had once taken in the works of
ancient poets, and in the exercise of his own art,[?] he will
not allow himself to feel that ' his capabilities of love'
are exhausted, or to forget what was due to living
friends. It is characteristic of his frank affectionate
nature, that while dead to all his old interests in life and
literature, he finds his chief consolation in unburthening
his heart to his friends. If all the rest of his being was
overpowered by his affliction, he still kept alive his unselfish and delicate kindness of heart. He cannot bear
that, even in a trifling matter, Hortalus should find him

[1] ' Whom now, far, far away, not laid to rest
Amid familiar tombs with kindred dust,
Fell Troy detains, Troy impious and unblest,
'Neath its unhallow'd plain ignobly thrust.'—LXVIII. 97-100.
[?] LXV. 10.   [?] LXVIII. 19.

faithless to a promise; and he tries to comfort his friend
Manlius in a great sorrow—apparently the loss of his
bride, in whose honour the nuptial song had been composed—which had overtaken him. Though all other
feelings were for the time dead, and neither love
could distract nor poetry heal his grief, his heart was
yet alive to the memory of former kindness, to the
desire for sympathy, and to the duty of thinking of
others.

The personal feelings and tastes of Catullus are displayed with great plainness and sincerity in his short
satirical pieces. These have scarcely anything in common with the reflective and didactic satire of Lucilius
and Horace. There is nothing of an ethical, and very
little of a political character about them. They arise
out of the sympathies and antipathies of the poet,
his sensitiveness to neglect or wrong, his indignation
against some actual instance of meanness or baseness,
the extreme fastidiousness of his taste, and his lively
sense of the ridiculous. He felt much more keenly
than most men not only personal affection but personal
antipathy. He is roused as much by any slight to his
friends as to himself. He assails the Prætor Piso, whose
selfishness and rapacity had stood in the way of his
friends, Verannius and Fabullus, with the same hearti-
ness as he had attacked his own former chief Memmius.
He writes in a spirit of bold independence and absolute
disregard of the claims of rank. His scornful advice,
'pete nobiles amicos,' expresses the revolt of his whole
nature against the bondage of courtiership. His rough
republican honesty breaks out in violent invectives
against Julius Cæsar and his associates. He asserts
his own entire indifference to and independence of that
man, whose single greatness was overshadowing the
world. There is nothing, however, in his poems to indicate that he ranked himself among the partisans of

Pompey. He unites 'soccr generique'[1] in one condemnation as the cause of the ruin of the Commonwealth. As a member of a class which recognised no social nor political superior, living apparently apart from public interests, and so blind to the inevitable tendency of things, he indignantly resisted the attempt of any one man to make his own will paramount in the State. Moreover, his fastidious taste inspired him with disgust towards the lives and characters of men like Mamurra and Vatinius, who rose to eminence under the shadow of Cæsar's greatness. But while there is every reason to admire the boldness and the honesty with which Catullus expresses his dislike, it is at the same time to be admitted that the virulence of his attack, and the extreme coarseness of his imputations, are among the worst faults which have left a stain on his impulsive and generous nature.

Many of the personal satires in these poems were written to expose licentiousness. There is unfortunately evidence enough to show that purity of life and speech was not one among the virtues either of Catullus or his friends. Yet he lays claim to some share of that virtue in his life at least, in such expressions as 'si vitam puriter egi,'[2] and in his strange apology for the freedom of his verse—

> Nam castum esse decet pium poetam
> Ipsum, versiculos nihil necesse est.[3]

The truth seems to be that the standard of conduct was, in that age, regulated by intellectual taste, and what would now be called gentlemanly feeling, not by any moral considerations. The iniquities which Catullus exposed were offences not only against morality and good taste, but against all natural human feeling. It is not possible to excuse and scarcely even to palliate

---

[1] XXIX. 24.   [2] LXXVI. 19.

[3] 'True poets should be chaste, I know ;
But wherefore should their lines be so ?'—XVI. 5-6.

the coarseness of language which he has allowed himself
to use in these careless or savage lampoons. It is one
of the strangest signs of the spirit of that age, to find
a poet with the clear eye and pure taste for beauty,
and the fresh feeling of life and capacity for natural
enjoyment, with which Catullus was endowed beyond
most poets of ancient or modern times, turning all his
vigorous force of expression to the vilest uses. There
can be little doubt that coarseness of speech pervaded
the social intercourse of his age to a much greater extent than during the early period of Roman literature
and during the Augustan age. In the former period, the
influence of the old Roman severity and of the virtuous
family life of the early Republic had not altogether
passed away. In the Augustan era, if there was as
little purity as in the age preceding it, outward decorum
was more strictly observed. The conservative instincts
of society, supported by external authority, shrank from
exposing to the light the symptoms of inward corruption. The impurity of the Augustan age, when it betrays itself at all, is expressed in tones of effeminate
refinement; it is associated with sentimentalism in literature; it was reduced to system and carried into action
as the serious and decorous business of life. The coarseness of Catullus is symptomatic rather of a more reckless
license in society than of greater or even equal corruption. Impurity is less destructive to human nature
when united with a rough masculine humour, and when
it vents itself in bantering or virulent abuse, than when
it clings to the imagination, unites itself with the sense
of beauty, and expresses itself in the language of passion.
Though the language of Catullus in his higher poems is
often ardent, it is little, if at all, sullied with impurity.
The errors of his life did not deaden his nature, nor
harden his heart, nor corrupt his imagination. It is
only in his careless moods, when he looks on life in the

spirit of a humorist, or in moods of bitterness when his personal antipathies were roused, or in his savage fits when he witnessed some inhuman lust or prosperous villany, that he casts aside those restraints which the better instincts of men in nearly every age have placed upon the use of language.

Many, however, of his satires and humorous pieces are entirely free from coarseness or indelicacy of expression. As he valued exceedingly good taste and courtesy, wit and liveliness of mind in his associates, so he is especially intolerant of all meanness, vulgarity, dulness, and pedantry. The pieces in which these characteristics are satirically exposed are marked by a keen insight into character, a lively sense of absurdity, sometimes by a hearty and boisterous spirit of fun ; they are expressed with wonderful vigour and directness ; but they want altogether the subtle and reflective irony which pervades the satires, epistles, and odes of Horace. Among the best of his lighter and more genial satires may be mentioned the poem numbered xvii.,

O Colonia, quae cupis ponte ludere magno,

which has some touches of graceful poetry as well as of humorous extravagance. It denounces the dulness and stolid indifference of one of his fellow-townsmen, who, being married to a young and beautiful girl

Quoi cum sit viridissimo nupta flore puella
(Et puella tenellulo delicatior haedo
Asservanda nigerrimis diligentius uvis)[1]—

was utterly careless of her, and insensible to all the dangers to which she was exposed. In order to rouse him from his sloth and stupor, Catullus proposes to have him thrown headlong from a rickety old bridge into the

[1] 'Though he's wed to a girl still in womanhood's dawn,
A creature more dainty and fine than a fawn,
One who guarded, like grapes that are red-ripe, should be.'
XVII. 14-16.

deepest and dirtiest part of the quagmire over which
the bridge was built—·

> Quendam municipem meum de tuo volo pute
> Ire praecipitem in lutum per caputque pedesque.
> Verum totius ut lacus putidaeque paludis
> Lividissima maximaque est profunda vorago.[1]

In another of these pieces[2] Catullus laughs at the affectation of one Egnatius - a black-bearded fop,[3] from the
wilds of Spain—who had a trick of perpetually smiling,
for the purpose of showing the whiteness of his teeth.
The poet represents this man, who seems to have excited
his jealousy as well as his ridicule, as wearing this eternal
smile in every place and on every occasion, even at a
criminal trial, during the most pathetic part of the advocate's defence of his client, or when standing beside a
weeping mother at the funeral pyre of her only son. In
another of his short pieces, written in the elegiac metre,
he gives expression to his feelings of thankfulness on
the departure, for the east, of a cockney and bore, who
afflicted the refined ears of himself and his friends by
the superfluous use of his aspirates—

> Chommoda dicebat, si quando commoda vellet
> Dicere et insidias Arrius hinsidias,
> Et tum mirifice sperabat se esse locutum,
> Cum quantum poterat dixerat hinsidias.[4]

The ears of men were just beginning to recover from
this infliction—

---

[1] 'There's a townsman of mine, whom I long to see sped
From that bridge to the quagmire clean heels over head,
And just in that spot I would manage his fall,
Where the sludge is the bluest and rankest of all.' xvii. 8. 11.

[2] xxxix. [3] xxxviii. 19.

[4] 'Whenever Arrius wished to name
" Commodious," out " Chommodious" came ;
And when of his intrigues he blabb'd,
With his " hintrigues" our ears he stabb'd ;
And thought moreover he display'd
A rare refinement, when he made
His h's thus at random fall
With emphasis most guttural.'—lxxxiv. 1-4.

Cum subito affertur nuntius horribilis,
Ionios fluctus, postquam illuc Arrius isset,
Jam non Ionios esse, sed Hionios.[1]

Like fastidious and irritable poets in other ages, Catullus waged a fierce war against all literary pretenders and the dull manufacturers of verse. He regards pedants and poetasters as the great bores of the age—

' Suscli incommoda pessimi poetæ.'

He thus writes with humorous exaggeration to his friend Licinius Calvus, who had sent to him a great collection of the works of these poets—

Isti dii mala multa dent clienti
Qui tantum tibi misit impiorum.
Quod si, ut suspicor, hoc novum ac repertum
Munus dat tibi Sulla literator,
Non est mi male, sed bene ac beate,
Quod non disperunt tui labores.
Dii magni, horribilem et sacrum libellum,
Quem tu scilicet ad tuum Catullum
Misti, continuo ut die periret,
Saturnalibus optimo dierum.[2]

In another poem he speaks of himself as offering to

[1] ' When suddenly came news one day,
Which smote the city with dismay,
That the Ionian seas a change
Had undergone most sad and strange,
For, since by Arrius cross'd, the wild
"Hionian Hooran" they were styled.'—LXXXIV. 10-12.

[2] XIV. 21.

[3] ' May Jove with countless mischiefs curse
The client, who on thee bestow'd
Of festian rascals such a load!
But if, as shrewdly I surmise,
That pedant Sulla sent this prize,
Of new and most recondite stuff,
I can't feel gratitude enough,
That all thy toil in his defence
Has had such fitting recompense.
Gods! what a book! and this you send
To your Catullus—to your friend;
His comfort wholly to undo,
Upon the Saturnalia too,
Of all our holidays the day
One most relied on to be gay.'—XIV. 6-15.

Venus a holocaust of the poems of Volusius, in token of his reconciliation with Lesbia.[1] In another,[2] he points out the absurdity and bad taste of one of his acquaintances, who, though a man of sense, wit, and agreeable manners, fancied himself a poet, and was never so happy as when he had surrounded himself with all kinds of literary materials, and was plying this uncongenial avocation.

All those poems in which Catullus expresses his personal likes and dislikes, show that he was, above all things, a man of singularly genuine nature. He scarcely seems at all to speculate or reflect on human life; but few poets have been endowed with more native force of feeling and perception. The charm of many of his small pieces arises from his strong capacity of enjoying the simplest and purest pleasures. Among the poems in which this side of his nature is most clearly revealed, may be mentioned the dedication of his yacht to Castor and Pollux, the lines on Sirmio, and those in which he gives vent to the buoyancy of his feeling, when, with the return of spring, he is preparing to start on his travels from the dull plains of Phrygia for the famous cities of Asia—

> Jam mens praetrepidans avet vagari,
> Jam laeti studio pedes vigescunt.[3]

The lines on his yacht—

> Phaselus ille quem videtis, hospites,[4] etc.,

express with great simplicity and freshness the feelings of affectionate pride which a kindly nature lavishes not only on living friends, but on inanimate objects, associated with the memory of past days of happiness and adventure. His fancy endows it with a kind of life, as

---

[1] XXXVL. [2] XLII.
[3] ' Already through each nerve a flutter runs
Of eager hope that longs to be away ;
Already 'neath the light of other suns
My feet, new-wing'd for travel, yearn to stray.'—
[4] IV. I. XLVI. 7.

he dedicates it to the twin gods, whose star is auspicious
to mariners, and allows it to rest in peaceful age on
the fair waters of Benacus—

> Sed hæc prius fuere : nunc recondita
> Senet quiete seque dedicat tibi,
> Gemelle Castor et gemelle Castoris.[1]

But perhaps the most perfect of all his smaller pieces is
that in which the love of home and of nature, — the
sense of rest and security after toil and danger,—

> Cum mens onus reponit, ac peregrino
> Labore fessi venimus larem ad nostrum
> Desideratoque acquiescimus lecto,[2]—

the glee of a boy united to the strong happiness of a
man, are expressed, or rather seem to live for ever, in
those few lines on Sirmio, of which it is impossible either
to analyse the charm, or adequately to render the language by which it is conveyed.

No poet has ever imparted so much life and grace to
the most trifling incidents.[3] The common experience of
all men and the ordinary intercourse of society were
much more to him than to other people, not by being
idealised but by being felt more keenly. He enjoyed
life so deeply, and received the gifts of the passing
hour so happily, that, in order to produce pure and
lasting poetry, it was enough for him to utter something
of the fulness of his enjoyment. He has no belief in a
life after death, or at best only some shadowy hope that
the sorrows of the living for the dead may in some way
be felt by them. He does not contemplate death with

---

[1] ‘But these are things of days gone past,
Now anchor'd here in peace at last ;
To grow to heary age lies she,
And dedicates herself to thee,
Who hast always her guardian been,
Twin Castor, and thy brother twin.'—IV. 26-7.

[2] XXXI. 8-10.

[3] Compare, for instance, poem X. —
‘Varus me meus ad suos amores
Visum duxerat e foro otiosum,' etc.

the stern self abnegation of Lucretius, but he seems to
have had so much enjoyment in this world as to be
unable to think of any state of existence unlike that of
his familiar associations. His interests were indeed very
limited in their range, but they were all very genuine
and very human. All that he writes about himself,
about his love and his friendship, his animosities and
scorn, his enjoyments and his sorrows, is expressed
without any appearance of effort. Natural language,
without ornament or involution, expresses most happily
the feeling with which his heart is full. It is perhaps
from the simplicity of his nature, and the limited range
of his interests, that he has succeeded, beyond nearly
any poet, in saying, on every occasion, exactly what
he wanted to say, with the happiest union of grace
and vigour. There are, indeed, even in the shortest and
simplest of his poems, many fine touches of imaginative
or poetical expression, as the following, for instance—

> Aut quam sidera multa, cum tacet nox,
> Furtivos hominum vident amores ;[1]

or again—

> Velut prati
> Ultimi flos, praetereunte postquam
> Tactus aratro est ;[2]

or

> Nec sapit pueri instar
> Bimuli, tremula patris dormientis in ulna ;[3]

or this—

> Puella,
> Asservanda nigerrimis diligentius uvis.[4]

But the great merit of his style in these shorter poems
is its simple genuine force. It has all the ease of refined
and vigorous conversation, combined with the grace of
consummate art. His power over metre is perhaps as
great as over language, and it has the same qualities of
force, simplicity, and directness. The higher manifestations of this power are to be sought in his longer and

---

[1] vii. 7-8.   [2] xi. 22-24.   [3] xvii. 12-13.   [4] xvii. 14, 16.

more artistic pieces. His adaptation of the music of
language to embody the feeling or passion by which he
is possessed is most vividly felt in the sky-lark ring of
his great nuptial ode, in the wild hurrying agitation
of the Atys, in the stately calm of the epithalamium of
Peleus and Thetis. But the metrical effect of many of his
smaller pieces also—as, for instance, the playfulness, the
gaiety, and the tenderness of his hendecasyllabic verses,
the lingering long-drawn-out sweetness of the Sirmio, or
the calm subdued sadness of the same metre in the poem,

Miser Catulle, desinas ineptire—

clearly indicates that the feeling and the melody were
born together in the poet's heart. Although his elegiac
verses are not written with the smoothness or the recurring chime of the verse of Ovid, yet those among
them in which his graver and sadder moods are recorded
have a true plaintive force and natural pathos, which
their comparative roughness seems even to enhance. It
is to be remembered also that, although not the inventor
of this metre, which had been previously employed in
the epigrams of Ennius, he appears to have been the
first among the Roman poets by whom it was used as
a continuous vehicle in narrative poetry, and in the
poetry of personal feeling.

The merits of Catullus as a poetical artist are most
apparent in his longer poems. Among these none is
more beautiful than the nuptial ode in celebration of
the marriage of his friend Manlius, a member of the
famous house of the Torquati. In this poem more than
in any other Catullus seems to pour forth the fulness of
his heart,

'In profuse strains of unpremeditated art.'

It is marked by all the excellencies of his shorter pieces,
and by poetical beauty of a much finer order. Resembling his slighter poems in being called forth by personal feeling, and by an event within his own experience,

it breathes the same spirit of warm friendship, and of
sympathy with beauty and passion. It is written with
the same gaiety of heart, blending indeed with a more
earnest and deeper sense of happiness. But his feeling
on this occasion does not merely express itself in graceful language, but awakens the active power of imagination, clothes itself in radiant imagery, and rises into
the completeness and rich melody of lyrical art. The
tone of the whole poem is one of joy, changing from
the tumultuous rapture of expectation in the opening
lines to the deep secure sense of happiness, expressed in
the closing stanzas. The passion is ardent, but free from
grossness or effeminacy. Even when, in accordance with
established custom, he abandons himself for a few lines
to the spirit of raillery and banter—

> No diu taceat procax
> Fescennina locutio[1]—

he does not allow himself to utter anything that might
cast a slur on the innocence of the bride. Thoughts of
her are associated with the purest objects in nature,—
with the ivy clinging round a tree, or the branches of
the myrtle—

> Quos Hamadryades deae
> Ludicrum sibi roscido
> Nutriunt humore[2]—

or with the hyacinth growing in the garden of some
rich man. Like the eager lover of beauty among our
own poets, he sees in other flowers,—

> Alba parthenice velut,
> Luteumve papaver,[3]—

the symbol of maidens,

> 'Whom youth makes so fair and passion so pale.'

He prized the grace of trees and the bloom of flowers

[1] LXI. 126-27.
[2] 'By the Hamadryads fed
For their sport with honey-dew.'—LXI. 23-25.
[3] 'Like the pale parthenium through
Poppy-beds of saffron hue.'—LXI. 104-05.

among the fairest things in nature. The chief charm
which he sees in woman is virgin innocence awakening
into love, or passion purified by a true and constant
heart. So too, in the epithalamium of Peleus and Thetis,
he compares Ariadne in her maidenhood to the myrtle
trees on the banks of Eurotas, and to the bloom of
vernal flowers—

Hunc simul ac cupido conspexit lumine virgo
Regia, quam suaves expirant castus odores
Lectulus in molli complexu matris alebat ;
Quales Eurotae progignunt flumina myrtos,
Aurave distinctos educit veris colores.[1]

In this poem he does not, as in the Acme and Septimius, express merely his sympathy with the joy and
passion of the moment. He acknowledges in marriage
a higher good than in the love for a mistress. He associates it with thoughts of the power and security of the
household, of the pure happiness of parental love, of the
continuance of a time-honoured name, of the birth of
new defenders for the State.

The charm of the poem does not consist in its tone of
feeling and its clear ringing melody alone. The bright
spirit of the day awakens the inward power that creates
pictures and images of beauty in harmony with itself.
The poet sees Hymenaeus coming from the distant rocks
of Helicon, robed in saffron, and wreathed with fragrant
amarcus, in radiant power and glory, chanting the
song with his ringing voice, beating the ground with
his foot, shaking the pine-torch in his hand. As the
doors of the house are opened, and the bride is expected

[1] ' Soon as the royal maid with wishful eye
Beheld him, she, who still was wont to lie
Within her mother's soft embrace, fed
And nourished by the balmy odours shed
From that chaste couch as myrtles sweet that grow
Where the clear waters of Eurotas flow.
Or scents exhaled from spring-tide's flowery vest.'
LXIV. 86-90.

by the singers outside, by one vivid flash of imagination
he reveals all their eager excitement—

> Viden ut faces
> Splendidas quatiunt comas ?'[1]

In no poet, ancient or modern, is there any picture of
old age, drawn with a truer hand than in these three
lines—

> Usque dum tremulum movens
> Cana tempus anilitas
> Omnia omnibus annuit.[2]

Still more perfect is that picture of infancy awakening
into consciousness and affection, contained in these lines
of infinite tenderness, purity, and beauty —

> Torquatus volo parvulus
> Matis e gremio suæ
> Porrigens teneras manus
> Dulce ridest ad patrem
>   Semihiante labello.
> Sit suo similis patri
> Manlio et facile insciis
> Noscitetur ab omnibus
> Et pudicitiam suæ
>   Matris indicet ore.[3]

The whole conception and execution of this poem, as
also of the Atys and of the epithalamium of Peleus and

[1] ' Behold
The torches, how upon the air
They shake abroad their gleaming hair.'—LXI. 77-78.

[2] ' Till hoary age shall steal on thee
With loitering step, and trembling knee,
And palsied head, that, ever bent,
To all in all things nods assent.'—LXI. 162-3.

[3] ' Soon my eyes shall see, mayhap,
Young Torquatus on the lap
Of his mother, as he stands
Stretching out his tiny hands,
And his little lips, the while
Half open, on his father's smile.

And may be in all he like
Manlius his sire, and strike
Strangers when the boy they meet
As his father's counterfeit,
And his face the index be
Of his mother's chastity.'— LXI. 216-23.

Thetis, prove that Catullus was very richly endowed
with the truthful eye and faculty of imagination as well
as with pure poetical feeling and the gift of musical
expression.

The poem which immediately follows is also an epithalamium, intended to be sung by young men and
maidens, in alternate parts. It is written in hexameter
verse, and in rhythm, thought, and feeling resembles
some of the golden fragments from the epithalamia of
Sappho. The whole poem sounds like a song in a rich
idyll. Its charm consists in its calm and mellow tone,
in the dramatic truth with which the feelings and
thoughts natural to the young men and maidens are
alternately expressed, and especially in the beauty of its
two famous similes. In the first of these a flower is
again the symbol of the bloom and innocence of maidenhood, growing up apart and safe from all rude contact.
The idea in the concluding lines of the simile—

> Idem cum tenui carptus defloruit ungui,
> Nulli illam pueri, nullae optavere puellae,[1]

may probably have been suggested by a passage in
Sappho, of which these two lines remain—

> Οἵαν τὰν ἰάκινθον ἐν οὔρεσι ποίμενες ἄνδρες
> πόσσι καταστείβοισι, χάμαι δέ τε πόρφυρον ἄνθος.[2]

In the second simile, which is supposed to be spoken
by the young men, the vine growing upon a bare field,
scarcely rising above the ground, unheeded and untended,
is compared to the maid who—

> ' Grows, lives, and dies in single blessedness ;'

while the same vine, when wedded to the elm, is regarded
as the symbol of the usefulness, dignity, and happiness
of a married woman.

[1] ' But pluck that flower, its witchery is o'er,
    And neither youth nor maid desires it more.'—LXII. 43-4.

[2] ' As when shepherds on the mountains tread down the hyacinth, and its
purple flower lies on the ground.'

The absence of all personal allusion in this poem, and its resemblance in tone and rhythm to some of the fragments of the Lesbian poetess, might suggest the idea that it was translated, or at least imitated, from the Greek. But, on the other hand, from its harmony with the kind of subject and imagery in which Catullus most delights, and from the close observation of nature shown in such lines as this—

Jam jam contingit summum radice flagellum,[1]

it seems more probable that it was an adaptation of the style of his great model to some occasion within his own experience, than that it was a mere exercise in translation, like his Coma Berenices.

The Atys is the most original of all his poems. As a work of pure imagination, it is the most remarkable poetical creation in the Latin language. In this poem Catullus throws himself, with marvellous power, into a character and situation utterly alien to common experience, and pours an intense flood of human feeling and passion into a legend of the strangest Oriental superstition. The effect of the piece is, in a great measure, produced by the startling vividness of its language and imagery, and by the impetuous and tumultuous rush of its metre. The subject may probably have presented itself to Catullus during his sojourn in Asia Minor. The poem may have been partly founded on Greek materials; but he has treated the subject in a thoroughly original manner. No translation ever written could produce that impression of genuine creative power, which is forced upon every reader of the Atys. There is nothing at all like the spirit of this poem in extant Greek literature. No other writer has presented so real an image of the frantic exultation and fierce self-sacrificing spirit of an inhuman fanaticism: and again, of the horror and sense of deso-

[1] 'Its topmost shoot
With nerveless tendril hangs about its root.'—LXII. 52.

2 A

lation which a natural man, and more especially a Greek
or Roman, would feel in the midst of the wild and
strange scenes described in the poem, and when restored to the consciousness of his voluntary bondage,
and of the forfeiture of his country and parents, and the
free social life of former days. A few touches in the
poem — as, for instance, the expressions, 'niveis mani-
bus,' 'roseis labellis,' and again, 'ego gymnasii fui flos'
—all introduced incidentally,—force upon the mind the
contrast between the tender youth and beauty of Atys
and the power of the passion which possesses him. A
similar contrast is produced between the false excitement and noisy tumult of the evening, and the terrible
reality and blank despair of the morning. The effect of
this drama of human passion and agony is intensified
also by the vividness of all its pictorial environment ;—
by the vision of the wild surging seas, through which
the swift ship and its mad crew were borne, and of
the gloom and horror of the woods that hid the sounding rites of the goddess, and the tall columns of her
temple.   Nothing can be more true and life-like than
that picture of the early morning—

> Sed ubi oris aurei Sol radiantibus oculis
> Lustravit aethera album, sola dura, mare ferum,
> Pepulitque noctis umbras vegetis sonipedibus.[1]

Everything is seen in those sharply-defined forms, which
are imprinted on the brain in moments of intense excitement or agony.

The 'Epithalamium of Peleus and Thetis' may be regarded as an epic 'episode,' or rather as an antique
'idyll,' in the true and original sense of that word, as it
was applied to the poems of Theocritus, which are by

---

[1] 'But when the sun's fresh steeds had chased the dark, and with his
radiant eyes
He gazed along the solid earth, the cruel seas, and golden skies.'
                                                    —XVI. 39-41.

no means limited to delineations of rural or pastoral life. In point of form, it may be compared to those 'idylls' in which our great living poet has painted the ideal of the heroic age of Christendom. It is too short to justify any judgment as to whether Catullus might, if longer life had been granted to him, have ranked among the great poets of human action. It is deficient in epical unity, containing, as it does, one poem within another. It shows the art of a poet who delighted in pictorial delineation, and in identifying himself with one particular passion, rather than in conducting a continuous story, and exhibiting characters dramatically acting upon one another. The ancient mythology had passed away as an object of real belief; but for Catullus it lived a new life in the forms of art. From his love of beauty and his power of imagination, he creates anew the beings of an ideal past, that he may represent, in forms more perfect than those of common life, the feelings and passions with which he had the strongest sympathy. He loved to contemplate the beautiful and stately creations of Greek poetry, and to breathe again the pure morning air of the golden age. The whole poem is pervaded by that calm light of strange loveliness which spreads over the unwakened world in the early sunrise of a summer day. He traces back the origin of the love of Peleus and of the Sea-goddess to the day on which the first ship, manned by the flower of the Greek warriors, broke 'the silence of the seas '—

Emersere freti candenti e gurgite vultus
Æquoreæ monstrum Nereïdes admirantes.
Illa, atque haud alia, viderunt luce marinas
Mortales oculis nudato corpore Nymphas
Nutricum tenus extantes e gurgite cano.
Tum Thetidis Peleus incensus fertur amore,
Tum Thetis humanos non despexit hymenæos,
Tum Thetidi pater ipse jugandum Pelea sensit.[1]

[1] 'Out of the creaming surges in amaze
Wild faces rose on that strange night to gaze,

On the appointed day the whole of Thessaly gathers
together to celebrate the nuptials, and to gaze on the
splendour of the palace, which was, on that day, to
receive the gods as its guests.

The marriage-bed is covered with a rich embroidery,
representing the tale of the desertion of Ariadne by
Theseus. It reveals her as just awoke from her treacherous sleep, and gazing,

Saxea ut effigies Bacchantis,[1]

from the shore of Dia, on the departing ships. The poet
then makes her utter, in lines of great beauty and burning passion, all her strong love and agony and desola-
lation. In another part of the tapestry, the advent of
Bacchus, with his crew of Satyrs and Sileni, is presented
with that life-like energy with which the Atys is animated.

When the crowd have satisfied themselves with the
sight of all the wonders of the palace, they make way
for the approach of all the gods and demigods. Among
them Chiron appears, bearing chaplets of all the flowers
that grew in the plains, and river-banks, and vast mountain chains of Thessaly. Next comes Peneios, leaving
the green vale of Tempe,

Tempe, quae silvae cingunt super impendentes.[1]

not empty-handed, but bearing huge trees, to plant before the vestibule of the palace. Among them, too,
comes the wise Prometheus,

> The Nereids of the deep ; and mortals then
> Beheld, what never they beheld again,
> The Nymphs of Ocean lift their rosy breasts
> Above the foam-flakes of the billows' crests.
> Then Peleus, then, with love for Thetis burn'd ;
> Nor was by Thetis mortal wedlock spurn'd ;
> And Jove himself approved the vows that gave
> The god-born maid to paramour so brave.'—LXIV. 14-20.

[1] LXIV. 61.

[1] ' Fair Tempe, girt with hanging forest shades.'—LXIV. 287.

Extenuata gerens veteris vestigia puros ; [1]

and lastly, all the gods and goddesses of Olympus, with the sole exception of Phoebus and Diana. Then follows an exquisite picture of the aged Parcæ, spinning the threads of destiny, and chanting their truthful prophecy of the happiness that awaits the bridegroom and the bride, and of the greatness and glory of their son. The concluding lines of the poem disclose the only vein of conscious reflection which can be traced in all the poems of Catullus. His genuine feeling of ideal purity and beauty forces upon him there the contrast presented by the guilt and utter corruption of his own age.

Much of the charm of the poem arises from its calm and stately music, changing to a more rapid movement in the lament of Ariadne, its rich pictorial power, and its blending of true human feeling and passion with outward representation. If it wants unity of incident, it is pervaded by a thorough unity of tone. The tale of the miserable love and passionate agitation of Ariadne seems intended to bring out, by contrast, the calm and deep security of love and happiness allotted to Peleus and his bride. There are several fine pictures of nature in the poem, drawn from mountain or sea-scenery, with a firm hand and with fine poetical discernment ; as, for instance, that of the clouds passing away from a snowy summit—

Cen pulae ventarum flamine nubes
Aërium nivei montis liquere cacumen ; [2]

and that more elaborate description at line 270 of the first ruffling of the waves by the morning breeze. Equally fine are his pictures from human life, such as those in which he paints the outward signs of the passion and anxiety of Ariadne.

---

[1] 'On whom
The scars still linger'd of his ancient doom.'—LXIV. 295.
[2] ' Like clouds, that from some snow-capp'd mountain's head
Are driven before the scudding gale, they fled.'—LXIV. 240-1.

> Quantum sæpe magis fulgore expalluit auri ; [1]

and of her agitation in finding herself deserted by her lover —

> Non flavo retinens subtilem vertice mitram,
> Non contecta levi velatum pectus amictu,
> Non tereti strophio lactentis vincta papillas,
> Omnia quæ toto delapsa e corpore passim
> Ipsius ante pedes fluctus salis alludebant. [2]

The picture of the bacchanalian train

> Euhoe bacchantes, euhoe capita inflectentes,

has suggested one of the masterpieces of modern art. [3] There is again a wonderful blending of passionate feeling with pictorial or even statuesque beauty in this stanza from the chant of the Parcæ —

> Adveniet tibi jam portans optata maritis
> Hesperus, adveniet fausto cum sidere conjunx,
> Quæ te flexanimo mentis perfundat amore
> Languidulosque paret tecum conjungere somnos
> Levia substernens robusto brachia collo.
> Currite ducentes subtegmina, currite, fusi. [4]

The only other poems of Catullus which it is necessary to notice, are his translation of a piece of Callimachus,

---

[1] ' How many and many a time more wan of hue,
Than the dull sheen of sallow gold she grew.'—LXIV. 100.

[2] ' Down dropp'd the fillet from her golden hair,
Dropp'd the light vest that veil'd her bosom fair,
The filmy cincture dropp'd, that strove to bind
Her orbèd breasts, which would not be confined ;
And, as they fell around her feet of snow,
The salt wave caught and flung them to and fro.'

LXIV. 64-68.

[3] Titian's picture of *Bacchus and Ariadne* in the National Gallery.

[4] ' A little while, and Hesper will be here,
And bring thee what is most to bridegrooms dear !
Comes with his gracious star thy bride, who will
With soul-subduing love thy bosom fill ;
Round thy strong neck her tender* arms entwine,
And sink into a sleep that blends with thine,
Run, spindles, run, and weave the threads of doom.'

LXIV. 329-334.

* The word *tender* hardly brings out the force of *levia*, which is properly *smooth, rounded, or ivory*.

and a long elegy, in which he blends an account of his
own grief, caused by his brother's death, and of his own
passion for Lesbia, with the tale of Protesilaus and
Laodamia. The subject of the first of these poems is
the 'Lock of Berenice,' which, having been dedicated to
Venus, as a votive offering for her husband's return from
war, and having afterwards disappeared, was declared
by the court astronomer, Conon, to have been changed
into a constellation. Neither of these poems throws any
new light on the genius of Catullus ; but they confirm
the impression that the favourite subject of his art was
the union of beauty and passion with truth and constancy of affection. The following passage from the
latter of these poems may be quoted, as exemplifying
his love of nature, and the truth with which he selects
and paints one of her fairest objects—

> Qualis in aërii perluceus vertice montis
> Rivus muscoso prosilit e lapide,
> Qui cum de prona praeceps est valle volutus,
> Per medium densi transit iter populi,
> Dulce viatori lasso in sudore levamen,
> Cum gravis exustos aestus hiulcat agros.[1]

The art of Catullus is thus seen to be very limited in
its aim, but very original and perfect of its kind. As a
lyrical poet he cannot indeed be placed on the same
level with Horace. He wants altogether the variety
and range of interests, the subtlety and irony, the meditative spirit and the moral strength of the great and
genial Augustan poet. But Catullus has a peculiar perfection of his own, to which it would be difficult to find
a parallel in ancient or modern literature. No poet has

---

[1] ' As some clear stream, from mossy stone that leaps
Far up among the hills, and, wimpling down
By wood and vale, its onward current keeps
To lonely hamlet, and to stirring town ;
Cheering the way-worn traveller as it flows
When all the fields with drought are parch'd and bare.'
LXVIII. 57-62.

ever surpassed him in the power of imparting a living
grace and beauty to the slightest incidents and most
transient interests of life. No Roman poet produces
such happy effects by the use of the simplest and most
natural language. All his shorter poems seem to flow
from his heart with the clearness, and ease, and sparkling
life of a mountain spring. To him alone among his
countrymen, graceful and musical expression seems to
have come without any kind of effort. In this excellence no modern poet has surpassed him, with the exception perhaps of Wordsworth in the happiest of his
lyrical ballads. The superiority of the English poet
consists in this, that he has expressed infinitely deeper
and nobler emotions with the same inimitable ease and
directness. Catullus has been, with much truth,[1] compared to another modern poet, one whose fortunes were
very different from those of the young Roman patrician,
but whose heart and nature were of the same warmth
and intensity—the poet Burns. There is, for instance,
a close resemblance in force and spirit between the one
short convivial song of Catullus—

> Minister vetuli puer Falerni
> Inger mi calices amariores, etc. ;[2]

and several of the songs of the Scotch bard.[3] Some of
his shorter poems may be compared with the fragments
of the earlier lyrical poets of Greece. The hymn of
Catullus to Diana—

> Dianae sumus in fide
> Puellae et pueri integri '—

---

[1] By the writer of an excellent criticism on Catullus in the *North British
Review*.

[2] xxvi. 1-2.

[3] Compare, for instance, the force and directness of these two lines with
the same qualities in the opening lines of one of Burns's most striking
songs :—

> ' Gae fetch to me a pint o' wine,
>   And fill it in a silver tassie,' etc.

[4] xxxiv. 1-2.

is very like, in tone and feeling, to a fragment of a
hymn of Anacreon, in honour of Artemis—

γουνοῦμαί σ' ἐλαφηβόλε.
ξανθὴ καὶ Διός, ἀγρίων
Μέσσω' Ἄρτεμι θηρῶν, etc.

The longer poems of Catullus, again, are marked by
higher, but not by rarer qualities of genius. Few poets
rank above him as pictorial artists. He selects his subjects simply from his delight in their beauty. He resembles some of the greatest among our recent poets in
his power of giving a true and yet ideal life to the
poetical creations of former times. He has shown also
great imaginative if not dramatic genius, in identifying himself with various phases of passionate emotion.
The simplicity of his nature is one chief cause of the
ease and perfection of his works. He was never turned
aside from his immediate object by reflective subtlety.
It was also one chief cause of the limitation in his art.
He shows no sympathy with the thoughts, the energies,
and the interests of mature manhood. His youth too
must be taken into account as determining the bent of
his genius. It may, moreover, be pleaded in extenuation
of the weakness and the errors which stained his life. It
would have been difficult for any one, especially one of
his ardent unreflective nature, to have risen clearly above
the religious unbelief, the moral corruption, and political
disorganisation of that age. His own poems, in which
he has given the world both of his best and of his worst,
leave no doubt that he shared the 'light half-belief' of
his contemporaries in the popular faith, and that he gave
himself up, without any after-thought, to the enjoyment
of his youth. But there is no reason to believe that his
life was in any degree worse than the common life of
young and gay patricians in a dissolute age. In kindliness and unselfishness it was much better than that
of men of pleasure in any age. In spite of all the

2 B

stains of ardent passion, his nature still remained fresh
and unworldly.   He never altogether lost his natural
love of purity and beauty ; he did not cease to find
happiness in simple things ; and he never seems to have
forgot the claims and duties of human affection.

SECOND EDITION.

In 2 vols. 8vo, with Maps and Illustrations, price 24s,

LIFE IN NORMANDY:

SKETCHES OF FRENCH FISHING, FARMING, COOKING, NATURAL HISTORY, AND POLITICS.

Drawn from Nature.   Edited by J. F. CAMPBELL, Esq.

" It is one of those books which at once fascinate and humiliate the reader—the former because it is full of good matter, put in a most interesting light; the latter because the material and the interest are derived from such simple and obvious sources that we wonder to think how these good things have been missed so long."—*Times.*

" 'Life in Normandy' is a most dainty work. To the intellectual epicure it will prove exceedingly appetising."—*Morning Post.*

" The freshness, the minuteness of description, the exuberant tone of feeling everywhere perceptible, the novelty given by the keen insight of the narrator, even in familiar objects, combine to render the book every way a satisfaction and a pleasure, whether to the naturalist, sportsman, or student of human nature."—*Globe.*

" A very pleasant and spirited account is this of the out-door and in-door life and occupations of our kith and kin across the channel."—*Reader.*

Third Thousand.

In 2 Vols. crown 8vo, price 24s., with Portrait and graphic Illustrations,

"CHRISTOPHER NORTH:"

A MEMOIR OF JOHN WILSON,

Late Professor of Moral Philosophy in the University of Edinburgh.

Compiled from Family Papers and other sources, by his Daughter, Mrs. GORDON.

" We do not believe that the most practised and able critic in Scotland could have done more to put Wilson's literary labours in a favourable light."—*Saturday Review.*

" We do not know that we have ever read a biography which has on the whole satisfied us better."—*Spectator.*

" The authoress has related its details with so much feeling and pathos, that, as a true expression of natural affection, to praise it would be impertinent."—*Times.*

" From his infancy to the hour of his death he displayed a force of character, a vigour of intellect, and a rectitude of conduct, deserving of admiration, and every portion of his life has been worthily recorded by his daughter."—*Observer.*

" His life was undoubtedly worthy to be written, and his daughter has written it in a manner which does justice to the subject, and does honour to herself."—*London Review.*

" Wherever the English tongue is spoken, will be hailed with pleasure this tribute to the memory of 'Christopher North.'"—*Sun.*

www.ingramcontent.com/pod-product-compliance
Lightning Source LLC
Chambersburg PA
CBHW021526110726
47902CB00004B/767

* 9 7 8 3 7 4 1 1 2 6 7 9 6 *